BETTER OFF WITHOUT HIM

Other Books by Dee Ernst

A Different Kind of Forever

BETTER OFF WITHOUT HIM

Dee Ernst

Montlake
Romance

Text copyright © 2013 Dee Ernst

Published by Montlake Romance, Seattle

www.apub.com

ISBN-13: 9781477809570
ISBN-10: 1477809570
Library of Congress Control Number: 2013938567

CHAPTER ONE

April, in general, is not a good month for me. Here in northern New Jersey, April can either be awash with daffodils or buried under a foot of snow, and waiting to see which way it will go kills me. I hate the April version of winter—some days, that nip of spring teases the air and gets you thinking about warm sunshine, but mostly it's just cold enough to be miserable. The snow turns black and ugly in about six minutes, and the salt used on the roads gets in between the pads of my dog's feet. Ever try washing the feet of a sixty-pound lump of wet fur? Whimpering, quivering wet fur? No fun at all.

On the flip side, what if it *does* get warm and sunny right away? That whole process of morphing out of winter woolies and sweaters and scarves that successfully hid my entire body for four months and getting into clothes that not only show skin, but also rolls, pouches, and wrinkled knees— it's excruciating.

Then, of course, there's the whole tax thing.

And let's not even discuss my allergies.

So it stands to reason that any given April day will not be a particularly good one. But the day my husband Brian told me that he was leaving me for somebody fifteen years younger and thirty pounds lighter was the worst.

That morning, Daughter the First, the sixteen-year-old, bitchy, bossy one, screamed from her upstairs bedroom that she had no clean clothes to wear, so she was *not* going to school. Since she, like her two younger sisters, is responsible for her own laundry, I screamed back that it was not my problem and she could go to school in her pajamas for all I cared, but she'd better be out of the house in fifteen minutes. She then came down stairs in full makeup and her pajamas.

"Miranda. Go upstairs. Put on real clothes."

"These *are* real clothes." She was wearing flannel pajama bottoms and a camisole.

"No. Those are pajamas."

"You just told me I could wear them."

The space right behind my eyeballs started to heat up. "*What?*"

"Just ten minutes ago, you said I could go to school in my pajamas for all you cared, as long as I got out of the house on time. You just said it, Mom." Her face was full of sudden concern. "You're not starting to forget things, are you?"

"No. Of course not. I remember what I said. I just didn't mean it. I was being facetious."

Miranda walked over to the cupboard, pulled out a bowl, walked to another cupboard, and found the cereal. The look on her face was one of fierce concentration. "What does that word mean again?"

"You know damn well what it means. It means I won't let you out of the house in pajamas."

"Just the bottoms," she pointed out.

"That still counts."

"All the girls wear them. Not just to school, either." She went to the refrigerator and pulled out the milk. "Remember the girls we saw in Kings?"

Yes, I remembered. I remembered thinking at the time that I'd die of embarrassment if my daughter walked around in public looking like she had just rolled out of bed. I also remembered telling my daughters that I would lock them in a closet before I would let them walk around looking like that. Did Miranda not remember that part?

"Don't you remember what I said about that? About locking you in a closet?"

She shrugged. "You didn't mean it."

"Yes. I did."

She defiantly poured Cocoa Puffs into a bowl. "I thought you were being facetious. Besides, I have nothing else that's clean." She poured some milk as I counted to ten.

"What about that outfit we just bought last weekend? The one with the camouflage skirt?"

Daughter the First, also known as Miranda Claire Berman, shrugged expressively. "I won't wear that. It's ugly."

"Then why did I spend all that money buying it for you?" I asked, although I should have known better.

"Well, I liked it in the store. But when I tried it on at home, it was really awful."

"And what," I continued, simply because I had to hear her answer, "is the difference between here and the store?"

3

She chewed, then swallowed. I could see that she was actually giving this some thought. "Maybe the light?" she suggested at last. "Yeah, I think the lights that they have in dressing rooms are trick lights so that everything you try on looks really cool, but when you put the same clothes on in, like, real daylight, it looks crappy. So I can't wear it."

And this is the girl who has problems in school, they keep telling me, because she's not working up to her potential. Any human being who can come up with an idea like that should be working in a brain trust.

"Real clothes, Miranda," I said in my best I'm-only-saying-this-once-then-I'm-killing-you voice. "Jeans. Or a skirt. Or Dockers. Not jammy pants. Then bring down the ugly outfit so I can take it back to Macy's for credit. Now."

Miranda knows when she can push and when she has to back down, so she actually dropped her cereal bowl and spoon into the sink before she flounced out of the kitchen in a subtle display of teenage compromise. I stirred lots of sugar into my coffee and waited for the second wave.

Daughter the Second and Daughter the Third are only separated by eight minutes, but that counts for a lot when you're fourteen. Daughter the Second is very sweet. Daughter the Third chews nails for breakfast then spits them out at people all day long. When they were little, they were kept in separate classrooms in school because they were impossible to tell apart. But sometime around the age of ten, distinct personalities began to develop. Now, to the casual observer, they could be two completely separate species.

Every morning, Lauren, the older and infinitely wiser, combs her shining, soft brown hair into neat little braids or ponytails, applies some mascara and clear lip gloss, then descends into the kitchen smiling, her books already in a neat pile by the door, her jeans freshly washed and actually ironed—which, I must admit, bothers me just a little—and her T-shirt always clean. That bothers me a little too, but she actually kisses me on the cheek each day as part of her morning routine. I tend to overlook a lot of her little foibles.

That particular morning, I could see a happy kitten face beneath her grey hoodie, and her hair was in a long braid. She carefully measured oatmeal and water into a bowl and set it in the microwave, then smiled as she poured her orange juice and said, in her very sweet, little-girl voice, "I put our DNA in Johnson already. Is that okay?"

I smiled. Of course it was okay. For those who need a translation, Johnson is our minivan. I call it Johnson after the actor, Van Johnson. I am a huge movie fan, and I watched a lot of old movies on television when I was a kid. The DNA she was referring to was the science project she and her sister had been working on for the past six weeks. The science teacher put a number of acceptable projects into a hat, and Lauren and her sister Jessica, who are both very smart in science and are lab partners, pulled out the DNA model as theirs. Jessica, with her warped sense of humor and her innate ability to take any mundane activity and turn it into something that will drive everyone crazy, insisted on a very large-scale model. The finished project was over five feet long and about as graceful to maneuver as a herd of water buffalo. So I was driving both girls and their project to school that morning.

On cue—that is, late—my youngest, my baby, my last chance of attaining perfection, clumped down the stairs. Jessica can't help clumping. She really can't. Her feet are encased in heavy boots that look like they're designed to protect SWAT team members from having their feet shot off by bazookas. And they are black, so they match the rest of her outfit, which is, of course, the important thing. Her pants, cut raggedly below the knee, are black. Her long-sleeved button-down shirt is black. The heavy eyeliner and clumpy mascara are black—are we all getting the picture? And her hair is black, the kind of dead, dull, artificial black that can only be bought. Very cheaply. Speaking of hair, her haircut is very one-of-a-kind, but for anyone who would care to duplicate it, here's how it's done.

1) Bend over and brush your long, silky, beautiful hair straight down.

2) Gather all your hair together and fasten with a rubber band as close to the scalp as possible.

3) Still bending over, grasp the hank of hair about three inches from the rubber band with one hand, and with the other hand, using very dull scissors, cut as close to the rubber band as possible.

4) Remove rubber band, stand upright, and shake your head.

5) Leave all the cut hair on the bathroom floor.

6) Mix one application of GothGirl Hair Color #666, Your-Mother-Will-Scream Black, in the bathroom sink, making sure to get a few flecks on the walls.

7) Apply half the bottle to your newly shorn head, leaving the rest to drip over the hair on the floor.

8) After rinsing, let hair dry without benefit of conditioner, gel, mousse, or blow dryer.

Ta-dah! The Jessica!

Jessica growled. She's not a morning person. She poured herself a cup of coffee, which she drank, of course, black, and started taking apart a bagel with her blackened fingertips, putting very small bits into her mouth a little at a time.

"I need a favor," she said. "It's really important." She was slouched against the counter, squinting at the sunlight like a vampire.

I sighed. "No," I told her, "you cannot get a tattoo."

"That's not it."

"And you can't get your nose pierced either."

"Wrong again, Mom." She sighed and munched more bagel, then asked, very casually, "Could I sleep at Billy's Friday night?"

Billy is her so-called boyfriend. He's a year older and lives six blocks away. He walks over to see her on the weekends and they go out for walks, sometimes into town, where there are places to eat and have coffee. He's a very quiet kid, with long hair that hides most of his face most of the time.

I put my coffee cup down very carefully. "Did you just ask me to spend the night at Billy's?"

She shrugged. "Yeah. He's having a sleepover party."

"A sleepover party?" I looked over at Lauren for some sort of verification. Lauren was actually nodding.

"Yes, Mom," Lauren said. "A lot of kids are having boy-girl sleepovers. It's kind of the new thing."

I tried not to hyperventilate. "Who else is invited?"

Jessica shrugged again. "I don't know. Kids. Jill, I think, and Avery. Maybe Matt."

"And his parents are going to be home?" This was sounding more interesting all the time.

"Don't know. Maybe."

"What are all of you going to do?"

"Don't know. Listen to music, watch a few movies, I guess." She shook her hair away from her eyes so she could actually look at me. "We'll stay up all night, Mom. It's no big deal. It's not like we're all going to be having sex or anything."

"Well, of course not," I said heartily.

"So, can I go?"

"As soon as I speak to Billy's mom, and Jill's mom, and of course, your father, whom I'm sure will be thrilled with the idea."

"Mom." Jessica started to whine. "You can't tell Daddy. He'll flip out. Can't you tell him I'm at Jill's or someplace?"

I shook my head. "Sorry honey, but what if I get struck by a bus on Friday night and wind up in the hospital dying? Your father would want to be able to bring you to my bedside so you can say a last goodbye. He needs to know where you are, Jessica. I don't lie to him about stuff like that."

She slammed down her coffee mug, then threw her bagel across the room where it landed, surprisingly, in the trashcan. She stormed out, muttering under her breath. I looked at Lauren.

"So, parents are actually letting their kids sleep over with members of the opposite sex?" I asked.

Lauren put her bowl and spoon in the sink. "Yes. It's okay, I guess, because everybody is in a big room together, and if anything was going on, everybody would know about it, and that would be really embarrassing, you know?"

I smiled, but was not convinced. I didn't think that a teenage boy, faced with the prospect of "getting some," would consider embarrassment a major obstacle. Lauren went upstairs and I sighed into my coffee cup.

I love my children. I really do. And I still have some control over their actions. But I can't help feeling that one day they'll figure out that there are three of them and only one of me, and it will be all over, like when the great lioness is taken down by a pack of lowly hyenas by force of their sheer number.

I drained my cup of coffee and began to put the girl's dishes in the dishwasher. I turned the kitchen tap slowly, then breathed a sigh of relief as clear water gushed out. Some days, that's a real cause for celebration in our house.

Earlier that morning we'd had a plumbing event. The claw foot tub in the girls' bathroom made a noise and coughed up something that looked like rusty water. That happened a lot.

We'd lived in this great big old house for about eighteen years, and it was almost finished. Brian and I originally thought that it would be fun to get an old fixer-upper and do all the work together. You know, bonding. However, older houses have things like plaster walls, so just trying to hang a picture requires expensive tools and titanium screws. We soon found it easier just to pick up the phone and ask for estimates. All our common living areas are beautiful, as are most of the upstairs bedrooms. The master bath has one lone toilet and lots of exposed beams, not to mention various lengths of copper pipe. And the walk-up attic, which was supposed to be my sanctuary, had plywood covering all the windows because the windows hadn't actually been ordered yet. It's not money that's the issue, but time, energy and the red-hot bloodlust that's needed to actually find the antique window store located down some dark alley in a strange little town and make the decision between four-over-four or six-over-six.

Why did I need a sanctuary? Because I'm a writer, and all writers need someplace quiet, peaceful and totally theirs where they can go to relax and be inspired. Actually, I'm an award-winning, *New York Times* bestselling author. Now, before you rack your brain trying to think of that beautifully written family saga that got shortlisted for the Booker or the thriller that Robert Redford optioned as his Next Big Thing, let me explain to you that the *New York Times* has *several* bestselling lists. There's the hardcover fiction and nonfiction list, the Holy Grail of lists. Then there's the trade paper, fiction and nonfiction lists. Trade paperbacks are those books that are the same size as a hardcover, but infinitely cheaper to publish. Then there's the mass market list. Mass markets are your basic small-enough-to-stash-in-your-purse-sized paperbacks. That's the list I made. I hung on to the number one spot on the mass market original paperback list for almost four months with one of my favorite titles, *Passion At Dusk*.

Yes, I'm a romance writer. When I started almost twenty years ago, romance novels were pretty much delegated to the back corners of bookstores. Since then, it's grown to be quite a respected, not to mention lucrative, genre. I write under the name of Maura Van Whalen, because my real name, Mona Quincy Berman, doesn't have a very romantic ring to it. Because I was a history major in college and am a sucker for old moldy ruins and rusty swords, I write historical romance. Maura's heroines are usually raven- or auburn-haired women with fair skin, clear green eyes, and warm trembly lips. They are usually named Clarissa, Isabella, or Honoria, have amazing breasts, and are strong-willed and daring. Their brooding, handsome counterparts are usually Drake, Trane, or Lord Aubrey Sinclair.

Being a history major, I'm big on historical accuracy, which is tough when you're writing not only about history, but about sex. Way back in the day, women were having all kinds of sex all over the place, pretty much the same as today, but the only ones who admitted it were either prostitutes, or, of course, royalty. I like to get my characters married off in the first chapter or two, often unwillingly, so they can then be separated and/or put through some trying ordeal together during which they realize how much they really do love each other. I write about a lot of arranged marriages, which were very common among the gentry. I also like to throw in the occasional duke who must hand over his gorgeous and willful daughter as payment of a gambling debt to an unscrupulous but amazingly hunky blackguard.

Lately, though, I'd been wanting to write for the twenty-first century, which would allow my characters to sleep with each other without even knowing each other's names. Their names would thus be Chloe, Zoey, Colton, or Paco, and they would have exciting jobs like magazine editors or undercover drug enforcement agents. I even had a new nom de plume picked out: Monique B.

As for my awards, well, let's say that there are roughly a gazillion groups out there related to the romance business, and they all love to have conferences and conventions, and prizes are awarded for everything from best plot, pluckiest heroine, or most frequent and imaginative use of the word "cock." I have a number of these awards. Considering what these awards represent, you'd think they'd be shaped like giant, erect penises, or maybe upright and breathtakingly full breasts. Instead, they are very abstract in nature, and tend to look like falling stars, soaring comets, or something a dog may have thrown up.

Speaking of dogs, and throwing up, that morning as the girls were heading out the back door, I heard Miranda mutter, then, moments later, Jessica growl. Lauren called over her shoulder about something gross on the floor. I wasn't paying a lot of attention because I had my head down, trying to dig the keys out of the bottom of my purse. Then I stepped in something. It was soft and made a squishy sound. I closed my eyes and sighed. Fred had left me another treasure.

My Golden Retriever is named Fred, after Fred Astaire, because I watched…wait, you already know that. Golden Retrievers are America's favorite pet because they are beautiful, loyal, and good-natured. Fred is beautiful, loyal, etc., but he also has a brain the size of a dried lima bean and is constantly eating the girls' underwear and then throwing them up all over my beautiful hardwood floors so I can then step on them and flatten them out into the shape of the Best Regency Romance Award I won in 1995.

∼

I returned from driving the girls to school, cleaned up the Fred-mess, and called Ben. I'm on a first-name, as well as know-all-his-kids-name basis with my plumber, Ben Cutler. We first met when one of my three then-interchangeable daughters, all toddling and wreaking havoc, flushed several socks down the toilet, causing the entire sewage system of Westfield to back up into my downstairs powder room. Since then, he's attended to several emergencies, as well as routine maintenance and upgrading activities. He's charming, polite, and always apologetic when handing me the bill. He also has a network of other highly paid professionals listed in his little black book, so when plaster/wiring/flooring needs to be replaced as a result of his work, he just calls up a buddy and takes care of it for me. Brian always maintains that there's probably a kickback in there someplace, but I try not to think about it. Oh, and did I mention that Ben is probably one of the five most beautiful men on the planet? He's a true inspiration.

In *Down To Desire*, he was the mysterious and charismatic Devlin Montry, Earl of Northumberland. In *Wednesday's Lover*, he was Philip Waters, the conflicted agent of the mysterious and dangerous Lord Buckingham. In *Passion's Eve*, he was Sir Jon Allenby, wrongly convicted of treason and on the run from the king's vengeful agents. Whenever I'm writing, I spend a lot of time thinking about Ben, usually in various states of undress. To be truthful, I spend a lot of time thinking about Ben even when I'm not writing. Then it becomes really distracting because, doing what I do for as long as I've been doing it, I tend to think of him in a romantic and historic context.

Usually when I call I get his machine, so I was pleasantly surprised when he answered his phone that morning. Even his voice was delicious, very deep, with the hint of a southern drawl.

"Ben, it's Mona, your favorite customer."

He grabbed her by the shoulders and shook her roughly. "You little fool," he said, his eyes glittering dangerously. "Don't you know what you mean to me? Do you really think I've been keeping away from you because I want to?" He pulled her close, his lips a breath away from her own. "Don't you know that I'm afraid of what I'll do if I'm alone with you?"

"Is it the downstairs toilet again?" Ben asked.

"No. The tub in the girls' bathroom puked up some rust earlier."

"Ah. Puking rust." He chuckled. "There's a lot of that going around. I can come by after lunch, if you'll be home."

"Yep. I'll be here. See you later."

I hung up the phone and was drinking my fourth cup of coffee, seriously thinking about getting some writing done, when Brian came through the kitchen door. Brian is an accountant. He's actually head of a department full of lots of other accountants, so he doesn't do much debiting or crediting himself, but he still calls himself an accountant, despite the CPA, MBA, six-figure salary and big corner office. He has a modest, self-effacing way about him that I've always liked. He doesn't look like an accountant anymore. He still wears a suit and tie to work, but they are very expensive, well-cut suits with sexy ties and splashy-colored shirts. He's a handsome guy for fifty-three. Tall, still slender, and not much gray because he's got that sandy blond hair—you know, the color that hides the gray really well until one day you look and say, "Oh my *God*, you're old." He hadn't gotten there yet. Something to look forward to, now.

So I was sitting in my big, old-fashioned kitchen, glowing in the mixed warmth of sunshine and hot caffeine, talking to the cat. I will not allow my cat on my kitchen counter. Ever. I'm sure when I'm not around, she makes it a point to rumba her way from the sink to the fridge, but when I'm home, she sits on the barstool next to me at the breakfast counter. She's very good that way.

I love my cat. She is pale orange and white and very fluffy, with big blue eyes and a tiny pink tongue. Her name is Lana. She is my favorite living being in the house, because although she pees and poops an incredible amount for such a small animal, she does it very neatly in a contained space, and sometimes spends as much as twelve minutes at a time sitting in my lap, purring in complete adoration. Well, maybe not adoration. Or, at least, not adoration of me. But she listens carefully to every word I say and never talks back. That alone elevates her to sainthood in my book.

But back to Brian. He came through the door. I was a little surprised. It was not an unheard-of occurrence, but lately midmorning returns home were few and far between. "Hey, hot stuff, back so soon?" I was smiling. I really loved my husband.

He shrugged. "Well, I left this morning just as the girls were screaming about a geyser in the bathroom, so I thought I might check it out. Still gushing?"

I shook my head. "Nope. Besides, I called Ben."

Brian had taken off his jacket and was leaning back against the counter. "Good. I like Ben. Nice guy. He coming by today?"

"After lunch."

Brian made a face. "He'll probably charge extra for the rush job. But he's still a nice guy. He's got kids, right?"

"Boys. His oldest starts Yale next fall."

Brian threw back his head and laughed. "I bet when he got off the phone with you, he called his kid right away and told him to go ahead and sign up for the next semester."

I laughed with him. "Probably."

Brian shook his head. "Remember when Jess tried to see if her Barbie could swim and tried to flush the damn thing? Ben was laughing so hard he couldn't get the wrench working."

"God, I'd forgotten that."

"A defense mechanism on your part, I'm sure. Usually you remember everything."

"Unlike you, who needs notes left on your shoes so you can remember which one goes on which foot," I joked.

Brian grinned broadly. "God, you're right about that. I have a hard time keeping track of so many things. In fact, there's something I've been wanting to talk to you about for weeks, and I just keep forgetting about it."

I sat up straighter, smiled, and tried the dutiful school-girl look. "Well, here we are, and you've obviously remembered, so shoot."

"Yeah. Well it's actually the main reason I came back. I wanted to tell you when the girls weren't here."

"Weren't here?"

"Yes. I didn't want them to see me pack."

I was still smiling. "Pack what?"

"My clothes. And my books. And everything. I'm leaving you, Mona. I'm very sorry. This is not about you, really. You've been a wonderful wife, but I've met someone else and I want to be with her. So, I'll just pack up my things and go."

He said this all very calmly. He might have been explaining why the little referee man threw up one of those flag-thingies during a football game. I stared at him, trying to latch on to something that actually made sense.

"You're packing?" I repeated. I was looking at him. Then I looked at Lana, still sitting patiently beside me. She offered no suggestions, so I looked back at Brian. "Your clothes?"

Brian cleared his throat and spoke very slowly. "Yes, Mona, I'm packing my clothes and moving out. I want a divorce." Then he stood up and walked out of the kitchen.

I looked at Lana again. She yawned. I followed my husband out of the kitchen and grabbed his arm as he started up the stairs. "Divorce? What are you talking about? Who did you meet? Where did you meet anybody? Except for your business trips, we go everywhere together. How could you meet someone?"

Brian ran his hand through his hair. "It's a woman at work, Mona. Dominique."

"What?" *Dominique?* Was he crazy? There were no real women named Dominique.

"You met her," Brian continued. "At the Christmas party. She transferred down from Boston."

Wait. Yes. Now I remembered. Her name was Dominique because she was from France, where the name Dominique is not outrageously pretentious, but actually as common as Nicole or Emily or Shanique. She was also about fourteen years old and roughly the size and shape of a bamboo shoot. I remembered her, quite clearly, because at the Christmas party she was wearing an amazing winter-white suit that I had tried on at Nordstrom, but decided against buying because it made my butt look too big, with very chichi red alligator pumps.

"Dominique with the accent? And the blonde hair? And red shoes? Are you kidding? You're old enough to be her grandfather."

Brian looked insulted. "She's thirty, Mona."

"Thirty? You're leaving me for a thirty-year-old bimbo?"

Brian pulled away from me and started up the stairs. "She is anything but a bimbo. She has an MBA from Georgetown. She actually interned at the White House."

"So did Monica Lewinsky," I yelled. "You can't leave me."

Brian turned on the stairs and looked down at me. Literally and figuratively. "I *am* leaving you, Mona. I've already spoken to a lawyer. You have a great deal of your own money, but I will be very generous. I'm not going to be a jerk about this. You can have the house and kids."

He turned back and marched upstairs. I stood there, watching him, feeling like a total loser. Then I screamed up to him at the top of my lungs.

"But I don't *want* the house and kids!"

∾

When Brian came back downstairs twenty-seven minutes later, I was calm. I was rational. I was the perfect Model of a Wife.

Things happened in a marriage. I knew that. And since I'd once been in therapy, albeit briefly, I knew that I could be a challenging person to live with.

I knew that there could be issues in a marriage that go completely unnoticed by a preoccupied spouse. I watch enough *Dr. Phil* to realize that things may have been going on that I was totally unaware of. Like that woman who didn't know that her husband was actually a cross-dresser until she threatened to sue her dry cleaner for all her missing clothes, and the poor guy had to confess. So, it's possible that there had been a blip on the radar that I didn't pick up on. I'm a big person. I can admit my mistakes. And I was perfectly willing to do whatever it took to get my marriage back to where I thought it was say, oh, two hours before.

Brian came back carrying all three of his suitcases and he dumped them in the foyer. I opened my mouth to speak, but he went back upstairs. I waited. He came down again, this time with my suitcases.

I narrowed my eyes. Did he really have that many clothes? "Those are mine," I said, trying to keep a possessive snarl out of my voice.

He nodded. "I know. I'll bring them back tonight."

"You're coming back tonight?" Was I surprised? Confused? Pleased?

"Well, yes. I think we should tell the girls together."

"Together? You want us to tell our daughters together that you're moving out to be with another woman?"

Brian looked uncomfortable for the first time. "Yes. Well, I think they need to hear the explanation from both of us."

"But both of us aren't leaving," I pointed out. "*You're* leaving. You're leaving because you're screwing a woman almost half your age. How can I possibly explain that when I don't even understand it myself?"

See, I was calm. No screeching.

He cleared his throat. "Now, Mona, I can't take total responsibility for this."

That just may have been the wrong thing for him to say. "And how, exactly, am I at fault?"

"Well, let's face it. Our marriage hasn't been the same these past few months."

I think at that moment I forgot all about being a big person. The entire unnoticed-blip-that-I-should-have-seen theory went out the window. "You're right. Apparently, for these past few months, one of us has been unfaithful."

"Well, yes, but before that, things were, ah, you know…" He looked at me hopefully. Like I was actually going to let him off the hook.

"Before that you and I spent a week in Aruba where we had monkey sex for six days in a row. Before that we talked about your coming with me to San Francisco this summer. We've been planning your sister's surprise fiftieth birthday party, which, I believe, is still scheduled for three weeks from next Saturday." I could feel the blood rising, and I fought the urge to scream. Had he actually thought I should admit mistakes? Was he crazy? "Two months ago you bought me a diamond necklace for our twentieth wedding anniversary." I took a few deep breaths. "So tell me. When, in the past few months, was I supposed to figure out that things were, 'ah, you know'?"

Brian shook his head sadly. "I'm going to take these out to the car." He picked up some suitcases and went out the front door. I sat down on our hall bench, gripping my knees with my sweaty palms. My eyes came to rest on our wonderfully quaint umbrella stand, an antique made to look like an elephant's foot, and I thought briefly about running him through with my Monet umbrella from the New York Metropolitan Museum store. I probably couldn't kill him with an umbrella, unless he agreed to lie down while I repeatedly stabbed him in the eye with it. My eyes moved to the cute bulldog doorstop. Also antique. Cast iron. Weighed a frigging ton. Capable of inflicting severe, possibly fatal damage. It was so heavy, one good swing would probably do it. It was so heavy, however, that I probably couldn't lift it high enough to hit him anywhere but on the foot.

He came back in to get the rest of his suitcases. My suitcases, actually. Could I call the police and report missing luggage? Would they actually arrest him for it? Now, there was a plan. What foreign woman, probably fishing for a green card or something similar, would want to associate with a convicted tote-bag felon? Why should I go to jail for murder when I could just as easily send him to jail for petty theft?

"I'm going now," Brian said. I had been so lost in the vision of my apparently soon-to-be-ex-husband in an orange jumpsuit that I didn't hear him come back in. He was looking down at me, actually smiling. "I'll be back around dinner. I'll talk to the girls."

"Where are you going?" I asked.

"To Dominique's," he said easily. "She has a condo in Hoboken, so I'll be close to work. And the girls, of course. I'll have my lawyer call your lawyer."

"I don't *have* a lawyer," I whined.

"You'll find somebody competent. Ask around. I'm not worried, Mona. I'm sure you'll be fine." Brian patted me on the head. Really. Can you believe it? Then he walked out the door.

I was so angry. Outraged that he could so serenely walk out and leave behind a wife and children and a dog and a cat. And I felt betrayed. I mean, there were vows taken. Love. Honor. Cherish. Till death. I wasn't dead yet.

I was also highly insulted that a person such as myself—attractive, intelligent, successful, respected in the community, great mother, and one hell of a cook—could be so easily replaced by a woman who was merely blonde, foreign, and who may or not have blown the president.

What I did not feel, and I only realized it long afterward, was brokenhearted.

CHAPTER TWO

The phone rang a few moments after Brian left. I have telephones in every room, and all the phones have caller ID, so I merely had to lean over from where I was sitting, hunched on the front hall bench, to see that Westfield High School was calling. That was not a good sign. But it was what I needed to pull me out of the pool of self-pity I was rapidly digging for myself.

"Mrs. Berman?" a man's voice asked after I said hello. "This is Vice Principal Arnold."

He didn't need to tell me who he was. Sadly, I recognized his voice from several previous phone calls.

"Yes, Mr. Arnold. What did Jessica do this time?"

Now, some parents with multiple offspring may not automatically assume that one child is more worth a phone call from the assistant principal than any of the others, but other parents don't have a Jessica. While her elementary and middle school careers might have been relatively undistinguished, she hit high school with an agenda. So far, in a few short months, she had incited her English class to walk out in protest of the banning of certain books in the library, managed to flip a calculator into the air—accidentally, supposedly—but *at* her geometry teacher, narrowly missing him but apparently damaging the calculator beyond repair, and had been permanently forbidden to use the upstairs annex of the library. So there was a little history here for me to go on.

"Actually," Mr. Arnold said, "it's not Jessica."

"Miranda? Did she get caught smoking again? Or is it about the missing trigonometry book? She swore to me—"

"Mrs. Berman," Mr. Arnold said firmly, "it's Lauren."

My heart stopped. I think, although there's been no scientific evidence produced so far to back me up, that the entire earth paused for just a moment on its axis.

"*Lauren?*" I whispered in disbelief.

"Yes."

"Is she okay?" My heart was pounding.

"She's fine, but there has been an incident and another student is involved. It's complicated. I'll explain when you get here."

I slammed down the phone, hand shaking. *Lauren?* I ran and grabbed my purse, slammed the back door behind me, hopped into Johnson and sped out of the driveway.

Normally, I can walk to the high school. It's several blocks away, but they are lovely, tree-lined blocks, with wide sidewalks and gracious homes, and I love the walk. Downtown Westfield, which is in the other direction, is another lovely walk. But today, I whizzed past Tudors and Victorians, blinded to everything but the gray pavement before me. *Lauren?*

I entered Mr. Arnold's office still trembling. He rose from his desk and took my arm, leading me to the sofa and sitting down with me. We faced each other, knees almost touching, and he actually patted my hand.

"Mrs. Berman, first let me repeat that Lauren is fine. That is, she is unhurt."

"You're sure it's Lauren?" I asked, reaching for any straw.

"Oh, yes. And she did confess."

"Confess?" My eyes started to well with tears. "Oh, Mr. Arnold," I whispered, "she was my best hope."

"Yes," he said, waving his hands helplessly in the air. "I know. She's always been a model student. An example for others, really. Which is why her behavior is so upsetting. I feel I must ask—is there anything going on at home that may have caused her to, well, act out?"

I took a deep breath and lifted my chin, blinking away the tears. "Well, as a matter of fact, my husband is leaving me. Us."

Mr. Arnold nodded his head. "Well, that might explain it. I'm sure that hit Lauren very hard."

"Well, no, because she doesn't know yet. He just told me himself, um,"—I glanced at my watch—"fifty-three minutes ago."

Mr. Arnold drew back. "Are you saying that your husband just now, this morning, told you that he was leaving you?"

"Yep."

Mr. Arnold looked amazed for a moment, then slipped back into his I-can-help-I'm-a-professional mode. "Well, you know Mrs. Berman, sometimes these separations can result in the strengthening of a marriage."

I looked at him rather coldly. "I don't think that will be true in our case."

He lifted one eyebrow. "Don't be too hasty, Mrs. Berman. Why, my wife and I recently had a bit of a problem, and the time apart did us a world of good."

I tilted my head at him. "Did your bit of a problem involve you schtupping a thirty-year-old French whore?"

Mr. Arnold looked shocked. "No, of course not."

"Then I don't think we're on the same page with this one, Mr. Arnold. Now, what about Lauren?"

"Yes. Well, she assaulted a fellow student, and as you know, we have a zero tolerance policy about that sort of thing. She faces an automatic three-day suspension, and we will insist she attend anger management classes."

"Assaulted? Are you telling me that she hit somebody?"

"Yes. I'm afraid so."

This was so not making sense. "Hit? She hit somebody with her hand?"

"Well, no. She hit them with her science project."

I made the leap from surreal to impossible with no effort at all. "Her science project? She hit someone with a five-foot-tall model of DNA?"

Mr. Arnold nodded sadly. "I'm afraid so."

I stared past Mr. Arnold to the wall behind his desk. Apparently, he had graduated from the University of Virginia, summa cum laude. I looked back at Mr. Arnold. "Why?"

"It really doesn't matter why she did it, Mrs. Berman, the fact is—"

"It matters to me," I interrupted.

"Well, I really don't know why. Let's bring her in, shall we?" He got up, spoke into his telephone, and a moment later Lauren walked into his office.

She looked miserable. Her shoulders were hunched, her eyes were red, and her perky braid had come undone. "Mommy, I'm so sorry," she whimpered, and started to cry.

I stood up and swept her into my arms. My poor baby. My heart was breaking for her. Really. I wiped the hair from her eyes and looked into her unhappy little face. "What the hell were you thinking?" I yelled at her.

She took a lungful of air. "It's just that she broke it," she wailed.

I shot a look at Mr. Arnold. "Who broke what?"

"Bernadette," Lauren explained at a gallop. " See, Jessica was supposed to carry the project from Mrs. Chambers's room, and when she brought it in, all the strands along the top, you know, the green ones, well, they were all broken off, so I started to yell at Jess, and Jess said she didn't do anything, and Ahmed said he saw Bernadette reach up and break them as Jess walked by, so I went to Bernadette and asked her if she broke our project, and she said yeah, she did, that it was a stupid project anyway, and then she started to laugh. So I grabbed the project from Jess and hit her over the head with it—hit Bernadette, not Jess. Jess just stood there with her mouth hanging open." Lauren moved her shoulders in a pitiful kind of way. "I was just so mad."

I was staring at Mr. Arnold, who had the good grace to look uncomfortable. "So, Bernadette ruined the science project that you and your sister spent six weeks working on?" I asked Lauren, but my eyes never left Mr. Arnold's face.

I could feel Lauren nod. I narrowed my eyes. "Let's hear Bernadette's side of this, shall we, Mr. Arnold?"

Mr. Arnold left the room. I shook my head at Lauren. "You bopped her with five feet of plastic straw and miniature marshmallows?"

A smile played along her lips. "Yes. I'm really sorry, Mom, but she is such a bitch. Honest. She is."

"Lauren, honey, I believe you. But you're the one who keeps me from running off to join the circus. If you start acting like your sisters, I don't know what I'll do."

"Daddy's going to be pissed, isn't he?"

I exhaled slowly. "Oh, dear. Well, I don't know. I have a feeling you'll be getting away with this one."

Mr. Arnold returned with Bernadette and Bernadette's mother, a shallow-faced woman I recognized at once. Sometime in the recent past, during a sixth grade PTA bake sale, she had given me a hard time because I only wanted six brownies and refused to pay for a whole dozen. Her name, as I recalled, was Bridget or Britta or Greta. I didn't like her.

"My daughter," she said at once, "could have been seriously injured. She called me on her cell phone as soon as it happened, she was so distraught."

"Your daughter," I spat back, "got hit with plastic straws held together by miniature marshmallows and craft glue. The only way she could have gotten hurt is if one of the straws went so far up her nose that it severed her brainstem. Who are you kidding? Injured?" I looked hard at Mr. Arnold. "So, what is going to be Bernadette's punishment?"

Mr. Arnold looked puzzled. Bernadette and her mother looked immediately on guard.

"What do you mean?" Mr. Arnold asked.

"There's a zero tolerance policy when it comes to assault. What's the policy about the deliberate destruction of personal property?"

Bridget/Britta/Greta looked nervous. Mr. Arnold still didn't get it.

"Those kids last year," I went on, "the ones who slashed the tires in the parking lot? Didn't they get an immediate suspension too?"

"Well, now, Mrs. Berman, this isn't quite the same thing now, is it?" Mr. Arnold could see the trap, looming wide ahead of him, and he was trying to steer as clear as possible.

"Oh, Mr. Arnold, I think it's exactly the same thing. You can't place a monetary value on what Bernadette destroyed, because it involved weeks of work, and that's so hard to calculate, not to mention the affect on both of my girls' grades. It's the same thing, isn't it? Personal property is personal property, and Bernadette deliberately destroyed my daughter's property. How long were those boys out? A week? And maybe Bernadette should also be required to seek counseling. After all, there may be some deep, underlying reason she sought out this particular science project, and if there are DNA model issues, we wouldn't want her to repeat the same grave error later on in life, would we?"

Mr. Arnold rolled his eyes in defeat. Bridget/Britta/Greta clenched her jaw. Bernadette looked clueless. I dared not look at Lauren, because I could feel her shoulders shaking with laughter, and I was afraid if I looked at her, we would both become hysterical.

"I can't suspend somebody for breaking a science project," Mr. Arnold said.

"Sure you can," I said, my voice steely.

"It's possible," Lauren suggested in a clear voice, "that Bernadette did it by accident."

"And it's also possible," Bridget/Britta/Greta said from between clenched teeth, "that Lauren tripped and the project just fell on my Bernadette."

Her Bernadette opened her mouth to protest, but got her foot stomped on. Mr. Arnold looked beaten. He took a deep breath and asked, "Does Bernadette wish to withdraw her complaint?"

Bridget/Britta/Greta nodded.

"Apparently, then, this has just been a little misunderstanding. Bernadette obviously overreacted, making a false accusation." Mr. Arnold clapped his hands together. "Okay, everybody, sorry for the commotion. Why don't we just get back to what we were doing, and forget all about this?"

Bernadette, still protesting under her breath, got dragged from the room. Lauren had turned to leave, but my hand shot out to stop her.

"What about the science project?" I asked.

Lauren looked back in surprise. Mr. Arnold just looked annoyed.

"Was Mr. Coopersmith able to evaluate the girls' work before the project was, um, accidentally destroyed?" I pressed on.

Lauren's face fell. "No. It was in Mrs. Chambers's room. Mr. Coopersmith never saw it."

I smiled sweetly at Mr. Arnold. "It would be a shame if my two daughters received a failing grade because their project was the victim of a little misunderstanding, don't you think, Mr. Arnold?"

Mr. Arnold sighed. "What would you suggest, Mrs. Berman?"

"Since it was sitting in Mrs. Chambers's room all morning, and Mrs. Chambers is also a science teacher, perhaps she can recommend a grade for the girls."

Lauren grinned. Even Mr. Arnold looked happy. "Excellent suggestion, Mrs. Berman."

"Yes," I agreed. "Isn't it." I gave Lauren a quick kiss. "Go back to class, honey."

I watched her go with a warm feeling. Kicking ass for the sake of my kids is something I do quite naturally. I don't send back bad food in a restaurant, and I've never returned an appliance if it breaks while under warranty. I even feel bad about telling the sales clerk at Chico's that she forgot my Passport discount again. But with my daughters, I grow an instant backbone.

Mr. Arnold put his hand on my shoulder as I started to leave. "Mrs. Berman?"

I turned. He looked the soul of sympathy and understanding.

"Is there someone who can be with you today? After that kind of news, you probably shouldn't be alone. A sister perhaps? Or a neighbor?"

"Darling," he whispered into her hair, holding her gently, "what can I do? How can I help you?" She leaned back to gaze into the dark tenderness of his eyes. "Just love me," she said, pulling down his head to meet his mouth with her own.

"Better than that," I said. "My plumber."

He looked confused, but then smiled. "If you ever feel the need to talk," he went on, "please think of me as a friend. I can understand that having your husband leave you for a younger woman can be a very humbling experience."

"Mr. Arnold," I said between clenched teeth, "looking into a lighted makeup mirror with a plus-seven magnification is a humbling experience. Having your husband leave you for a younger woman just plain sucks."

And then I left.

~

When I got back home, everything looked exactly the same. The furniture gleamed softly. Fred was stretched out in his favorite patch of sunshine on the living room floor. Lana was curled up on the softest pillow of the window seat. I could sense a vague feeling of something missing, probably my luggage, but my home looked the same as it did when Brian was still living in it.

I sat down in the hall and called my best friend, Patricia Carmichael. Everyone needs a best friend like Patricia. She's very rich. I mean, she's a Carmichael, born and raised on the North Shore of Long Island, the same neighborhood Jay Gatsby lived in. That's the kind of rich she is.

Now, you might ask, why would I, being a Quincy by birth, be impressed by that? Because I'm not one of *those* Quincys. My Polish great-grandfather, coming over to America and standing in line on Ellis Island, was told that his name was too long and too hard to pronounce. The clerk helpfully suggested that my GGF take five letters from his last name, and use those as his Americanized name. GGF looked at his wife, who picked out Q, N, Y, C, and I. They rearranged the letters, and presented the new name to the same nice, helpful clerk, who pointed out that, in America at least, if you really wanted a Q in there, you'd need a U as well, and the Quincy family, later of Belleville, New Jersey, was founded. If those were the letters they wanted to keep, you can imagine the ones they left behind. Surprisingly, the DAR has never approached me or any other members of my Quincy family tree. Those DAR babes know the score.

Back to Patricia. She is very beautiful, which, in addition to the really rich part, is a little hard to get past, but once you do, she's a wonderful person and the best friend you could ever want. We're friends because, being a Carmichael, she's a patron of the arts, and in Westfield, New Jersey, writing historical romance is actually considered art, and about fifteen years ago we met at a Westfield Salutes the Arts festival. I didn't know who she was, I just knew by looking at her that she was way out of my league. You've seen the type, probably in Bloomies or Saks. She's one of those impeccably dressed women, with very expensive-looking ash blonde hair, amazing bone structure and knock-your-eyes-out diamonds in very classy settings.

She approached me, a martini glass in one hand, and when she found out who I was, she told me she was a fan of my books. I didn't believe her. I thought I knew my demographic, and it didn't include her. But she insisted, smiled, and leaned in very close.

"You must tell me," she asked in a low and husky voice, "all those marvelous sex scenes you write? Do you really have that good an imagination, or are you the luckiest woman in New Jersey?"

After an icebreaker like that, I was smitten. We met a few times for coffee after that, but our friendship was cemented one afternoon when we had lunch at the Highlawn Pavilion and she taught me how to drink.

The Highlawn Pavilion, for those who don't know, is a breathtaking mansion with an even more breathtaking view of the Manhattan skyline. She picked me up for lunch in her baby-blue Mercedes, and we were soon ensconced in a deep banquette, surrounded by quiet, luxury, and the promise of excellent food. The waiter, a very proper-looking gentleman who knew Patricia and addressed her by name, which impressed me like you would not believe, asked what we wanted to drink. I said a Tequila Sunrise. The silence at the table fell like a dead hippopotamus. The waiter did not write anything on his little pad but instead turned to look at Patricia. So did I.

Patricia leaned forward and spoke gently. "Really, darling, wouldn't you rather have a martini?"

I was game, but ignorant. "What's in a martini?"

Patricia took a small breath. "Well, it's very simply made, you see, which is why it's so perfect. There's gin, very cold, and a splash of vermouth, also very cold, and an olive. Very cold."

"Hm." I looked back at the waiter. "It sounds lovely, but I don't like gin."

The waiter's face actually cracked, as though I had just told him his mother died. He looked back to Patricia. So did I.

Patricia, being extremely well bred, smiled serenely. "No problem," she said. "Vodka?"

Ah.

"Vodka martini," I said obediently, and the waiter, looking like he had just been spared having to throw himself in front of a speeding train, bowed and left.

We've been drinking them together ever since.

Patricia does not have caller ID in her house. She has staff to screen her calls for her, so it took a minute or two to get through. "Mona? Love, how are you?"

"Oh, Patricia," I started, then found I could not go on.

"Mona, what? Is it Jessica?" (See, I'm not the only one.)

"No. Well, there's Lauren. She hit a student over the head with her DNA."

Patricia, who had been over last week and had the girls preview their project for her, took a sharp intake of breath. "Oh, I'm sure she must have had a good reason."

"She did. And it's fine now, but actually it's Brian. He left me."

There was silence. "He left you? But, darling, why?"

"He met someone else. Dominique."

More silence. Then she chuckled. "Oh, Mona, not to worry. Obviously, this is some feeble cry for attention. There are no real women named Dominique."

This is why she's my best friend. "Yes, she's real. She's French."

"Oh, my God. Mona, darling, I'm coming right over. Make sure the vodka is cold." Another reason why she's my best friend.

I went into the kitchen and sat. Four years ago, when we did our big kitchen/family room remodel, I insisted on a full-sized refrigerator and, right next to it, a full-sized freezer. I told Brian it was so that I could stock up on sirloins and swordfish from Costco, and could always have more than

just one flavor of ice cream on hand, but the real reason was
so that I could stash four one-liter bottles of Grey Goose at
the bottom, where they would always be perfectly cold and
ready for anything.

It took Patricia fourteen minutes to arrive, which meant
she hit all the lights. I was still sitting in the kitchen when
she burst through the back door. She gave me a very long
and hard hug. Then she stepped back. "Mona, I'm here
now. We'll get through this. Do you have olives?"

I nodded. Patricia knows her way around my kitchen,
and in no time flat, had the martinis made. She poured
mine and slid it across the countertop. I took a long,
icy swallow.

The classic martini is a very simple thing, but they always
taste better to me when Patricia makes them. I have tried
her technique many times, but it's never quite the same. I
think it's something in the way she fondles the ice. Here's
how she does it:

1) Open freezer, removing vodka (or gin) and taking
enough ice to fill a tall glass pitcher, preferably from
Tiffany's.
2) Plunge martini glasses, also preferably from Tiffany's,
into the indentation made from taking out the ice.
3) Open a bottle of vermouth. Add one capful to the
pitcher, swirl gently three times, then pour whatever vermouth not clinging to the ice down the drain.
4) Pour cold vodka into the pitcher, counting out one
one-hundred, two one-hundred, three one-hundred,
four one-hundred, five one-hundred.
5) Stir slowly.

6) Dry two or three pitted but unstuffed olives with an imported Irish linen towel.

7) Remove glasses from freezer. Drop in the olives.

8) Pour vodka mixture carefully into glasses. Sip or gulp as needed.

The best thing about a martini is that I usually only need one to make everything all better. That day, I knew I was in for a long, wet afternoon.

"So, tell me, when did this happen?" Patricia always speaks in a very low and cultivated voice. She often goes into what I call her Junior League mode, when she barely moves her lips and her jaw is frozen shut. She can have lengthy conversations this way, without ever really opening her mouth, not even for vowels.

"This morning," I croaked. The first jolt of icy vodka tends to cause my vocal cords to seize up. By the third sip, I'm usually all right.

"What? This *just* happened?"

I nodded. "Yes. He came home in the middle of the morning to tell me and to pack all his stuff.'"

"And her name is really Dominique?" Patricia asked, her eyes bright. Being the gracious person that she is, she'd poured my drink first, then her own. She can fill her glass to the absolute top and never spill a drop when picking it up. I don't know how she does it. She always holds her martini glass the same way, with the bowl resting in her upturned palm, held slightly away from her body so in case she's jostled by some clumsy oaf she won't suffer any damage. Just like June Allyson in *The Women*.

She took a quick sip. "You poor thing. Does MarshaMarsha know?"

MarshaMarsha is my next-door neighbor and another one of my very best friends. I call her MarshaMarsha to distinguish her from Brian's sister, MarshaTheBitch. MarshaTheBitch used to be plain old Marsha, a tolerable sister-in-law, a kindly older sister to Brian, and a very generous aunt to the girls. When my father-in-law died ten years ago, Marsha realized she was Jewish and decided to do something about it. The Bermans had always been members of the Ultra-Non-Observant Temple, which means they remembered the High Holidays, but didn't necessarily do anything about them. But when Marsha decided to embrace Judaism, she wanted the rest of the Berman clan to join in.

My mother-in-law, Phyllis, the new widow, patted Marsha's hand and explained that for over forty-five years she had been faithfully praying to God that she would die before her husband, or, better yet, have them die together, hand in hand, and since God had chosen to ignore her, she wasn't going to start making the extra effort now. Rebecca, the younger sister, who was a practicing Wiccan and had been for almost ten years, may have done something involving burning herbs grown at the waning of the moon, because Marsha developed a mysterious and nasty rash that lingered for weeks. Brian laughed, the girls balked, and I, being a non-observant Catholic, refused to get involved in any way. Of course, Marsha blamed me for the family's eventual descent into hell, and she began referring to me as the Goy Slut who Brian had (insert heavy sigh here) married. This after being in my wedding party all those years ago. So, she easily became MarshaTheBitch

But MarshaMarsha remained MarshaMarsha. She didn't mind, although I'm sure she inwardly winced at *Brady Bunch* reruns. Her real name is Marsha Riollo, and she is an absolute doll.

As I shook my head, Patricia went to the back door, yanked it open, and yelled for MarshaMarsha. MarshaMarsha, having four boys under the age of twelve and the reflexes of a Navy SEAL, was in the house before the echo died away.

"What?" she asked. "Did something happen?" Her eyes went quickly to the martini glasses. It was a familiar sight in my kitchen, actually, but since it was barely one in the afternoon, she realized that something must be amiss.

"Brian left," Patricia announced. "Can I get you a drink?"

MarshaMarsha sat beside me and grasped my hand. "Oh, Mona, really? Is that why the car was here this morning? I saw Brian drive up and I thought, well…" She shrugged. I know what she thought. Her husband, Alphonse, a successful chiropractor with an office right in town, often walked home for a nooner with his adorable Italian wife. And she *is* adorable, round and pretty, with curly dark hair and big, brown eyes.

I sniffed and knocked back what was left of my drink. "He left me for Dominique. She's thirty. And French. And a size four. My life is over. I'm going to die with eight cats and no husband." And then I put my head down on the table and really started to cry.

I don't know how long I sobbed, but when I finally lifted my head, MarshaMarsha handed me a much-needed wad of tissues. I dried my eyes, blew my nose a lot, and took several long, deep breaths. Then Patricia handed me another martini, which went down much more smoothly than the first one. The second always does.

"You," Patricia said distinctly, "need to call Brian's mother."

I stared at her. "Phyllis? Why do I need to call Phyllis?"

"Because," MarshaMarsha said, "she's his mother, and in her eyes, he can do no wrong. You need to call her and tell her what happened before he does so she knows what a snake he really is. If he gets to her first, she'll think this is all your doing and start telling all the relatives how happy she is that he finally got out of his hellish marriage."

"Oh, my God. Really?" I was shocked. "No, Phyllis likes me. She would never approve of his leaving."

MarshaMarsha shook her head. "Honey, believe me. When it comes to mother's-in-law, the Italians and the Jews are only separated by their opinion of pork. I know. Call her. Tell her. And then ask for her help in getting him back, so your family doesn't end up on the cover of *Broken Homes Monthly.*"

I looked at Patricia for confirmation. She was holding the phone in her hand. I nodded. She hit speed dial and handed me the phone.

Phyllis Berman, at seventy-eight, is still physically spry, mentally agile, and happily living in Bay Ridge, Brooklyn, in the same sprawling, three-bedroom apartment that she raised her family in. When her husband Lewis, died, we were all a little worried about her living alone. But Phyllis posted an ad on the bulletin board at Brooklyn School of Law. She had two empty bedrooms and an extra bathroom, so she turned them into a very nice suite and, for the past ten years, has had a series of young and accommodating law students living with her. She charges them an incredibly nominal rent, and in exchange, they help with errands, keep her company at mealtimes, and make sure she takes all her required medications. It's a perfect arrangement. And she gets free legal advice whenever she wants or needs it.

Phyllis is another one without caller ID. I don't know how people do it, but she says she likes being surprised.

"Phyllis, it's Mona."

"Mona, my favorite daughter-in-law," she said. It's an old joke, but she loves it.

"Phyllis," I said, my voice a little shaky, "I've got some not-so-good news. Are you sitting down?"

"Yes. Mona, is it Jessica?" My poor daughter.

"No. Phyllis, I don't know what to do. Brian has met another woman."

There was a very long pause. "My Brian? Another woman? No, Mona, I think you must be mistaken. Brian works very hard, you know. If he hasn't been coming home some nights, I'm sure there's a reasonable explanation."

"He's been coming home fine, Phyllis," I said, my voice getting stronger. "That's not it. He told me himself."

Pause. "What did he say exactly, dear? I mean, men are entitled to have friends. If he met somebody nice, so what? Don't jump to any hasty conclusions. Invite her to dinner. I'm sure that once you get to know her, you'll find her to be a delightful person."

This was becoming much harder than I had anticipated. "Phyllis. Listen to me. Brian told me that he has met another woman and that he's in love with her."

"Hold on, dear. I need to get a drink of water." I could hear a thud as she set the phone down. I stared at the receiver in amazement. I glanced at MarshaMarsha and Patricia, both of whom had that I-told-you-so look.

Noise on the phone. Phyllis was back. "Now, Mona, sometimes men reach an age where they, well, question their manhood. Sometimes they need a little fantasy to get over the hump."

"Phyllis, this is not a hump. Well, actually it is, but it's not any hump that I'm a part of. Brian came home this morning, packed his clothes, and left the house." I was almost shouting. "He told me he was leaving me for a thirty-year-old French woman he met at work. Her name is Dominique and he's moving in with her." I forced my voice back down to a normal pitch and managed to conjure up a little sob as I drove it home. "He's got a lawyer."

"Lawyer? He's got a lawyer?" Phyllis finally got it. "Probably that slime-bucket Hirsch Fielding, who thinks nobody knows he changed his name from Feldstein. I knew his mother, Sadie. The poor woman turns over in her grave every time her worthless son takes on another client." She was silent. "I can't believe that my son would do this, Mona. I am ashamed. For a man to leave his wife and family like this. Thank God Lewis isn't alive to see this day." She had been sounding a little frail, but she suddenly got back into gear. "If you need anything, you let me know. I know you've got money of your own, but you call, okay? And if my daughter the religious fanatic tries to give you a hard time, you tell me. Okay?"

"Oh, Phyllis, thank you," I said gratefully. "I was afraid for a minute that you wouldn't understand."

"What's to understand? You two got married by a rabbi in sight of God and the family. Brian should know better.

He is a disgrace. And I'll tell him that when he calls." She slammed down the phone. I hung up more gently.

"Well?" Patricia asked.

"Thank God I went with a rabbi instead of a priest," I said.

MarshaMarsha nodded. I noticed that sometime during my crying spell, she had acquired a martini. She patted my hand again. "Everything happens for a reason, honey. Honest. You may not know what the reasons are, but it will all become clear."

Patricia, who does not necessarily hold to the life-is-a-cosmic-plan idea, rolled her eyes. "Whatever. But I know who you should call next. David West."

I squinted at her. "Who's David West?"

"My divorce lawyer. Believe me, with all the business I give him, he'll probably take on your case pro-bono." Patricia just finished up with Husband Number Three. I think the reason she has always kept her maiden name is that she values economy of motion, and who wants to keep filling out all those name-change forms?

I nodded. Now, you may be asking why, in such a time of stress, I didn't do what every other woman would immediately do, which is call my mother. Sadly, the wonderful and ever-supportive Evelyn Quincy passed many years ago, shortly after the death of her beloved husband, Jerry. Now, I do have a sister, who, being older, might have been a good substitute, but Grace and I are not really that close. She lives on a commune in Oregon. She's lived there since she ran away from home in 1976 with a hash-smoking sitar player named Shadow. She's a grandmother now, and Shadow makes handmade musical instruments that sell for several thousands of dollars, but she is still just a little bit flaky, and has never forgiven me for not giving up my Nestlé Crunch bars years ago, when there was a big to-do over something, I forget what, but it really got under her skin. I just shrugged it off and kept on eating chocolate.

Just then, there was a rattle at the back door. Somebody was turning the doorknob. I flew out of my chair and threw open the door, shrieking, "Brian!", but it was not Brian. It was Ben Cutler, my plumber. He stopped smiling as I dissolved into tears again.

"Mona? What's wrong?" Ah, Ben. He's tall, maybe, six foot two. He's almost forty, but in great shape, with broad shoulders and amazingly sexy arms. Muscular, you know, from throwing all those toilets around. He's got very dark, straight hair and bright blue eyes and a dimple you could get lost in. In a work shirt and tool belt, he stops traffic.

"Brian's gone," I wailed, and threw my arms around his neck, sobbing some more. He put his arms around me, very nicely too, and patted me on the back.

She could feel the heat of his hands through the sea-green silk of her bodice, and the long, hard length of him as his arms tightened, drawing her closer, his lips in her hair. Her heart was pounding, and she could feel the rush of blood as she lifted her mouth to his.

"There, there," he murmured, or something equally ineffective. We stood like that for a few seconds then he, as I would have written, "gently disengaged himself" from my desperate grasp.

He looked down at me sternly. "Take a deep breath, Mona."

I did, several times, and wiped my eyes with the back of my hand. Ideally, he would have handed me a starched white handkerchief, smelling faintly of tobacco, musky sweat, and old whiskey, or, better yet, wiped my eyes for me, but men don't carry handkerchiefs anymore, whiskey-smelling or otherwise.

"Where did he go?" Ben asked.

"To Dominique's. With all his clothes."

Ben looked around. He knew both Patricia and MarshaMarsha, of course, not just because he's spent so much time at my house, but because I have recommended him to all my friends and he has seen the insides of their bathrooms as well.

Patricia folded her arms across her breasts. "It's true, Ben. The stinker took a powder. We were just discussing lawyers."

Ben frowned, and then his eyes lit on the martini pitcher. "Any extra?" he asked. Patricia, a born hostess even if it's not her house, jumped to the task of finding another glass and cracking open a new jar of olives.

Now, before you get the wrong idea, Ben does not usually waltz into my kitchen and settle in for a cocktail. But between my hysteria and Patricia's pronouncement, he probably figured it was a good move.

Ben steered me to my chair and pushed me back down. Gently but firmly. His hands were on his hips and his head tilted slightly to the side. The sunlight was behind him, casting his handsome, rugged features into dark relief.... But wait. Perhaps I'm getting a bit off track. He looked down at me, shaking his head in disbelief.

"Are you telling me that Brian has left? Really?"

All three of us nodded. MarshaMarsha, I noticed, was sitting up a little straighter and was slowly caressing the long, smooth stem of her martini glass.

"I can't believe it," Ben continued. I gazed up at him, waiting for his next words of comfort, but Patricia handed him a martini, momentarily distracting him. He took a sip, nodded his approval, and drank some more. "This is terrible, Mona. Terrible. Why any man in his right mind would leave a woman like you is beyond all belief."

If I had been on my third martini, instead of my second, I very well might have thrown myself at his feet in gratitude, not to mention a teeny bit of lust. As it was, I just nodded and tried to look brave and plucky.

Ben appeared to be thinking about something. He frowned slightly, sipped slowly, and finally nodded. "You need a good lawyer," he said at last. "First thing. My last wife had a great one. Cleaned me out."

MarshaMarsha leaned forward. "Oh, you're divorced, Ben? I never knew that."

"Oh, yeah. About four years now." He was running his tongue over his lips, relishing the memory, or perhaps going for that last bit of martini, and all three of us women took in a long, collective breath.

He set down his empty glass. "I came over about the tub. But I'll come back. This must be awful for you."

Awful? Why was he saying awful? Sitting there, looking up at him, I was having a lovely time. I realized, with a jolt, that I had never been around Ben while under the influence of two Carmichael Martinis before, and that my judgment was, to say the least, severely impaired. Brian had left. I was despondent. I had no right to be smiling up at my plumber.

"It's okay, Ben," I said at last. "You'd better go up. I want things around here to be as normal as possible for the girls."

Ben nodded and headed up the back staircase. Patricia slumped slightly against the freezer as he left.

"Has he always looked that good?" she asked.

MarshaMarsha nodded. "Oh, yeah."

"God," Patricia muttered. "Why did I never notice?"

"You were probably married last time you saw him," I said. "And sober."

"I'm sober now, darling, not to worry. You're slurring a bit, though. Speaking of the girls, how are you going to tell them?"

"He wanted us to do it together," I told her. "Miserable bastard." I gazed into my empty glass and felt a new swell of misery. "They're going to be so upset. They love their daddy."

MarshaMarsha pushed her empty glass toward Patricia with significant force. "Your daughters will be fine. They're really very good kids."

"Miranda will say it's my fault," I said in a muffled voice.

Patricia tut-tutted as she played with the ice. "Darling, be reasonable. How can she possibly blame you for this?"

"She'll find a way. Remember last January, when the blizzard closed down the roads and she couldn't get to the Green Day concert? That was my fault. And it was my fault when the cat coughed up a hairball on her dress for the Freshman Formal last year." I sank my head back down on the table. "She blamed me when Heath Ledger died."

"Mona, when things are the worst, people rise above. I bet your daughters will surprise you," MarshaMarsha said.

I heard Patricia make a noise that, in another, less genteel person, might have been called a snort. Patricia has no children, and while she takes a keen interest in all her friends' offspring, she harbors no delusions about the human spirit, especially the human spirit as found in teenaged girls.

We all sat drinking in silence for a few minutes. My lips, during this time, became completely numb. Patricia, recognizing the signs, took charge.

"We need lunch," she announced. "We need lots of food, soon, or we'll be passed out when the girls do get home." She opened my refrigerator and began hauling things out. I watched her with keen interest.

I am a very good cook. I am also a very good eater. I have to work hard at not ballooning up to a size 22W. By working hard, please don't misunderstand me. I'm not talking exercise. No, not at all. Although I do walk a great deal, including up to town and the Yoga Center, where, about once a week, I stretch and moan to Navajo flute music and very bad incense. No, by working hard I mean that I stay away from white food and ice cream except on weekends, and I try to eat a healthy balance of protein and complex carbohydrates, as well as low-fat fats to keep my skin and hair looking good.

Patricia is an excellent cook. Gourmet stuff. Without ever having to look at a recipe. And she's bone thin. She once explained to me that her weight had never been an issue for her, that her whole family was just naturally slender and she could eat whatever she wanted whenever she wanted. I still like her.

In a remarkably short time, she presented us with a platter of open-faced sandwiches, hot and bubbly from the broiler, lots of lovely salad and big glasses of cold water. She called up and asked Ben if he was hungry. Then we all sat and waited for him to come downstairs.

Now, Ben coming downstairs is not nearly as impressive as Ben going upstairs, as you can imagine, or maybe you can't, but it's still a show worth watching. He sat down with us, smiled politely, and we all began to eat our lunch.

My first bite was asparagus and roasted red pepper under melted Fontina cheese. "This is really good," I told Patricia. "Where did you get the cheese?"

Patricia waited until she had swallowed to answer. "From your fridge, dear. Where else?"

"And the asparagus?" I asked.

"Where do you think?" Patricia doesn't get angry at stupid questions, only stupid people.

"I don't remember buying it," I said, trying to explain myself to Ben. Ben smiled.

"I'm surprised you still remember your name at this point," MarshaMarsha said. "How are you feeling?"

I thought about that. Aside from a very big buzz that was filling me to the eyeballs, I was really pissed off.

"I'm really pissed," I said.

They all stopped to watch me.

"Really angry," I continued. "He's not just leaving me. He's leaving his family. His daughters. And for what? That's what I don't get. If he wanted to screw her, he could have done it and I probably never would have even known. He's always working late and going on business trips. He could have had his little thing on the side and gone on with us at the same time. Why did he have to tell me?" I felt tears again. "Why did he have to hurt me like that? It's just so—

49

well, *mean*. Mean. Why would he do that?" I looked around at three kind and sympathetic faces.

"Oh, honey," MarshaMarsha said softly.

I took another sandwich. Crumbled bacon, mushrooms, and hot blue cheese. I took a few bites, chewing carefully as no one said a word. I was starting to feel more focused. I took several gulps of water.

"I don't know how he's going to explain this to the girls," I said. "Is he going to tell them the truth? I mean, come on, a thirty-year-old girlfriend?" I viciously stabbed my salad with a fork. "And the thing is, I thought everything was fine. I mean, we weren't fighting. We were still having sex. We were planning his sister's birthday party. It's a surprise party. Here. I didn't know anything was wrong. If I thought we were in trouble, I'd have been more prepared, or something. But he just came home and said—" I stopped and drank more water. I looked fiercely at Ben. "You didn't cheat on your wife, did you?"

Ben shook his head. "No. She wanted kids. I already had the boys from my first wife." He never talked about his first wife, adding an air of mystery to his past. Like he needed to add anything. I could see Patricia starting to move her hand to touch his, then pulling back. Luckily, I was closer. "I'm glad," I murmured, patting the back of his long-jointed, strong hands, feeling the soft and springy hairs on his fingers...never mind.

Ben pushed back from the table and Lana jumped up onto his lap. She rubbed her head against his abdomen a few times, kneaded her paws into his well-muscled thigh, and settled into his lap, licking her whiskers with a tiny pink tongue and purring.

Slut.

Ben absently scratched her head, causing all three of us at the table to tilt our heads slightly to the side, as though his fingers might then catch a good spot behind the ear.

"He'll come around," Ben said assuredly. "Guys get stupid at a certain age. He'll realize what he left behind and come to his senses."

"Yes," Patricia said silkily. "But the question is, should Mona take him back?"

I thought about that. "Of course. I mean, there are the girls, and the life we've built together. I want to save that."

Ben was nodding. "Naturally. You're a smart woman, Mona. Be patient, and I promise, you'll get what you want."

Luckily, the food and water had their desired effect, or I would have added that I also wanted a weekend away with my favorite plumber, preferably spent naked.

MarshaMarsha swooped in and started clearing the table. She probably wasn't sure if I had reached a sobriety point that could be trusted.

I took a long breath in and shook my head. "This hasn't really sunk in yet," I told them. "I'm having a hard time getting my head around all this. I need to sit someplace quiet and try to sort this out before the girls get home."

"Absolutely," Ben said, picking up Lana as he stood and holding her against his chest. She looked so smug. I swear, she was smiling. "I need to go down to the basement and finish this up, but I should be out of here in less than an hour."

"I'll clear this up," MarshaMarsha offered. "Why don't you go into the living room and just sit for a while?"

"Excellent idea," Patricia chimed in. "I'll help you, Marsha." She looked with regret at the martini pitcher. "I don't think you'll be needing any more of these today."

"Oh, no," I said. "I need a clear head for the rest of the day." I was getting up and starting toward the front of the house when the doorbell rang. We all looked at one another, and moved as one to the front door.

I opened the door and there stood my Aunt Lily. She was paying off a tired-looking taxi driver who had apparently hauled at least six pieces of luggage from his cab up the walkway to my front door. She smiled brightly as she stepped over her Louis Vuitton makeup case.

"I'm sorry I didn't call, Mona, but I didn't want to get into an argument over the phone, so I just came on over."

"From Brooklyn?" I asked, as I took her coat. "With all this?"

"Everything else is in storage," she explained. "Hello, Patricia, how are you? And Marsha? Did I interrupt something? Ladies' lunch?"

"Sort of" I said. Ben was gallantly moving several suitcases into the hall. "Aunt Lily, what's going on? Why are things in storage?"

Lily adjusted her sweater. "I sold the apartment."

My jaw dropped. She had, for years, lived in a two-bedroom co-op in Prospect Park, Brooklyn. "Sold?"

"Yes."

"You're moving?"

"Well," she shrugged. "Eventually. I don't know where, exactly. So I just thought I'd stay with you until I figured it all out." She smiled serenely. "I know you won't mind. I just hope Brian isn't too upset." She looked at Ben. "Those go up in the guest room, dear. I don't know who you are, but I do hope you're going to stay for a while." She swept past us into the living room. At that moment, Fred, who finally figured out that the doorbell he'd heard was his doorbell, came bounding out of the den, barking furiously and knocking over two large suitcases. The phone, mercifully silent until now, began to ring. And the carbon monoxide alarm, hung at the top of the stairs, inexplicably began to wail.

I looked at Patricia. "Forget that clear-head crap. Make more."

Chapter Three

My Aunt Lily is my father's only sibling, his younger sister, and she is also my godmother, born of a generation who took the duties of godmother very seriously, so she has always been a keen and, I must admit, welcomed presence in my life. Every year, from my fifth birthday until I went away to college, she would spend a whole day with me in New York City: a fancy lunch, a trip to a museum, and a carriage ride in Central Park. She took me to my first ballet. For my sixteenth birthday, she gave me a strand of pearls. I'm quite sure that, had I been a boy, she would have taken me to a discreet whorehouse and bought me my first woman instead. After the death of her husband, my sweet Uncle Larry, twelve years ago, she sailed gracefully into old age without him, traveling to all the places they had dreamed about together, and keeping two season tickets to the Metropolitan Opera. I know she loved Uncle Larry very much. It's a tribute to her strength and zest for living that the mourning process did not interfere in any way with her desired lifestyle.

Aunt Lily is tall, thin, stooped, and dresses like Miss Marple, in straight skirts, soft blouses, and cardigan sweaters. She wears stockings and low-heeled shoes in all weather, and although I had seen her in a bathing suit once, she generally keeps most of her skin covered in public. Her hair is snow white, cut short and carefully permed. She'd hit seventy-two that winter and thankfully had not appeared to lose any of her mental agility. She had, however, lost what Brian called the "couth gene." She says whatever she wants whenever she feels like it, and often leaves a room with several open mouths behind. I really do love her.

But at that moment, with bells ringing and the dog barking and the faint snarl of an impending headache at the base of my skull, I really wanted her gone.

MarshaMarsha answered the phone, Ben bounded up the stairs, and Patricia grabbed Fred and yanked him back to the den. I stood for a moment in the hallway, taking a few breaths, then went after Aunt Lily.

I love my living room. It's long and broad, with tall windows and a beautiful fireplace. All the furniture is what Ethan Allen calls "transitional." Comfortable, but not formal. Cushioned without being overstuffed. Elegant but welcoming, in soft taupes and grays and creams. I often just sit here with a book and look around in pleasure. Brian and I had many times come here just to talk. It's a talking kind of room. The dog is not allowed on the furniture and there are never any empty soda cans around.

Aunt Lily was sitting in my favorite chair, still adjusting her clothing, smiling at me. "I did interrupt, didn't I? I'm sorry, Mona, but, I felt it best to just walk through the door. If I tried to explain what it was I was planning to do, I was afraid we'd argue, because I don't have a clue what to do next."

"I see." Although I didn't. "So, you sold the apartment?"

"Yes. For 1.3 million dollars."

"Oh." That's the kind of information that could stop any conversation. At the same moment, MarshaMarsha stuck her head in.

"Your sister-in-law is on the phone," she said. "Marsha."

Good Lord, those tribal drums were quick. "Tell her I'll call her tomorrow," I said to MarshaMarsha. I turned back to Aunt Lily. "You were saying, ah, 1.3 million?"

"Yes. I could have held out for more, but I wanted a quick sale. I've become very concerned about the impending arrival of Martians in Prospect Park and wanted to get out of Brooklyn as quickly as possible."

That's also a big conversation stopper. My jaw may have been hanging open.

Patricia sailed back in, looking totally unruffled. "Lily, we were just finishing up lunch. Can I get you something? The trip must have been horrendous in midday traffic," Patricia said, looking at Aunt Lily as though Aunt Lily were a normal person.

"Patricia, that would be lovely. I am famished. And, truthfully, I'd love one of those famous martinis of yours."

Patricia looked modest. "Certainly. We were just discussing another round as you came in. Perfect timing."

"Aunt Lily," I said loudly, "was just saying that she felt the urgent need to leave Brooklyn because of the impending Martian invasion of Prospect Park."

Patricia blinked. "Well, then, we'd better get you a double," she crooned, and swept out. MarshaMarsha, hovering in the hallway, stuck her head back in.

"Martian invasion?" she asked. I don't blame her. I mean, honestly, who wouldn't be curious?

"Yes. It's not generally talked about, but those of us on the Park know." Aunt Lily tightened her lips. "The media, of course, refuses to listen."

I didn't know where to look. Luckily, Ben came in, shaking his head.

She watched as he came towards her, his stride long and purposeful, his dark hair curling beneath the brim of his hat, his broad shoulders pushing aside the crowd. He caught her eye and smiled, and she felt a slow pounding in her veins as he came closer.

"I think there's a short in the alarm," he said. "That's why it went off. It's hardwired in, you know, so I had to disconnect it at the electrical panel. I'll call Alex tomorrow and have him take a look, okay?" Alex, I vaguely remembered, was an electrician, short and red-haired. Wore a Rolex. Ben turned to Aunt Lily. "I've put all your bags in the guest room. Have a pleasant visit."

Aunt Lily began to visibly flirt. "Why thank you, my dear man. And who are you again? I don't believe we've met."

"This is my plumber, Ben," I explained, sinking wearily into a chair. "Ben, this is my Aunt Lily."

Ben actually walked over and kissed her hand. "A pleasure. May I call you Lily?"

"Oh, but of course. So, you're Ben? Why, the girls have told me all about you."

I looked over in alarm. "The girls? My girls? Have told you all about Ben? What have they told you?"

Lily smiled mischievously. "They've told me that he has the most marvelous ass. My dear man, could you possibly turn around and bend over?"

Ben was, understandably, speechless.

MarshaMarsha looked at me in complete amazement, took a deep breath and spoke, very heartily. "Ben, are you done in the basement, or are there still a few things to finish up?"

Ben smiled woodenly and backed out of the living room. I think that only his iron will prevented him from clasping his hands protectively over his marvelous ass.

Aunt Lily was craning her neck to watch him disappear around the corner. "My heavens," she said, "if I were twenty years younger, I'd ride him hard then rub him down slow." She smiled wistfully. "Then I'd ride him again."

Before I could say anything—not that I was capable of reasonable speech, but still—Patricia came back in, carrying a tray laden with sandwiches and, thank the Lord, another pitcher and some more glasses. She had broken out the second string as far as the martini glasses went—the shorter ones, with smaller bowls and thicker stems. Still perfectly adequate, of course.

"Now, Lily," she said as she handed Aunt Lily a plate of food and began pouring, "tell me all about the Martians."

"Well, they're not really Martians," Aunt Lily said, nibbling the corner of something topped with more melted Fontina.

My shoulders slumped in relief. Thank God. Of course, there were no Martians. She probably was thinking of the conservation group that camped in the park last year to protest the spraying of the white-winged moth or something.

"Well, of course there are no Martians coming," I agreed, gratefully taking a very tiny sip.

"No. I don't know what they're called, exactly," Aunt Lily continued. "Their planet, you see, is very far from here. So Mr. Knapper, you know, from down the hall, just called them Martians. But I'm sure they have their own proper name. You know, like the Muslims and the Iowans do." She sipped her martini and nodded in appreciation. "Excellent, Patricia. I really needed this. And the sandwich, too. I did interrupt something, didn't I? I'm sorry, Mona dear. A celebration, perhaps? Is it someone's birthday?"

"Brian left me," I blurted. "Today. This morning. For another woman."

Aunt Lily stared at me. "Really?"

"Yes." I drained the entire contents of my glass without a blink.

Aunt Lily put her glass down and sighed. "Well, thank heavens for that. You're lucky to be rid of him, Mona dear. He was without a doubt the worst husband ever."

Patricia, I could see, was visibly moved. That didn't happen to her very often. Her lips actually parted and her hand, bringing her glass up to her lips, stopped midway.

"Aunt Lily," I sputtered. "I thought you liked Brian!"

"Oh, I do dear. Very much." Lily had put her plate of food down on the coffee table to take her drink from Patricia, and was now squinting at the sandwich selection, her hand wavering between the cold prosciutto and the hot blue cheese. "He's so charming. Funny, but not too obvious. Good at parties. And he's generous. That necklace he gave you a few months ago? Very well done." She frowned and looked up at me. "But as a husband he really sucked. I never could figure out why you stayed with him for so long."

"He was a great husband," I roared. "And a wonderful father. He has always been a great partner." Right up until he started screwing around, that is.

Aunt Lily took a few moments to swallow her sandwich, then sipped her martini again, delicately. "He never did a thing to help you, dear. Let's face it, you ran this home and took care of the girls, and aside from bringing home a great paycheck, he never lifted a finger. You have always done it all, dear. My heavens, you even had to schedule his colonoscopy last year. I mean, the man couldn't arrange for a tube going up his own ass. Useless. Of course, he was probably a good tumble, but that can only go so far." She smiled sweetly. "Not to worry, dear. You're much better off without him."

"Aunt Lily," I was breathing heavily, "you're wrong. He was my best friend."

She shook her head. "No, Mona. You're very lucky to have two best friends right here in this room with you. But Brian was never your friend. Brian never thought about anyone but Brian. He was always the most important person in the room. A best friend is someone you can call up in the middle of the night because you're afraid or mad or in jail, and that person will drop everything to help. Brian wouldn't even get up to answer the phone. He never once put anything or anybody ahead of his own needs. Didn't you ever notice that? I mean really, Mona, you were married to him, what, twenty years?"

I nodded dumbly.

"And what I really didn't like was how he never took you seriously," she went on. "As a writer. We talked about it a few times, you know. He thought it was some little hobby of yours. He never respected all your hard work. He just liked going to all the award parties."

"Not true!" I yelled.

Aunt Lily set down her glass and looked at me very seriously. "Dear Mona, I'm so sorry. But I bet if you asked him, he couldn't name one of your books."

I looked at Patricia and MarshaMarsha, and something in their faces stopped my anger. Aunt Lily was right. Brian had been a lousy husband.

I had never thought about it much, because he *was* very charming. We were always laughing together about something. He would stretch his legs out in front of him and start waving his hands around, and soon the whole room would be smiling along with him.

But he wasn't big on helping around the house. Or running the girls to various sports events or rehearsals. He never had dinner ready if I came home late from the city, not even take-out. He never called anybody for anything, not the doctor, or our broker, or Ben Cutler. He didn't walk the dog or feed the cat. He let me hire the cleaning people and the lawn people and the painting people and the snow-plowing people and he never bought me a birthday or anniversary card. There was always something attached to a beautiful bouquet, of course, but nothing was ever signed by him in his own hand, and I knew for a fact that there were standing orders with our local florist to automatically send those beautiful bouquets because I had given those orders myself years ago.

What a bum.

"But I loved him," I said.

"I'm sure you did, dear," Aunt Lily said sadly. "But it doesn't look like he loved you."

"I think I need to rest for a few minutes," I said slowly. Why on earth had I finished that last martini? Was I crazy? I had almost been sober after lunch, and now I was back in that let's-spin-a-few-times-around-the-world mode. I needed somewhere quiet.

I wasn't going to get it. The back door slammed open, and I heard a familiar clomping. The girls were home already?

"They don't know yet," I hissed to Aunt Lily, and I pulled myself upright and forced myself to stand straight as Jessica rushed into the living room.

"Mom, did you really kick Mr. Arnold's butt?" Jessica asked.

Her face was beaming, her eyes bright, and she looked like she actually approved of me. I shrugged. "Well, I guess," I muttered modestly. "Where are your sisters?"

"Late bus. Lauren has yearbook and Miranda's chasing after some senior in the Spanish club. Did you really threaten to take Bernadette to the Board of Ed?"

Ah, urban legend. "I thought about it."

"That is so cool." Jessica dropped her backpack, which landed with enough force to cause a few priceless figurines on the fireplace mantel to jump. "Hi, Aunt Lily. Did Mom tell you what she did?"

Aunt Lily stood and swept Jessica up in a warm hug. "No, dear, we didn't get around to that yet. Let's blow this pop stand and head for the den, and you can tell me all about it. Are your nails supposed to be that color?"

Jessica grinned happily and trailed after Aunt Lily, pulling her backpack along behind her. I slumped back down on the couch and closed my eyes.

"She's right," I said. "Brian was a shitty husband, and I had a miserable marriage."

"Well, no," MarshaMarsha said. I opened my eyes and looked at her.

"Every marriage is different," she continued. "What you and Brian had worked for a long time. You've been very happy with him. What Lily said might have been true, but we all pay a price for what we want. You wanted Brian. If that meant running the show, you obviously never minded because you did it beautifully. You've been a great wife, even if he wasn't such a great husband."

Patricia nodded. "She's right, darling. He's the one losing here, not you. He'll never find another woman who's as accomplished and capable as you are. The man's an idiot. He'll probably figure it out for himself in a few months, when he has to start doing things like picking up his own dry-cleaning and remembering to take out the garbage." She tilted her head at me. "This is a lot for one day. Brian is coming back tonight? Why don't I hang around until then? You just rest for a while. I'll deflect the girls."

I swallowed hard. "Thank you."

MarshaMarsha got up and looked at me. "The boys are going to start coming home. I've got to go. I've got eggplant parm in the freezer. I'll have Joey run it over. The girls will want something hot for dinner, and Lily shouldn't have to cook her first night. I'll be by again tomorrow, okay?"

I nodded, stretched out on the couch, and closed my eyes. The room was still unsteady, and my lips were back to being slightly numb. My brain was racing, but thanks to all that vodka, I actually napped a little, hearing snatches of conversation that fit into odd, unhappy dreams. The cat curled against me, and I could have sworn Ben Cutler came in and kissed me on the cheek, but that may have been wishful thinking. I became fully awake quite suddenly when the room was turning dark and I could hear Brian's voice.

I jerked up from the couch, brushed down my hair, and tried to look like I was just sitting in the dark. He came into the room at a rush and angrily turned on the overhead light. I stood up and raised my chin proudly.

"You called my mother?" he snarled.

I nodded defiantly. Then, I crumpled just a little. I pointed to Patricia, who was standing right behind him.

"It was her idea."

Brian's eyes narrowed as he turned to look at her. "I should have known. Patricia, you are such a bitch."

She smiled. "Oh, darling," she cooed, "I know."

Aunt Lily came downstairs. She had changed from her sensible shoes to sensible slippers. She looked at Brian coldly. "I never did like you," she spat, then swept past him to sit by the fireplace, picking up a magazine from the side table and making quite a show of reading it.

Brian clenched his teeth. "My mother called me at work. I can't believe you told her."

"I just told her the truth, Brian," I said.

"We need to talk to the girls," he snarled.

I squared my shoulders. "No, Brian. *You* need to talk to them."

He wheeled around and headed back, yelling for the girls. I could hear protests coming from upstairs, but eventually they all came down and followed him into the den. I sat back down. Patricia sat with me. We waited.

They were in there for almost twenty minutes when I started to worry. Why wasn't anyone crying? Shouldn't somebody have started throwing things by now? Weren't they angry? Sad? I was trying to figure out how they were taking things when the doorbell rang. I got up, crossed the hall, and opened the door. It was Dominique.

My jaw dropped open. She was standing very stiffly, her tiny body wrapped like a sausage in a black suit, her very blonde hair swept up into a perfect twist.

"I got tired of waiting in zee car," she said. "Is everyzing okay?"

Now, in my novels, I know exactly what to say when the Other Woman has the balls to make an appearance. When Millicent Dupree realized that she actually loved her husband of three months, the silent but devastatingly handsome Geoffrey, Earl of Marchkirk, and came face to face with Syllabyne Combs, the earl's former mistress, Millicent put that Syllabyne whore in her place with a few scathing observations of character and one well-appointed insult. Amanda Sinclair, newly engaged to Wentworth, Duke of Briarcliff, sent Justine Rutledge, who had very serious designs on the duke, scampering off after a war of words that went on for two and a half pages. So in theory, at least, I knew the long and short of it. Looking at Dominique, however, I couldn't think of a single word to say. Lucky for me, I had Patricia and Aunt Lily.

Patricia went into her Junior League mode. I could tell by the stiffening of her neck and the way her jaw clenched. She let loose a barrage of words that sounded spiteful and insulting, but, since they were in French, I had no idea what they were.

Dominique, on the other hand, understood completely, because she went white.

"Non," she whispered.

Patricia moved her shoulders in a decidedly Gaelic gesture. Then, the real bombshell fell. Aunt Lily, coming up behind, also said something in French. Her accent, I could tell, was not as perfect, and Aunt Lily's lips actually moved when she spoke, but the effect was still pretty good.

Dominique visibly shrank. She took a few steps back. Then she turned and ran back to the car. Brian's car. The Mercedes.

"What did you say?" I asked.

Patricia smiled evenly. "I told her that there was a law in this country against husband-stealing and that if you pressed charges she would be sent back to France."

"Really?" Oh, that was rich.

"Yes," Aunt Lily said. "And I told her I did it to my husband's mistress. Had her deported back to Poland." She shook her head. "I wouldn't believe such a thing, but Dominique certainly did."

I was still laughing when Brian came bustling into the hallway, clasping his hands and looking rushed.

"What's so funny, ladies? And did I hear the door?"

"No, no door," I sputtered. "How are the girls?"

"Fine, just fine. I really have to get going, so—"

"Wait." I narrowed my eyes at him. "Why are they fine?"

"Ah, well, I just explained to them—"

I marched back to the den. My daughters were all on the couch watching *American Idol*. They did not look upset.

"Why aren't you upset?" I yelled.

Miranda hit the remote, silencing Contestant Number Three. "What's to get upset about, Mom? Obviously, this is what you and Daddy want, although I can't understand why you'd be so willing to let this family fall apart, so what's the point?"

She was blaming me. Of course.

"Brian!" I yelled. He came sheepishly into the room. Obviously, he had been hoping for a quick escape. "The girls seem to think," I said, "that this is something we both want." I looked at him hard. He started to blush.

"Ah, yes. Well, I told the girls that things had been not right for some time."

I bit my lip. "Did you tell them I had no idea that things had not been right?"

"No."

Lauren looked interested.

"What else did you tell them?" I asked. I was chewing the other side of my lip now.

"Just how, well, you know, people grow apart and that you and I had talked about this and you didn't disagree with me moving out."

I had to hand it to him. That wasn't exactly a lie. He just left out a whole bunch of other, relevant parts. "Did you tell them about Dominique?"

"Who's Dominique?" Miranda demanded.

"So, you didn't. Okay, then, did you tell them that I didn't know we had any problems until this morning?"

"Who's Dominique?" Miranda asked again.

"Did you tell them that I was sailing along thinking everything was fine while you were carrying on behind my back?"

"Daddy?" Jessica looked shocked. "But you said you two just drifted apart."

I was in Brian's face now. I might have been screaming. "Did you tell them I didn't disagree with you because you just walked in, packed up your things, and told me we were finished without giving me a chance to even give you an argument?"

Brian looked disgusted. "See," he said, "now they *are* going to be upset. You just had to get your two cents in, didn't you?"

If I had owned a gun, I would have shot him.

"Brian," I barked at his departing back. He turned. "Name one of my books."

He frowned. "What?"

"Name one of my books. I've published twenty-seven books in the past eighteen years. Name one."

He looked at me like I was a crazy person. "What the hell are you talking about? I don't know the names of any of your stupid books." Then he walked out.

I couldn't look at my daughters. The blood was running through my body so hard and fast I could barely hear beyond the rushing in my ears. I closed my eyes and took several deep breaths. Then I looked over at my three little girls.

Jessica was white. Lauren was in tears. Miranda looked pissed.

Miranda spoke. "I can't believe he'd do that to you," she said in a small voice.

And for the first time in that long, long day, I thought that maybe, just maybe, we'd be all right.

CHAPTER FOUR

When I awoke the next morning, there was a warm, unfamiliar presence in the bed. I opened one cautious eye.

Fred. Right. Fred had often asked to be let up on the bed, but Brian always said no. During the times when Brian had been away for extended business trips, I had not given in because I knew that Brian would eventually be back and Fred would face even more disappointment. Last night, Fred got the invite.

As a sleeping companion, Fred was commendable. He didn't snore. His legs didn't twitch. When I snored, he didn't shake me on the shoulder and insist I turn over on my side. He didn't steal the covers or get up three or four times to pee. He didn't fart and stayed on his side of the bed. He had it all over Brian.

I smelled coffee and knew that the previous day had not been some bizarre Kafka-esque nightmare. Brian, in the twenty years we had been married, had never made the coffee.

I got out of bed and stumbled across the hall to the bathroom. On the way back, I caught a glimpse of myself in the full-length mirror beside the dresser and almost had a stroke. I looked awful. My first thought was, God, no wonder he left.

I forced myself to take another look, then began to process my figure logically. I usually didn't look this bad. My eyes, for instance, were only bloodshot because of all those Carmichael Martinis. That was also why my skin looked so pasty, except for the red splotch on the side where the sheets had bunched up beneath my cheek and left an imprint. Normally, my hair was carefully brushed, not sticking straight up on one side.

I squinted. A few years ago, my eyelashes had completely disappeared. They could be coaxed back with two or three applications of black mascara, but without that, my face looked lash-less and bland. Not quite this bland, but still.

I pulled back my lips in a forced grin. There was not a forest of pine growing between my teeth after all. It just felt that way. The Carmichael Martini again.

I threw back my shoulders. I had always been proud of the fact that I had only gained ten pounds in twenty years of marriage. Of course, redistribution had become a bit of a problem. My arms were not sleek, but rather rounded, almost puffy. But then, Liz Taylor, in that scene in *A Place in the Sun*, where she first meets Monty Clift playing pool, and she's in that gorgeous white dress with her arms and shoulders bare, well, her arms aren't very buff either, but you don't even notice because of all that cleavage. I've got cleavage too, but, without proper support, my breasts sag so badly that unfettered, my nipples hover about four inches above my waistline. I'm naturally short-waisted, by the way, but it's still a pretty impressive drop.

My thighs rub together. And my butt wobbles.

I stepped back from the mirror, hoping that a little distance would improve the situation.

It didn't.

But I clean up well. I had a headshot done a few years ago, for a conference or some such nonsense, and boy, did I look good. Black and white, with the light just right on my eyes, which are, with enough mascara, my best feature. My cheekbones looked sculpted, my chin and jawline firm, my dark hair beautifully styled, my smile seductive. Almost Ava Gardner. That old-fashioned, glam look.

Not that morning, however.

I smelled bacon. I suddenly remembered Aunt Lily had offered to get up and make breakfast for the girls so I could, as she put it, "sleep off all that Grey Goose." But I felt the need for normalcy, so I slipped into sweats and slouched downstairs.

My daughters were all sitting around the table, smiling and chatty. As I rounded the corner and entered the kitchen, silence fell. They all looked guilty, torn between the bliss of eating good, hot food that someone else had prepared for them, and the knowledge that this was Day One of Life Without Father.

Aunt Lily had found the waffle maker in the appliance graveyard that was my pantry, and the kitchen smelled of baking and hot grease. I began to salivate.

"Good morning," Aunt Lily said cheerfully, thrusting a mug of hot coffee at me. "One waffle or two?"

"Two," I mumbled, sipping gratefully. "How is everybody this morning?" I asked, feigning real interest in something other than the prospect of crispy bacon.

"We're fine, Mom," Lauren said, smiling bravely.

"Did you return my outfit?" Miranda asked.

"Can I go to the sleepover?" Jessica also asked.

Oh, my wonderful kids. So much for being devastated by their parents' breakup.

"Yesterday," I reminded them coldly, "I was a little distracted, so I didn't get the chance to do what I had planned to do. Hopefully, today will be a more normal kind of day, and I'll be able to attend to all your needs. If not, you will all just have to deal, okay?'

They nodded, but not very convincingly. Thank God for the emotionally recuperative powers of selfishness.

They didn't go back to chatting, but they started smiling again as they ate. The waffles, when smothered with syrup, were delicious.

"Why don't you ever make waffles?" Jessica asked.

"Well," I explained, "you girls usually aren't down here at the same time on school mornings, and on the weekends, you all sleep really late. When you were little, though, we used to have Pancake Saturday, remember?"

They all nodded. Brian had made the pancakes. I paused for a moment, expecting some fond sentimental memory to sweep over them.

Jessica snarled. "It was the only fucking thing Daddy ever cooked."

Normally that kind of language is not tolerated, at the breakfast table or anywhere else, but since I totally agreed with her, I let it slide.

"Well," Aunt Lily suggested, "we could always do brunch. You know, eleven-ish. That way everyone can sleep in, but we can all have something really yummy together. What do you think?"

The girls nodded. Out with the old, in with the new. Aunt Lily was starting her own traditions under my very nose. I'd have to think how I felt about that. But not now.

"I'm going to take a shower," I announced, "so everyone have a great day. No assaults, please, or any other digressions. I can't handle any more drama." I kissed each of them on the cheek and went back upstairs. Quick shower, no blow-dry, back into sweats and slippers. I grabbed Lana off the living room couch, yelled to Aunt Lily that I was going to work, and went out the back door, down the driveway, and climbed the stairs to my office over the garage.

All of the houses on my block have a huge, detached garage with a finished upper story where, I'm sure, the help once lived. My own personal help comes every week with a minivan, so the upper story was converted to an office space when we first bought the house. I wanted a place to write that was away from the house, and that worked well for the first year, until I had my first kid, and then I couldn't leave the house except for food shopping or other emergencies. As the girls got older, I hired a long succession of mothers' helpers to watch my daughters while I crossed the driveway to go to work. It's not at all like my long-planned attic oasis, it's just a really good place to write in. It's one long, narrow room, with bookshelves covering the one tall wall, and a bathroom and kitchenette against the opposite tall wall. The other walls are cut short by the roofline, and on one side is a long desk and worktable, and across from that is a huge, shabby sofa covered in rose chintz that Brian said was too hideous to put in the house after I went out and bought it without asking him first. It's the kind of pouffy, pillowy couch perfect for curling up in on rainy afternoons. In front of it is an old trunk I use as a coffee table. It's the same trunk I took with me when I went away to college, and back then I spent an entire summer cutting things out of my favorite magazines and decoupaging them to the trunk, so that even today I can look down and see Lauren Hutton smiling from the cover of an old *Seventeen* magazine. There are a couple of skylights and an ugly linoleum floor. I love it.

I went over to the kitchenette and made coffee. Lana settled into the couch. She loves "Take Your Cat to Work" days. I turned on my computer, but didn't read anything. I took my coffee mug, snuggled into the couch, and waited for Anthony.

Anthony Wood is my personal assistant. About ten years ago, my agent suggested I hire somebody to deal with book-signing schedules, conference appearances, and the like. I hired Anthony part-time, back when he was a high-school senior who wanted to be a painter. In the ten years he's been working for me, he's gone on to graduate from Parsons School of Design, where he received a Masters in Fine Arts. He is now a very successful painter of what he calls "interior landscapes," which are really big murals on people's living room walls. He also paints exquisite watercolors, but you can't make nearly as much money doing that as you can, say, painting a replica of Monet's *Water Lilies* for a really rich stockbroker.

He continues to work for me two days a week for several reasons: I pay him a lot of money and he can adjust his own schedule around his painting jobs. He loves telling people that he's an artist who dabbles in publishing, and he loves to travel to all those conferences and conventions with me. In return, he is an invaluable deduction on my income tax return. He is an excellent assistant. He's gone on to do proofreading and editing, as well as making significant contributions to the actual writing process.

He also manages my website, filling readers in on my day-to-day life. He leaks clues about the next book, tells them where I'll be putting in an appearance or doing a signing. He coordinates all my online activities: blog conferences, discussion groups, online book clubs. I answer all my own e-mails, but he juggles MySpace and Facebook.

Anthony is gay. Not one of those obvious, flamboyant gay men, but he's a real expert on male sexuality from both the giving and receiving end. Since he has also become a real friend and confidante, I have no problems asking him "If you do this to a penis, does it feel good?" (FYI, according to Anthony, there is pretty much nothing you can do to a penis that doesn't feel good).

Anthony is also my head cheerleader. He has a very high opinion of himself, and has told me on several occasions that even if he didn't work for me, I'd be the only writer of flashy, trashy historical smut that he would ever read.

He is so sweet.

I sat stroking Lana between the ears until I heard Fred barking hysterically from the house. A car must have pulled into the driveway. Thank God, Anthony at last.

Anthony is a very beautiful man. He has those classic golden-boy looks—think Redford in *The Way We Were,* but without the mole or crooked nose. Anthony's nose, in fact, is perfectly straight. So are his teeth. His eyes are green, his jaw is firm and square, and his hair is dark honey blond and swept off his high, broad forehead. Since I know him so well and since he is so very gay, he has never been a character in any of my books.

I could hear the door downstairs slam shut, and Anthony came upstairs. Even though it was a cool, cloudy April morning, Anthony had dressed for a golden June afternoon. He was wearing white cotton pants that tied just at his hips with a drawstring and came to just above his ankles. His shirt was blue-and-white striped, sailorish, tight enough to show off his very nicely muscled arms and short enough to reveal his flat-as-a-board abs. He was also wearing blue canvas slip-ons with rope soles and a straw sunhat.

Okay.

So, remember what I said about him not being flamboyant or obvious? Forget all that. You could spot this man across a crowded room and know immediately what side his bread was buttered on.

"Hello, Mona," he sing-songed. His look was swift and accurate. "Absolut-itis?"

I nodded. He put down a large straw tote bag and poured himself some coffee.

"Trish?" he asked.

Anthony has a nickname for everybody. He calls Patricia "Trish." I have never heard anyone, not even her parents, whom I have met several times, call her anything but Patricia, but Anthony calls her Trish, she calls him Antoine, and they get along famously.

I nodded again while he shook his head. "And on a weekday? You should know better. How are my girls?"

Anthony loves my daughters. He thinks they are three of the brightest and most charming individuals of earth. They in turn, love him, but I can see where that comes from. He's beautiful, non-threatening, will drive them to the mall anytime they want, buys them expensive coffee drinks that end in –*ino*, and will talk for hours about clothes, cute boys and makeup.

Anthony is their designated guardian. If Brian and I should both tragically be killed in an airline crash, or if, for instance, I try to blow up his car and can't get away fast enough and get blown up as well, he will be their guardian. Our first choice had been my parents, and after their deaths, Brian's parents. After Brian's father died, and Phyllis said she would not want the responsibility of all three of them by herself, we looked around for an appropriate person, preferably someone who had an outside chance of outliving us. In the end, Anthony was the obvious choice. Some people, on hearing this, wonder why we didn't choose some other close family member. But the only ones who ask that have never *met* any of our other close family members.

The girls don't know. As certain as I am of their love and devotion, Brian and I both believe that Mommy's money + Daddy's money + Anthony helping them make important decisions might be too great a temptation.

"Miranda thinks that the lighting in dressing rooms is designed to make clothes look better than they really are," I told him.

He settled into the other side of the couch and waved his hand. "Of course the lights are fixed. Everyone knows that. Something about the fluorescents. What else?"

"Jessica wants to go to a boy-girl sleepover."

"Well, she can't. I read all about those things. Parents think there will be no sex going on, but believe me, orgy city. Do you want me to talk to her?"

See, I told you he was sweet. I nodded. "A girl named Bernadette broke the DNA project on purpose, and Lauren hit her over the head with it."

He looked shocked. Not because Lauren did the hitting, because he's always said that Lauren has a very dark side, but because he had personally gone on several mini-marshmallow and plastic-straw searches at Kings.

"Somebody broke the DNA? Good for Lauren. That girl needs to shake it loose more often. Who's been in the house, by the way? Is somebody homesick, or do you have a ghost washing dishes?"

"Aunt Lily has moved in. She sold her place because she's afraid that once the Martians land in Prospect Park, property values will go down."

"I bet she got a bundle. How long is she staying?"

I gawked at him. Did he not hear the word "Martians"?

Just then, Fred began to bark again. I closed my eyes tightly against the uproar. "What is that stupid dog barking about now?" I muttered, opening my eyes slightly to look at Anthony.

He cupped his hand behind his ear and tilted his head, listening. He frowned, then said, "Timmy and the well again. Should we call the sheriff?"

Patricia came sailing up the steps, carrying a plain white shopping bag that smelled like heaven. Anthony jumped off the couch.

"Bettinger's, Trish?" he asked, taking the bag.

"Antoine," she murmured, kissing his cheek. "Yes. Crumb cake. And strudel." She looked at me sternly. "You didn't tell him?"

Anthony looked up from inside the bag. "Tell me what?" he asked, his eyes narrowing, a large piece of crumb cake in his hand.

"Brian left me," I told him, looking hopefully at the bag.

He looked puzzled. "Brian who?"

"My husband," I said loudly. "Brian, my husband, left me."

"Ohmygod. When? Why?"

I reached forward and snatched the crumb cake from his slender fingers. "Yesterday. For Dominique."

"The Frenchwoman from Boston?" Anthony asked.

Patricia and I both stared. "How did you know that?" I finally asked.

He shrugged and rooted around in the bag again. "You told me you had met her. At the Christmas party, remember? I wanted to know what everyone was wearing, and you said that a Frenchwoman from Boston named Dominique was wearing the winter white suit we had seen at Nordstrom, you know, the one that you wouldn't buy because of your body image issues, with red alligator pumps."

I was impressed. His memory for fashion-related conversation was phenomenal. "Well, yes. That Dominique. He packed everything and is living at her place in Hoboken."

"I hope her place in Hoboken is big enough for all the party guests," he said, pulling out another piece of crumb cake.

I have a hard time following Anthony sometimes. "Party?"

"Yes. The surprise party for Glinda." He refers to my sister-in-law Rebecca as Glinda, the Good Witch. Rebecca must not mind, because she hasn't given him warts or anything. My other sister-in-law, MarshaTheBitch, is Miss Gulch. His nicknames can get a little silly.

I still wasn't following. "I'm not following."

Patricia was. "Brian can't possibly expect you to still have a surprise party for his sister. He doesn't live here anymore. It's not unreasonable to assume that Dominique will take over the responsibility as hostess."

"But I love Rebecca. I don't care who the hostess is. I planned her party to be here."

Anthony shook his head at Patricia. "She doesn't get it," he said.

Patricia sighed heavily. "I know." She smiled patiently at me. "Mona, you need to tell Brian that the seventy-five people who were going to be spread over your spacious and elegant backyard will now have to be crammed into Dominique's condominium. And that the caterer you have engaged doesn't travel, so she—that is, Dominique—will have to arrange for another person to take care of the food. And the drinks. And the rented tables and chairs. Not to mention that someone will have to call all the guests and inform them of the change of address. And why."

"Oh." I smiled. "I'm starting to feel better now. Anthony, why don't you just fax the guest list to Brian this morning?"

He licked crumbs off his fingers. "With pleasure. I'm very sorry, Mona. This is terrible. But you don't seem, ah, too upset. Aren't you angry and hurt and tortured?"

"I am angry." I was. Maybe I'd be hurt and tortured later, but that morning I was still just really pissed off.

Patricia had sat down next to me and taken the half-eaten crumb cake from my hands and put it on the trunk. "I hope this isn't too presumptuous, but I've made an appointment for you with David West. He's my attorney. One week from today."

"Already? I'm seeing a lawyer already?"

"The sooner the better," she said calmly.

Anthony was looking at Patricia with frank admiration. "How," he asked, "did you get her an appointment with the best divorce lawyer in the state?"

Patricia looked smug. "He's handled three divorces for me in the past twenty-one years. I reminded him that I'm only forty-eight and could very easily manage another three."

Patricia doesn't mind telling people her age because she looks ten years younger than she is, and knows it, so whenever she mentions how old she is, somebody inevitably says, oh, but you look so much younger, and Patricia loves that. I, on the other hand, don't look forty-five, but I look about forty-three and a half, so I never mention my age. To anyone. Ever.

I held out my coffee cup and Anthony dutifully reached for it to pour me more. "I'm not sure I'm ready to talk to a lawyer."

Patricia looked into my eyes. "Tell me."

"It's happening too fast. What if he lives with this woman and decides she's a bitch and wants to come back?"

"He's an asshole," Patricia said indignantly. "Are you saying you'd take him back? After he cheated on you for months, left you, lied to your children about everything, and after you yourself admitted that he wasn't much of a husband in the first place?"

"Well, God, Patricia, when you put it like that, I'd be stupid to take him back."

"So, how would you put it?"

Anthony sat down on my other side and I reached for more caffeine. "I liked being married," I said at last. "I won't like being alone."

Anthony was shaking his head. "You have three daughters, lots of good friends, a demented aunt who has apparently moved in, and me. When will you ever be alone?"

"It's not quite the same, Anthony," I said patiently. "I like having somebody to, you know, rely on. Pick up the slack. Help me out."

"And when," Patricia asked, "did Brian ever do that?"

"Okay, so maybe not that." I was feeling a little frustrated. "What about sex? God, I might have to start dating again. One of the things I liked about being married was that I never had to worry about shaving my legs or explaining about my appendix scar. Who would want to see me naked now? I'm forty-five and I droop."

Patricia waved a casual hand. "Darling, there will always be somebody out there who'll want to see you naked, believe me. In fact, after his performance yesterday, I'd bet that Ben would stand in line."

"Ben?" Anthony whispered, setting down his coffee cup so quickly that it spilled a little on the table. "Ben was here yesterday?"

Anthony has a little bit of a crush on Ben. Well, okay, a huge crush. It's kind of funny, because he gets all tongue-tied and silly when Ben is around, which is very unlike the normal Anthony. I've told Anthony many times that when he's around Ben, he's fine, but that's not true. Ben even asked me once if Anthony had ever seen a professional about his stutter. I'd never tell Anthony that, though. He'd be very upset.

"Yes," I told him, "Ben was here yesterday. The morning started with the girls' tub puking up rust."

Anthony leaned forward. "What was he wearing?" he whispered.

No matter how badly I'm feeling, I can't help but string Anthony along. I puckered my brow, pretending to try hard to remember. "A leather G-string and his tool belt?" I said at last.

"No," Anthony whispered in disbelief.

"No," Patricia said firmly, giving me a hard look. "He was wearing the usual jeans and T- shirt."

Anthony looked crushed. "Oh. Well, did he look good?"

Patricia rolled her eyes. "Antoine, really, is the Pope Catholic? Does a bear shit in the woods? Does Ben Cutler look good?"

Anthony grinned.

I grinned too. "He looked great. Lana sat on his lap during lunch."

Lana had found a comfortable perch on the back of the couch. Anthony looked at her enviously. "How was he?" he asked her. Lana purred.

The door opened downstairs again, and MarshaMarsha came up, looking adorable and concerned.

"Mona, how are you? You look awful, like you haven't slept at all," she said, stooping to kiss me on the cheek. "I worried about you all last night. I still can't believe it. Is that strudel from Bettinger's?"

Patricia nodded. "Yes, have some. We're trying to talk Mona into seeing a lawyer. She says she's not ready."

MarshaMarsha managed to pour herself a cup of coffee and snag a piece of pastry while she continued to look adorable and concerned. "I can understand that. This is a big shock, and is totally unexpected." She looked and sounded sincere even as she was stuffing her face with strudel. "Mona needs time to think and weigh her options. And there's always a chance that Brian will see the error of his ways and come crawling back on his hands and knees begging forgiveness. Not that she could ever forgive him for being such a piece of shit husband, but still." She smiled, showing dimples. "Right, Mona?"

"Right," I said, not sure what I was agreeing to, but then God, with his usual sense of timing, not to mention humor, stepped in. My fax machine began to hum.

Anthony jumped up and raced over to the machine where he began diligently reading whatever was coming through.

"It's from somebody named Herschel Fielding," he announced.

Why was that name familiar? I looked at Patricia and frowned, trying to think.

"Apparently," Anthony said as he read the fax, "he's Brian's lawyer. He's faxing over a proposed separation and visitation agreement."

"What?" My jaw dropped as I scrambled up and stood next to Anthony, staring at the fax machine. "A separation agreement? Already? Is he crazy?"

"No," Patricia drawled, "just very insensitive."

It took a few minutes, and we all watched in silence as the fax machine hummed and slid out one sheet of paper after another. Patricia made another pot of coffee. MarshaMarsha perched on the edge of the trunk and chewed strudel one tiny mouthful at a time. Finally, the machine fell silent and I grabbed the stack of paper and shoved it into Anthony's hands.

"What do they say?" I asked.

Anthony shuffled everything together neatly and squinted in concentration. "He wants to see the girls one night a week and every other weekend. He's being very generous about child support, two thousand a month. That's way above the average, I believe." He read on. "He doesn't want to pay alimony, and instead will let you keep the Westfield house, which is in both your names. And you get the shore house." *Well, of course,* I thought. I bought the shore house with my own money twelve years ago, and it was in my name only, and Brian, although he spent family time there, never gave a red cent toward renovation or upkeep.

"But he wants to keep the Hoboken condo," Anthony went on in a very confused voice. "When did you buy a condo?" He looked at me. I would have looked back, but I was too busy seeing red.

"I never bought a condo," I said finally. The room fell into a hush, and I could feel, rather than see, everyone shrink back in silence.

I cleared my throat. "Is there an address?"

Anthony nodded. "Yes. I can go onto the county tax page and see when it was purchased, if you want me to."

"Yes." I walked back to the couch and sat down hard. I didn't look at MarshaMarsha or Patricia. I couldn't.

It took Anthony about three minutes to find it. "He bought it last September," he said at last. "Her name is on the deed as well. Dominique's condo and his condo are one and the same."

September. He bought it with her last September. What a total son-of-a-bitch. I went over to the phone and dialed the direct number to Brian's office. He answered on the second ring.

"Hey, it's me." I kept my voice very even.

"What did you say to Dominique last night?" he asked, sounding angry.

I clenched my jaw. "I didn't say anything to her."

"Then what did Patricia say? And Lily?"

"I haven't a clue," I lied. "They were speaking in French."

"Lily speaks French?"

"Apparently. I just assumed, by the way she bolted out of there, that they were letting her in on a few of your less attractive personal habits."

He sighed. "That's not funny, Mona."

"No. Neither is this fax I just received from your lawyer."

"Well, Mona." He switched gears suddenly, sounding very calm and relaxed. "Hirsch and I happen to think that I'm being very fair and generous. The state has guidelines for child support, and I'm way above their monthly amounts. And I am giving you both houses."

"I noticed that. Of course, the shore house was bought and paid for by me alone, but still. You're being very generous. And thorough. In fact, you must have spoken to this Hirsch several days ago to have him draw up something so complete."

Brian sounded cool. "As a matter of fact, yes."

"So the divorce idea was something you remembered to talk about with other people. It was just me you had a problem telling."

"Now, Mona, let's not get bogged down with unimportant details."

"Okay, I won't. I just have one question. When you told Hirsch about the condo, didn't you make it clear to him that I didn't know anything about it, and that he shouldn't have mentioned it in the proposal he just faxed over?"

There was a moment of silence. I glanced at Patricia, who winked and raised her coffee cup in salute.

"He put the condo in the agreement?" Brian asked, his voice sounding not so calm and relaxed. "The man is a fucking idiot."

"No, Brian. You are a fucking idiot. Do you know what my lawyer is going to do with this?"

"I thought you didn't have a lawyer."

"Yeah, well I do. David West. The best divorce lawyer in the state. I'm seeing him next week, and I'm going to make sure he gets me every single thing I'm owed, and then some." I slammed down the phone and closed my eyes, taking deep, slow breaths.

They had bought a place to live. Together. In September. Over six months ago. Which means they must have been seeing each other before that, unless they met each other, fell in love and decided to live in adultery all within a few short weeks. Why hadn't I ever noticed anything different? What was wrong with me?

"What's wrong with me?" I said softly. I heard a flurry of activity and opened my eyes.

MarshaMarsha grabbed the bag off the trunk, fished out another piece of strudel, and pushed it into my hand. Patricia hopped up and ran over to snag the coffee pot. Anthony waved a tissue box.

"What did he say?" he asked breathlessly.

"I need to see David West," I growled, and sipped my coffee.

"Absolutely," Anthony said. "What did Brian say?"

"He said that Hirsch was a fucking idiot. I need to see my lawyer." I looked at Patricia. "Next week?"

She nodded as she refilled my cup. "Yes. One week from today. At ten thirty."

I took a deep breath. "One week. God, what am I going to do for a whole week?" I moaned.

"Well," Anthony said uncomfortably, "you might try working a little. Your first draft is due in about six weeks. Oprah sent an email asking how things were going."

Oprah didn't really send me an e-mail. Anthony called my agent Oprah. My agent is Sylvia Snow, and Anthony calls her Oprah because Sylvia is a fiftyish black woman with lots of smarts and brass balls the size of the QE2.

In the late sixties, Sylvia got into Radcliffe through affirmative action, and got out with a degree summa cum laude and a big attitude. After kicking around New York publishing houses for ten or so years, she decided to go it alone. I was her first client. She sold my first book. Over the past several years, we have made each other lots of money. She now has a very impressive client list, including celebrities, internationally known psychologists, and one romance/mystery/chick lit author who has her very own section at your local Barnes & Noble. She calls me her favorite author. I am, if nothing else, her first author.

Sylvia does not get me free houses in the Hamptons or front row seats to sold-out Broadway shows. We don't exchange confidences or spend hours chatting away like good buddies. She tries like hell to sell my books for the most possible money, and I try to write stuff that's good enough for all her efforts. We get along just fine. Usually. But now she wanted an update on the new book, which was supposed to be complete and on my editor's desk by June first, and the news was not so good.

I stared at Anthony, stricken. "What can I tell her?"

Anthony shrugged. "Mona, I don't know what to say. I've been trying to talk to you about this for weeks. You kept blowing me off."

Patricia was frowning. "What's going on?" she asked.

"I'm having a bit of a problem with the new book," I said

Patricia looked indignant. "That's ridiculous," she declared. "Mona, you write the best creamy thigh stuff out there. What kind of problems could you be having?"

"Well, I'm trying to write something different this time," I said.

MarshaMarsha tilted her head. "A Scottish one? I love those men-in-kilt things." MarshaMarsha had been a fan before she ever met me, and she not only has read all my books, she is a long-time member of a romance-only book group that's carefully scrutinized some of my most interesting love scenes. MarshaMarsha always scores big with her group when she brings me along so I can give a firsthand account of the hows and whys.

I shook my head.

"One of those supernatural romances?" she asked hopefully.

Patricia frowned. "Supernatural?"

"Yes," I explained. "They're actually called paranormal romances. Sex with ghosts. Werewolves. Vampires. It's very in right now."

"That's disgusting," Patricia murmured.

"That's what I thought," I said. "I can't write about ghosts, because I believe in ghosts and I'd creep myself out. Forget time-traveling, because I'd never be able to keep all those centuries straight. Shape-shifters are very hot, and so are vampires and witches, but I personally know a witch, Rebecca, and I know for a fact she hasn't had sex in years, which is not very inspiring."

Anthony swiveled around in the desk chair. "I wanted her to write about Lizzie and Fitz."

Both Patricia and MarshaMarsha stared at him blankly.

"You know." Anthony waved his hands around. "Elizabeth Bennett and Fitzwilliam Darcy. *Pride and Prejudice?* The bookstores are full of sequels."

Patricia raised an eyebrow. "And you actually thought Mona should write a book using somebody else's characters?

Like those people who write about *Star Trek* or Jessica Fletcher?"

Anthony looked a little hurt. "Well," he muttered, "when you put it that way…"

Patricia sat back down beside me on the couch. She patted my hand. "Our Mona is better than that."

I smiled gratefully. "Actually, I started writing a contemporary romance."

"Well, that's very exciting," MarshaMarsha said brightly.

"It is. And I was doing really well. My character is a twenty-something who has her own graphic design firm in Manhattan, and her husband of just a year leaves her, and she becomes involved with two very different men, and then hubby comes back and wants to try again."

"That sounds full of possibilities," Patricia said. "You should be taking those ideas and running all over the place with them."

"I know I should, but I'm stuck. I can't decide who she should end up with. And I'm having a hard time getting into the head of a twenty-seven-year-old metro girl. Now I'll never be able to finish. How can I write about a woman who lives happily ever after with some man when right now I think all men suck?" I looked over to Anthony. "Except you, of course." Anthony smiled.

"Well," MarshaMarsha said, "why don't you write about a happy ending where she doesn't end up with anyone. She's just happy by herself."

I frowned at her. "Happy by herself?"

"Sure. Have her be one of those women whose life changes so much for the better after she's dumped. It happens all the time."

I shook my head. "Whose lives are so much better?"

MarshaMarsha pursed her lips. "Well, there's my cousin, Vicki, who fell apart after Dan left, but ended up getting a scholarship to law school and she's a junior partner now, with a great place on the Upper West Side and a hunky boyfriend. Ellen Mitchell? Down the street? When she divorced her husband, she was forced to go into business for herself, and that's how she ended up with her catering business. You know how well she's doing."

"There's also a client of mine," Anthony put in. "I just did a gorgeous Parrish in her bathroom, a take on *Dinkybird*, you know, the one with the nude on the swing? When her husband left, all she could do was babysit kids, and now she owns six private daycare centers and is absolutely rolling in it."

I looked at Patricia. She shrugged. "Darling, all the women I know see marriage as an investment. They always ended up better off than they were before."

I shook my head. "I still can't get into this girl's head."

Anthony shrugged. "So don't make her a girl. Make her somebody more like you. Make her forty-something instead."

I rolled my eyes. "Nobody wants to read about a middle-aged woman who gets dumped."

Patricia looked thoughtful. "Maybe that's because nobody's ever written about a middle-aged woman who gets dumped, unless she's a ridiculously rich middle-aged woman who ends up getting lots more money, revenge and some hot boy-toy. But really, how many real women can identify with that?"

MarshaMarsha was nodding in agreement. "She's right. All you get right now in books are young single girls who spend half their paychecks on shoes. The women who are over forty are all in quilting clubs or knitting clubs or solving mysteries with their cats. Maybe it's time for a real person to have a real crisis and get over it. And live happily ever after all on her own."

I stared into my coffee cup. "So, she's in her forties and ends up alone. But a better person? Let me think. This is not a romance. It could still be a love story. This might be a very good idea. She could still have a great life, and lots of sex. I mean, divorced isn't the end of the world. At least I hope not."

"Of course it's not," MarshaMarsha said stoutly. "And you're going to be just like your character. You're going to have a much better life alone, with lots of sex."

That sounded good. That sounded great. Maybe if I wrote about it, I could make it true. I raised my coffee cup.

"I can write this," I said.

"Of course you can," Anthony agreed.

"And even better, I can live it."

"Hear, hear," Patricia murmured.

"To a better life," I said.

We all clinked cups. MarshaMarsha smiled. "Don't forget lots of sex," she said.

Chapter Five

The week after Brian left felt, strangely enough, just like the week after my mother died. There was an overwhelming sense of loss and sadness, but it felt oddly abstract. Both of my parents had lived in Florida since the eighties, and I saw them only two or three times a year. After my father died, my mother spent a little more time with me, but her death left a gaping hole in my heart, rather than in my actual life. On a day-to-day basis, I barely missed her. It was knowing that she was no longer a part of my physical universe that broke my heart.

With Brian leaving, it was the same kind of feeling. He'd worked long hours and took many business trips, so he wasn't around the house much anyway. It's not like I suddenly had to do things for myself, because I'd always done things for myself and my daughters without much help from him at all. But knowing that he no longer loved me, that he had chosen another woman to spend his spare and precious time with, made me incredibly sad. So sad, I almost forgot how mad I was about the whole thing. Almost, but not quite, because he kept doing things to piss me off even more.

The Friday afternoon after he left, he called Miranda on her cell phone and invited her and her sisters to have dinner with him. And with Dominique. Miranda was in the kitchen when the call came, wolfing down the first of two peanut butter and banana sandwiches she often made when she got home from school. Lauren was with her, drinking a Diet Coke. Jessica was upstairs slamming things because she was not sleeping over Billy's house, when apparently everyone else in the world was.

When her phone rang, she looked at it, made a face, and looked at me.

"It's Daddy," she said in a tight voice.

I remained silent. I was slicing pepperoni for pizza. We were supposed to be having homemade pizza for dinner. I was in charge of making and baking. The girls would be doing the eating. Typical mealtime.

"Answer it," I said calmly.

She flipped open the phone. "Yeah?"

She listened. I watched her out of the corner of my eye, almost chopping off my thumb in the process of trying to be cool.

"What?"

More listening.

"Why would I want to meet her? She broke up our home. And she's French. They hate us."

I was so proud.

"Okay, Dad. I'll ask. But don't hold your breath." She hung up and started in on the other sandwich.

"Well?" asked Lauren. "What did he want?"

Miranda looked nonchalant. "He wanted to pick us up and take us all out to dinner so we can meet Dominique. Wanna go?"

Lauren shook her head. Miranda got up, left the kitchen, and went upstairs, presumably to ask Jessica. The slamming above stopped for a few moments, then began again, followed by what can only be described as a loud but hollow laugh. I was guessing Jess said no. Miranda came back into the kitchen, opened the refrigerator, and took out a Sprite. She sat next to Lauren at the breakfast bar and watched me slice.

"What did Jess say?" I asked casually.

Miranda was no fool. "Guess, Mom. Like you couldn't hear her." She made a rude noise.

"Are you going to call him back?" I asked, still cool.

She shrugged. "I told him not to hold his breath."

I was torn. On one hand, the pending divorce was between Brian and me. The girls, while of course affected, were technically not involved in our issues. They still had two parents who loved them and who would continue to be a part of their lives. As their parents, we deserved their love, and more importantly, respect. Whatever animosity I may have felt toward Brian, and whatever feelings he still had for me should not spill onto our daughters. Neutrality was best all around.

On the other hand, I couldn't help but feel a bit happy. Let's face it: I'd won.

I sighed. "Call your father and tell him what's going on."

Miranda rolled her eyes and dialed. "Dad? It's me. No."

She listened. "I mean, no, we don't want to have dinner with you, and no, we don't want to meet Dominique."

She handed the phone to Lauren. "He wants to talk to you."

Lauren looked pained, but took the phone. "Hi Daddy." Pause. "But I don't want to meet her." Pause. "I don't care." Pause. "Mom, he wants to talk to you."

This I was not ready for. I cleared my throat and took the phone. "Yes?"

"Mona, this is Brian."

"Really? I would have never guessed."

"Don't be a smartass, Mona. What's wrong with Miranda and Lauren?"

"Nothing. Why?"

"They're being very bitchy about this."

"Maybe they both have PMS."

Brian exhaled loudly. "That's no excuse. I want them to be ready in an hour so I can pick them up and take them to dinner. Dominique wants to meet them."

"So this is about Dominique?"

"Yes, of course it is."

"Gosh, Brian, maybe it should be about your three daughters. Maybe what they want should come first. What do you think?" I was still holding the knife in one hand, and I started stabbing the slices of pepperoni with the tip of the blade.

Brian sounded a bit impatient. "Mona, the sooner the girls get used to the whole idea, the better. Just have them ready."

"Sure. Just as soon as you tell me how."

"What?"

"We're talking about three teenaged girls. How do I get them ready? They don't want to go. Do I threaten them?

Ground them for two weeks? Do I bribe them? Maybe I should physically drag them out the front door and sit on them until you show up, and then you could force them into the car. Of course, I could only drag one at a time, and while I'm doing that the other two could scatter, but I'm sure together we could hunt them down." The pepperoni slices were becoming pepperoni hash.

"Mona, you're being difficult. Just have them ready."

"I'm not being difficult. I'm being practical. You know your own daughters, Brian, or at least you should. How hard is it to get them to do something they don't want to do?"

He was silent. "You're a bitch," he snarled, and hung up.

I handed Miranda her phone. "Turn it off," I said in a shaking voice. I overturned the box of mushrooms and began furiously chopping them.

"Way to go, Mom," Jessica said behind me. She must have come downstairs during the conversation with Brian. She was actually smiling. "I turned off my cell, too. How about you, Lauren?"

"I'll do it now," Lauren said, running out of the room.

I was starting to calm down. "Jess, honey, want to take the dough out of the fridge? It needs to come to room temperature."

Jessica went over to the refrigerator, and we all spent the next few minutes in companionable silence. Lauren came back in and set the table without being asked. My blood pressure was getting back down to normal when the house phone rang, and I recognized the number on the caller ID as Brian's cell.

"Aunt Lily," I called. She came in from the den, where she'd been watching the Food Network. "Can you answer the phone? It's Brian, and we don't want to talk to him."

Lily smiled, and reached for the phone. "Hello?" Pause. "This is Lily. Who's this?" Pause. "Brian who?" Pause. "What the hell do you want?" Pause. "You want Mona? You mean your wife? The one you just ruthlessly abandoned for some cheap French tart?" Pause. "Well, she's not here." Pause. "Now really, why would I lie about a thing like that?" Pause. "Brian, I really don't have to listen to that kind of abuse." She hung up.

"What's for dinner?" she asked.

"I'm making homemade pizza," I explained happily.

The phone rang. Lily answered it and said, in a distinctly Hindi accent, "Hello?" Pause. "Sorry? No speak American?" Pause. "Sorry? Telemarketer?" She hung up again.

"Maybe," she said, smoothly, "we should put this away until tomorrow night, and walk into town for burgers at the pub. My treat. What do you think?"

We were out of there just as the phone began to ring again.

~

The next day, Saturday, a bouquet from Incredible Edibles arrived. Incredible Edibles is a company that creates what appear to be bouquets of flowers that are actually made from food. This particular bouquet consisted of chocolate chip cookies, chocolate covered strawberries, sugar cookies in the shape of oak leaves covered with green icing, and candied orange and lemon slices sprinkled with sugar. All the items were on the end of long skewers and stuck in a festive pink vase. Quite pretty. Immediately, the girls began to fight over who got what, and after half an hour of constant sugar consumption, they were all spitting like cats. When I suggested that perhaps they should save a little something for later, Miranda hissed. Then I hinted that perhaps one of them should at least call their father and acknowledge the bribe.

Jessica shrugged. "If we ignore him, maybe next time he'll send cash," she said.

Later that afternoon, it occurred to me that I had a standing account at Incredible Edibles, so I called and spoke directly to the owner. Sure enough, Brian had charged the whole thing, meaning that sometime next month I would be getting the bill. Luckily, the Hoboken address had burned itself into my brain, so the correction was made quick enough.

Sunday, Miranda almost caved. She came down after lunch, tracked me into the den, sat down, and took my hand.

"Mom, if I ask you to take me to the mall so that I can meet Daddy for lunch and he can buy me a new pair of Uggs, will you take it as a sign of betrayal?"

I just looked at her. She rolled her eyes, sighed heavily, and left. Good girl.

By Sunday night, I think Brian had admitted defeat. At least in Round One.

~

David West looked the way a lawyer should look. I'm not talking Gregory Peck in *To Kill a Mockingbird.* Or even Jimmy Stewart in *Anatomy of a Murder.* If Susan Hayward had gotten him on board in *I Want to Live,* she would have gotten, ten, fifteen years, tops. Think Kirk Douglas, in that movie about the soldiers raping the girl in that little German town, and how Kirk turns into a barracuda. *That's* how David West struck me. In fact, when he shook my hand, I figured that when he went swimming, instead of doing laps he probably made slow, lazy circles on the bottom of the pool.

His office was also just right. It took up a whole floor over a row of retail shops in Morristown, and overlooked one of the true village greens that remained in New Jersey. Thick carpet muffled any intrusive sounds, and the smell of coffee made me feel right at home.

I sat across from him and sniffled. Sometime during the previous weekend, something somewhere had bloomed— maybe a daffodil, maybe a tulip, maybe a maple leaf had unfurled, but whatever it was, it set off my allergies. My eyes had turned red-rimmed and puffy, my throat felt scratchy, causing my voice to sound froggy, and my nose was filled to capacity. So sitting in his office, I looked the picture of emotional distress. What I was feeling was closer to murder.

I had spoken to his secretary and gotten a list of information to collect, and had it all in a neat manila folder that I handed to him. He looked quickly at the file.

"Tax returns? Excellent. Bank statements, credit card bills, mortgage papers. I can see you've done your homework. What's this?"

"That's what my husband's lawyer faxed over to me last week," I croaked.

His eyes scanned quickly. "Well, child support looks generous, and visitation is about standard. He's giving you the family home, how nice of him. This house in Harvey Cedars? Tell me about it."

I cleared my throat. "It's mine. Just mine. Brian giving it to me is not as generous as it sounds. I bought it twelve years ago because I'd started to make money writing, and my accountant thought it would be a good idea. It's right on the border of Harvey Cedars. In fact, the houses across the street are in the next town. A while back, my neighbors and I made a pact that we'd never tear down our houses and build McMansions in their place. So it's a very modest block. Cape Cod-style homes. Mine has three bedrooms and two baths."

David West flashed me a look. "But it's still a sizable asset?"

"Oh, sure. I mean, it's on the beach block. On Long Beach Island, which is a prime New Jersey shore location. I could sell it for the lot alone and buy a whole island in the South Pacific."

"Is it a rental? Do you derive income from it?"

I reached for a tissue and dabbed my nose. "No. I spend the summers there. With my daughters. We go down after school lets out and stay 'til Labor Day. We've done that for years. Brian comes down—that is, came down—on weekends and for a week or two at a time."

He was nodding. "Okay. Now, tell me about the condo."

"I don't know anything about the condo. Brian bought that without my knowledge."

His eyebrows went up. "Now, that's interesting. I don't know this particular address, but I know the neighborhood, and he probably paid a pretty penny for it."

I sniffled again. "According to the tax records, he paid $875,000 for it."

He actually smiled. "Really? That required a substantial down payment. Did you notice any money missing from any accounts?"

I shook my head. "No."

"Very interesting. Good. Now, Mrs. Berman." He folded his hand together and looked legal. "I'm seeing you today, on such short notice, because Patricia Carmichael called and asked a favor. Which I was more than happy to do for her. She has been a client for many years. In fact, I've known Ms. Carmichael a very long time. I might even venture to call her my friend." He stopped, thought for a minute, frowned, and shook his head hard. "Well, no, not really friend. But I know her. Very well. She can be, ah, determined, and ah…." He was still frowning.

"Strong-willed?" I suggested.

"Yes," he said gratefully. "Very strong-willed. And, well frankly, ah…."

"Intimidating?" I offered.

He smacked his hand, palm down, against his desktop. "Exactly. Intimidating. At times."

"Well, she's very beautiful," I said, by way of explanation.

"Oh, yes. That she is."

"And smart. Not just intelligent, but street smart."

He leaned back in his chair and nodded his head. "Absolutely. You don't expect someone of her, ah, background and appearance to be so savvy."

"Yes, that throws people off." I smiled at the poor man. "Then there's the whole more-money-than-God thing."

He made a small face. "Yes, there's that too. The point is, because of who she is, and the type of person she is, on the basis of her referral I'm not going to bother with the usual screening I do with potential divorce clients. I'm going to assume you are here in good faith and have every intention to go through with this. My hope is that you're not just trying to scare the shit out of him."

"Nope. I want out."

"Good. Now, just so you know, I don't do revenge. I don't do public humiliation. I'll get the best settlement possible for you and your daughters. That is my only job. I'm very good at it."

"I know. That's what Patricia said. And other people. I'm very grateful that you could see me on such short notice. I don't know how I would have found a good lawyer otherwise. In fact, my original plan was to hang out in front of Family Court until some guy came out crying, 'Oh God, I'm ruined,' then grab his wife's lawyer."

He decided to get the joke and smiled. "Well, that might have worked. But this way is much better. I'll need a fifteen-thousand-dollar retainer."

I smiled back. "Done. Have the agreement sent over and I'll have a check ready."

He stood up and reached out to shake my hand again. "A pleasure, Mrs. Berman."

"Mona. Call me Mona. Mrs. Berman is soon to be a thing of the past."

～

When I got back to my office, Anthony was busy on the computer. He flashed me a gorgeous smile and stood up, dumping Lana onto the floor where she stretched, yawned, and gave me a dirty look.

"I had lunch with Lily again," Anthony reported. "She's an absolute fruitcake. Are you sure you want her staying with you?"

"Where else is she going to go?" I grumbled.

"She's loaded. How about a nice assisted living place in, say, Duluth?" He handed me a steaming mug of coffee. "How's the lawyer?"

"Kirk Douglas in *A Town Without Pity*."

"Perfect. Can I go next time?"

I sank into the couch. "Maybe. Anything I should know about?"

He arranged himself on the other end of the couch and handed me the cordless phone. "Glinda called."

Glinda, my favorite sister-in-law. I reached over, took the phone, and dialed her number.

"Mona, I just heard. I was in the Ozarks doing a spring cleansing, and I just got back last night. I am so sorry about this," she gushed as soon as she picked up the phone. Rebecca has the same attitude about caller ID as I have: if you know who's calling, why waste time pretending to be surprised? "My brother is a real stinker. I'm on your side, honey. What can I do?"

I loved Rebecca. "Nothing, I guess."

"Does the house feel empty?"

"Well, it would, but Aunt Lily is here."

"Oh, how nice. I think she's just great. How long is she staying with you?"

I sighed. "Apparently forever. She sold her co-op because of the aliens that are scheduled to land in Prospect Park."

Rebecca made a sound. "That old chestnut has been driving people out of Park Slope for years. Does she really believe it?"

"I guess. She's here with a gazillion suitcases and no permanent address."

"Well, she's got good timing. At least she'll be able to help out with the girls. How are they taking this whole thing? Or are they over it already?"

Rebecca does not have any children of her own, but as a strict observer of the human condition, she knows exactly how the teenage mind works. "I think they're trying to figure out what double birthday parties are going to be worth."

"Figures. That reminds me. What about my surprise party? You're not still having it there, are you? I mean, not even Brian is that uncouth."

"Rebecca, how did you know? It's supposed to be, well, you know. A surprise."

Rebecca laughed. "Oh, Mona, come on. Have you ever known Phyllis to keep anything a secret?"

True. I loved my mother-in-law, but the woman's mouth never quit. "Anthony faxed the guest list over to Brian's office," I explained to her. "It's his problem now. His and Dominique's."

"That's her name?" Rebecca squealed in delight. "Really? Oh my stars, how funny. I bet she's skinny and blonde and a real bitch."

I laughed with her. "Rebecca, you really do have supernatural powers." A thought suddenly struck. "Rebecca, speaking of powers...."

"Yes?" She sounded a bit tentative.

"I don't really know much about your, well, religion."

"I like to think of it as a complete way of life."

I sighed. "That sounds nice. But answer me this. Do you, well, you know, perform...um...." I bit my lip. How could I ask this delicately?

"Perform?" she coaxed.

"Spells. Do you do spells?"

She chuckled. "Do I do spells?" she repeated, apparently in disbelief.

"Yes. Potions and chants and things."

"It's more complicated than that, Mona. There are certain things that can be done with the help of certain items that can bring about positive changes in a person's life. I don't have a cabinet with jars of rat dung and eye of newt. What is this all about?"

I took another track. "What about transfiguration?"

"Mona," Rebecca said patiently, "that's a word from the *Harry Potter* books."

"Yes. You know it?"

"I've heard it, yes. You do realize that those books are fiction, right? And that something like transfiguration can't be done in the real world?"

"Well, of course I know that."

She must have heard the disappointment in my voice. "Mona. Did you want me to turn Brian into a frog or something?"

Was that an offer? "Well, that would be good. Can you do that?"

"No," she said shortly.

"Oh." How disappointing. What is the point of having a witch in the family if she's only good for tasty cider and herbal cough syrup?

"And even if I could," she continued, "I wouldn't, because it would break my mother's heart."

I sighed. "True. And I love your mother. So, maybe you could do a little something to Dominique? Or to Brian that would affect Dominique?"

She made a thinking-about-it sort of noise.

"Rebecca?"

"If you want," she said, chuckling, "I can make him impotent."

"Oh my God." Now, that's a payoff. "Can you really?"

"Well, I wouldn't do it myself. After all, he's my brother. But I'll ask somebody in my Wiccan support group."

"You have a Wiccan support group? I didn't realize that. Since when?"

"A couple of years now, why?"

"Is that your, well, coven?"

"I belong to a coven, of course, although I like to think of it as my family. But my support group is different. It's where I go to bitch and moan."

"Just like regular therapy?" I was intrigued.

"Almost. We also spend a lot of time talking about the rabid misconceptions and bizarre expectations of those outside the circle."

"Well," I said brightly, "that sounds like fun. Do what you can, Rebecca. I'd really appreciate it."

"Hang tough, Mona. I love you."

"I love you too." I hung up and gazed wistfully at the phone. I loved Brian's family. Except MarshaTheBitch, of course. How did he end up being such a shit?

"How did Brian end up being such a shit?" I asked aloud, to the world at large. Anthony shook his head. "Don't know, babycakes, but it's really time to call Oprah."

He was right. I needed to talk to my agent. It was time.

Once I had decided to change the focus of the book, everything became surprisingly easy. I had spent the past few days writing in spurts of amazing speed and, more importantly, clarity. I knew exactly who was who and where the story was going. But I was nervous about talking to Sylvia. The manuscript was due on June first. My publisher had given me a very nice advance. I was worried about finishing the book on time, because in between those moments of speed and clarity, I sat around a lot, almost in tears, feeling sorry for myself. It was hard, I was discovering, to be creative and miserable at the same time. I had never needed extra time to finish a manuscript, and under normal circumstances I might have easily gotten an extension. But these were not normal circumstances. The book I was writing was not the book I had been paid for, and that could be sticky.

Sylvia picked up on the second ring and, having caller ID, cut right to the chase. "Mona, you've been avoiding me. What's wrong with the book? Is it going to be finished on time?" she asked, putting first things first as always.

"No. Things have happened. I've made some changes."

I could hear her settle in for a much longer conversation than she originally anticipated. "Okay. What changes?"

Anthony had refilled my coffee cup, knowing this would take a while, and that, unlike some people, I am not a pacer when I talk on the phone. I like to sit in one comfortable spot for the duration. "Well, first is the title. It's no longer going to be called *So Many Men, So Little Time.* The new title is *Better Off Without Him.*"

"Ah-huh. That does indicate a lot of changes," Sylvia said slowly.

"Yes. Sydney Karloff no longer has her own graphic design company, she's a children's book writer and illustrator. She's not twenty-seven either. She's forty-five. Her husband still leaves her, but they'd been married twenty years, not just one. And she doesn't have a walk-up in SoHo. She moves from her Upper West Side co-op to a small town in rural New York."

Sylvia was silent. "So I guess this eliminates the sexy undercover cop working on a major heroin bust."

"Pretty much. Jack is now a high school science teacher who paints houses in the summer. She hires him to paint her new house."

"Ah-huh. What about the millionaire who wants a new logo for his charitable foundation to help underprivileged kids?"

"Brock? Now he's a fifty-year-old bank president and volunteer at the local youth center."

"And the ex-husband? Does he come back begging for forgiveness?"

"No. That never happens in real life. Even in romance novels, it's a cliché. He's a schmuck and he's out of the picture by page thirteen."

"Ah-huh. Okay, so who does she end up with?"

"No one. That is, it's vague. Could be either guy. It ends when she realizes that her life alone is more important and

111

meaningful than her marriage ever was, and her friends and family mean more than some man."

"Ah-huh."

"But she still has lots of sex and there's a happy ending."

Sylvia was silent. I closed my eyes and tried to hear what she was doing on the other end of the line, but there was dead silence. Finally, she said, "This is a significantly different book than the one you proposed last fall."

"I know."

"And it is significantly different than the one you'd received a very substantial advance for."

"I know, Sylvia. But it's good. Really good. Better than anything I've ever written."

"When we discussed you writing something other than historical romance, this was not like anything you mentioned."

I was feeling a little desperate. "I know, Sylvia. But this is a good book. I've got the first fifty pages, and they are amazing. Talk to Frannie. Please." Frannie was Francine Welles, editor extraordinaire, who had been holding my hand for over ten years.

"Okay. I'll try calling her right now, and I'll call you back."

I clicked off the phone and looked over at Anthony. He's been with me long enough to know the consequences of making major changes to a book you'd already been paid for. He smiled at me.

"Mona, this really is the best work you've ever done. I love the way you write, you know that, but this is really something special. Your characters are real and honest and funny. I laughed out loud at some of this stuff. And I'm in love with Sydney. If I were an old straight guy, I'd be all over her."

"Oh, Anthony, thank you. Your opinion really matters to me, you know that. I love Sydney, too. I want her to be strong and happy. She deserves it."

He leaned across the couch and kissed me on the cheek. "So do you, babycakes. So do you." He looked thoughtful. "Maybe you could convene the Mavens?"

Ah, the Mavens. Let me explain. As a romance writer, I'm a member of the Romance Writers of America, a group of people, mostly women, who support and encourage the romance-writing industry. And believe me, it's an industry. Romance is really big bucks. We all meet once a year to congratulate each other, give awards, eat lots of good food, and network like crazy. Considering we're all technically competitors, we get along very well and are generally supportive of each other's efforts. Over the years I'd become friendly with a group of writers who all happen to live in the New York metropolitan area. We're all members of our local RWA chapters.

Anthony refers to us as "the Mavens" because between us, we've written every type of romance novel known to *Publisher's Weekly*. We're experts. We're popular with fans. We're financially successful. And we love to get together to have a long lunch, exchange ideas, and, as Anthony says, shovel deep shit.

"Good idea," I said. Talking about the new book with those women would give me serious feedback. "Actually, it's a great idea. Send an e-mail to all of them and see if we can get a date."

Sylvia called back less than an hour later. "Fran is concerned. She wants a complete synopsis and whatever you've got written. She wasn't happy."

"With what?"

"Well, for one thing, there's no happily ever after with Mr. Perfect."

I rolled my eyes. "Sylvia. This book is about a woman who does not need a man to feel complete and valuable. She is happy with her life as a single person. How can that be a problem?"

"Listen, Mona, I think it's great. In fact, even as we speak, therapists and feminists all over the country are giving you a standing ovation. But we're talking about book editors here, Mona. You know how they think."

I sighed. Yes, I did know how they thought. "Anything else?"

"Forty-five is a tough age to sell. Can she be younger?"

"No, she can't. What's wrong with forty-five? Not every woman who reads a book is twenty-three."

"I know that. But there's marketing to deal with, and forty-five is a hard sell."

"What happens to all the forty-year-old marketing people? Are they all sent to the large print division, or just given a walker and shown the door?"

"Don't shoot the messenger, honey. I'm just saying."

"I'm sorry. Listen, I'll deal with Frannie. I'll send her the stuff right away, and I'll convince her. I have faith."

"Okay, Mona. Then I'll have faith too."

Chapter Six

My daughters and I have been going down to the Jersey shore for the summer since the twins were still in diapers. We go down to Long Beach Island, a long sliver of sand dotted with tiny towns and miles of beach and homes that have become so overpriced it's like the Hamptons but without the pomp and circumstance. Going down there year after year has resulted in a number of summer-only friendships for the girls and me, so the house is always noisy and happy and crowded. I love the long mornings with coffee on the porch, listening to the sound of the ocean. I love grilling fish and making salad and dicing fruit and pretending I'm being healthy. Fred loves romping on the beach every night, chasing seagulls, and being walked everywhere we need to go. The girls love sleeping late, Froot Loops for breakfast, trolling on the beach, and wearing as little clothing as possible. They also love the Keegan boys.

The Keegan boys are now seventeen, sixteen, and fourteen. They are all tall and very good looking. I've always assumed they took after their mother, although I never met her. Doug and his ex-wife parted right after the youngest, Mike, was born. Doug apparently made a boatload of money designing a very popular video game, and when he sold his tiny company to Sony, the ex-wife imagined a lifestyle quite different than what Doug imagined. So she took half the loot and did the Paris-London-New York thing. Doug stayed in Pennsylvania. His one concession to wealth was a house on the Jersey shore where his boys stay with him for the summer. He and the boys arrived three years after we did, and the kids grew up together.

Doug is the ugliest sexy man I know. Or maybe the sexiest ugly man. I'm not sure which comes first, the ugly part or the sexy part. He's short—no more than five foot six—with a wedge-shaped head, high forehead, small close-set eyes, and very high cheekbones. All in all, a fairly hideous package, except for his mouth. May I, just for a moment, wax rhapsodic about Doug's mouth?

His lips are wide and full, a bit too wide, some may argue, but wide enough that the ends are turned up in a quirky, slightly naughty smile. His lips are also full, Botox full, but they've been like that since before Botox was a twinkle in some plastic surgeon's eye. His lips are also red, and smooth, and very soft looking. And moist. They always look like he just licked a little something off his lips.

He's also very sexy. His body is amazing—he spends all his time playing with his sons. They ride bikes every morning to the community pool where Doug does a bunch of laps while the boys score with the cute female lifeguards. They rollerblade, shoot hoops, throw Frisbees, windsurf, and bodysurf. As a result, Doug has a broad chest, muscular arms, washboard abs, and an ass that's tight as a drum. All the man has ever worn are shorts and half-buttoned Hawaiian shirts. The kind Magnum PI wore.

Doug also has great hair: thick and curly, a little too long, a beautiful chestnut color barely shot through with gray.

But the sexiest thing about Doug Keegan is that he makes you feel like you're the most important person in the room. He looks right at you, talks right to you, listens to every word, and laughs in all the right places. Consequently, he always has a string of very attractive, usually much younger, and always intelligent and successful women who hang around him like bees around a hive.

After his wife left, Doug started another business and made another bunch of money on another video game. But during the summer, he leaves his company to spend time with his sons, where, on rainy days when they can't be outside doing healthy things, they stay inside and test all of the new games Doug is developing on any one of the four or five different game systems Doug has scattered around his house.

I once had a brief flurry of worry that the two families would suffer a summer romance that would ruin the carefully built and very successful friendships we'd established. But the girls talk about the boys like brothers, and the three boys always seem to have other girlfriends to keep them busy.

Every summer, it's the same routine. We leave early in the morning, stop at Costco and spend half the summer's food budget on steak, fish, and junk food, get to the shore house by one P.M., have lunch, and spend a few hours cleaning and opening windows. By late afternoon, my daughters take Fred for the first of many long walks around the neighborhood as they wait for the Keegan clan to return from whatever activity they're engaged in. Then, the girls pile over to the Keegan house, Fred drags his hot and tired butt up onto our tiny, shaded side porch, and Doug comes over to welcome me back to the shore.

This year, just like clockwork, he yelled hello from the front door and came into the kitchen just as I was finishing stowing away all the freezer food. Doug never seemed to realize that we had not seen each other for nine months. Or perhaps it just didn't matter to him.

"I have discovered," he announced, "the perfect use for all that mint we planted a few years ago. The Mojito. You smash together lots of fresh mint with sugar and lime, then add white rum. Top with seltzer. It will make our summer perfect."

"It sounds wonderful. Can we make it by the gallon?"

"Sure." He rooted around in a cardboard box, pulled out Doritos, and opened the bag. "So, the girls tell me you finally got rid of that asshole husband of yours."

I stared at him. "Doug, I thought you liked Brian. I thought you two were, well, friends."

He crammed a few chips into his mouth. "Hey, I love Brian," he said after a few chews. "Brian is the perfect friend. Funny, knows sports, good drinker, a great talker. But let's face it, Mona, as a husband, he must have really sucked."

I nodded and cleared my throat. "Doug, all I've heard for the past two months is what a shitty husband Brian was. Why didn't anybody tell me? Why didn't you?"

He wiped Dorito schmutz off his chin. "Come on, Mona, what was I going to say? 'Hey, I think your husband is a great guy, but he's treating you like pond-scum?' What would your reaction to that be?" He settled his still-admirable butt against the counter. "You'd deny it, yell at me, call me jealous or something equally ridiculous, and we wouldn't be friends anymore." He shrugged. "I just figured you were smart enough to figure it out yourself, eventually."

I munched a Dorito. I had just stashed eighty dollars worth of swordfish steaks into the freezer, so I could start the healthy eating thing later. "But, Doug, that's the thing. I didn't figure it out. Didn't the girls tell you? He left me. For another woman. Younger, skinnier, blonder. French."

"Hmmm. French, ah?" His eyes narrowed, and as they're pretty small to begin with, they practically closed. "He's such a moron. He mentioned her."

"Mentioned her?" My voice rose three or four octaves. Fred, out on the porch, lifted his head and actually whimpered. "He mentioned her? When? What did he mention?"

Doug looked apologetic. "Last summer when he was here. We were drunk, of course, and he told me there was a French woman that he was, well, infatuated with. I told him he was a fool. I told him to stop before it was too late. That he couldn't risk losing you." Doug shrugged. "Moron."

"You didn't tell me," I yelled. "Why didn't you tell me?"

Doug sighed patiently. "Would you have believed me? No. You would have thought I was jealous and all that other crap and, bingo, not friends." He shrugged. "I thought he'd outgrow her, just like he outgrew all the others."

I froze. "Others?"

Doug sighed again. "Oh, shit. Now I'm the moron."

"How many others?" I asked carefully.

He tried to look nonchalant. "Oh, three or four. Maybe six. Usually he met them on business trips, and they lasted just a few weeks. Seven. No more than ten." He swallowed. "Ten."

I tried to think. "Doug, we've known you for ten years. That means that every summer that Brian came down here, he told you about a new one?"

"No, no, Mona. That's not how it was at all." He thrust the bag of chips in my face. "Have another Dorito."

I munched rebelliously. "Okay, then, how was it?"

"It's only been in the past, oh, five years. He just started talking one night how he had gone to New Orleans for something and met a woman, and he said—"

"Said what?"

Doug took me gently by the arm. "Let's sit outside," he suggested.

My house is a converted Cape, the whole first floor a combination living-dining-kitchen with a bathroom and my bedroom tucked into the back. I have a tiny side porch off the kitchen, but the whole back of the house is a screened-in porch with comfy wicker furniture, ceiling fans and white Christmas lights. It's where we spend most of our time. That's where Doug and I sat as he told me all about the Great Adventures of Brian Berman and his Marvelous Wandering Penis.

Doug is a great storyteller. He's bright, very articulate and has a terrific sense of humor. If he hadn't been relating my own husband's infidelities, it would have been a very entertaining visit. As it was, I sat there and started feeling angry all over again, angrier than I had been for, say, sixty-seven days. Ever since Brian walked out of the house.

"Mona, I'm sorry," Doug said at last. "I'm sorry Brian was such a prick. I'm sorry I had to keep this from you because I've always considered you a much better friend than Brian. And I'm really sorry that I told you all this. But I think that you needed to know, because Brian is going to want you back. I don't care how hot or skinny or blonde this one is, she's nothing compared to you, and even a jerk like Brian will figure that out. You need to know so that when he comes crawling back, you can tell him no."

"He's not coming back," I said dully. "Didn't the girls tell you? He's happy as a pig in shit. Dominique has him puttering around the house singing. He even cooks when the girls visit him for the weekend. He never cooked a day in his life with me. He never did any of the things for me that he does with Dominique—the ballet, chick flicks...God, he even walks her dog."

"Exactly," Doug said. "He hates shit like that. So how long do you think he's going to continue to do stuff that he hates just to impress this broad?"

I had stopped considering the possibility of Brian coming back. Brian and the girls had reached a truce by the middle of May, and the tension of their relationships had lessened, taking quite a bit of pressure off me. After their first few visits to their father's new residence, they spread fantastic tales of domestic harmony and bliss. They tried not to appear too obvious, but Brian was deliriously happy and wasn't shy about spreading the word.

I looked at Doug through narrowed eyes. Maybe it was the sun. Maybe it was the white of Doug's teeth gleaming from between those amazing lips. Whatever. "You really think he'll want to come back?"

Doug nodded. "Yes. And you have to promise me, Mona. When he does, you have to say no. Can you do that? Can you promise?"

I nodded. "You betcha."

~

Life at the shore is always relaxed. No pressure to get anything done, no place to go, all the people you want to see are right there, so it's always a time for me to let go of the reins and let the girls go pretty much their own way. I usually managed to be between books in the summer, and it had been years since I'd had to write while down at the shore, but this summer I'd be writing like I never had before. Frannie had gotten me until the first of October to turn in a new manuscript, and it had been a long and hard battle. Everyone liked my first idea, and couldn't understand why I felt the need to change anything.

"Mona," Frannie had said, "you've got the makings of a nice little success here. Sydney is very appealing, has an exciting job, terrific wardrobe, and lots of sex appeal. You've got two great guys for her to fool around with, sexual tension, a little danger and suspense, and a happy ending. It's practically perfect."

"But Frannie, that book has been written a million times. Did you read the synopsis of the new book? Didn't you like it?"

"Yes, Mona, it sounds fine, but older female characters usually aren't featured in romantic stories, you know that."

"This isn't a romance. Just because she has sex doesn't make it a romance."

"Exactly. That's the whole problem, Mona. You say she's involved with two men, but since she doesn't end up with either of them, it's not a romance. Is it a comedy? Because there were a couple of times in those first few chapters that I laughed out loud."

I felt the spot behind my eyes start to burn. "No, it's not a comedy. Sydney happens to have a sense of humor about her life, and the people around her also have a sense of humor. Characters don't have to be so deadly serious all the time."

"Okay. Not a comedy, not a romance. Maybe you could give her a series of obstacles, you know, maybe with her house, bad plumbers and faulty wiring, that kind of thing. We might get by with hen lit."

I closed my eyes and took a cleansing breath. "Hen lit?"

"Well, not chick lit because, frankly, she's too old."

"There's such a thing as hen lit?"

"Have you thought about a ghost? Or a vampire?"

We finally agreed that I would send additional chapters, and by the time the June deadline came and went, I'd been granted another four months. Four months sounded like a lot of time, but I was still plagued by bouts of sadness, anger, and a total loss of self-esteem. My only hope was that down the shore, away from the home that Brian so carelessly broke apart, I might be able to crank out some serious work.

I'd also had lunch with the Mavens a few weeks before. Trying to get a group of busy women to find an open afternoon for lunch may not sound complicated, but it really is. We had, years ago, tried to establish a regular luncheon date, but with all our crazy schedules, no one wanted to commit to any set time. So now we just e-mailed each other whenever someone got the urge, and whoever could make it, did, and those who couldn't didn't.

We had settled on an afternoon in mid-May at the Pierre Hotel. We like hotels because the food is always great and we can settle into the bar afterwards and talk for hours with little or no interference, as long as someone is buying a drink or two. And since we never drive ourselves to these luncheons, we all end up buying a drink or two. Or three. Or six. But those were white wines and shouldn't count as much as, say, six vodka gimlets.

At the end of the afternoon, there were four out of ten of us left. Amanda Witt was one of those women rightfully referred to as a "Grande Dame" of romance, and she played the part to the hilt. She was always perfectly coiffed, dressed to the nines, and accessorized with fabulous pearls. She had been a great supporter of mine for years, and could truthfully be called a good friend. She was, at sixty-eight, sharp and quick as she had been when I first met her fifteen years ago. She was caustic, insightful, and could write a love scene that would make a Bangkok hooker blush.

"So what do you all think of this year's Rita Lifetime Winner?" Amanda asked. Allow me to translate. The Rita Award is the award given annually by the Romance Writers of America, the RWA, at their annual conference. The Lifetime Achievement Award goes to an outstanding writer with at least fifteen years of publishing history. This year's honoree had left the table just minutes before, having to drive all the way back to Greenwich, Connecticut for her grandson's Little League game.

"She deserves it," said Jan Gleeson, who is just about my age and working on Husband Number Five. "The woman writes like a fiend, and all that research? My God, all those little islands in the Caribbean, not to mention shipwrecks and slave uprisings? Of course, she gets to write off all her trips to Antigua, but still."

Amanda shrugged. She narrowed her eyes at me. "Mona, I would have thought it was your year. Is that why you're not coming to Nationals?" she said to me. She signaled the waiter. "You had signed up for a workshop that I was running, and I just heard you dropped out."

Nationals, or the yearly RWA conference, was in San Francisco this year. I had indeed volunteered to work one of the workshops, but had withdrawn from the event just the week before.

"Mona," Jan gasped, "you've never missed a conference." Jan wrote about romance in the Wild West. Her pairings often involved feisty pioneer brides-to-be who were abducted by handsome Lakota braves. Jan was an absolute stickler for historical detail, and had actually studied Lakota. We often teased her that her elaborate and beautiful-sounding Indian names actually meant "Hung Like Buffalo" and "Horny Hottie Seeks Same."

I cleared my throat. "Well, I'm missing it this year, and it's not about the award. I don't deserve a Lifetime Achievement Award. At least not yet. I don't have half the output of some of these women."

Amanda nodded. "True. So, is it about your idiot husband?"

"What about your husband?" Jan also signaled for another drink. "I've met your husband. Is he really an idiot?"

"He left her," Amanda said. "Of course he's an idiot."

I shrugged and fiddled with my empty glass. "I just can't come this year. I mean, seriously. My husband left me for a French blonde fifteen years younger than me. Hasn't that plot device been used by half the people who'll be there? "

Chloe Radisson frowned. Chloe was only twenty-seven, and had a string of successful NASCAR romances to her credit. "You're right," she said. "Mary Bancroft used that exact storyline last year. The wife wasn't a writer, but still."

"And Lu Chisholm," Jan said slowly. "Didn't she have a contemporary stand-alone two years ago? Lawyer husband runs off with client? Blonde client? French blonde client?"

Chloe nodded. "Yes. And MaryAnn had that artist-model thing."

"Right," Jan countered. "And Liz Clayton, doctor-nurse."

"See?" I said. "My God, I'm practically a cliché."

"Yes," Amanda said. "So, your life has become your work, Mona. That doesn't mean you leave the work behind."

"I'm not leaving anything behind," I told them. "I'm just sitting this year out. Besides, I don't want to leave my girls for a week." That was a flimsy excuse, since in previous years, Brian had come with me and Lily watched them.

Chloe reached over and grabbed my hand. "I'm so sorry, Mona. So, have you started seeing anyone?"

"What? God, Chloe, it's only been six weeks."

"Really? Oh."

Jan make clucking noises. "Give yourself time, Mona. I know how hard it must seem, but believe me, you'll soon start to take an interest in other men."

Easy for her to say. She's had lots practice.

I shrugged. "Right now I'm just trying to stay focused on the new book. That's my priority."

Amanda lifted an eyebrow. "New book? Care to elaborate?"

"Yes," I said slowly. "I'd be interested in what you all thought." I took a deep breath and gave them the storyline. It took several minutes, as I tried to flesh out several plot points and explain the characters. When I was done, I looked around expectantly.

"Well? What do you think?" I asked.

Amanda looked thoughtful. "So, you're leaving the fold?"

I sighed. "No, I'm not. Honestly. I love writing romance, you know that. I was going for a stand-alone contemporary, but got sidetracked. I just couldn't bring myself to write about happily ever after."

"I don't understand, Mona," Jan said. "She doesn't end up with one of the men? How is that even possible? The first rule of romance is a happy ending."

Chloe sniggered. "I thought the first rule of romance was sex by page thirty."

Amanda reached over and smacked Chloe's hand. Then she turned to me. "There's nothing wrong with writing straight fiction. And it sounds like a good story. I bet your editor is giving you hell."

I nodded. "She's a little resistant. Romance is such a strong sell. I don't think they want to take a chance on upsetting the fan base. She's already told me I'll be writing as Mona Quincy, not as Maura Van Whalen. She's protecting the brand, I know. Anthony has started working on a new website."

Chloe tapped her fingers against the table. "What about feedback on your old website?" she suggested. "Have you put out anything about this new book yet?"

"No." I thought for a moment. "That's not a bad idea," I said. "I could have Anthony throw out a few feelers, see what the fandom reaction is."

Amanda smiled. "Good. Now, what else are you working on?"

Amanda knew me well. I wasn't happy unless I had the next book somewhere in the back of my head.

"Well," I said, leaning in and lowered my voice, "I was thinking about a spoiled younger sister who's promised to an Irish lord, but since she doesn't want to leave London, she talks her bookish but beautiful older sister into going in her place."

Chloe nodded. "Very nice."

Amanda beamed. "That's my girl."

~

On the divorce front, David West assured me that everything was going along just fine. The state of New Jersey had very liberal divorce laws, with none of that eighteen-month waiting period or sleazy photos needed to prove adultery. All that had to be agreed upon was a financial settlement, so it appeared I would be a free woman by the fall.

While I was trying to find a rhythm for the summer, the girls slipped right back into their old patterns. Miranda refuses to expose her skin to the sun because of wrinkles, cancer, and other ozone-related hazards, so she tended to sit on the beach in the smallest bikini I'll let out of the house, under a huge beach umbrella and a big hat and Jackie-O sunglasses. She had her iPod in her ear and her eyes on all the cute guys. She spent a fortune on artificial tanning products and moisturizers, and ate like a bird. She was very happy.

Lauren played softball every morning and volleyball most afternoons. She also likes to slather on the sunscreen, but her skin turns naturally golden and her hair gets bronze glints and her teeth seem to sparkle and boys were all over her all the time. She was also very happy.

Jessica, believe it or not, found a group of black-clad, sun-and-sand hating friends who walked all over the island in Doc Martens and old canvas army hats. I don't know where they went, but I think pinball and other video and arcade type games were involved. She smelled of tobacco occasionally, but never of pot, so I tended not to get too excited. She wasn't really happy, but then, she never is.

The only thing that has ever thrown a kink in all the wonderfulness that is summer is rain. Rain at the Jersey shore is a cruel and killing thing. Luckily, the Keegans have so many video games that my girls can hang out there for the day with little or no interruption of mood. But this year, it started raining on the third day after our arrival, and it rained for four days straight. I knew that something had to give. And it did.

They approached me as a group. Never a good sign. They sat in a row on the bench in the kitchen, the rain outside pouring down the sliding door behind them. Miranda, the natural leader, spoke first.

"Mom, we've been doing some talking during the past few days."

Talking. They'd been talking. I cursed the rain and smiled at them. "And?"

Lauren cleared her throat. "Well, it's just that it's been about three months since Daddy moved out."

I nodded encouragingly. Maybe this wouldn't be too bad. Maybe they wanted to finally talk about their feelings of anger and betrayal. Maybe they wanted to tell me how they really hated visiting their father because they realized what a horrid man he was. Maybe they wanted to thank me for being such a fabulous mother.

"Yes, honey. Three months. That's about right."

They all nodded. No one spoke.

"So?" I prompted.

Miranda straightened up. "So we think you should start dating again."

"Let's face it, Mom," Jessica leaned forward. "Dad and Dominique are a sure thing. They're getting married as soon as they can. You can forget about happily ever after with Dad, okay? And you're not getting any younger. We figure if you start now, maybe you can get somebody before it gets too late."

"Dating?" I said again.

Lauren gave Jess a dirty look. "What she means is we don't want you to be alone. In the next few years we'll all be out of the house, and, well, we don't want you to be living with just Aunt Lily and the dog and the cat."

"Dating?" I was having a bit of a hard time with this.

"Mom." Miranda spoke again. "Yes. Dating. As in, going out with men. We think you should start. I know you're not really divorced yet, but we thought you could just, you know, practice. This summer, I mean. Here at the shore house. So when the divorce is final and you're serious about finding Mr. Right, you'll know what to do."

"You want me to practice dating. Before the looking-for-Mr.-Right dating."

"Exactly," Jessica said happily. "That's just what we want you to do. It's been a while, right? Since you dated? And it's a whole new world out there, Mom. Men your age are usually looking for hot young babes, so you need to polish the old charm before you get out there. Otherwise, you won't have a chance."

"Really?" Her faith in me was touching. "So I need to practice? And whom, exactly, am I supposed to practice on?"

"Mr. Keegan," Lauren said.

I frowned. "Who?"

"Mr. Keegan, Mom," Lauren rolled her eyes. "Across the street?"

"Doug Keegan? You want me to practice dating on Doug?"

"It makes great sense, Mom." Lauren stood up and started pacing up and down the kitchen. "First, he's an old friend, so there'll be none of that awkward first-date stuff. He's funny, and he's really good at dating because Devlin is always talking about all his girlfriends." Devlin is the oldest of the Keegan boys, followed by Liam and Mike. "Not only that, he's safe. I mean, he won't try to pull any funny stuff, and if he did, well, I mean, I like Mr. Keegan and all, but he's kinda ugly. You'd never want to do anything with him anyway."

I had no idea how to respond to all this. The fact that my daughters were not only eager to have me find a man but were even planning elaborate scenarios to prepare me for the actual hunt floored me. They had obviously spent too much time unattended.

"Lauren," I began, "first of all, I see Doug Keegan almost every day. He's either here or at the Wilsons' next door, or I'm at his house or at Scott and Steve's."

"See?" Lauren said excitedly. "You're with him all the time anyway. He's perfect."

"Honey, what I meant was, since I see him all the time, why would he ever ask me out? Why would he want to?"

"He thinks it's a great idea," Jessica said. I could tell she was getting bored because she began twirling her hair around her index finger.

"How do you know that?" I asked cautiously.

"Well, we asked him," Miranda said. "We told him our idea and he said he'd be happy to be your guinea pig. All you have to do is give him a call."

"Oh?" Doug also thought I should start dating? More interestingly, practice dating? Practice for Mr. Right? Who the hell was he anyway? He of the many women and no commitment?

I cleared my throat. "Well, I think I'll just go over there right now, if he thinks it's such a good idea."

"Mom," Lauren said. "It's raining like crazy outside. Why not just call him up?"

I smiled down at her as I headed for the door. "You'll understand some day," I told her, and hurled myself into the rain.

I was a real idiot, because by the time I'd crossed the street and hit Doug's porch, I was drenched. I pounded on the screen door, and when he yelled to come in, I banged it open and dripped puddles all the way to the kitchen.

His house is the twin of mine, and his was also remodeled into an open floor plan on the first floor, but off the back of his kitchen is a large family room with two flat screen televisions hooked up to various gaming systems and lots of bean bag chairs on the floor. It reminds me of a frat house game room.

Doug took one look at me and began unrolling paper towels. "You're dripping. Is something wrong? Are the girls all right?"

"They want me to start dating," I said, my voice low, because his three sons were looking at me instead of the TV screens.

"Ah," he said. Soaking wet I did not feel charming and vulnerable like Kate Winslet in *Sense and Sensibility*. I did not feel sexy and mysterious like Gene Tierney in *Laura*. I felt chilly and wet. I needed to be wrapped in soft, scented towels, swept in front of a roaring fire, and handed a snifter of very fine brandy. I did not need to be patted down with crumpled Bounty.

Doug took my arm and led me out of earshot of the boys. "Listen, Mona, don't be mad at your daughters. They are really concerned about you, and they talk to my guys about stuff, and I'm usually in the same room, so, you know." He looked concerned. "They love you."

"I know that. I'm not mad at them. But who the hell are you to agree to 'practice date' me? I do not need a mercy date from you or anybody else. If I want to go out with a man, I'll ask him myself."

"Oh. That. Well, the girls were trying to find somebody you'd be comfortable with."

"I got that. But you've gone through more women in the years I've known you than most men go through in a lifetime. And they've all been young, flippy things who never stayed longer than a few months, according to your war stories. So to think that I'd—that you and I—well, I mean, God, Doug. It's insulting."

"How? Aren't I good enough for you?"

I was flabbergasted at his response. "That's not what I mean."

"Then what do you mean? I'm more than happy to take you out to dinner or dancing or whatever you want to do. I'm offering to spend an evening or two or more in your company. I'm actually looking forward to it. So what's the problem?"

"The problem is that the girls want me to practice on somebody. Somebody safe. And they picked you, and you agreed."

A smile played across his soft, full lips. "You don't think I'm safe?"

I could smell his skin. Salty, slightly musky. His hair was a little frizzy from the rain and haloed out from his scalp. His shirt was, of course, mostly unbuttoned, and the skin on his chest looked dark and smooth. "I'm pretty sure you're not," I said slowly.

"Good. Then how about tomorrow night? The rain is supposed to stop, and we'll walk someplace for dinner. Seven?"

I cleared my throat. "Seven is good."

"Okay. Since this is a date, remember to dress nice and brush your teeth."

I grinned, "Yes, teacher."

"Be polite and don't pick your nose."

"Anything else?"

"You might want to shave your legs. Just in case."

I stopped grinning.

"Only kidding," he said holding out both hands in front of him, as to stop a speeding train. "Honest. Kidding."

I walked back home. Drenched. But I had a date.

～

That night I called Patricia.

Patricia also spends her summers within sight of the Atlantic, but she does it in South Hampton, about twenty minutes, with no traffic of course, from the house she was born in. Her place is a fourteen-room shingled beauty, right on the beach, a gift from her godmother upon her graduation from Sarah Lawrence.

Some of us, when we graduated from college, got U.S. Savings Bonds.

Patricia is surrounded by the very rich and famous. The Spielbergs. Billy Joel. Martha Stewart. But Patricia comes from a class of people who think that *they* should be impressed upon meeting *her*. What's-his-name was right. The rich *are* different.

But she can be very patient. "The girls suggested this?"

"Yes."

"The same girls who wanted you to have your eyebrow pierced to protest the war?"

"Yes."

"Who bought you spandex running shorts for Mother's Day?"

"Ah, yes."

"And who signed you up for a fashion feng shui class last Christmas? I can't believe you're taking dating advice from these people."

I sighed. "I know. But they're so sincere. They mean well, honestly."

"Darling, they all mean well, going way back to the Pope trying to save all those poor infidels from eternal damnation by torturing them all and cutting off their heads. Meaning well is universal. It's also the worst reason in the book to take anyone seriously."

"How do you feel about dating?"

She laughed. "For myself or for other people?"

"Either. I don't know. That lady shrink on the radio says that you shouldn't date anyone for at least a year. And that's after the divorce. She says you haven't gotten over being married for at least that long."

"Anyone who takes a whole year to get over a bad marriage isn't trying very hard. This Keegan person, the one the girls want you to practice on, is he that neighbor of yours? The rich, short one?"

"Yes. Doug Keegan. He goes through women like you go through shoes. He doesn't need practice."

"And he would what, give you pointers? Make sure you're up to speed on dating etiquette?"

"Something like that. The thing is, Patricia, honestly, it's not a date that I need. Or want. But I've got to tell you, I'm so horny I could scream." There, it was said. It was out there, floating in the cosmos. I was so desperate for sex, I was starting to look at dildos in online sex stores.

Brian and I had always had a great sex life. Actually, even before Brian, I had a great sex life. Not that I was a loosey-goosey. Before Brian, I was involved with a few other nice, serious young men. And with all of them I'd had good to great sex. I was never one of those women who needed to be seduced. My idea of foreplay was someone saying, "So, you wanna?" With Brian, I really hit my stride. That was the best part of being married at first—all that sex whenever I wanted, and if I happened to get pregnant, I wouldn't have to kill myself. And I really came to want sex. Especially when I was writing. It wasn't just those long descriptive passages of the erotic physical manifestation of emotional love, it was the whole creative process that turned me on. The past weeks of writing had been torture, and now, surrounded by half-naked bodies and glistening skin, I was near hysteria.

"Hm. Yes, I know how you get. How well do you know this Doug person? Maybe you could work out a deal."

"Deal?"

"A fuck buddy. That's what you need. Do you think you could ask him?"

"You mean, 'Hey, Doug, forget the lobster, let's get laid?'"

She made a noise. "Mona, please. You've made a career out of romantic give and take. I'm sure you can come up with something a little more subtle than that."

Sex with Doug. It's not like I'd never thought about it before. In all honesty, I thought about it every summer when I watched him rollerblade down the street with his kids, bare-chested, with thigh muscles to die for. I'd think about it, then jump Brian. Now there was no Brian, but there was still the bare-chested, muscle-thighed rollerblader setting my little heart aquiver. Did that mean I could jump Doug?

"Well, whatever. We're going out on our first practice date tomorrow night. I can't wait for MarshaMarsha to get here."

MarshaMarsha spent a month with her parents, in a bay-front house twelve blocks away, every summer. She had since she was little. In fact, her sun-drenched childhood memories prompted me to look for a summer house in the first place. She and her boys were due in a few weeks.

"You'll be fine, Mona," Patricia soothed. "Have dinner with this person. It might not be such a bad idea. And if you want, have sex with him as well. You're a grown woman, for God's sake. You can do as you please. You don't have to explain yourself to anyone. Go. Do. That's what freedom is all about."

We hung up. Freedom. Is that what I'd been feeling these past few months? I'd recognized anger, and sadness, and crushing loneliness. Freedom hadn't popped up yet.

Maybe it was time.

~

You would think that there is nothing in the world more embarrassing, not to mention humbling, than taking dating advice from your teenaged daughters.

Well, there is.

Try taking fashion advice from your teenaged daughters.

Jessica struck from the kitchen table. "What are you wearing?" she said around a mouthful of the chocolate Pop-Tart that was her breakfast.

I was peeling an avocado. For my lunch. It was, after all, past noon, but the girls and I were on very separate dining schedules during the summer. "What am I wearing when?"

"Tonight. With Mr. Keegan. He's a very young-thinking guy. All his other dates have been twenty-somethings, so he's used to fashion-forward women."

"Are you suggesting I'm not fashion-forward?"

She looked at me with skepticism. To be fair, I was wearing khaki walking shorts with frayed cuffs and a navy T-shirt that said "Republicans for Voldemort."

"Black would be good," she said. No surprise there.

"I'm not going to a funeral," I pointed out. "Besides, wearing black may suggest a pre-assumption of a dreary experience. I'm trying to be optimistic."

"You could wear my black pencil skirt. With high, spiked heels. And a red camisole. I could lend you the whole outfit. I even have some great necklaces."

Perfect. The Goth-Whore look. "I'll think about it," I promised.

Lauren was next. She came in a few minutes later from her tennis game with Devlin Keegan, all glowing and sunny. She swigged from her water bottle and eyed me critically.

"You look good, Mom," she said at last.

I was folding towels at the time. My "Republicans for Voldemort" shirt was covered with lint. I sensed a trap. "Thanks, honey."

"Maybe it's time for a haircut," she said.

"I just got it cut two weeks ago," I reminded her. I'd had it cut pretty short, as a matter of fact. Brian always liked my hair long, down past my shoulders, which required constant maintenance. This summer, I decided I wanted something easy, and I'd gotten it. All I needed after a shower was a half-teaspoon of hair gel and a few licks with a comb.

"Well, then maybe you should let it go all curly. Kind of an afro. That would be different," she suggested.

"Yes, it certainly would. Why do I need to be suddenly different?"

"For Mr. Keegan, of course. He sees you all the time. You need to, well, surprise him."

"I'll keep that in mind."

"So, what are you wearing?"

"Jess suggested a black pencil skirt, red camisole, and spiked heels."

Lauren shook her head sadly. "She's so lame. You'd look like a hooker. That's too much of a surprise. How about a twirly skirt? And that pretty pink ruffle blouse you bought last week?"

I took a deep breath. Next, she'd be suggesting white gloves and a poke bonnet. "I'll think about it."

Miranda, coming in from the beach that afternoon, took the most direct approach. "Mom, we really need to bring you up to speed. You've got four hours until your date. Let's go out to Bay Village and see if we can find something that makes you look like someone other than a forty-five-year-old mother of three who hasn't had a date in over twenty years."

"I'm not buying a new anything for this."

"Mr. Keegan sees you almost every day. He knows all the clothes in your entire wardrobe. Don't you want him to think you've made an effort here?"

"Jess wants a black skirt, red cami and heels. Lauren wants a junior-league prom skirt and ruffles. Those are two looks he's never seen."

She chewed her lower lip. "Well, wear hot pink. It will show off your tan. A skirt would be good, you've got nice legs. And open sandals, 'cause your feet are pretty. No panty lines, okay?"

"I'll think about it."

In the end, I actually borrowed Jessica's skirt. On her, it hung down around her hips and ended mid-calf. On me, since we're built very differently, it settled right around my waist and came just above the knee. Hot pink sleeveless linen shirt. My tan did look great. Also hot pink sandals. As for my hair, I used Lauren's mousse and put a diffuser on the hair dryer, creating a halo of soft curls instead of my usual slicked-back hairstyle. Why not?

The bell rang at seven. The girls were politely on the back porch, not hanging around the front door. I straightened my shoulders and marched out to meet Doug Keegan.

I stopped on the threshold and stared. He was wearing a white button-down shirt, actually ironed, with the sleeves rolled halfway up his forearms. Navy walking shorts with a slim black belt around his narrow waist. Leather loafers with no socks.

"Nice," I blurted.

He grinned. "Yeah. I clean up pretty good. You look very pretty. Like the hair. Ready to go?"

I nodded, flustered. I was so used to seeing his bare chest and equally bare feet that seeing him so clothed was disconcerting. "Where are we going?" I managed.

"Harvest Tavern. I made reservations. It's too far to walk like we planned, but it's great for first dates." He flashed a wicked grin. "But first I thought we'd go to Scott and Steve's for a drink."

Scott and Steve are our resident gay couple. There are a total of twelve houses on our little block, and eight of us live here all summer. The four houses that are rentals have interchangeable families going in and out. The rest of us have become pretty good friends over the years, and it's generally accepted that any time after four in the afternoon is cocktail hour, and that any of us can go over to somebody's porch or deck for a few drinks. But at least once a week, a formal party turns up somewhere, invitations issued as we walk to and from the beach, and Scott and Steve usually throw a real shindig.

Their house is the epitome of what they like to call beach kitsch. Stone mermaids on either side of the front door. A wide assortment of pink flamingos on the tiny lawn. Crushed shell walkway. Potted palm trees in the front yard and paper lanterns out back. They are very generous hosts and Scott is a great cook. I love going there.

They both came to meet us as we came around to the back yard. Scott, very short and bleached blond, kissed me on both cheeks. "I love the idea of you two dating," he gushed. "Even if it is just for practice. You're perfect together. Really. My blessings on you both."

Steve, much taller and also bleached blond, rolled his eyes. "I can't wait for the he-said, she-said. You both need to report in tomorrow. Mona, you come early for coffee. Doug, sometime after lunch."

I looked at Doug. "Did you tell the whole block?"

"I posted it on the community bulletin board." He laughed and wandered off, returning with two tall drinks, colored bright pink and tasting of rum. We sipped and scanned the crowd. Scott and Steve tended to invite anyone they happened to meet, not just the usual suspects, so there was always someone to giggle about.

Doug spotted her first, and whispered wickedly in my ear. "Look. It's Our Lady of the Bodacious Ta-Tas."

"Oh my God," I whispered back. "And I think they're real."

I recognized her as the woman renting the house at the corner. Her breasts were stupendous. And I am a keen observer of breasts. Since I've spent so many years writing about them, frantically searching for the right adjectives and, in some cases, adverbs, to describe them, I've become an expert observer. In fact, for a heterosexual woman, I spend an inordinate amount of time looking at and thinking about women's mammaries. But this woman was off the scale.

They started about four inches below her chin, jutting out like the prow of a ship, then cutting back in about three inches above her belt buckle. She was showing ample cleavage, enough to reveal not the perfect rounds of flesh so easily identified as silicone, but the soft, undulating skin that God alone can create.

She glanced our way, must have seen us staring, and waved before working her way through the crowd to where we were standing. I imagined that, in her head, each step was accompanied by a little brass band playing "ba-boom, ba-boom."

"Hi," she said breathlessly, "I'm Vicki Montrose. I'm renting the Keller place. You're Mona Berman. I love your books. I can't believe I'm meeting you. I've never met anyone famous before."

I tried to look modest. Doug tried to look anywhere but down the front of her shirt. "Thank you, Vicki. It's nice to meet you. This is Doug Keegan. He lives right next to Scott and Steve. He's famous too. He invented Death Ride 66. Ever hear of it?"

She turned to Doug, forcing his eyes up. "Yes. My sons play it all the time. It's terribly violent, isn't it?"

I could see the strain of keeping his eyes on her face. "Yes. But it made me a lot of money. You should have your sons come over. They can test Death Ride 2000. My own boys are loving it."

She fluttered a perfectly manicured hand. "Oh, they're staying with my mother this summer. I'm going through a divorce right now. I feel the need to be alone. I have to try to gather all my inner strength and focus on healing. It's been a terrible ordeal."

"I'm so sorry," I said instantly. "I know how you feel. I'm going through a divorce myself."

She had very pretty blue eyes that widened and filled with tears. "Isn't it terrible? The feeling of abandonment and isolation? I'm completely at a loss. How are you coping?"

"It's getting easier." I sighed and took a long drink.

She got a little closer. "So tell me," she murmured, "what are you doing for sex?"

I must have looked a little taken aback, because she suddenly fluttered her hand again. "I'm only asking because, well, your books and everything. You must be very enlightened about sex. Open, you know. Free. I'm going crazy, myself. Especially when I see happy couples together. All I can think about is—" She lowered her voice. "You know."

"No, I don't know," Doug said innocently. "Tell me."

144

She ignored him. "I mean, how will I ever start even dating again? It's a cruel world out there."

"I'm practice-dating," I said, taking another gulp of my drink. Pineapple and cranberry. Very refreshing.

She looked interested. "Really? With who?"

Doug smiled. "With me. If you like, I can book you for next Thursday."

She tilted her head, looking him over carefully. "Let me think about it," she said to him, very seriously. Then she switched back to me. "I have a brother."

"Oh? I have a sister."

"I meant," she fluttered her hand again, "in case you're interested. He's younger than us, of course." I felt flattered. She was probably in her late thirties. Did she think I was that young?

"Really?"

"Yes. Cute, too. I don't know why he isn't more successful with women."

"Maybe," Doug suggested, "he's Scott's type."

She frowned. "No, I don't think so. He's got no game, you know? No confidence. Maybe I should have him call you?"

I didn't know what to say to that, exactly, so I just smiled and, thankfully, the Wilsons swept through, taking Doug and me with them, where they sheltered us and kept us laughing until Doug said it was time to officially start our date.

We had to drive to downtown Beach Haven for dinner, where the fish was, of course, fabulous, but they also had steaks to die for. We had a very nice dinner, and conversation came easy. When Doug is on, he's really a charmer. I had spent hours sitting and laughing with him on my back porch, and with the quiet candles, soft music, and great food, I felt very comfortable with him. And also very uncomfortable. We were both in new roles, and I wasn't sure how this evening was supposed to end up.

Neither did Doug, because as we drove home, he suddenly broke our nice, warm silence. "So, what are you doing for sex?"

"Thinking about it way too much," I answered truthfully. "I'm opening an account at BigHonkingDildos.com."

"Am I supposed to make a pass at you?" he asked as he turned into his drive.

I sat there, thinking. "Well, that's an interesting idea, but where would we go? I know that my daughters are probably looking at us right now from the upstairs window. If we go into your house, they'll probably freak. If we go to my house—well, we won't go to my house."

"Ever have sex on the beach?"

"The drink?" I asked. "It made me puke."

"No. The real thing."

"No. I was always worried about getting sand up my butt."

He grinned. "Look. Let's walk. No pressure, okay?"

So we walked up to the beach. There was no romantic full moon, and the tide had left behind a slimy assortment at the water line that reeked faintly of fish. Not ideal seduction circumstances. We sat for a while up near the dunes. It was cool, dark, and I had goose bumps everywhere.

"Well," he said at last, "what do you think?"

"I generally don't put out on the first date," I told him. "At least, I didn't when I was eighteen."

"Okay," he said, and stood up, brushing sand from his shorts.

I reached up, grabbed his hand, and pulled him back down next to me. "I'm not eighteen anymore," I told him.

"I know." It was too dark to see his eyes. Or even much of his face. But he smelled good, salty and musky. And there was a faint heat coming off his body.

"What would it mean, exactly?" I asked.

"Us having sex?"

I nodded.

"Well, see, the good thing about me is that I'm perfectly comfortable being the rebound guy. The revenge-fuck guy. The mercy-fuck guy. It doesn't bother me that you're still married, technically speaking. It doesn't bother me that Brian probably thinks of me as a friend. When it comes to sex, I'm very straightforward. I love it 'cause it feels good. So, what would this mean?" He turned on his side, facing me, propping himself on his elbow. "Whatever you want, Mona. I happen to think you're an attractive woman. I want you. Do I want happily ever after? Probably not. I've never considered you in that way before. Do I think we could have a good time? Yeah. And that's pretty much as complicated as it gets for me."

"My friend Patricia thinks I need a fuck buddy."

"Your friend Patricia sounds like a wise woman."

"I haven't been with anyone other than Brian in twenty years."

"We're pretty much built the same. And things work the same way. "

"Would we use a condom?"

"Absolutely. And trust me, they're much improved."

"What about this dead horseshoe crab right next to me?"

He reached over and pulled me across his own body, until I was lying down on his other side. He leaned in close. "See, all gone." And he kissed me.

Kissing someone other than Brian was a shock that lasted about three seconds. Then, biology kicked in and I kissed back.

I got sand up my butt.

I didn't care.

CHAPTER SEVEN

Ever notice how much more brightly the sun shines after really good sex? How the birds sing sweeter, water tastes fresher, air smells cleaner? I walked over to Scott and Steve's the next morning, sat down at their kitchen table and said, "That coffee smells great. And did you hear the gulls this morning?"

Scott looked at me. "You screwed him," he said.

"What?" I tried to bluff.

Steve squinted. "He's right. You had sex with Doug last night. And it was good." He sat down and looked at me. "It was good, wasn't it?"

"Guys," I stalled, "you don't know what you're talking about."

"Oh, yes we do," countered Scott. "Come on. He's coming over later, so we'll hear about it all anyway. So, where did you guys go?"

"To dinner at the Harvest Tavern."

149

"No, I mean after," Steve said impatiently.

I sighed. "For a walk on the beach."

"What?" Scott said. "But it was dark and windy last night. And there was all kinds of sea gack on the sand. It smelled pretty gross."

"Yes," I agreed. "I was sitting right next to a dead horseshoe crab."

Steve looked uncomfortable. "I'd have thought Doug had a little more class than that." He sniffed.

"Really," said Scott. "But, was it good?"

If I hadn't known these guys for almost nine years, I might have been offended. "It was great. He was great. I felt like Deborah Kerr with Burt Lancaster in *From Here to Eternity*."

"Oh," Scott sighed. "I knew it. I always knew he'd be great in the sack. After all these years of just fantasizing, to finally know for sure." He may have gotten teary at this point. "And he's really hung, right?"

"Oh, stop it," I snapped.

Steve made little clucking noises. "Okay, that's enough. I'm happy for you, Mona. Very happy. Somebody like Doug is just what you need right now, to help you feel young and sexy again. After all, you got dumped for a hot young thing. I'm sure your ego was in need of a boost."

"My ego has been just fine, thank you very much," I said dryly.

"I'm sure," Steve said soothingly. "But isn't it nice to have it, well, stroked?"

I grinned. "You bet. And Doug is a good stroker."

Scott beamed. "Make sure you e-mail Anthony. He'll be so proud."

"Anthony? My Anthony?" Anthony usually spent a week or so with us, and knew Scott and Steve well. "What has Anthony got to do with anything?"

"He's got a crush on Doug," Scott said smugly. "Has for years. Know what his nickname for Doug is? Surfer Ken."

Crush? I thought it was Ben Cutler he had a thing for. Was Anthony attracted to all the straight men in my life? Did he ever have a thing for Brian? "Anthony is in love," I told them. "He may not even come down this year. He may be going sailing with his new beau."

"Really?" Steve poured more coffee, and we sat and gossiped happily for the next hour, then I went back across the street. Doug's house was all closed up. He and his sons were off doing some ridiculously strenuous activity, like they did every morning. I sat at my desk for a while, trying to answer e-mails, but I kept drifting off to Doug-Doug Land. I thought, briefly, of calling Brian and telling him all about it, but reconsidered.

"Mom." Lauren was in the doorway, tennis racket in hand. "I'm off to meet Devlin. Did you have a good time last night?"

I was suddenly stricken with guilt. My daughter would surely see the signs. She would know what I did last night. She would be shocked.

"Yes. We had dinner at the Harvest."

"That's nice. You got in late."

"Yes. We walked on the beach."

She made a face. "It was yucky on the beach last night. Dead horseshoe crabs everywhere."

"Yes. I noticed."

"Do you think you'll go out with him again?"

Good question. Last night, as he walked me to my door and kissed me hard, crushing me against the doorjamb, with his hand up my shirt and mine down the back of his shorts, I asked him when we could do this again and he said whenever I wanted.

"Maybe tonight. Who knows?"

"Okay. Good. Well, see you later."

"Have a good game." I smiled as she left. She hadn't a clue. Thank God. She said she was meeting Devlin. That meant all the Keegans were back. Would Doug have the energy for a nooner?

Instead of calling him to ask, I went to the beach and lay out on the sand, baking. Miranda drifted by, set up her umbrella and all her other accoutrements, and settled under the shade.

"So, tell me everything," she said.

"Everything? Okay. We started with a cocktail, then salad. I had house with balsamic, and he—"

"Mom." She sighed. "Did you have fun?"

"Yes."

"Good. I think you should continue to go out with him, until you feel comfortable being in the company of a man other than Daddy. I realize you may have difficulty opening up to somebody else. But let me know when you're ready for Phase Two."

"Phase Two?"

"Yes. That would be a date with a stranger."

"I'll keep you posted."

She slathered herself with lotion, brushed her hair up to the top of her head, arranged herself in a sand chair, plugged in her iPod, stacked five magazines neatly in the sand next to her chair, took a long swig of her water bottle, and settled back, eyes closed. Fifteen minutes later, she sat up and told me she was going for a walk. I nodded, and as soon as she was gone, I moved to her chair under the umbrella and snoozed until Doug sat down beside me.

His appearance was more of what I was used to. His faded shirt had parrots on it and was opened to his navel. His jean shorts were cut so high that the pockets hung down lower than the frayed cuff. He was barefoot, his hair was wooly, and he was wearing sunglasses.

"I had lunch with Scott and Steve. They're very happy for us. They say I need to be gentle with you. I didn't have the heart to tell them you practically tore my skin off last night."

"Did I?"

"Yes. I'll have scars forever. Or at least until next Monday."

"Poor baby. I promise to never do that again."

"Please, don't promise that. I enjoyed it."

"Mm. Me too. Miranda thinks I should continue dating you until I feel comfortable opening up to someone other than Brian."

Doug chuckled. "Yeah, well, keep me in the loop."

"Will I see you tonight?"

"Listen, Mona, are we sure we're doing the right thing?"

I sat up and looked at him. "What are you saying?"

He pushed his glasses to the top of his head. "I like you, Mona," he said.

"Thank you. I like you too. I thought we'd established that."

"No. What I mean is, I like you as a friend. That doesn't happen to me much. In fact, you've always been one of the few women I like talking to even with your clothes on. Most women need to be naked for me to spend much time with them."

"I've noticed that about you."

"So, you see where there may be a problem."

"No, I don't. Unless you're suggesting that now that you've seen me naked, you don't like me anymore, which, I've got to tell you, would be kind of a huge blow."

"You're fine naked. Very fine. It's not that." He made a face.

Oh shit, I thought.

I had never been unfaithful to my husband. Never. Even when I was much younger and, I must say, something of a hot babe. I mean, I'd get hit on all the time. But I was always steadfast. I loved Brian. I was happy in our marriage. I'd taken vows. So for twenty years I never seriously thought about sex with another man, despite my continuous daydreaming about it. Maybe my sturdy resolve was due to the fact that, because of the nature of my writing, I was having constant fantasy sex with hoards of men endowed with various degrees of unbounded attractiveness and sexual prowess. But whatever the reason, I'd been faithful.

And, to tell you the truth, things had gotten a little too comfortable the past few years with Brian. After all, there are only so many combinations available. Even the Kama Sutra ends.

But now I was a free woman. Sure, there were still papers to sign, but it would only be a matter of months. For all intents and purposes, my marriage was over and I was free to have sex with whomever I wanted. And the perfect Guy-After-Brian was right there, sitting next to me. He was safe and friendly and, if last night was any indication, extremely talented. And he was the kind of guy who could have sex without any emotional complication. Exactly what I needed and wanted.

And now, suddenly, he's developed a conscience?

"Wait a minute. What happened to the rebound guy? What happened to the revenge-fuck guy? Last night you didn't care that I was still legally married to someone who might consider you a friend, but today you're concerned because you like me? Is that it?"

He looked sheepish. "Yeah. I guess when you put it that way, it seems a little silly."

"It is silly. Very silly. Listen to me, Doug. I've been having sex pretty regularly for over twenty years, and I've got to tell you, last night was memorable. I couldn't write something that good, and believe me, I'm an award winner when it comes to fantasy sex. So please don't go all noble on me, Doug. You've slept with women for years and never gave them a single thought. Let me be one of them. I'm begging you."

He chuckled again. "I don't want you to stop being my friend, Mona. I'd miss that."

"I promise, Doug, that no matter how many times you screw me senseless, I'll always be your friend."

"Okay." He looked relieved for a moment then tilted his head so he could look over the tops of his sunglasses. His eyes were so squinty I could barely see them, but I knew that expression anywhere. "Want to go back over to Scott and Steve's? They just left for Cape May and let me have their key. Or we could use their outdoor shower."

"If we used the shower, we'd have to be quiet."

"Yes, but it would be warm and wet and there's no roof, so we'd be in the sunshine."

"Let's go."

Even better without the sand up my butt.

~

MarshaMarsha's family used to have a big cookout their first day down to the shore, but five years ago her father died of a heart attack and her mother had a stroke. So I invited the whole crew to my house that year, and every year after that.

MarshaMarsha always arrived the weekend after the Fourth of July, so they were due in town about ten days after Doug and I started dating. And to be honest, we did go on real dates. Four of them. The rest of our time together had been in the relentless pursuit of someplace safe and comfortable to have sex, someplace we wouldn't be discovered by my kids, his kids, or any passing strangers. It had become a challenge, but one we were fully prepared to meet.

The Riollo family arrived just at four on a Sunday afternoon. I was sitting on my back porch with the Wilsons, my down-the-shore next-door neighbors. They were retired teachers with no children who had been spending their summers in the same house for over twenty years. They were good friends. When I told them about Brian, the very first night after we had come down, Tom looked shocked and sputtered about what a great guy Brian had been and how awful everything was. Annie just rolled her eyes and shook her head, finally telling me that she had always thought I deserved better. They hadn't mentioned Brian since that day. They knew that Doug and I had gone to dinner, but if they were curious about anything else, they kept it to themselves. One of the reasons I loved them.

MarshaMarsha was carrying an armful of fresh corn. Al, her husband, was walking beside MarshaMarsha's mother, Celeste D'Annello. Mrs. D. was about four feet tall and, in the manner of all old, tiny Italian ladies everywhere, had permed steel gray hair and a unibrow. She walked slowly and had been going deaf for years. She had a tendency to drift into her own little world, only to take a sudden interest in a conversation five minutes after it was over, at which point she would ask a number of questions at concert pitch. She was a lovely lady, but a bit trying.

I stood up to shake her hand as she came onto the back porch and offered her my chair. The Wilsons had also stood. There were kisses and handshakes all around, then Mrs. D. sank into my chair, smiled dreamily, and focused on some point in the yard just left of the garage. Al, seeing her settled, pecked me on the cheek and made a beeline for the red plastic tub filled with ice, beer, and soda, then popped the top off a Bud Light and took a long pull.

"Good trip down?" Tom asked brightly.

"I'm gonna kill them all," Al snarled. He sat down. "They're animals," he muttered. "They should be in cages."

I took the bag of corn from MarshaMarsha and she followed me into the kitchen. "The boys not behaving?"

She sighed. "It's getting harder and harder. They don't want to leave their friends, Nick got tapped for All-Stars but I had to tell him no. Jack wanted to be in a summer theater production, and I had to say no to that as well. I don't know how long I can keep dragging them down here. Thank God for Doug Keegan and his sons. The boys are already over there getting ready to windsurf or something equally exhausting." Something must have flickered across my face because she suddenly looked sharp. "What?"

I cleared my throat. "Doug."

"What about Doug?"

I glanced over my shoulder. Tom and Annie had Al relaxed and laughing already. The girls, I knew, were still on the beach. "Doug and I are having sex."

Her mouth dropped open. "*What?*"

"It was the girls' idea, actually."

"The girls told you to have sex? With Doug?"

"No, of course not. They decided that I needed to practice dating."

"What are you talking about?" She had dumped the corn in the sink and was shaking off all the dried corn silk.

"Practice dating. Apparently, they're convinced that Brian is never coming back, and they wanted me to practice dating somebody in preparation for the actual dating I may do in the future. They picked Doug as my first sample. And we ended up having really great sex. Then we had it again. And again."

"Isn't that more like practice sex? This is very confusing."

"No, not really. He's my fuck buddy."

"I didn't think you had it in you."

"I didn't either," I admitted.

"So are you doing any actual dating?"

"Dinner, once. Drinks. A movie. Mini-golf."

"Well, that sounds fun. And the sex is good?"

"Great."

"Well, there you go." She frowned again. "The girls?"

"They know about the dating part. I don't think they've figured out the rest. In fact, the reason they picked Doug was because they didn't think there'd be any, uh, temptation."

She had arranged all the ears of corn in rows in a big baking pan, in preparation for shucking. Now she shrugged. "Well, he is kinda ugly."

"Yes," I agreed.

"But he's got a great body. And all that curly hair. His eyes are squinty, but that mouth of his…." Her voice drifted off, and she looked thoughtful.

"Exceeds expectations."

"Well. Yeah, I'd do him." She picked up the corn. "Shall we?"

We went back on the porch and shucked the corn and chatted happily. The girls came back and took turns in our outdoor shower, which is not nearly as nice and private as Scott and Steve's, but gets the sand off. Finally, Doug showed up with all seven boys, in a line like so many dwarves. We ordered the kids outdoors to sit at the long picnic table under the scrub pines in the back yard, while the adults stayed on the screened-in porch. We ate burgers, hot dogs, corn and potato salad, and had cut into the second watermelon when suddenly Fred, who had been comatose for most of the afternoon, lifted his head and barked.

We all stared at him. He knows everyone on the block, and anyone he doesn't know he still considers a best friend.

"Hello," came drifting around the corner of the house, and Fred barked again. Someone came teetering up to the porch in spike-heeled sandals and a fuchsia sundress. Vicki Montrose.

She was looking quite pretty. It was hard to get past the boobs, of course, but she was thin everywhere else and was attractive, with bouncy blondish hair and big eyes.

"Hello everybody," she said somewhat breathlessly. "I hope you don't mind, but I heard all the laughing and thought, well...."

I stood up. "Of course, Vicki. Have you eaten? We haven't put anything away yet. Or maybe some watermelon?"

She smiled. "Maybe just a teensy drink."

Doug leaped to his feet. "Allow me." He bowed, looking directly into her considerable cleavage. "What can I do you? Get you?"

She batted her lashes. "A Cosmopolitan would be divine."

He took off into the house.

The Keegan boys had been seeing Vicki in various states of dress and undress for almost two weeks, so they weren't staring too hard, but the Riollos were having a tough time of it. The boys were falling off the picnic benches trying to get a better angle. Even Al didn't quite know where to look. Tom Wilson immediately put his sunglasses back on so no one could accuse him of anything later on.

"So, Vicki," I began, "does this mean you'll be staying another week?" All rentals ran from Saturday to Saturday, and today would have meant a changing of the guard.

"Actually, I took the place for the whole summer. I told you, I really needed to have some alone time. But I came over to tell you that my brother will be joining me sometime near the end of the month, and I thought the two of you might go out."

I stared at her blankly. "Out where?"

"Now, you, stop teasing me. You told me all about it, remember? Practice dating? Well, now you can practice on Mitchell."

Doug returned and handed her a drink. "Mitchell?" he asked politely.

"Yes," Vicki explained. "Mitchell is my brother. I think he could really help Mona and her practice dating."

Al Riollo looked puzzled. "Mona, are you really dating again? That's great. I had no idea. But, of course, Marsha never tells me anything."

"Actually, honey," MarshaMarsha said gently, "I just heard about it myself today."

"Honest? Practice dating, did you say? What is that, exactly?" Al looked around hopefully.

MarshaMarsha turned to me and beamed. "Tell Al all about it, Mona. Go on."

I cleared my throat. Doug, I could see from the corner of my eyes, seemed intent on scratching Fred's ears. "My daughters seemed to think that I needed some practice before diving into the dating pool, so they suggested that Doug and I go out a few times, just as, you know, a warm-up."

"Honest? What a great idea." Al was genuinely interested. "And how did that work out for you both?"

MarshaMarsha began to choke on her drink, and Tom Wilson patted her gently on the back.

"Yes, you never did tell us," Tom said. "How did that go?"

"Fine," I said smoothly.

"We've been having a great time," Doug said. "Tuesday we played mini-golf."

"I'm just not sure I'm ready for Phase Two," I explained to Vicki. "You know, going out with a stranger. My daughter Miranda says I need to work up to that gradually."

"Excuse me," Mrs. D. suddenly yelled at Vicki, "but don't they hurt?"

Vicki looked confused. "Don't what hurt?"

"Your boobies. Your back must be killing you."

Vicki turned red. So did MarshaMarsha.

"Mom," she said loudly, trying to tactfully divert her, "Mona is dating Doug. Isn't that interesting?"

"Mona? Dating Doug?" Mrs. D. was successfully sidelined. "Doesn't Brian have anything to say about that?"

Vicki frowned. "Who's Brian?" she asked.

"My husband." I sighed.

"Mom, Mona's getting a divorce, remember?" MarshaMarsha plowed on.

"Divorce? Did you tell me that?" Mrs. D. asked.

Al tried to help. "Yes, we told you all about it, Mother D. Remember? Brian left last spring."

Mrs. D. suddenly smiled. "Yes, I remember. He was cheating on her. Is Big Boobie over there the one?"

"No," MarshaMarsha said quickly. "Vicki is renting down the street. She wants Mona to go out with her brother."

"But isn't Mona dating Doug?" Mrs. D. frowned again. "How many men is she going out with anyway?"

Al tried again. "They're practice dating, Mother D."

"Practice? What the hell is that? Who needs to practice dating? You go out, and it clicks or it doesn't." Mrs. D. shook her head. "What the hell is so hard about that?"

Vicki leaned in. "He cheated on you?" she breathed. "Oh, you must be devastated."

I conjured up my Joan-of-Arc face. "It's hard," I admitted.

"How brave of you to soldier on," Vicki continued.

"Yes. Well." I managed a weak smile.

"But I think Mitchell would be a good step for you." Vicki was smiling again. "He's a very successful entrepreneur."

"Next thing you know," Mrs. D. yelled, "they'll be having practice sex."

MarshaMarsha buried her face in her hands. Al downed the rest of his beer. Tom and Annie Wilson both snapped their heads in my direction.

"Entrepreneur?" I asked. "How interesting."

"Yes." Vicki was bursting. "He owns three comic book stores. He's thinking about trying to franchise."

"Imagine that." My head hurt. "Doug, he owns comic book stores."

Doug was keeping a straight face. "Whereabouts?"

Vicki held out her empty glass and waggled it at him. "Hoboken. Jersey City. And Chatham. That was his first store. The Chatham one. That's where he lives. With our parents."

"Oh?" Doug finally broke into a grin. "He still lives with his folks? Hard to figure."

Vicki shrugged. "It's not like he doesn't have lots of money, you understand, but Mom is so good to him, you know?"

"Oh." Doug chuckled. "I know." He got up and took her glass. I finally glanced over at Tom and Annie, who were looking as though the sun had suddenly risen on an entire new world. I smiled weakly at them, then turned to Mrs. D.

"Can I get you more iced tea?" I asked her. She shook her head, then frowned again.

"Are you going to have sex with Big Boobie's brother too?"

I could not even begin to formulate a response.

"Mother," MarshaMarsha was trying to insist, "it's not about sex."

"The hell it isn't," Annie muttered.

Tom frowned. "Mona and Doug?" he asked his wife, who rolled her eyes and knocked back the rest of her drink.

"Mom." Miranda, who had been sitting on the back picnic table surrounded by the Riollo and Keegan boys, appeared on the porch, cell phone in hand. "Can I ask you something?"

"Oh, God. Please," I said.

"Dad wants to know if we can spend a few days with him. He says he hasn't seen us in a month, and he'll take off a few days. He said he'll take us to the city. Can we go?"

Now my stomach hurt. "How do your sisters feel about this?" I asked.

"They're cool. He wants to take us shopping. Is it okay?"

I took a long breath. Far be it from me to keep my children away from their only father if they really wanted to spend time with him. "Of course it's okay, honey. Whatever you girls want to do. When can he be here?"

"Hold on." She put the phone to her ear, turned her back, and mumbled. She snapped the phone shut and turned back. "He's crossing the bridge."

"What? He's crossing the bridge? What bridge are you talking about?" I felt a sudden rush of anxiety.

"You know. The bridge. Onto LBI. We'd better pack," she yelled to her sisters, and the porch was suddenly full of girls, then empty again. My jaw was still somewhere on my chest when Doug reappeared, Vicki's new drink in hand.

"What did I miss?"

"Brian is coming to get the girls for a few days," I told him.

"So? Why do you look so upset? When is he coming?"

"In about fifteen minutes," I told him.

I had not seen Brian since he walked out of the house in April. We had phone conversations, e-mails, and plenty of lawyer-related exchanges. I even left a message for him at his office that he could come and pick up an assortment of items, ranging from his golf clubs to his high school football trophy, that I thoughtfully had thrown into a huge pile in the garage. But nothing face-to-face. He picked up the girls and returned them home without leaving the Mercedes, and all I had seen of his actual person was his silhouette.

Al and MarshaMarsha were gathering up Mrs. D. and calling for their boys, and the Wilsons were standing and shaking hands, murmuring goodbyes. Vicki gulped her drink and hugged me.

"I'll call about Mitch," she whispered, and left.

MarshaMarsha gave me a quick kiss. "I'll call you tomorrow," she promised.

And Doug and I were sitting alone.

"Can I clear a room or what?" I said at last.

"Do you want me to stay?" he asked.

I shook my head, and he left, brushing his hand across my shoulder.

I sat a few minutes longer, looking around the porch. Everyone had arranged their empty glasses neatly on the coffee table, so I gathered them onto a tray and went into the kitchen. I wasn't sure what I was supposed to do. Brian was coming. Would I actually see him this time? And if I did, how did I look?

I ran into the bathroom and looked in the mirror. Damn, I looked pretty good. Tan coming along nicely. Hair soft and curly. I'd put on my I've-got-company bra, so the girls were high and in place. Manicure and pedicure intact. And I looked great in blue.

I went into the living room and turned on the reading light, then sat and began to read a magazine, so that when Brian pulled up, he was sure to see me sitting there alone. I turned the pages, listening to the girls squabbling upstairs, and finally car lights swept up the drive, a car door slammed, and Fred went crazy, racing up from the kitchen and flinging himself against the screen door, barking like a mad thing. I heard Brian talking to him from the other side of the door, so I casually called for him to come in.

Brian looked thinner. And tired. He stood in the center of the room, hands in the pockets of his khakis looking down at me as I continued to carelessly turn the pages of my magazine.

"Hello, Brian." I sounded cool. Composed. Totally detached. "How are you?"

"Good. Good." He spoke heartily. "Doing fine. Thanks for letting me get the girls on such short notice. I was on my way back from Atlantic City. A bunch of us from work brought Joe Heddon down for his bachelor party last night. I just took a chance I'd be able to scoop them up."

"You hate Atlantic City," I said. "You always bitched and moaned when we went there."

He shrugged. "It's not that bad."

"And you hate Joe Heddon."

He looked shocked. "Whatever gave you that idea?"

"You once called him a malevolent rat-bastard with a really tiny dick," I said.

He became thoughtful. "Really? When?"

"When he fired Susan Lucas."

"Yeah, I remember now. Well, people can change."

"Oh? Did he grow a bigger dick?"

He chuckled. "No. He's Dominique's boss."

"Ah."

He frowned. "What do you mean, 'ah'?"

"Nothing. Doesn't matter. You're here now, that's the thing." I smiled tolerantly as I flipped another page. "They haven't seen you in so long, and they seem very excited. Miranda mentioned shopping."

He cleared his throat. "Yeah. I thought I'd take a few days, you know, take them on a little spree."

I turned to a fascinating article on the benefits of cranberry juice. "And how's Dominique? Will she be shopping with you?"

"No," he said shortly. "She's taken off to see some friends in Phoenix."

"Phoenix? I hope she doesn't fry. The heat in Phoenix in the middle of July can be brutal."

He shrugged. "That's what I told her, but she was determined to take a few days for herself. They're going to some spa out there."

I finally looked at him, one eyebrow raised. "Trouble in Paradise?"

"No. No, nothing really. Well, just a little dry patch, that's all. Nothing that can't be, ah, managed. Every couple has them. You know, dry patches." He walked over to the staircase and yelled upstairs to the girls. I could hear a rumble of activity above me. He turned to me and cleared his throat again. "You look great, by the way. How are things going? I mean, are you getting out and around? I'd hate to think you're down here just, you know, sitting around."

I smiled. Smugly. "Actually, I've started dating."

"Oh." He looked alert. "How do the girls feel about this?"

"It was their idea. Although, it's very funny, because they insisted that I practice first. On somebody familiar. Before I went out with a stranger."

"Practice? How cute. So you found somebody to practice on, then?"

"Yes." Flipped another page. "Doug Keegan, actually."

"What? Doug?" He laughed. "Come on, Mona, Doug doesn't date. He just takes women out so he can sleep with them."

I looked modest and continued flipping.

He sat down across from me. "I mean, seriously, Mona, that guy is a lot of fun, but he's only out for one thing. I mean, you don't want to get involved with somebody who's only interested in recreational sex."

"Well, maybe that's all I'm interested in. You know, being married for so long, it's nice to have some freedom. To do whatever I want. Whenever I want." I smiled at him. "Wherever I want."

"Mona." He was suddenly serious. "I know I can't tell you what to do, but I hope you're not having sex with somebody when our daughters are right in the next room."

"Of course not, Brian," I assured him. "Just as I'm sure that you and Dominique never have sex when our daughters are in the next room."

That stopped him. And just then, the girls spilled down the stairs and they were gone in a flurry of waves and kisses and half-opened backpacks. I watched them go out the door, and turned back to Brian.

"You looked like you were about to say something, Brian. What was it?" I asked sweetly.

Brian opened his mouth, closed it, and took in a deep breath. "Goodnight, Mona," he said, and left.

Fred sighed and hauled himself up on the couch. I heard crickets.

A few minutes later, Doug let himself in and sat down next to Fred. "How did he look?" he asked.

"Tired. Worried. He said he and Dominique were having a dry patch."

Doug flashed a grin. "That's guy-talk for not being able to get it up."

I brightened. "Really? Remind me to send Rebecca flowers."

He looked puzzled. "Rebecca? Isn't she Brian's sister?"

"Yeah. She's the best."

He patted Fred between the ears. "Do you want me to stay a while?"

I tilted my head at him. "Yes. And you want to know why?"

"I can guess."

"Besides that. With the girls gone, we can actually use a bed."

"A bed? What an interesting idea."

It was. Especially since Fred forgot to read the memo and kept getting in the bed with us. We finally gave up trying to push him off, and we ended up on the floor, with him watching from the top of the mattress. I'm glad he finally had a good story to tell all his doggie friends.

CHAPTER EIGHT

I was falling into a comfortable writing routine. Although I'm an early riser during the school year, I always tend to sleep in summer mornings. I found that sticking to my old schedule was working out pretty well. I got up every morning at six thirty, walked Fred for two miles, had breakfast, and got in two or three hours of uninterrupted writing time before the girls even cracked open an eye.

I had set up shop on the back porch, my laptop on a battered rattan table, iced coffee at the elbow. After the morning rush, and a few hours beach time, I was back for at least two hours before dinner. In the few hours before bed, I'd go over what I'd written earlier, make changes, and e-mail everything to my best critic and first line of editorial defense, Anthony. Anthony was still at the Westfield house twice a week, going over what I sent him, answering mail, making entries to my website, and fielding phone calls. He was also dating a yoga instructor named Victor, keeping me informed of community events, preventing Lily from burning down my house, and offering his usual brand of invaluable advice on everything from the improper use of the possessive to my sex life.

To: Mona
From: Anthony
Date: July 8
Subject: Crazed relation

Victor and I are fine, thanks for asking. And I'm thrilled to hear about you and Surfer Ken, although this whole practice dating idea sounds a little strange, like something a crazy teenager would think of—whoops! I forgot. A crazy teenager did think it up. There you go! And in response to your last e-mail, no, I don't have a crush on every straight man in your life. Just Ben, because he's so heartbreakingly beautiful that I can't even give him a nickname, and Surfer Ken, because he's built like a Greek god. Too bad his face is like the Minotaur, LOL.

I sent two dozen roses to Glinda, as you asked. I can only imagine why. Some things I really don't want to know.

Work on the new website is almost done—I just need artwork, which I'm attaching for your approval. I've announced the new book, and the fact that it will be released as a Mona Quincy title. I'll start giving hints as soon as you have a final draft approved.

In case Lily forgets to mention it, you're finally getting a new master bathroom. She's worked out some deal with Ben. Lily would have the place looking like a Las Vegas brothel—an extremely tacky Las Vegas brothel—but luckily Ben is so handsome and charming he has her eating out of his hands. Ben snuck me in yesterday while Lily was off planning to overthrow the Garden Club for refusing to serve Planter's Punch at their luncheon last week. Lily has surrounded herself with every paranoid crackpot in town, and I swear, they'll be running the place by the time you get back. Every time she sees me, she gives me a very odd look. I keep waiting to show up and find the police waiting to arrest me for trespassing. She does know I work here, right?

Lily has expanded the family by taking in two new kittens. They are adorable, but Lana keeps picking them up by their little necks and dropping them into the toilet. Ben told me he's had to duct tape a few toilet lids closed, because Lana seems determined to drown these interlopers before they reach puberty.

I read the new chapters and they're just terrific. I am so loving this book. Sending you a hard copy with all my little notes, but I have no serious complaints. I'm so glad you're able to write down there.

Must go. Anthony

To: Mona Quincy
From: Your Aunt Lily
Date: July 8
Subject: How I Spent Your Summer Vacation
Darling Mona;
Ben was kind enough to show me how to work the computer in your den so that I can e-mail you. I've been taking a class at the library with a few of the ladies from the neighborhood, and I must say I really enjoy the World Wide Web. The things that are available are truly amazing, and now that I can use the house computer, I don't have to worry about all those silly restrictions that the library has on cer-

tain sites. I would think that an institution that prides itself on intellectual development would not be so closed-minded about some subjects.

Ben and I are working on that master bathroom of yours. I'm paying for it, as a gift to you for all your warmth and generosity in letting me stay here. I wanted it to be a surprise, but Ben insisted I tell you about what was happening. He also wanted you to know that he was exercising prudent judgment in the selection of all the fixtures. In other words, he nixed the marble columns and the gold plated faucets shaped like little naked angels. He's a very attractive man, but with very pedestrian taste in bathroom décor. I would personally love to sit in a big, red tub and watch naked baby boys pee water into the bubbles, but Ben went in another direction. We have been arguing over tile, and he won't budge an inch, so I told him he should drive down to Long Beach Island and discuss the issue with you personally, and he's going to give you a call. I hope you agree with pink iridescent.

Anthony continues to come to work two or three days a week, even though you are no longer here. I assume this is all right with you, as he does have his own key. But if he's trespassing, please let me know so that I can call the police and have his ass thrown into jail.

I have adopted two little kittens. I promise to take them with me when I go. Lana has adjusted fairly well. Knowing your fondness for old movies, I've named them Olivia and Joan, as they are beautiful sisters and great drama queens. Just last night Joan threw a hissy fit just because I tried to pose her sitting in one of your martini glasses holding a speared pearl onion in her little mouth. Virginia, who lives on South Maple and who was having a few cocktails with me at the time, was trying to get a picture on her new digital camera, so she could win one hundred dollars from *Star* magazine's "Cute Pet of the Week" contest. The glass was unbroken, thank goodness, but I still haven't found the onion. I think it rolled under the couch, and I'll ask Ben to look for it tomorrow.

Please let me know how you're doing. I've always loved sending and receiving mail. Now that our government needs more money and is raising the price of stamps again, it's nice to know we can keep in touch without funding the Pentagon's diabolical plan to annex southern China. What they intend to do with all those extra people, I have no idea, but it might be nice to get those little televisions for less money.

I haven't heard anything else about what's happening in Prospect Park. As soon as the landing starts, I'll let you know.

Love, Aunt Lily

To: Aunt Lily
From: Mona
Date: July 9
Subject: Anthony
Dear Aunt Lily – I'm so glad that we can chat back and forth like this. Please don't arrest Anthony. He's working, honest he is. Even though I'm not there, he answers e-mails, keeps up with my professional correspondence, helps with book-tour dates—he does everything, for God's sake, so leave him alone and let him do his job in peace. Please. As

for our president, I wouldn't worry about the China thing. He's got enough on his plate right now. Mona

To: Anthony
From: Mona
Date: July 10
Subject: Whatever

Yes, Anthony, I'm still "seeing" Doug. I asked him last night how old he was, and he's fifty-one. Then I asked him about his, well, endurance. I mean, aren't men supposed to slow down after a certain age??? He just laughed and said he had slowed down—I should have known him at 30! Very funny. No, not funny. More like Ripley's Believe It or Not. But interestingly enough, the word of my practice dating experiment has spread across all of Long Beach Island. Bobby the Fish Guy, who owns the place three blocks down where I grab fish dinners to go a couple of times a week, has set me up with his brother, Jack, the art teacher. I've met his brother quite a few times, as he spends a few weeks down here every summer helping Bobby out at the shop. As I recall, his brother is reasonably attractive and kind of funny. He called and we had a nice conversation, and we're meeting for drinks and possibly dinner Wednesday night. I'll keep you posted. Ben is coming all the way down here on Monday—he and Lily are having Tile Wars, and he insisted I weigh in. I guess he's right—I hate to think about Lily unchecked. Your comments on the book were great, by the way. You're right about Sarah—I don't want to get too schmaltzy. Cancer and three grandkids may be a bit much. Can she have just one grandkid? Maybe an adorable charmer with missing front teeth, so that Sydney will have somebody to look after? I'll have to think about this one. Miss you too, Mona

~

Ben knocked on my door early Sunday morning. He had warned me he was hitting the Parkway before seven, but he caught me before my second cup of coffee and in the middle of a dicey scene in my book involving two naked people in a rowboat. I squinted at him through the screen door, then shifted my gaze to two teenaged boys slouching behind him.

"I hope you don't mind," Ben said, "but my sons asked to come with me. They were a little insistent."

I grinned. "I bet." I opened the door. "Come on in, guys. I'll get some badges so you won't have to pay on the beach."

They filed in quietly. Ben introduced David, going to Yale in the fall, and Ethan, starting his junior year in high school. The two boys looked so much like their father I felt lightheaded. I almost asked Ben if we could sign the marriage contracts right then, but couldn't decide who would get Ethan: Jess or Lauren.

The boys thanked me politely, said they wouldn't need to be back to use the bathroom, since they usually just peed in the water, then clattered out the door and tore up the street to the beach. Ben watched them for a minute, then sighed. "I really hope you don't mind. They bushwhacked me as I was leaving this morning, and I didn't want to call you so early to ask if it was okay. We'll be going on down to Wildwood Crest to see their grandmother as soon as we're done here."

"No problem," I told him, waving him onto the back porch. "Can I get you coffee? No? Okay, where's this tile Lily can't stop talking about?"

He had a messenger bag slung over his shoulder, and he opened it onto the coffee table, pulling out a dozen or so tile samples. He separated out a piece of pinky-mauve, glazed to look like the inside of a seashell.

"That's Lily's choice," he said.

I looked at it. "For what?"

"Everything," Ben said. "She wants the entire shower, including the ceiling, as well as the backsplashes over the sinks and the tub surround."

I stared at him. "It would glow," I blurted. "It would look neon."

He nodded. "I know. I think that's the effect she's going for."

"Ben, can you tell me what everything else looks like?"

He pulled a laptop out of his bag. "Here. Take a look."

Everything that Ben had picked out was perfect. Period looking pieces, almost in the Craftsman style, all simple and elegant. A deep claw-foot soaking tub, two pedestal sinks, and the classiest-looking toilet I'd ever seen. He'd taken digital pictures of the work so far, and I could tell it was going to look just great. I looked at him at last and shrugged. "I don't know, Ben. I'm thinking plain white subway tile. Is that too dull?"

Ben looked relieved. "Not at all. But I'd like to add a pinstripe. Very narrow. In sage green. Here." He pulled out a thin piece of tile that looked like Depression glass. "Just for a punch of color."

"Perfect." I said, leaning back. "I'll call Lily and tell her that from now on, whatever you say goes. I'm giving you complete control."

He pushed her onto the bed, pinning her wrists over her head with one hand and grinning down at her. "Does that mean I can do whatever I like?" he asked, untying the ribbon at the neck of her nightgown. "Because if it does," he murmured, sliding his hand over her breast, "we could be here quite a while."

"Then I'm ordering those 24-karat gold faucets," Ben said, straight-faced. "And the emerald showerhead."

"Lily might forgive you," I laughed. "Really, Ben, it looks great. But you didn't have to come all the way down here. I'd have trusted your judgment over the phone."

He put everything back into the bag before he looked up at me. "Well, I also wanted to see how you were getting on. I was a little worried about you. How are things going?"

I was so surprised that for a moment I could think of nothing to say. "I'm fine," I finally managed. "Better than I thought I'd be, actually. Thank you so much for asking."

He settled back in the chair. He was wearing denim shorts and a faded green polo shirt. He had on scuffed leather topsiders with no socks, and his legs were, well, great. He looked tanned and relaxed, and I briefly wondered what he would do if I went over and pulled his shirt off and started—

"Mom, who was at the door?" Lauren was yawning, her hair rumpled. "Isn't it really early?"

"Sorry." Ben stood up. "That was me. Believe it or not, your mom and I had emergency bathroom issues."

She giggled. "I've never heard of emergency bathroom issues that could be resolved on a porch, but if you say so…" She wandered back into the house.

I cleared my throat. "So, your mom lives in Wildwood Crest?"

Ben shook his head. "No. Ellen's mother. Ellen, my first wife. The boys used to spend weeks with her when they were little, but now with them both working, they don't get the chance to see her too often. That's why when they found out where I was heading, they pounced."

"It's nice that they feel so close to their grandmother. My girls sometimes go weeks without remembering they even have a grandmother."

Ben shrugged. "Bonnie, Ellen's mother, never really approved of me. Not that I blame her. After all, I got her nineteen-year-old daughter pregnant. But when Ellen got sick, Bonnie changed a little. I guess she realized that I really did love Ellen after all. After that, she went out of her way to get in good with the boys. I'm sure that when they spent time with her, they were bombarded with soda, chocolate, and endless television. That kind of bribery makes a lasting impression."

I finished the rest of my coffee and we sat there in silence for a few minutes. Finally I said, "You're a good dad, to spend your day off driving your kids to see somebody who probably doesn't like you very much."

He shrugged. "Isn't that what it's all about? Having kids? You spend lots of time doing things you don't want to. The best thing about David going off to college is that now I can spend Saturdays doing what I want instead of driving all over the state in search of a travel soccer game."

I stood up and stretched. "Thank God my girls are only interested in spectator sports. And shopping." I watched him unfold and hoist his bag over his shoulder. "Seriously, you all can hang here for a little longer. I'm just writing and the girls are still asleep. Nobody would mind."

He flashed me a smile that could have guided fogbound ships to shore. "Thanks, but no. I'm going up to grab the boys, then we need to get going. But thank you. And I'm glad you're doing okay."

I followed him out, simply because the view from the rear was outstanding. He threw his bag into the truck, pulled out a towel, peeled off his shirt, and shrugged out of his shorts, revealing red swim trunks underneath. I watched with my heart in my throat, wildly hoping for one outrageous moment that he would in fact be naked beneath the denim. He wasn't. He walked up towards the beach as I slumped against the side of his truck for support.

As he disappeared over the rise of sand, Anne Wilson came running out of her house and grabbed me by both arms.

"Who was that?" she asked in a hushed whisper.

I sighed. "Ben. My plumber."

She turned to stare where he had vanished. "Will he be coming back?"

"Sure. This is his truck."

"No, I mean, is your plumbing fixed? Or should I drop something down my toilet so I can call him myself?"

I patted her gently and drew her inside, explaining that he didn't work nearby. Poor woman, she was so disappointed.

∼

Doug thought it was funny that I had decided to expand my dating pool. It was, of course, Miranda's idea. I don't know in what little notebook she had written down her plan, but there seemed to be an established course of events somewhere. After my fifth date with Doug, I had reached some sort of benchmark. I'm assuming she didn't know about all the times we had sex and therefore didn't factor that in. Anyway, Miranda announced that it was time to practice with somebody new, and she had the ideal candidate in mind. It was her idea that I talk to Bobby Kuschke, the fish guy.

There's no table service at Bobby's, only a long line of people waiting for the freshest, hottest fried fish platters anywhere. Ideally, you take your order directly to one of the outdoor picnic tables, splash on lots of malt vinegar, and eat everything while it's still hot enough to burn your fingers. My daughters don't like the noise and crowds, so my dinners are usually packed in Styrofoam and plastic and whisked home.

The Friday before MarshaMarsha was due to come down, Bobby pulled me out of line to the back of the shop. He's a red-faced, sweaty guy, but maybe that's because he's cooking in a one- hundred-degree kitchen ten hours a day.

"So, Mona, I heard about you and your old man. Tough."

"Thanks, Bobby."

"And I hear you're doing a little dating around, trying to get back on track?"

I wanted to ask where he'd heard that, then decided I really didn't want to know. I couldn't believe that Miranda had actually approached him about fixing me up. I preferred to think there was just a little birdie flitting around who told him. "Yes, I am dating a little. But only with men I already know."

Bobby nodded approvingly. "Smart. Don't want any whacko strangers when you're just pulling out of the box. So how about Jack?"

I thought hard, then gave up. "Jack who?"

"My brother. You know Jack. He spends five, six weeks down here, helping out. He's a teacher the rest of the year. An art teacher, but he's not no fancy boy, just 'cause he's into painting and all that shit. He's a little out there, you know? And he can be a pain in the ass sometimes, but a good guy. He'll be here next week. What d'ya think?"

An out-there pain in the ass good guy who's not a fancy boy? What a referral. But I did know Jack. He seemed smart and funny. He also had beautifully shaped hands, thick straight hair, and a very attractive smile. He always wore sunglasses and gave me extra-crispy fries.

"Here," I said, scribbling my phone number down on a napkin. "Have Jack call me. We'll see.

Jack called Monday night after Brian had come by to pick up the girls. More precisely, he called as Doug and I were enjoying what we romance writers like to call a postcoital languor. I had to get off the bed, because Doug kept doing things with his tongue that made it hard for me to concentrate, but Jack and I agreed to meet for drinks that Wednesday at seven. As I hung up the phone, Doug flashed me one of his naughty grins.

"Cheating on me?"

"It's a drink. I won't be screwing him. In fact, I'll probably come home and screw you."

"This could work out well for me. Other men can wine and dine you, and I'll get you in the sack."

"I didn't think it would be possible to cheapen this relationship any further, but I believe you've found a way."

"It's a gift."

~

Jack and I had arranged to meet at a great little place on the bay where, if you were lucky enough, you could sail your boat up to the dock and walk up to your table. I drove, of course. Jack, apparently, flew.

He was just where he said he'd be—at the bar. He may have been there for days, because when I approached him, he had to squint at me for several seconds before recognizing me. He grinned broadly, began to slide off the bar stool, and slipped down to a heap at my feet.

Not an auspicious beginning.

But I was willing to assume the best, so I helped him to his feet, directed him to a small table overlooking the bay, and even held his chair for him while he cautiously sat himself down. I sat across from him, face carefully arranged, and said hello. He squinted again. Then looked out over the water.

"If we sit here, I may get seasick," he said slowly.

"Seasick? But we're not on a boat."

He nodded at this piece of information. "That may be true, but I feel like I'm on a boat. Can we sit on the other side?"

This proved to be an exhausting exercise, because aside from navigating through several closely grouped tables, we also had to avoid getting run over by anxious waitresses carrying trays laden with food and drink. When we finally got to another table, safely away from the sight and sound of water, he squinted again, looking equally distressed.

"We're not near the water," I pointed out.

"I know. That's not the problem. We're too near the parking lot."

The spot between my eyes started to burn. "What's wrong with the parking lot? Do you get carsick too?"

"The fumes," he explained. "I don't like the fumes."

"Do you want to go and get a table inside?" I asked.

There may have been a little something in my voice, because he looked suddenly hearty and eager to please. "No, not at all. This is fine. Drink?"

He waved his hand frantically in the air until a waitress hurried over. She was smiling at him like he was an old friend. Which, as it turned out, he was.

"Maggie, honey, how are you?"

"Oh, Jack." She giggled. "I heard you were back."

"Just this week, honey. Give me my usual, and whatever the lady wants."

The lady wanted to get the hell out of Dodge, but I asked for a club soda. "I'm driving," I said to Maggie, by way of explanation. Then I turned back to Jack.

"So, I guess you're a regular here?"

"I live here."

I laughed. "Really?"

"Yep. Really. In the spare room over the kitchen."

I stopped laughing. "You live over the bar?"

"Yep. Have for years. Could stay with Bobby, of course, but he doesn't like me smoking pot with his kids around, so it's just easier to stay here. Maggie there? She's the owners' daughter. She, well, kind of looks after me when I'm here."

"Does she now?"

Maggie returned with my club soda in what looked like a giant water goblet. Jack had something in the same sized glass. Clear, on the rocks. I stared as he took a long gulp.

"What is that?" I asked.

"Gin."

"And what?"

He frowned. "And ice."

"A classic," I said.

He grinned broadly. "I find the simple things work out best for me. I don't like a lot of stuff, you know? Stuff crushes the creative mind."

I saw the straw and grasped at it. "Yes, Bobby says you're an artist. Do you paint? Sculpt?"

"Right now, I'm working in what I like to call mixed media."

"How interesting." Here we were, having a real conversation. I felt a little proud of myself. "Is it difficult to get the supplies you need here on the island?"

He waved his hand. "Nope. That's the thing. I'm using local material."

I tried to be encouraging. "Such as?"

"Well, last night I found three dead jellyfish and a great piece of driftwood. As soon as everything dries out, we'll see what develops."

Maggie had hurried over. Probably in response to his expressive hand-wave. He looked at me. "Want to order some dinner?" he asked.

Dear God. No. "Not right now, the club soda is just great. Maybe in a few minutes."

Jack winked at Maggie, who trotted off. He grinned at me again. "So, you're a writer? I knew I felt a spark. All those times you'd come in for shrimp specials, I knew you and I had more in common than preferring cocktail sauce over tartar. A fellow artiste, you know?"

I swallowed club soda and nodded. "Oh, yes. Absolutely. So, where do you teach?"

He shrugged and drained the rest of his gin. I wondered why his speech wasn't slurred. While he was managing to sit relatively upright, I noticed that his left elbow kept slipping off the table. "I'm kind of between positions right now," he said.

"Oh?" Well, no wonder. "Are you looking for another job?"

"Well, the thing is, most schools want a drug test."

"The nerve."

"Yeah, like, who the hell cares what a person does on his own time, right? So, I'm going to wait things out for a bit. I haven't told Bobby yet, but he'll let me stay the whole summer, I'm sure. May even work through the winter. I bet this place is something in the off season."

"I bet." I had always imagined the whole of Long Beach Island to be something of a ghost town in the off season, but I kept my mouth shut.

"But enough about me. Heard you were getting a divorce."

"Yes. I am."

"That sucks. Unless it was your idea, of course."

"No, it wasn't my idea, and yes, it does suck. But it's been really hard on my daughters, so as much as I hate to cut this short, I should get home. They get a little needy."

"Of course. Understand perfectly. Let me walk you to your car." He stood up.

I could see my car from here. Less than two hundred yards away. The path was free of physical obstructions, not too sandy, and in a fairly straight line. How much trouble could he get in? "That would be lovely. Thanks."

He didn't manage to get around to pulling my chair out, but he did let me go first and didn't lean on me as we walked. He was frowning, and I assumed it had to do with his concentrating on putting one foot in front of the other. We were about halfway to my car when he suddenly stopped, put a hand on the nearest car, and bent over. I jumped away from him and he threw up all over where my left foot had just been. I closed my eyes and prayed for rescue. Impossibly, rescue was right behind me.

"Hey, is everybody okay here?"

I opened my eyes at the voice. It was a very nice voice— deep, strong, slightly amused. I turned around and found myself face-to-face with a Viking.

I'm sure he wasn't a real Viking, but if I had been gathering wood on some distant shore a thousand or so years ago and saw this guy row up, I'd have immediately assumed that pillaging would ensue.

He was tall, well over six feet, with what might be considered a receding hairline, or possibly just a high forehead, and red hair. His eyes were icy blue and looked like they spent a lot of time squinting into the sun. He was very tan, wore white jeans and a pale blue shirt, open halfway down his chest, showing a lot of reddish chest hair and impressively rippled muscles.

"Jack and I were having a drink, but Jack had a bit of a head start, and I don't think he's feeling very well," I explained.

Viking looked at Jack. "When did Jack get here, last Sunday?"

I tried not to laugh. "Probably."

Viking shook his head. "Not to worry, Mona. I'll get him inside."

I stared at him. "How do you know me?" I asked. And then it clicked. "Oh, of course. Peter."

He really was a Viking. He was Peter Gundersen.

Every year when Brian had come down, he rented a boat for all his friends from work and spent a day deep-sea fishing. He always used Peter's boat. Two years ago, I had foolishly agreed to go with Brian, and spent the entire day watching a bunch of grown men drink like teenagers and lie about their fishing prowess. By the end of the day, Peter and I had formed the kind of friendship that happens between two total strangers who are thrown together during the course of a natural disaster, say, an earthquake, and have only each other to rely on.

Peter grabbed Jack by the shoulder and pushed him back toward the bar. I waited a few minutes next to my own car, and when Peter came out of the bar, I waved at him. He was grinning.

"Your friend Jack lives here. They knew exactly what to do."

"Thank God somebody did. Poor guy."

"Poor guy hell. He was soused, and they say he gets that way every night. How the hell do you know him anyway?"

I sighed. "I just know him from The Fish Shack. Bobby's place? We were supposed to be on a date."

Peter tilted his head as he looked at me. "So you and Brian did split up?"

I nodded. "Yes. Does the whole island know?"

Peter laughed. He had very white teeth. "Pretty much. It's a very big small town in the summer. Everybody knows what's going on, especially with the long-timers, like you. Never liked Brian, by the way."

"It seems that nobody did." I started fishing around in my purse for my keys. "Well, thanks for helping out, Peter. I'm sure Jack will appreciate it in the morning."

"Hey, no problem. Busy Saturday?"

I jerked my head up. "Me? Busy? I don't think so. Why?"

He shrugged. "I had a cancellation. They paid in advance, and because of the contract, they lost all their money, so I've got a free boat this weekend. We could do a little sailing, maybe have dinner out in the bay. What do you think?"

He met the criteria. I knew him. Not as well as I knew Doug, but much better than I had known Jack. He looked sober. And sexy. "You won't be drinking, will you?"

He looked shocked. "I never touch the stuff on the water. Never."

"Then I think it sounds great."

"Okay. Meet me at the marina around three. Slip 43. The weather's supposed to be perfect."

"Okay. See you then."

Another date. I had another date. Jack had proven to be a disaster, but with a guy like Peter, what could go wrong?

~

The next morning, I had coffee with Scott and Steve. Their kitchen was very 1955. White enamel and chrome cabinets. The table had a red Formica top and red leatherette chairs. Every time I sat down, I expected Donna Reed to serve the coffee. Steve had made oatmeal scones with dried cranberries, and I was trying to take tiny bites instead of shoving the entire thing into my mouth.

I had been telling them about my evening with Jack. They remained silent throughout, except for Scott, who kept sniggering. "And then he threw up." I reached for a second scone. "I considered that officially to be the end of the date."

Steve reached across the table to squeeze my hand. "I'm so sorry, Mona. But Jack is a drunk. And a total pothead. Didn't you know that?"

I stared. "He is? No, I didn't know that. Why would I know that?"

Scott was brushing imaginary crumbs from the table. "Everybody knows that," he muttered.

"I didn't. And you guys couldn't warn me?"

Steve sighed deeply. "Everybody knows, we thought you did, too."

"Then why would I go out with him?"

"As an act of kindness?" Scott suggested. "After all, you're still practicing, right?"

"Maybe I am, but really, guys, you should have at least given me a heads up." I munched some more scone. "So, what can you tell me about Peter Gundersen?"

Scott lit up. "Very Nordic."

Steve smirked. "Yes, very."

"Is he a drunk? A druggie?"

Steve looked thoughtful. "No, not that I've heard. He's very successful with his charter business. Takes the boats down to the Florida Keys every winter, goes after sharks or something."

Scott smiled dreamily. "I love a man with a really long pole."

I snorted. "You are disgusting. Steve, but where did you get this recipe? I may live on these for the rest of my life." I found my fingers hovering over scone number three, and had to force them back onto my lap.

"Off the Web. I'll give it to you," Steve said. "What does Doug think of your, um, branching out?"

I shrugged. "He seems to think he'll save a bunch of money on wining and dining, and still score big. Which is true. After I came home last night, I felt so depressed I jumped him behind Scoops Away. Got ice cream all over my, well, everything."

Steve squeezed my hand again. "Well, good luck with Peter."

I sighed and looked longingly at the remaining scones. "Thanks."

~

To: Mona
From: Anthony
Date: July 14
Subject: Playing catch-up

Mona—a few things that keep slipping my mind—Ben keeps asking about you. Particularly about when you're getting a divorce, and when you're back from the shore, and if you've decided to start dating. Of course, I haven't said a thing to him about your sexual exploits, but I did tell him the divorce has been fast-tracked. Is something going on here that you're not telling me? I know he always spent way too much time here to just be fiddling with pipes. Also, Lily wanted three more kittens I said NO. Ben can keep Lily in line, but she ignores me as much as possible. Can you tell her no more kittens? I'd hate to have you come home to a swarm. Love to my girls – Anthony

To: Aunt Lily
From: Mona
Date: July 14
Subject: Kittens
Dear Aunt Lily. The girls say hello. The weather here is fine. Anthony says you want to get more kittens. Please don't do that. I'm begging you. I think that the three cats we have now are more than enough. When you decide to get your own place again, of course it won't matter, but I don't want any more pets in my house. Please. I mean it. I've asked Anthony to keep an eye on things. I know that you are more than capable of taking care of yourself, but I'd feel so much better knowing that someone is keeping tabs on things, just in case of an emergency. So please be nice to Anthony if he stops by the house to say hello. He's doing it as a favor to me. And no more cats. At all. Thank you. Love, Mona

To: Anthony

From: Mona
Date: July 15
Subject: Aunt Lily

Dear Anthony—If you want a tremendous raise, just do the paperwork yourself, but can you please look in on Aunt Lily? I know it's asking a lot, but I told her you'd be doing it as a favor to me, and asked her to be nice. I also told her no more cats. I was very clear on that point. As for Ben, you're being silly. Ben, besides being the best looking plumber in the world, is also one of the nicest people, period. But he has no interest in me other than as an inexhaustible source of work. I'm sure his main concern as to my marital status is whether or not I'll be able to afford him if I'm my sole source of income. Talk to you soon, Mona

To: Mona
From: Anthony
Date: July 15
Subject: Lily

I plan on buying a small island off Antigua with the raise I just gave myself. I stopped in with perfectly good tuna sandwiches and iced tea to have lunch with Lily, and she hustled me right out of the house to go to a class at the YMCA. Now, I don't want to alarm you too much, but when she first arrived here back in April, she had no objections to having lunch with me. In fact, a few times it was her own idea. Now she treats me like an IRS investigator. I don't know if she resents the fact that I am now the designated babysitter, or she's just becoming paranoid and delusional. Ben says she treats him just fine, but, well, that's Ben. Who has shown up wearing shorts a few times and I almost had a heart attack.

Who still asks for you all the time. I'm telling you, he's got an eye on you, babycakes. Play your cards right and you'll be sharing your new Jacuzzi tub with the best legs in New Jersey. In the meantime, have fun with your fishing captain. Love you – Anthony

~

On Friday, I got a very fat manila envelope from David West. It was my divorce agreement, or his version of it anyway. He sent long detailed list of all assets and debts, and beside each item was an MQ or BB. At the end of several pages was a line that read something about miscellaneous household items already determined. I assumed David was referring to the garage filled with Brian's stuff that he had not come by to collect. It was a very sad document, neatly dividing twenty years of living and loving into what boiled down to two big piles. I read it three times before signing the bottom. Now, it had to go to Brian's lawyers, who would pick it apart and come up with what I'd like to think of as a reasonable counter-offer, although David seemed to think there might be a bit of a fight. I called Doug, who sent his boys to the movies, made a pitcher of Mojitos, and suggested we get naked. He was very sweet about everything, because instead of having wild sex, I ended up crying all over his sheets and he kept handing me tissues.

"Can I get you some water?"

I shook my head.

"How about food? Maybe if you ate something, you'd feel better."

"I'd feel better if my husband wasn't so eager to get rid of me that he'd agree to give me all the IBM stock."

"Brian is an idiot, remember?"

"Yes, I know. This is your fault. You got me drunk."

"It's worked in the past."

"True. But I think tonight is a bust."

He gave me a hug and kissed my sticky cheek. "I'm not worried. After a sail on the bay and a sunset dinner, I expect you'll be easy pickings tomorrow night."

Miranda, after hearing that her candidate Jack had thrown up in a public place, had declared she was out of the matchmaking business for the rest of the summer, and that all future dates would be my responsibility. She did want to be kept in the loop, however, and thought Peter was ideal. In fact, she was in love with the idea of his owning what she kept referring to as "a fleet of ships," and wanted me to wear white bell-bottoms and a blue-and-white-striped shirt, a la Marlene Dietrich.

I was thinking that Peter was ideal as well, because after parking my car at the marina and following the dock to Slip 43, I found myself staring at a sleek yacht, not at all like the fishing boat Brian had rented. This baby looked like it could mosey around the French Riviera and feel right at home.

"Hello," I yelled, then remembered *Gilligan's Island*. "Ahoy. Permission to come aboard?"

Peter bounded onto the deck. "Permission granted. Let me show you around."

It was a beautiful boat. Not very big, but definitely rich. It had a small but beautifully decorated cabin with tiny stainless steel appliances in the galley and a flat-screen television in the living room. He invited me up to the pilothouse where I sat as he smoothly took the boat out of the marina. He talked at length about horsepower and knots per hour, but I was so impressed with the white leather deck chairs I was hardly paying attention. It seemed to be a rather large boat for just one person, but he explained that there were no sails involved, and that with the computer equipment aboard, he could handle it all himself. Then he suggested some champagne.

"I thought you didn't drink," I said.

He flashed a smile. "Not for me, Mona. For you. Go below and check out the fridge."

I went back down below and checked everything out, including the bathroom—tiled, with a walk-in shower—and the bedroom. The bedroom was one very large bed with a satin comforter and barely enough room to walk around it. I headed back to the galley and took champagne out of the baby fridge, as well as a platter of cheese and crackers and a champagne flute made of pink acrylic.

I brought everything topside, Peter opened the bottle, poured me a glass, and snagged a piece of cheese for himself before returning to the wide bank of dials and knobs that I guessed ran the whole boat.

I took a sip. It was lovely, cold and fizzy and slightly sweet. I was stretched out on a deck chair, having kicked off my sandals, and closed my eyes against the afternoon sun.

"This is great," I said loudly. The noise of the engine was loud. Peter, looking over his shoulder at me, suddenly reached down, cut off the engine, and stepped away from the steering wheel. He sat next to me on a second deck chair.

"What were you saying?" he asked.

"I was saying this was great. Shouldn't you be driving or something?"

He shook his head. "No. We're not in the regular travel lanes, so we shouldn't have to deal with lots of traffic." We had only been cruising along for about twenty minutes, but as I looked around I was surprised to find myself surrounded by nothing but sea. There was no shoreline, no buoys, no passing ocean liners.

"I thought we were going to stay in the bay," I said.

He shrugged. "Why should we?"

Good question. The answer was that I felt very nervous and alone out here in the middle of the ocean with just him, but I didn't think I should tell him that, so I just smiled and drank more champagne.

"So, some people cancelled?" I asked him.

He nodded. "Yes. German tourists, eight of them. They sounded like a rowdy group, so it's just as well."

"Does that happen much?"

He shrugged. "No. But I make sure the contract calls for money up front, so when it does happen, I'm covered."

I swirled champagne. "This is a much nicer boat than the one Brian usually rented."

"Yes. Everything is top of the line. It took me over a year to get it. Special order."

I was kind of waiting for him to maybe ask me a question, or talk about something other than himself or his boat, but so far, no luck. "How many boats do you own?"

"Three." He ate some more cheese. "Want to go swimming?"

I looked at him, surprised. "I didn't bring a suit."

He grinned. "So? We're alone out here. Just strip down and dive in."

Ah oh. "No, thanks."

"Mind if I go in?" he asked, suddenly standing up.

"Not at all."

He was wearing blue and white floral swim trunks and a short-sleeved denim shirt. He grinned down at me again and pulled his shirt over his head. He had a very nice back, well muscled and tan. Then he reached down and pulled off his swim trunks. He stepped out of them, turned to give me a little wave, and dove off the edge of the boat.

I was shocked, of course. But not that shocked. I was suddenly aware that I didn't find red pubic hair very attractive. I noticed that he had a great butt with no tan line, so he must have spent a great deal of time trunk-less. He was also hung like a horse.

This was interesting. Here I was, in the middle of the ocean, with a man who had no apparent personal interest in me outside of getting me naked. I drank some more champagne.

Two years ago, when Peter and I had spent an afternoon together in a much smaller pilothouse, we had laughed and traded wisecracks about his passengers, my husband and his band of wannabe sport fisherman types. Peter and I were united against the equivalent of a common enemy, so of course we felt connected. But now, today, alone with nothing in common but the open ocean, we were total strangers. One of us was drinking champagne, one of us liked to swim in the nude. One of us could travel around the world by the stars in the heavens, and one of us needed a GPS to find north. One of us had probably eaten whale meat in a previous life, and one of us didn't know a damn thing about boats.

I poured some more champagne and added some cheese to a cracker. I took a bite. Very sharp cheddar on multigrain. I glanced up at the sky. Maybe a chivalrous helicopter pilot would come by, and I could flag him down. How would he know to drop down a ladder so I could escape like Jamie Lee Curtis in *True Lies*? Could I carve out a message of some sort on the deck?

Peter was pulling himself out of the water and climbing up the side of the boat by way of a rope ladder. He was dripping wet and, I must say, looked like a water god. Sleek. Sun-kissed. Glistening.

He walked past me and the pile of his clothes on the deck and went below. I listened for a few minutes, and sure enough, he called for me. Crap.

He was lying in the middle of his giant satin-swathed bed. He was still glistening. He was smiling. He had an obvious hard-on. Holy crap.

"Peter, listen." I chewed my lip. I didn't think he would rape me, but it's wise not to get on the wrong side of the only person in the world who can get you back on dry land.

"Peter, I'm very flattered. Really. And you are quite the man, obviously. But the thing is—" Think fast. I needed something that was not so much as a rejection as a turn-off. "I didn't bring any condoms."

He was still smiling. "Don't need 'em. I got snipped. Come on over here, Mona."

"But what about, you know, spreading something?"

"We're wasting time here, Mona. Not to worry. I'm clean as a whistle."

"But I'm not. I'm actually in the middle of, uh, a flare-up right now. And without a condom, well—"

He sat up. "You've got—?"

"Oh, yeah." I made a careless gesture with my hand as I watched with some satisfaction his reaction to the news, the anatomical equivalent of the sinking of the *Titanic*. "But, if you're willing to take the chance…" I started unbuttoning my shirt, and he scrambled off the bed.

"No, Mona, honest. I don't think I, uh, I mean *we* should risk anything." He went past me and pounded up the stairs. I followed him slowly, and when I got topside he was back in his clothes, looking very nonchalant, munching on a cracker.

"More champagne?" he asked.

"Sure." I sat back down and drank some more. He sat, nodding his head occasionally, for about ten minutes. I was watching the ocean, feeling very relieved and quite impressed with myself. Finally, he suggested we head back.

"What about dinner?" I asked, trying to look hurt.

He cleared his throat. "To tell you the truth, I'm not feeling so good. Maybe too much sun. Next time?"

Forty minutes later, I was in my car heading home, shaking with a mixture of rage and hysteria. When I pulled into my driveway, I parked, threw myself out of the car, and ran to Scott and Steve's. They were in their backyard with, of course, Doug.

Scott got to his feet. "What happened? Why are you home so soon?"

"He was a sex fiend," I yelled.

Steve frowned. "We knew that."

Scott nodded. "Everyone knows that."

"I didn't." I was still yelling. "I didn't know that. I asked you guys."

"Well," Scott said reasonably. "You asked us if he was a drunk."

"Or a drug addict," added Steve. "You never asked if he was a sex maniac."

Doug was laughing.

"*You* knew?" I shrieked at him. "You knew and you just let me go off on a boat with him?"

Doug composed himself. "I figured you could take care of yourself."

"I had to tell him I had a sexually transmitted disease."

Scott clapped his hands in delight. "Excellent. Quick thinking. Can I get you a drink?"

I was still standing over Doug. "I could kill you," I said, my voice still shaking but much quieter.

Doug grabbed my hand. "I have a much better idea."

I snatched my hand back. "You thought I'd be easy pickings?"

Doug nodded. "Sure. The guy's crazy, but he's got a great boat and I've heard he's well, physically well-endowed. If that's not a turn-on, what is?"

I turned and started to walk away, but Doug's voice stopped me. "Tom and Ann took your daughters for pizza in Beach Haven. They mentioned the water park."

I turned.

"They just left. Fifteen minutes ago. They'll probably be gone 'till nine."

I narrowed my eyes at him. "Nine?"

Doug nodded.

"That's hours from now."

"Yes."

I looked at Scott, who was trying to look totally disinterested.

Steve cleared his throat. "So," he asked, "was Peter, well, as impressive as they say?"

"Dirk Diggler in *Boogie Nights*."

Doug stood up and stretched elaborately. "I think I'll say goodnight, boys. Thanks for the drink."

He walked past me and around to the front of the house, I followed him, grabbed his hand, and pulled. He followed me across the street and into my house.

Easy pickings.

To: Anthony
From: Mona
Date; July 22
Subject: GRRRR
All men are scum. I hate men and don't think I can make a go of it with women. Is there a third sex? Mona

To: Mona
From: Anthony
Date: July 23
Subject: Practice date
Oh, babycakes, I hope you aren't angry, but I told Marty to call you this week. You know Marty, right? Starbucks Marty? He runs the place, may even own the franchise. He's always behind the counter. Anyway, Marty has always been a big fan of yours. Victor and I have been logging in serious coffee time, and I got to know Marty pretty well, and when

he told me he was down in Beach Haven for the next two weeks, I mentioned you were down there too, and he told me he thought you were a very nice woman, so I gave him your number. You like Marty, remember? You said he was a real sweetie, and he is. He's also kinda hot in that pseudo-Mafia/ Michael Corleone kind of way. Please don't be mad. I love you, Anthony. PS – if there was a third sex, believe me, I'd have slept with it.

To: Anthony
From: Mona
Date: July 24
Subject: Marty

Oh, Anthony, of course I'm not mad. And you're right, Marty is a sweetie. When he calls, I'll be charming and I bet we have a great time. I love you, too. Mona

~

Starbucks Marty and I agreed to meet at a very popular Italian restaurant that was around the corner from the house he was renting. It was also within walking distance of my house. Public place, close to home. The restaurant was a bring-your-own-bottle family place, so he couldn't get drunk before I got there. And he probably wouldn't be naked. I was hoping I'd be safe.

We had to wait for a table. We sat on a bench with a bunch of other hungry diners and I got a chance to take a look at him without his requisite Starbucks black-with-snaz-zy-green apron. He was attractive in a very macho-Roman kind of way. Thick wavy hair, dark, sprinkled with gray. Olive skin, black eyes, heavy brows, red mouth, and very white teeth. Dressed in the standard summer uniform: khaki shorts and white polo shirt. Very respectable-looking. We smiled politely without saying a word until we were seated across from each other.

Marty frowned, centered the vase of plastic flowers, placed the salt and pepper shakers on either side of the vase, and said, "Well."

"Yes. Well. How are you Marty?"

"Fine. You?"

"Good."

The waitress came by, declared her name to be Tina and that she'd be our server for the evening, and filled our glasses with water. Marty ordered an iced tea, and we looked at the menus.

"Have you ever been here before?" he asked.

I nodded and sipped water. "Yes. Everything's good. I think I'll try the Veal Marsala."

"You eat veal?"

I looked up from the menu. "Eat veal? Yes. Don't you?"

He sighed. Very heart-felt. Deep. "What they do to those baby cows..."

Okay then. The waitress came back, set Marty's iced tea on the table, and looked at us expectantly.

"I'll have the Chicken Marsala, with pasta on the side. Ziti. Small salad, oil and vinegar. A side of garlic bread. Marty, do you want to split an appetizer?"

Marty lifted his shoulders. "They don't have those little rice balls, do they?"

I looked at Tina. She shook her head.

"No, Marty. How about calamari?"

He shrugged his shoulders. "I really wanted rice balls."

I turned to Tina. "No appetizer, I guess. Marty, what will you have?"

Marty cleared his throat. "No osso buco?"

Tina shook her head. "No. Only what's on the menu."

Marty sighed. "No lamb chops either?"

Tina smiled patiently. "Is it on the menu?"

Marty shook his head. "No. So I guess I'll have the pork chops. Can he make those with hot peppers?"

Tina was still smiling. "On the menu?"

Marty's face could not have looked more morose. "No."

Tina remained chipper. "Pasta?"

"No, thanks. Baked potato."

Tina's smile finally cracked. "No baked potato. Sides are pasta, steamed veggies or rice."

Marty looked close to tears. "Pasta. No, rice. I'll have rice, please."

Tina wrote happily. "And on your salad?"

"Balsamic, please."

Tina snatched up the menus. "Not on the menu. Oil and vinegar okay?"

Marty shrugged his shoulders again and waved her away. He took a sip of iced tea, grimaced, and shook out his napkin. He examined the hem of the napkin, shook his head, and settled it on his lap. He rearranged the silverware, making sure that the edges of each piece were the exact same distance from the edge of the table.

"So," he said, "the food is good here?"

"It's okay," I backpedaled. "Nothing great, but okay. I like it because it's close to home."

Marty nodded. "Yes, it's close to where I'm staying as well."

"Great. How's your place?"

He rolled his eyes. "The mattress is lumpy. There may be bugs. There's a sticky place on the kitchen floor. Don't get me started on the bathroom."

I wouldn't dream of it. "Have you spent time down here before?"

"No. Usually I go to Ocean Beach. Maryland. But the house I usually rent burnt to the ground over Christmas, so I thought I'd take it as a sign and try someplace new."

"And how are you liking it so far? Aside from the house being, you know, icky?"

He took another sip of tea. "The water is really cold here. The sand looks dirty. I know it's not, I mean, not any dirtier than any other sand, but it looks dirty. And it's very coarse. Gritty. I stepped on a shell and I think my heel is infected. I'm also allergic to the sunscreen I bought."

We had already ordered dinner. I was trapped. Back in Westfield, behind the counter of Starbucks, Marty was smiling, sweet and engaging. Here and now, he was the most depressing man I had ever met. The good news was that the service was usually good here, and I could be back out on the street in about an hour.

I looked around the room. No sign of Tina and our salad. "Have you met anyone down here? People are usually friendly. Any nice neighbors?"

He sipped more iced tea, making another face. "The people next door had the police there Monday night. Across the street is a three hundred pound woman who sunbathes in her front yard every morning. In a two-piece. And the

couple on the corner had a fistfight on the sidewalk yesterday around dinnertime."

"Oh." Where the hell were our salads?

"Anthony tells me you're getting divorced," Marty said,
breaking a small silence.

"Yes. I am. My husband left me for another woman."

"My second wife did that," Marty said.

"Oh? Left you?" Can't imagine why.

"Yes. For another woman."

Ouch. "That must have been very hard."

"It destroyed me, I gotta say. We'd been married
six years."

"Well, it must have been difficult for her to suddenly
realize, after all that time, that she was really a lesbian."

Marty lifted his shoulders. "She said she wasn't before
we were married. She told me I drove her to it."

How long did it take to make a couple salads? Were they
growing them a leaf at a time back there?

"So, you've been divorced?"

He nodded. "Four times."

Mercifully, Tina appeared with salads and my garlic
bread, as well as the oil and vinegar, extra butter for the
bread, and a shaker of parmesan cheese. She set everything
down, left, and I sat for a few extra moments while Marty
rearranged the plates and condiments. We finally began to
eat, and Marty shook his head sadly.

"Iceberg," he muttered.

"Excuse me?"

"Iceberg lettuce. I hate iceberg lettuce."

"There's also green leaf in there, and red stuff, what is
that, radicchio? It looks fine."

He looked skeptical and tasted. He lifted his shoulders. "Oh well."

"Well, here, have some garlic bread."

He took a bite, and smiled for the first time. "Good."

Thank God. "We could get another order, if you like."

"No. I'll just have this piece."

I ate some salad, which was quite good, by the way. "So, you were talking about being divorced. Did you really say four times?"

"Yes. Can you believe four different women divorced me?"

What I couldn't believe was that four different women married him in the first place, so I just shook my head and kept my mouth full.

He took another piece of garlic bread. "My first wife took off in the middle of the night and left a note. She said she had to go and find herself. She went to Alaska. Then Diane left me for Joan. Maryanne went back to her first husband. While they were still married, she had a restraining order against him, but she told me he'd gotten help and was a lot better. Sarah, well, she was drinking so bad in the end, it was just as well."

"Oh my." This called for an immediate change of subject. "How did you get attached to Starbucks?"

"Well, I had a degree in chemistry, but after I'd been at my first job for a couple of years, there was a small, well, accident. No one was hurt, but the owners of the company didn't handle things well, and I was basically blackballed from the industry. I tried teaching, but too many parents complained about test scores, you know how that goes. Then I went into sales, pharmaceutical sales, because that's the future, right? But the company went belly-up. Very unexpected. And for a while I was with an Internet company, very promising. I was actually partner. Lost everything. So I was looking for a sure thing, and I think Starbucks is the answer."

I glanced around. Might a car come careening through the front window? Would a bolt of lightening crack our table down the center? Was that actually a black cloud hovering over Marty's head?

I took a deep breath. "I hope you're right, Marty. Starbucks is a great company. I'd hate to see anything happen to it. My daughters are there all the time. And I hear Anthony and Victor are putting in a lot of time down there. Are you sure you don't want your own order of garlic bread?"

"No, thanks. Just one more piece. Yes, Anthony is lovely, very charming. Victor, well, not so much. He's into all that metaphysical stuff, you know, karma and auras and things. Always talking about positive energy. He actually said I had a negative vibe. What kind of crap is that?"

Tina appeared, dishes in hand. She set down mine, then Marty's, and smiled at us both. "Can I do anything else?"

I picked up my plate and handed it back to her. "I'll take mine to go."

～

Jessica found me on the back porch, eating Chicken Marsala and drinking a tall vodka tonic. She sat down across from me, watching for a while, before she spoke.

"Another bum date?"

"I cannot," I told her in all honesty, "even begin to describe it. Let's just say we can never go into Starbucks again."

She shrugged. "Maybe you can't, but we can. He doesn't know who we are. He hates all the kids. He's just nice to the old rich folks."

"I'm not having much luck with this dating thing."

"I noticed that. We have to figure out what you're doing wrong."

"Me? Why would it be me doing the wrong?"

She shrugged. "Well, Mom, anybody is allowed one crappy date, it's just a mistake, you know? And even the second time can just be a matter of poor judgment. But after the third time, you've got to wonder if maybe it's you instead of, you know, them."

"It's them. Trust me. I get along fine with Doug."

"Well, if I were you, I'd start getting along with somebody else. I don't want Mr. Keegan for a stepdad." She hauled herself up out of the chair and skulked off into the house. I sat for a while longer, drinking. Maybe she was right. Was there something wrong with me?

To: Anthony
From: Mona
Date: July 26
Subject: Marty
Anthony, really, is there something wrong with me?? I found Marty to be the most depressing and depressed person ever. Did you know he drove several companies into bankruptcy, and has been married four times?

To: Mona
From: Anthony
Date: July 27

Subject: Marty

Oh, honey, there's nothing wrong with you. I thought you knew about Marty. Everyone knows he's been through four wives. Where have you been? I didn't know about the bankruptcy curse, or the depression thing. He's always so cheerful behind the counter. But he'd have to be. But this is still practice, right? Don't take it so seriously.

To: Mona
From: Aunt Lily
Date: July 27
Subject: Brian

Hello, dear. I just thought I'd let you know that the worthless piece of shit you're divorcing called me this morning and said he was coming by tomorrow before lunch to collect all his belongings that you had set aside for him in the garage. Now, I don't mind him being here as long as he stays outside, but what if he wants to come into the house? I'm thinking about calling a friend of mine from Brooklyn to act as sort of a bodyguard. I can't imagine what I'd do if that miserable asshole tried to force his way in. I don't believe Anthony works on Thursdays, not that he'd be very effective in the protection department. He's a lovely boy, but don't you think he's a touch effeminate? Lana chased a kitten, Olivia I believe, up the living room drapes yesterday and the poor little thing had to jump for her life. Lana is not adjusting as well as I'd hoped to her new little family.

My love to the girls, Aunt Lily

CHAPTER NINE

The day after reading Lily's e-mail, I left the house at four thirty in the morning so I could be sure to arrive in Westfield before Brian. Traffic on the Parkway can be a crapshoot, but I got lucky and slid into the driveway just at seven. The sun was coming up, birds were chirping, all looked peaceful and perfect. I slid down behind the steering wheel and promptly fell asleep. I was in the middle of a rather nice dream, something to do with eating cracked crab with that cute guy from *Dirty Jobs*, when a very deep voice woke me up.

"Hey, lady."

I opened my eyes. It was much brighter. I glanced at my watch. I'd been asleep for over an hour. I turned my head toward the voice.

It was Luca Brasi from *The Godfather*.

"Hey, lady, you supposed to be here?"

I struggled to sit upright and find my voice. "I live here," I said.

He looked at me with suspicion. He was a young Luca, but he had the same cold look in his eye. "I thought Lily Martel lived here."

Lily? He knew my Aunt Lily? "She's my aunt," I explained. "It's my house. She lives with me."

He stuck his tongue out of the side of his mouth as he pondered this information. I was beginning to think that what he had in abundance in the brawn department, he perhaps lacked in other areas. "So, then, how come you're sleeping out in your car instead of in your house?"

"I've been living down the shore all summer, and thought I'd come up today, but I got here early. I didn't want to wake her. Do you know my Aunt Lily?"

"She's a friend of a friend. I was sent down here in case she had trouble. Don DeMatriano told me to keep her safe."

It took me a second to realize that Don was not Mr. De-Matriano's first name. "Can I get out of the car?" I asked.

He thought about it, then backed away. He opened the car door for me, closed it behind me, and followed me around to the kitchen door. The fact that I had a key made no impression on him.

Lily was sitting at the breakfast bar in the kitchen, a steaming cup of coffee and the morning paper on the counter. She looked up as we entered, and registered no surprise at my appearance, nor at the appearance of a total stranger wearing a gray pin-striped suit and a black fedora.

"Coffee, Mona? You must have left awfully early. And are you Mr. Guerrano?"

Luca smiled. "Yes, ma'am. You Mrs. Martel?"

"Yes. But call me Lily. Everyone does."

"Sure. And you can call me Mickey. Please."

She slid off the stool and pulled out some cups.

"Aunt Lily," I said in a surprisingly calm voice, "I really need to speak with you. Right now."

"Of course, dear, as soon as I pour this nice young man some coffee. Banana bread? I baked it myself just yesterday."

Mickey smiled. There was a gap between his two front teeth so large that I detected a glint of silver on his molars. "Thank you, ma'am. That's very kind of you."

"Now, Aunt Lily."

She scowled, set the food in front of Mickey, and swept out of the kitchen.

I followed her into the living room and, with a quick look over my shoulder to make sure Mickey had not followed us out, hissed, "Did you hire that gorilla as a bodyguard?"

She shook her head sadly. "Now, Mona, just because he's a rather large man, that's no reason to call him names. I'm sure he's very sweet."

"He's hired muscle from Don DeMatriano."

She frowned. "No, Mona, you're mistaken. It's Joe DeMatriano."

"Joe may be his name, but Don is his title. How did you meet a Mafia kingpin?"

"I'm sure Joe is not a kingpin. He sat next to me a few years ago during a lecture at the Brooklyn Botanical Garden. It was about the migration patterns of the monarch butterfly in North America. Fascinating stuff. We started talking, then went out for coffee. We would see each other once in a while after that, usually for coffee."

I clutched my chest. "You *dated* a don?"

She chuckled and waved her hand. "Don't be silly, I'm old enough to be his mother. Besides, he's very happily married. Five children. All boys. The oldest—"

"Aunt Lily. Stop. I don't care about his family. Well, actually, I do, because I think a member of the enforcement branch is having banana bread in my kitchen. You called this guy? Joe?"

"Well, yes. Joe told me that if I was ever afraid, or worried about my safety in any way, I should call him and he would make sure I was taken care of. I called him last night about Brian, and he told me to expect Mickey. Just as a precaution."

The thought of Mickey escorting Brian down the driveway kept my mind in a happy place for several seconds, then common sense kicked in. "Aunt Lily, now that I'm here, why don't we let Mickey go back to whatever cave he came from."

"Now, Mona, that seems to me a very rude thing to do. He just got here. Let him stay for a while, to feel useful."

"Maybe." I turned around and went back into the kitchen. Mickey was sitting at the breakfast bar and scratching the ear of a black kitten who had jumped on the stool beside him. I watched as his massive fingers curled around the tiny ear, and he made little kissing noises. He caught me watching him and blushed.

"I love kitties," he said.

"That's Olivia," Lily said, bustling back into the room. "Lana hates her most."

The back door opened, and Mickey rose to his feet in a movement so abrupt that Lily and I both jumped and Olivia bolted from the stool. Mickey's hand actually went into the opening of his jacket as Lily yelled.

"It's okay, Mickey. That's not him."

It was Ben Cutler, frozen in the doorway, his eyes wide and fixed on Mickey's face.

"Ben, what a surprise." Lily smiled at Mickey. "That's Ben. He's a plumber, and quite welcome. Come on in, Ben. I didn't expect you back until next week."

Ben hadn't moved. He smiled at Mickey. "Are you a friend of Lily's?"

Mickey had sat back down and picked up his coffee cup. "In a manner of speaking."

"Good. Hi, Mona. I didn't expect you either."

"Come on in, Ben. If it weren't seven thirty in the morning, I'd offer you a drink. Coffee?"

He finally moved his eyes from Mickey to me. "That would be great. So, Lily, yes, I didn't think I'd be around today either, but I knew that Ray had finished up the sheetrock yesterday, and I wanted to check it out. Did Lily tell you, Mona, that we're working on your bathroom?"

"Yes. I don't suppose I can take a peek?"

Lily made a cluck-cluck sound. "No, dear, it's a surprise. Banana bread, Ben?"

"No, thanks, Lily."

I sipped my coffee and looked at the happy domestic scene before me. My beloved aunt, in a modest housecoat of pale pink roses, was pouring herself another cup of coffee. Mickey, the hired help, calmly munching on banana bread, was thoroughly prepared to kill the next person to walk through the door. And Ben, no longer looking nervous but alert and seriously hot.

He leaned against the fireplace mantle, one hand on his hip, the other holding the dagger carelessly. His dark eyes glinted in the firelight as he smiled. "Quite an interesting situation," he said, his voice soft and deadly. She knew she should be frightened, but all she could think about was the long, strong line of his throat above the open linen collar, and the way the leather of his boots hugged his muscled calves.

"Aunt Lily," I said, "now that Ben is here, perhaps we can relieve Mickey of his, ah, assignment."

Lily frowned. "But he's come such a long way."

Mickey glanced around. "Hey, it's no difference to me. Stay here, drive back to Brooklyn, I still get paid. It's up to you, ma'am. If you think you still need me, I'll be happy to stay."

Ben looked clueless, but game. "Lily, I don't know what you could possibly need me to stay for, but I will. All day. And tonight. I've got nothing to do tonight either."

Lily pursed her lips. "Mickey, I suppose I'll be fine with Ben here. Would you mind going back home?"

He lumbered to his feet, wiped crumbs from the front of his suit, and shook his head. "I don't mind at all. I'll be on my way. If you ever feel the need of my assistance again, just let Mr. DeMatriano know. It was a real pleasure meeting you." He bowed, surprisingly graceful, and walked out. The room seemed suddenly very empty.

Ben turned to me and blurted. "What the hell just happened?"

"That was Mickey," I explained, laughing shakily. "Brian told Lily he was coming by today to get his things out of the garage, and Lily got a little panicked, so she called her good buddy, the Mafia don, who sent one of his assassins to protect her."

Ben turned to Lily in amazement. "You know a Mafia don?"

Lily shrugged. "I think Mona is exaggerating a little bit. Joe is just a local businessman who knows a few people, that's all."

Ben frowned. "Joe?"

Lily nodded. "Joe DeMatriano."

Ben's jaw dropped. "Joe DeMatriano? As in Big Joey 'Two Shoes' DeMatriano's son? He's head of one of the biggest organizations in New York, one of the Five Families."

"Oh dear," Lily murmured. "He told me he was a shoe wholesaler."

Ben put down his coffee cup and leaned forward against the breakfast bar. "Christ, Lily, he's one of the biggest criminals in the state. And yeah, he is a shoe salesman, that's how his father got his nickname. It's one of their fronts, the shoe business. That was their tagline, back in the seventies. Big Joey would appear in his own commercials, saying if you came to his shoe stores, you could buy two shoes for the price of one. Then he was indicted for money laundering, trying to bribe a government official, and several counts of murder. Don't you ever read the newspapers?"

Lily sniffed and straightened her shoulders. "Of course I do. But I don't read that kind of unpleasantness. Organized crime." She sniffed again. "I need to get dressed. If you both would excuse me, I'll be upstairs." She turned, and with great dignity left the room.

I looked at Ben and burst out laughing. "I can't believe her."

Ben was shaking his head and chuckling, his beautifully formed shoulders shaking. "I can't believe her either. God, what a summer this has been, with that old lady." He straightened up and looked at me. "You look terrific, by the way. I really like your hair short like that."

I was so flustered that I almost dropped my coffee cup. "Thanks, Ben. It's good to see you, too, because Brian really is coming over here, and I could use a little moral support."

He spread his arms wide. "Well, I'm here. Let me run upstairs and check out the work they've been doing, then we can sit and wait for him together."

We didn't wait long. I puttered around the kitchen, had a conversation with a sulky Lana, and had barely settled into the living room with a magazine when I heard the front door open.

Brian came into the living room, saw me, and came to a stop. "Mona, what a surprise. I didn't know you'd be here. Lily didn't mention it."

"Well, it is my house, Brian."

"Of course. It's just that you're usually at the shore house."

I smiled. "Yes, I am. Which makes me wonder why you didn't try to contact me there to let me know you were coming by today."

He smiled broadly. "Mona, don't talk like that. It makes it sound like I need your permission."

"Permission would have been good, Brian. You don't live here any more, remember? And all your things are in the garage, which is open. There is no reason for you to be in this house at all, especially since you never told me you'd be here, and didn't even bother to ring the doorbell."

He was still smiling, but his eyes narrowed. Not a good thing. "You're becoming quite the bitch about this whole thing, aren't you?"

"Not at all, Brian, but we've both paid our lawyers lots of money to work out a settlement, and in the division of property, this particular property is going to be all mine. And everything that's in it. Anything that's yours is outside, where you should be. I don't think they'd like it if we messed around with all their hard work."

Brian sighed and stuck his hands in the pockets of his khakis. "Mona, don't get too stuck on all that legalese. I'm sure we can renegotiate if we want to."

I'd stood up and walked over to him. "I don't want to renegotiate. I like things just as they are. Your stuff is in the garage. I'll be happy to help you move it into the car."

He tilted his head to the side. "Mona, did I tell you your hair looks great short like that? In fact," he leaned in, "you look great altogether. Very sexy." He reached out and put his hand against my cheek. "I'd forgotten how hot you could look."

I stepped back from him, suddenly shaky. I had not expected anything like this. "What do you want, Brian?"

His smile turned. "What are you offering, babe?"

"Nothing." My voice was pitchy. I hated that. "Nothing at all."

His smile vanished. No more Mr. Nice Guy. "There are a few things I forgot about, that's all. Small stuff. I'll just get them and leave."

"Like what?"

"Like the print in the bedroom. The Audubon. That was my father's."

"It was a gift *from* your father. To *me*. For my birthday. It's mine and you can't have it. And that certainly isn't a small thing. It's worth thousands."

He sighed, lifting his shoulders. "Yeah, well, what about the mirror in the den, you know, the one we bought in Napa?"

"You mean the Art Deco antique that *I* bought in Napa? That's also worth a fortune, and it's also mine."

"I'm starting to think that maybe it isn't."

"Then call your lawyer and tell him about it. Then he can call my lawyer, and they'll hash it out for a few weeks, and I'll still get it because I kept the bill of sale because it had the appraisal on it, and it's in my name only."

"Bitch isn't even the word, Mona. You're—"

"Brian, I think you should leave now."

"Listen, Mona, this is still legally my house, and I can walk into it and be in it for as long as I like, because I still have certain rights. And you're still legally my wife, so watch your mouth, because I can still do what I want with you, too."

I was suddenly frightened. Really. Who was this man? I think at that moment I would have cut off my little finger to have Mickey come lumbering out of the kitchen. But I didn't need Mickey. I had Ben.

She pulled away in terror, running for the stairs, and suddenly Phillip was there, his dark cloak whirling behind him as he hurtled down the steps. He drew his sword in one swift, fluid motion, its sharp tip against Griffin's throat. "Did he hurt you?" he asked, his eyes glittering. "Did he even touch you?"

"Brian," Ben said quietly, coming in from the hallway. "Good to see you. Mona, you okay?"

Brian narrowed his eyes and looked from Ben to me and back again. "Got the plumber on your side?" he said in a nasty tone.

Ben spread his hands. "Side? Are there sides, Brian? I thought the two of you had settled everything quite amicably."

Brian leaned in to me and whispered, "You screwing him too?"

I stepped back, angry and shaken. "Leave, Brian, before I call my lawyer and see if I can arrest you for something."

Brian lifted his shoulders, then dropped them as he turned away. "Whatever, Mona. I'll get my stuff from the garage. There's nothing here I want anyway." He slammed the door behind him.

Ben crossed over to me and put both his hands on my shoulders. "You okay?"

I nodded. "Yep. Fine."

"Why don't I go and help Brian with whatever moving he needs done. You stay right here, alright?"

I nodded again and he left. I sat back on the couch, and after a few minutes Lana came up on my lap. A few minutes later, she jumped back down again. Olivia came by, and in the manner of all kittens everywhere, started chasing a dust mote in the most adorable way possible, quite distracting me until Ben came back.

"Well, he's gone. Where's Lily?"

I shook my head. "No clue."

Ben disappeared upstairs, then returned a few minutes later. "She was watching Brian from her upstairs window. She wished Mickey had stayed."

I thought about it. "Me too."

Ben laughed. "No, you did fine without Mickey. Look, it's early for lunch, but let's go and get some coffee or something. What do you think?"

I looked up at Ben. "I think that's the best idea I've heard all week."

~

We ended up taking Ben's truck to a diner where I was suddenly, ravenously hungry and ordered French toast with eggs over easy, hash browns, sausage, and coffee. Ben ordered coffee and a muffin. A blueberry muffin. How cute.

"So, how's your summer going, Mona," Ben asked when the waitress had left.

I looked into my coffee. This was my fourth cup. I'd have to think about cutting back. "It's going okay, I guess. The girls are all fine, having a great time, as usual. The book is going along really well. I'm almost finished with a first draft."

"Wow, that's great news. Congratulations, Mona. But what does that mean?"

"It means I'll send the manuscript off to my agent, she'll give me ideas about what needs to be changed, and then hopefully I'll have something worthwhile by October."

"I'm sure it will be terrific."

He was so sweet. "I'm also dating. Trying to, anyway. It's not going so well."

Ben sat back. "Anthony mentioned something about that. What's been going wrong?"

I sighed. "I think it's because I have rotten taste in men and keep picking the wrong ones to go out with. It's all Miranda's fault. She wants me to practice on men I already know, but apparently I only know sex fiends and whack jobs."

"Well," Ben said easily, "you know me."

The waitress set our plates down in front of us, but I didn't even notice. Yes, I did know Ben.

"That's right," I managed at last, starting to shovel food into my mouth. I felt like I hadn't eaten in a week.

I knew Ben.

"So," he continued, breaking off a piece of muffin, "maybe this could be one of your dates."

I almost stabbed myself in the cheek with my fork. "A date? With you?"

"We're out, and eating, and I'm willing to pick up the tab. What do you think?"

I stared at my plate. On a date with Ben.

Now I may or may not have mentioned it, but I had done a lot of fantasizing about Ben. In all my imagining, however, not even one scenario involved food. Well, maybe grapes, ice cream, or strawberries dipped in chocolate, followed by champagne. Then there was the warm honey and—never mind. The point is I never pictured us on a normal, let's-grab-a-bite kind of date. And as fate would have it, suddenly we were on exactly that kind of a date, and I was eating a breakfast big enough to feed the entire defensive line of the Green Bay Packers.

"I've been up since four thirty this morning, which is why I'm so hungry." I explained. "If this were a normal date, I would have stopped after the French toast."

He laughed. "Not to worry. I'm flush."

I had to decide how to act. I'd had dozens of conversations with Ben, all comfortable and usually a little flirtatious, but what about now? Was I still allowed to flirt? Should I be serious? I took a leap.

"Well, then, we have to talk about date stuff."

"Like what?"

I stared at him. "Don't you know? I mean, you must go out all the time."

He was stirring lots of sugar into his coffee. "No, not really. It's hard to find somebody to, you know, connect with. There has to be a spark, you know? Something to pique the interest."

"Do I pique your interest?" I blurted.

He looked at me evenly. "You are by far one of the most interesting women I know."

"And I burn for you, every inch of my being. I can't stand it. I must have you." He looked into her eyes. "Please, do not deny me any longer."

"Is that because of my myriad of plumbing problems?"

He laughed again, and chewed more muffin. "Partly. I must admit, professionally speaking, your house represents a major challenge. But you're a funny and smart woman. And you're a writer. I find that fascinating. I love to read, mostly nonfiction, and I just can't imagine having the ability to put down words on paper in such a way that holds the mind, captures the imagination. It's a great gift."

I would have preferred his being fascinated by my dark and sexy eyes, or perhaps my sweetly irresistible mouth, but hey, from Ben I'd take anything.

I had to say something. It was my turn. "Thanks for saying that. It means a lot to me. I take my work seriously. It feels good to be appreciated."

He smiled. "So, is this good date conversation?"

"Yes, it is."

"So, do you mind telling me why you felt the need to leave the shore at four thirty to meet Brian?"

I set down my fork. I needed to take a break from chewing anyway. "Lily sent me an e-mail that he was coming, and she did sound a little nervous, and I really didn't trust Brian. Things had been going *too* smoothly, you know? I figured he might try something, if for no other reason than to piss me off. And I was right. If I hadn't been there, he might have tried to take stuff, and I would have hated to put Lily in that position."

Ben grinned. "If you hadn't been there, Mickey would have broken all of Brian's fingers, and it would have made Lily's day."

I laughed. "Yes, you're right."

He put his hand over mine. His skin was rough but warm, and my pulse, I've got to tell you, went through the roof. "You're a real class act. Brian is and was a jerk, and you did just fine, Mona."

"You were my backup, though. Thanks."

He pulled his hand away. "We make a good team," he said lightly. I almost swooned.

"You think?"

"Of course. Are you finished? Because I do kind of have to be someplace else."

"So that offer to spend all day, and night if need be with Lily, was for Mickey's benefit?"

"He really scared me," Ben said, his voice suddenly serious. "I think he had a gun."

"I think you're right. Okay, I'm done, let's go."

He paid the bill and we drove back to the house. He pulled up in front of the driveway, and as I opened the door, he spoke.

"So, when is the divorce final?"

I shut the door then leaned against it, my head in the cab. "Sometime in the fall. Maybe by Christmas. It's all about reaching a financial settlement, and Brian is getting picky. We don't have a date yet, but I should know soon."

He nodded. "Well, maybe I'll see you before then. I hope so. We should keep the team together. Good luck. And have a good rest of the summer."

I stepped away from the truck, and he drove slowly away. I stood and watched until the road was empty.

Ben and I. We'd had a date. And it had not been a disaster. In fact, he'd said we should keep the team together. Which proved there was nothing wrong with me after all.

CHAPTER TEN

Some days at the shore are perfect—clear skies, cool breezes, the bracing smell of salt in the air. Some days are not. Some days, the humidity is so high the air weighs a ton, the sky is beige and seems to press down on the ocean, and all you can smell is fish. Days like that, the girls hide in their air-conditioned rooms and watch soap operas. I usually lie out on the back porch and sleep over a not-so-good book.

It was that kind of day, just at the end of July, when, half-dozing, I heard a tentative voice say hello. I opened an eye. There was a figure standing outside my screened porch door. I opened the other eye.

He was a very nice-looking man. Tall, maybe six feet. Broad shoulders, narrow waist, great forearms, with dark hair and eyes, even features, well-shaped eyebrows. Not traffic-stopping, but definitely worth a second look.

"I'm sorry," he said, "but the front door was open, so I figured somebody was home, but no one answered the bell. I just came around back. Did I scare you?"

I sat up and yawned. "No. Excuse me. It's the heat. We're all stupid today."

He grinned. He had a great smile. He was wearing long khaki shorts and a polo shirt. "Yeah, I know that feeling. Stupid is what I usually do best. I'm Mitch Wallace."

"Hi, Mitch Wallace. What can I do for you?"

He shrugged. "Well, my sister thought I should come over and introduce myself."

"Your sister?" I frowned, thinking, then it hit me. "Mitch? Mitchell? You're Vicki's brother Mitchell?"

"Yeah. That's me."

I struggled out of my chair. "Well, hi." I opened the screen door. "Come on through."

I was suddenly aware that I had bad humid-day hair, was wearing no bra under my T-shirt, and that I'd been snoozing in my own sweat for a while. I ran my fingers through my hair, hit three snags, and gave up. "I'm Mona. Have a seat. Can I get you a drink of something? I've got a pitcher of Mojitos in the fridge."

He nodded and sat. "Sounds great. Thanks."

I went into the kitchen, pulled out the pitcher, took a quick side trip to the bathroom, and groaned at my reflection. I had big red crease marks on my cheek from sleeping on the rough chair cushion, and my lips were very chapped. I was also glowing. Think severe-exposure-to-radiation type glowing. I splashed water on my face, gargled, and tried not to think about my frizzy hair or floppy breasts.

I went back into the kitchen, put the pitcher and a couple of glasses on a tray, and hurried back onto the porch. I poured us both a drink, and took a big gulp. "You're not what I expected," I told him. "I mean, you're nothing like your sister."

"Yeah," he shrugged. "No man-boobs."

I froze for a moment, then laughed. "Yes, there's that too. But you don't look alike at all." I wanted to add that he didn't look like a still-living-with-the-folks-type loser who sold comics for a living, but I wanted to be tactful.

He sipped his drink and looked thoughtful. "Well, with Vicki, you have to make allowances. We actually resemble each other quite a bit. Or at least we used to. But she's changed her nose, her teeth, dyed her hair, wears colored contacts and has had work done to her face. A lift or peel or something." He grinned again. "She calls it creative use of available technology."

"Well, good for her. Go down fighting, I say. Do not go gently into that good night."

He frowned. "Isn't that Dylan Thomas?"

I nodded. "Yes. It's one of my favorite poems."

"But wasn't he talking about death?"

I nodded again. "Death, old age, it's the same thing. They're going to have to drag me kicking and screaming."

He lifted his glass in salute. "Here's to kicking and screaming."

I took another gulp. "Amen to that. So, you're down visiting Vicki?"

He shook his head. "Just stopping by on my way south. I deal in animation art on the side, and there's a guy in Virginia with what sounds like an amazing collection of stuff.

Animation stills, drawings, that sort of thing. His father used to be a background artist for the Fleischer brothers."

"Oh?" I asked politely. "Should I know who they are?"

He shrugged. "Probably not. Unless you were a big fan of *Gulliver's Travels* when you were a kid."

I sat up. "The cartoon? I loved that movie. The cute little guy with the nose, screaming, 'There's a giant on the beach,' and the two songs...." I actually sang "Faithful, Forever," the whole first verse, before I realized I was making an ass of myself in front of some guy I didn't even know.

But Mitch was applauding. "That was amazing. Really touching. A real tribute to one of the great love duets of modern cinema."

I bowed my head modestly. "Like Nelson Eddy and Jeanette MacDonald."

He nodded. "Fred Astaire and Ginger Rogers."

"Judy Garland and Mickey Rooney."

"Shirley Jones and Gordon McRae."

I put my hand over my heart and closed my eyes. "Annette Funicello and Frankie Avalon."

He laughed. "Them too."

He liked old movies. And he seemed so nice. "Well, the collection sounds exciting," I said. "But that seems a long way to travel."

Mitch shrugged again. "He says he's got a bunch of original stuff, as well as discarded drawings. Collectors go nuts for that sort of stuff. I could make a bundle."

I frowned. "By selling the stuff in your store?"

He shook his head. "No. I've got an internet business that's really taking off. The stores are fun, and they're my bread and butter, but the real money is on the Web."

Three stores. A website. Real money. He was sounding less loser-like all the time. I was mulling over the faint possibilities when I was rudely interrupted.

Miranda slammed open the door. "Mom, I need to go home this afternoon so I can go with Megan to New York to see My Chemical Romance. She's got an extra ticket. We'd take the train in, right to the Garden, and then go home after the show. Oh, and I need some spending money, too."

I turned to my daughter. "Miranda, this is Mitch Wallace. Mitch, this is Miranda, my oldest daughter, who is no way going into New York by herself, and I don't care if God himself is playing with a heavenly orchestra and full celestial choir."

"Mom, Megan goes by herself all the time. The train is so safe, you know it is, and besides, you owe me for not letting me go to Green Day last winter."

I counted to three. "You didn't go to Green Day because there was a foot and a half of snow on the ground, and the only way to get into New York was by dogsled. I don't care what Megan does by herself all the time; that's Megan's mother's problem, not mine. And the train may be safe for sixteen-year-old girls, but wandering around Penn Station in the middle of the night is not. No."

"Well, what if you drive me and I meet Megan there? It's a free ticket, Mom, please?"

"Drive? You want me to drive to New York and drop you off in front of Madison Square Garden, and do what? Sit in my car for three or four hours? And then drive back here?"

"Well, yeah, you're not doing anything else, are you? I mean, you've just been sitting here sweaty and cranky all day."

"No."

"Mom, it's My Chemical Romance! I really love them."

"Then buy the CD."

"It's a free ticket."

"Then you've nothing to lose."

"It's not that far a drive to the city"

"Yes, it is, and it costs a fortune to park, and you know how temperamental Johnson gets in traffic. And if you argue any more, you'll piss me off. No."

She stomped out. I glanced over at Mitch.

"Johnson?" he asked."

"That's the van. It's been having radiator issues."

"Why did you name your van Johnson?" He suddenly grinned. "The actor?"

"Yeah. I love old movies."

"Me too." He sipped. "Sixteen is a tough age," he observed. "You have other kids?"

"Twins. Fourteen. That's a tough age too."

He whistled. "Twins, huh? Are they identical?"

I sighed. "They used to be." I heard a familiar thumping on the stairs. I looked at Mitch. "I think they waited all day until they saw you come to the door, then drew straws to see who would come down first."

Jessica slunk onto the porch. "Mom, can you take me up to Sandy Hook? They're thinking about closing down the nude beach there, and a bunch of us want to go up to protest."

I looked at her. She had decided not to re-dye her hair Ghastly Black, so there was a wide strip of soft brown at her roots, then black, and then a fringe of what was supposed to have been hot pink, but which against all that black had only gotten as far as maroon. Since henna tattoos were all over the Jersey shore, she had three: a chain around her left calf, a spider on her wrist, and a green heart on her cheek. I refused to give her permission for any more piercings after the fourth hole in her left ear, but the fake nose ring looked very convincing. She was dressed in a black long-sleeved T-shirt, black shorts that came below her knees, and black high-top sneakers. Her typical beachwear.

"Jessica, you won't even show your navel. What do you care if they close down the nude beach or not?"

"God, it's not about me, it's about the freedom to express yourself." She put her hands on her hips. "Listen, I know it's hot, and you're probably cranky, but try to think of somebody other than yourself. A lot of people use that beach every day, and it's not fair to close it."

"It's also not fair that I have to drive up there and sit around and watch a bunch of naked people carrying signs, either. No."

She looked horrified. "Mom, we aren't going to be naked."

"Of course you are. It's a nude beach, for God's sake. As a show of solidarity, everyone will have to be nude."

"But that's gross."

"Oh, I know. I've seen some of the people who go to that beach. Lots of old guys. Gray and pudgy."

"The women," Mitch added, "are pretty gray and pudgy too. I remember going there as a kid, hoping to see a bunch of hot girls, and everyone was about sixty and sagging."

"That's really disgusting," Jessica said. She looked at him with interest. "Who are you?"

"Mitch. Who are you?"

"Jessica. And you really used to go there? I mean, you're not just trying to gross me out?"

"I really used to go there," Mitch continued. "And when there were young girls around, all those old men got, you know, excited."

"Yuck," she growled, then skulked back into the house.

I gave him a look. "Did you really used to go to the nude beach?"

He shook his head. "Nope. Never. I'd have been too embarrassed. I was kind of a nerdy kid."

"Well, good bluff," I said as I gazed at Mitch approvingly. "Very well done."

He shrugged. "No problem. I was just following your lead, which was quite good."

I tried to look modest. "Well, with three of them, I've developed skills beyond those of mortal men."

"I take it that was the evil twin?"

"You could tell?"

He nodded. "The cloven feet were a dead giveaway."

I sighed. "Yes, that's usually what does it. Here comes her Bizarro World counterpart now."

"Mom." Lauren looked apologetic. "Mrs. Wilson is volunteering at the soup kitchen on Thursdays, and I told her I would help in the morning, but I saw her just a few minutes ago and she's going over now, so can I drive over with her? I can always walk back if I want to leave before she does."

"Honey, you don't have to walk. Just call me, and I'll pick you up. Unless you want to throw one of the bikes in the back of her car? Then you can bike home."

She brightened. "Great idea. Thanks, Mom." She smiled at Mitch. "I'm Lauren."

He nodded. "Mitch."

"Nice to meet you, Mitch. Okay, Mom, I'll call if I'm going to be late." And off she bounced.

Mitch whistled softly. "Wow. I bet she makes you crazy in a whole different way."

I laughed. "Oh, God, yes. Another drink?"

He nodded, and as I was pouring I saw his eyes go over my shoulder and his eyebrows go up in surprise. "Wow," he said. "She looks like a million bucks."

I turned. Patricia was standing outside, wearing a yellow sundress and sunglasses, looking cool, sleek, and beautiful.

I looked at Mitch. "You," I told him, "are not even close."

I stood up and flew out the door. I hadn't seen her all summer. I gave her a hug and kissed her cheek. "I'm so glad to see you," I gushed. "But how on earth did you find me?"

She smiled knowingly. "I just got a new car and it's got one of those GPU things in it that tells you where to go. Very nice. And the voice sounds just like Cary Grant. I had to pay extra for that, but it was worth it." She followed me onto the porch.

Mitch had stood up. Such a gentleman. "Actually, it's a GPS. Hi, I'm Mitch Wallace."

She took his hand. "Patricia Carmichael." She looked around. She'd never been to the shore house in all the years we'd been friends. "This is charming, Mona. I could live on this porch. Of course, I'd need something to cool me off."

I grinned. "Coming up." I went back into the kitchen, grabbed another glass for her Mojito, and was back on the porch in time to hear them laughing over something that somebody said that I hadn't heard because I was in the kitchen, and I felt a twinge. Of what, I wasn't sure. But it was a definite twinge.

"Thank you, darling," Patricia said, floating over to the table. "I'll pour. You look done in, poor baby. The heat is ghastly. How are the girls?"

"Good," I told her. "They were hibernating in the air conditioning upstairs until they realized Mitch was here. Then they trooped down like little soldiers."

"Yes, well, that's understandable. God forbid something should be happening and they're not in the loop."

"I'm really glad to see you, Patricia, but what the hell are you doing down here?"

"My goddaughter is getting married in December, I think I told you that, and her insufferable mother is throwing her a shower this weekend. The whole mess is in Philadelphia, and although it's not exactly on the way, I so infrequently get down this far I thought I'd swing by." She took another long sip and settled herself in a chair. "This is heaven. You can hear the ocean from here." She tilted her head dreamily. "Heaven." She took a sip of her drink. "A Mojito, right? How splendid."

"Thanks," I said modestly. "It's Doug's recipe."

Patricia leaned forward. "Well, it's yummy," she said. "Are you married, Mitch?"

Mitch shook his head. "Nope."

She looked thoughtful. "Are you gay?"

Mitch smiled. "Nope again."

"Then what is it? You're attractive and well-spoken. You aren't one of those hopeless types still living with your parents, are you?"

I closed my eyes and groaned inwardly, but Mitch laughed.

"Actually," he told her, "my parents live with me. I've got a big old Victorian, complete with an old barn and a guest house. A few years ago, my Dad had a pretty bad heart attack. I had the whole guest house done over for them. Everything's on one level, handicapped accessible, because my dad has a real problem with steps now. So they live behind me, and I can keep an eye on them. My mom still bakes me cookies every Sunday. It works out well for all of us." He shrugged. "I just ended a relationship with a woman who'd been telling me for eight years she didn't believe in commitment, and then she broke off with me to marry her boss. I think I have bad taste in women."

Patricia looked sympathetic. "Yes, well, I'm sure there's a twelve-step program for that." She smiled, then frowned as a shrill voice made its way around the corner of the house.

It was Vicki, tottering up the steps and through the screened door on very high heels.

"Mitch, are you here?" She was wearing a floaty sort of sleeveless dress and a huge sunhat. "Did you find Mona?"

Mitch did not look thrilled to see his sister. "No, I'm not here. And I'm still looking for Mona. Any helpful hints?"

She had that "Oh, you silly thing" look on her face. "I just stopped by Scott's house, and you know what he told me?"

Mitch thought a moment. "'Luke, I'm your father?'"

She was still being patient, and she waved the book that she was holding in her hand. "No, Mitch."

He frowned. "Luke, I'm your mother?"

"No," she said flatly, patience apparently gone. Although Patricia looked highly amused. "He said you turned down his invitation to dinner tomorrow night."

Mitch explained. "I was walking to the beach, and a bleached blond guy in a Speedo comes running out from a forest of pink flamingos and insists I stop by for hand-rolled lobster chimichangas. Of course I turned him down."

Vicki made a tut-tut noise. "Not very friendly of you," she scolded. "Especially since I've heard he makes killer chimichangas."

"He does," I said to Mitch. "The lobster ones are to die for."

Mitch frowned. "But he didn't even know who I was. Why would he run out in the middle of the street to invite a total stranger to dinner?"

I thought. "He probably liked your legs. Scott's like that."

"Anyway," Vicki said loudly, "it was rude. You shouldn't be rude to my neighbors."

I looked apologetically at Mitch. "She's right. Rude is bad."

"Bleached blond guy," Mitch said very slowly, as though trying to explain physics to a first-grader. "In a Speedo."

Vicky would not be swayed. She scowled at him, then she turned to Patricia and amped up her smile. "I'm Vicki Montrose. Thrilled to meet you."

"Thrilled? Really?" Patricia chuckled. "I'm Patricia Carmichael. But I can't imagine why you'd be thrilled to meet me. I'm barely famous."

Vicki faltered, but just a bit. Then she handed me the book in her hand. "I saw this and thought of you. Maybe we could try out a few of the recipes."

I looked at the title. "Mocktails," I read slowly. "What are 'Mocktails'?"

Vicki simpered. "They're drinks. They have no alcohol in them, but they taste like the real thing."

Patricia, who was pouring again, whipped around. "No alcohol? Making drinks with no alcohol? Whatever is the point?" Her eyes narrowed at me. "Who is this person?"

Vicki managed to look sincere and condescending at the same time. "Well, it's just that people around here seem to drink an awful lot, and since I've been hanging around with everyone, I've been drinking an awful lot too, and I don't handle drinking as well as some other people, so I thought with a 'mocktail' I could look like I'm fitting right in, but not wake up with a splitting hangover."

Mitch hauled himself up and put down his empty glass. "That's what club soda is for, Vicki. And I'm sure Mona is thrilled by your suggestion that she's a raging alcoholic." He looked at me. "I've got to get going, but can I ask you something?"

"Uh, sure." I said. "I'll walk you out." We walked off the porch and around to the front. The heat was brutal. Drops of sweat rolled down my back.

"Look," Mitch said. "I'll be back up here from Virginia next week. Would you like to go out to dinner with me?"

I squinted at him. "I'm sweaty, cranky, and apparently have a drinking problem. Why would you want to have dinner with me?"

He grinned. "You're the first woman I've met who can sing 'Faithful, Forever.'"

I grinned back. "Good enough. You want my phone number or anything?"

He pulled out a cell phone and entered my number. Then he waved and walked down the street, where he got into what looked like a gull-winged Mercedes. Silver. Very shiny. I'd started back to the house when Vicki came whizzing by, waving frantically at Mitch's disappearing car. I went back onto the porch, sank into a chair, and looked at Patricia.

"I like your hair," she said.

"Thanks. It usually looks better without all the frizz, but I like it too."

"And how are things going with the rich, ugly guy across the street?"

"He had some sort of computer-systems related emergency and left yesterday, along with his sons. The girls are bereft."

"What about before he left?"

"Things were fine. I mean, he's good at what he does, and I can appreciate it. That's the beginning and the end. When I leave at the end of the summer, it will all be over."

She raised an eyebrow. "Maybe before the end of the summer?"

I sighed. "Maybe. Mitch seems like a very nice guy."

"He's forty-two. A good age."

"How on earth do you know how old he is? You were only with him for two and a half minutes."

She looked smug. "Darling, if nothing else, I know all the right things to say. And the right questions to ask." She made a face. "That's his sister?"

I nodded.

"He might be worth it."

I nodded again. "Yes. He might"

She sighed. "I finished the rough draft."

"Did you?" Patricia is one of the few people who read my books as they are being written. She loves the idea of seeing each version change. She also likes reading the manuscript before anyone else. Because I trust her judgment, she gets every draft. MarshaMarsha always waits for my books to be released, but Patricia likes to read them hot off my computer. "What did you think?"

"It's the best thing you've ever written. It's one of the best things I've read this year. Really wonderful, Mona. Sydney is a terrific character, and it's a great story."

Patricia is not just my best friend, she's my most honest critic. "Oh, Patricia, thank you." I took a breath. "I'm really worried about it tanking."

"Why? It's wonderfully written, funny, real, and it brings tears to the eye. Not my eye, of course, but I can sense the potential. Why on earth would it tank?"

"I've had a loyal fan base for years. This is not what they'll be expecting. What if they're upset?"

"Mona, give all those people a little credit. They haven't been reading you all these years because you know how to describe eighteenth-century dresses, or even because you write good sex. They read you because you write characters that they love. And everyone will love Sydney."

"That's what Anthony says. He's been leaking bits and pieces onto Maura's website, and he insists the feedback has been very positive."

"See? And I love the character of Stella. She's very familiar." She looked at me through narrowed eyes.

"Well. Yes, she's you. I could never put you in any of my other books, because you're such a contemporary person. But this time, it seemed right."

She raised an eyebrow. "So, a single parent of an autistic son who throws pots in a small town seemed right for me?"

I laughed. "Perfect for you."

"Well, whatever. I'm very flattered, of course. But I'm telling you right now, if this book is ever made into a movie, I want Michelle Pfeiffer to play my part."

"Also perfect for you."

Patricia winked. "Bet your ass, baby."

Doug came back the same day as my scheduled date with Mitch, so I had to decline his offer to get together and fuck like bunnies. Instead I had a manicure, pedicure, and touched up my roots. The girls watched with interest. They made the usual helpful suggestions, which I ignored. Mitch picked me up in his cool silver car. I felt like a Bond Girl.

We drove to the northern tip of the island, just past the lighthouse, to a small, shabby-looking place with fabulous seafood and tables huddled right out on the water. He had made a reservation, and we were seated right away. The breeze was perfect, tiny white lights climbed the pole next to our table, and the waiter was attentive. We ordered, and after the first awkward three minutes, Mitch began to talk.

Mitch had bought everything the guy in Virginia had stashed in his garage, and had arranged for it all to be shipped to a temperature-controlled warehouse, which took him several minutes to explain to me. I managed to prop my chin up with my hand to keep my head from crashing to the tabletop from boredom. When he was apparently done, I said "Golly."

"Shit," he said. "I probably just cranked the geek meter all the way up to 'Danger Will Robinson.'"

I had to laugh. "Possibly. But you're very cute when you get excited, so it was almost worth it."

"It is exciting. Even if it's exciting just for me. This is art, really. This guy had a background piece, done all in watercolor, that was breathtaking. You could have framed it and put it in a museum."

"I believe you. And I'm glad you love what you do. You'll be a much happier person in the end."

"Do you love what you do? Vicki says you write. Anything I'd have read?"

"Probably not. I'm a writer of historical romances. At least I was. My latest book is kind of the anti-romance. And yes, I do love it. I'd do it if I never got a thing published, and spent my life shuffling manuscripts to friends and family members."

"You didn't order anything to drink, not even wine. Are you sure you don't want something?"

"No, thanks. I don't want you to think I'm a closet alcoholic."

He made a face. "Don't worry. I don't believe much of what Vicki says. She's a great person, really. I mean once you're her friend, she'll give you the shirt off her back, but she sees everything through a haze of self-doubt. She grew up having a body both men and women would kill for, and she thinks that's the best part of her. It's hard."

"In that case, I'll have six shots and a beer."

He laughed. "Vicki said you were funny."

"Yeah? What else?"

"Going through a divorce."

I made a face. "Yeah. Hopefully, things will be final in a couple more months. We, uh, speeded things up, since there was obvious desertion, adultery, etcetera, but I'm still signing things and waiting."

"That really sucks." He tilted his head. "So, okay, what did she tell you about me?"

"Hmmm. She said you were an entrepreneur."

"True."

"And that you had no game, no self-confidence. And that you lived with your parents."

"What? God, why didn't you just shoot me when I came to your house?"

I shrugged. "Because I didn't know who you were. If you'd have been wearing a nametag, it would have been a different story."

He laughed. Then he started telling me stories of his childhood, and I started telling him stories about mine, and by the time we were arguing about who had a worse prom date, I was floating. What a nice guy.

We had finished dinner and were sitting in the bar of the restaurant, looking out over the bay and talking about boats—he loved to sail! Me too!—when my cell phone rang. Now, I carry a cell phone at all times, but very few people know the number. Brian knew it, of course, but I doubt he'd have anything to say to me at this point. Anthony knew it, but he and Victor were up in Lake George, so I doubted it was him. That left one of my girls. So when it rang at 10:47, I panicked just a little. Caller ID told me it was the house.

"Hello? Who is this? What's wrong?"

"Mom." It was Jessica. "Look, I'm sorry to bother you, but it's an emergency."

I was reaching for my purse, getting ready for a quick exit. "What? What happened."

"The printer is out of ink."

I stopped. Took a breath. Put down my purse. "What did you say?"

"The printer. The ink cartridge is empty and you don't have another one."

I looked over at Mitch. He was looking concerned. Ready to help. What a nice guy. "The ink cartridge is empty?" I repeated.

Mitch sat back and grinned.

"Mom, this is serious. I need to print this out."

"Honey," I said, trying to keep my voice even, "it's almost eleven at night. What is so important that you need to print it right now?"

Heavy sigh over the phone. "Mom, it's too complicated to explain. I just really need another cartridge."

"Okay, honey. Listen. Take the old cartridge out of the printer. Can you do that?"

I heard muffled sounds. "Okay, Mom. Got it."

"Good girl. Now, set it down on the floor."

"Really? Okay, hold on. It's on the floor."

"Good. Now, walk slowly around the cartridge three times, chanting 'Ink Fairy, Ink Fairy, bring me more ink.'"

Mitch chuckled. Jessica made a different kind of noise. "Oh, right, Mom. Like a real Ink Fairy is going to drop a cartridge out of the sky."

"Jessica, there's just as much a chance of that happening as there is a chance of me leaving my date and driving around Long Beach Island trying to find an all-night office supply store."

She was silent. "Yeah, well," she said at last.

"Listen, Jess, are the Keegans still up? Check to see if the lights are on and the front door's still open. I'm sure they have two or three printers over there."

I heard more muffled sounds. "You're right. They're still up."

"So go over and ask Mr. Keegan to help you, okay?"

"Okay. But what should I tell Mr. Keegan if he asks where you are?"

I felt my face get red. "Don't worry, he knows I have a date." And I hung up.

I looked up and met Mitch's eyes. They were very still.

"So, you've mentioned him a few times. And Vicki's talked about him," Mitch said. "What about this Keegan guy, anyway?"

Now, we all know what a hypothetical situation is, right? So, let's put this in a hypothetical setting. Suppose, just suppose, there's a woman in her forties, going through a divorce, who has just had a lovely dinner with a sweet, thoughtful man who, incidentally, gave her butterflies in her stomach. And let's also suppose that this same woman has been having a purely physical relationship with the man across the street for a number of weeks, because the woman felt lonely and vulnerable and really just needed a hand to hold. Figuratively speaking, of course. Not literally. Literally, she needed to get laid.

So what happens when the woman gets questioned about that purely physical relationship? And the question is asked by the sweet, thoughtful man? What to do?

Option One: Lie

Deny any and every allegation. After all, the sweet, thoughtful man is a visitor, and the woman may in fact never see him again. By lying, the man thinks the woman is pure and saintly. Even though what she really is is a liar.

Option Two: Confess all

Even though the sweet and thoughtful man is a visitor, the purely physical affair is pretty much common knowledge among the adults on the block, and the sweet man's own sister probably got details from any one of several valid sources. By confessing, the woman may appear to be a real slut, but an honest slut. There's something to be said for honesty.

Option Three: Burst into tears

Men usually react when a woman starts to cry. And they usually react badly. They don't know what to do, what to say, or how to gracefully exit the room without looking like a real schmuck. Also, sobbing and talking at the same time allows a woman to say just about anything without having a single word understood. So, while crying, a lie or the truth sounds just about the same. There is the vanity factor at play here, though. Very few women look good while crying.

I looked out over the bay, looked down at my drink, and decided to go for it. "Doug Keegan is the man across the street. I've known him for years."

"Yeah," Mitch said encouragingly.

"I've been sleeping with him." That came out badly. Too abrupt. I cleared my throat and tried again. "He and I, ah, have been, well, you know. Just, well, sex. I mean, we're friends and all, but us, ah, together it's just. Well. Sex."

Oh, that came out so much better.

Mitch also looked out at the bay. "Would you call this a phase?"

"Yes," I said gratefully. "Exactly. A phase. See, when I got down here, I was just so hurt and mad, the best way to get it out seemed to be with Doug. Doug is the perfect rebound guy. The perfect revenge-fuck guy. He'll tell you that himself. He's a very uncomplicated man. And I needed an uncomplicated solution. We've both known that at the end of the summer it would be all over. I just needed a little something to get me through a rough spot, you know?"

"Vicki said you'd gone out with a few other men. Did you sleep with them too?"

That stung, but it was a fair question. "No, I didn't sleep with any of them. I didn't even like any of them. In fact, I physically resisted a few of them."

"And what about me?"

I felt a little squishy. "Mitch, you are such a nice guy. And I'm not saying that so I can tell you I think we should just be friends. I'm telling you that because I can't think of any other man I'd rather spend time with. You're great. Really great. But I'm still married, sleeping with a guy just to keep the emotional bogeyman away. I've just written a book that may very well fall completely flat, and although I would have written it out of pure love, if it does fall flat, it could ruin my career, and I happen to value my career very much. My daughters are ignoring the fact that their home is now broken, which I think is a bad thing. When I think of Brian, my husband, the first emotion is still anger. I should be over that part by now. I'm kind of a mess."

"I noticed. But you're a terrific mess. You're a smart, funny, lovable mess." He smiled wryly. "You're exactly my kind of mess."

"Is that a good thing? Didn't you say you had bad taste in women?"

"Yeah. But I think my luck is changing. Can I see you again?"

I felt a flutter. "Sure. When?"

"I really have to get back to work and take care of a few things. But I could drive down next Tuesday."

"I have plans next Tuesday, as it happens. Some very good friends of mine are taking their boat down to Atlantic City for dinner, and I was invited along. Could you join us?"

"I'm not a big gambler."

I laughed. "I'm not either. But I bring a roll of quarters and let myself go crazy at the slot machines."

"That sounds great. I'll call you at the end of the week and let you know for sure."

He drove me home, gave me a very nice goodnight kiss, and drove off, leaving me standing on my front porch, doing the happy dance.

~

Doug Keegan took his fall from grace-or-whatever with style. He came over early the next morning after my dinner with Mitch and poured himself some coffee. He perched on my kitchen stool and looked at me sharply.

"So, how did your practice date go last night?"

"Doug," I said slowly, stirring in cream and sugar, "I don't think it was practice. I think it was the real thing."

He raised his eyebrows. "The geek comic-book seller? The living-with-Mom-and-Dad guy? We've been making fun of him for weeks."

"Yeah, I know. But he's none of those things. He's…" I looked straight at Doug. "He's really nice."

Doug whistled silently through his lips. 'Wow. That's deadly."

"No, Doug, I mean it. He's a terrific person."

Doug nodded his head. "Okay, then. So I suppose this means we won't be having any more sex-on-the-beach?"

"I don't think so," I said slowly.

"Well, Mona, I gotta tell you. We had a great run."

I nodded. "Yes, Doug, that we did."

"Shall we have a favorite-moments recap?"

I laughed. "No, not necessary. But thank you. Really. This could have been the crappiest summer of my life, but because of you, it wasn't."

"So, listen, when you write the book, make sure I'm taller. And handsomer. But you may have to tone down my sexual prowess, because no one would believe you."

And that was that.

～

Mitch called me on Sunday. "Hello," I said.

"Is this Mona Berman? Quincy? Mona?"

"No, I'm sorry Mona-Berman-Quincy-Mona was admitted to a padded cell yesterday because some guy who was supposed to call her at the end of the week didn't."

"Oh. This is Sunday. Isn't Sunday the end of the week?"

"Not really. She was referring to the end of the *work* week, which would have meant Friday. The end of the calendar week is Saturday. Either way, you're too late."

"Wow. That's too bad, because I was planning on driving all the way down to see her on Tuesday. Can this date be saved?"

"Possibly. I spoke to my friends and you're welcome to come along. They want to start down around noon. Can you be here by then?"

"No problem. See you then."

I gave him directions to the marina, hung up and did the happy dance again.

∼

MarshaMarsha was very excited. "You met a nice guy? Oh, this is great, isn't it great, Al?"

Al was busy stowing things below deck, but grunted in approval.

"This is going to be our second date," I explained. "I figured you guys could help with any awkward pauses."

Al grunted again, then came up from below deck with a bottle of Sam Adams.

The Riollos' boat was nothing like Peter Gundersen's yacht. It was a sturdy, scruffy little cruiser, with a blue canvas canopy for shade and one seat behind the controls. You sat on bench seats along the side of the boat, and when the tide got low, you got out and helped push the boat off the sandbars. Brian and I had gone with them on many a trip to Atlantic City in past years, and it felt strange to have Mitch along this year when only last year we had splurged on champagne for the trip home after Al hit it big at the blackjack tables.

Al took a long swig of beer. "So, you aren't seeing Doug anymore?"

MarshaMarsha shushed him. "Al, don't be nosy."

"What the hell, you're dying to find out too. Well, Mona?"

"Doug and I agreed to end our most current relationship and return to our previous one."

Al nodded approval. "Good. Cause I gotta tell you, Mona, Doug was a bit of a come-down for you. You deserve somebody a lot better looking."

MarshaMarsha rolled her eyes. I grinned. There was no point in trying to explain to Al that what I needed—and got—from Doug had nothing to do with his looks.

I had been watching the parking lot for Mitch, and saw a flash of silver. There was a lot of silver in the lot. The official car of New Jersey is a silver SUV, but Mitch's long, sleek car stood out. I watched as he came onto the pier. He was dressed in shorts and a polo shirt, with a Mets baseball cap on his head and a faded blue tote over his shoulder. I smiled at the sight of him.

Al waved for him to come on board. "It's a good thing you're wearing that hat, 'cause if you were a Yankee fan, I'd have to throw you overboard."

"If I were a Yankee fan," Mitch said, climbing down, "I'd throw myself overboard."

Ah, sports. The only thing two men need to become best friends is the love of a common team. Or the hatred of one.

We had a wonderful time. The ride down was smooth and sunny, we wandered around the dark, noisy casinos, and Mitch won three hundred dollars on a dollar slot machine and treated us all to a very expensive dinner. We had eaten early so that Al didn't have to cruise back in the dark, and we docked back in Long Beach Island just after eight.

Al invited Mitch back to the house for a drink, but Mitch backed off, citing the long ride home as an excuse. I walked him back to his car.

"You have great friends," Mitch said, running his hands up and down my arms.

I pulled him close, very close, and kissed him. He kissed back. Wow.

"So, next Tuesday?" He whispered in my ear, his hands still moving.

"Tuesday? What about next Tuesday?" I was having trouble concentrating. I kept kissing him.

"I could drive down again."

"That would be good."

More kissing.

"Good," he agreed.

I could feel the handle of his car door pressing into my back. It should have hurt, but it didn't. Now I was having problems breathing. "Maybe we should stop," I gasped.

"Maybe."

I could feel other things pressing into my front. I took a deep breath and pushed him away. "I'll see you next week," I said with difficulty.

He cleared his throat. "I'll call you. Maybe tomorrow. Definitely by Thursday."

"Right."

He called the next morning. I was on the back porch, busy reading Sylvia's notes on Chapter Three, but when I saw his number, I jumped up to answer.

"Hey, Mitch. Hi."

"Hi yourself. Am I interrupting anything?"

"What? No, not at all. Well, yes. Book stuff. But it can wait."

"What kind of book stuff?"

"Seriously?"

"Yeah. I'm interested."

"Well, I sent my agent my first draft, and we had a long conversation last week about her suggested changes, and I took copious notes that I can't understand because I was writing in my lap, and so now I'll have to call her again and ask her what 'sex, Jack, ladder' means."

"Jack has sex with a ladder?"

"Don't think so."

"Jack has sex on a ladder?"

"Maybe. I had a great time yesterday."

"Me too."

"How do you feel about caller ID?"

"What?"

"Caller ID."

"This is a test, right?"

"No, of course not. Not in the sense that there's a right or wrong answer. I'm just curious."

"None of my phones, except my cell, have caller ID."

"Not even your business phone?"

"No. Do you have strong feelings about caller ID?"

"Me? No." I took a sip of iced coffee. "Nope, not at all."

"I seem to be missing the guy gene that makes me want to use all available technology, even stuff I don't need. I have a cell phone, a flat-screen, and an iPod, but no caller ID or electronic ignition on my gas grill. I also don't have a home theater system. Does this mean I can't come back down next Tuesday?"

"Actually, your disinterest in all things electronic is a plus. Brian couldn't take a shower without some new technological marvel helping out in some way. But caller ID, well, that's another story."

"Every year, on Margaret Mitchell's birthday, I watch *Gone with the Wind.*"

"Good save. Come on down."

He called again Monday. "I can't come down. My store manager broke her leg last night, and my assistant manager is in Nova Scotia. The manager from my other store is still in rehab. I can't get away."

I was surprised how disappointed I was. "Of course, do what you've got to do. I'll be home in two weeks anyway. I'll see you then."

"I'm going to miss you."

"Me too. Call me, though. You can call, right?"

He laughed. "I'm not a big one for talking on the phone. I don't do small talk."

"So, we'll have short conversations instead of small talk. Please call me."

"I will."

He did. What a nice guy.

～

Amanda Witt called me. We normally e-mailed each other when we wanted to chat, or actually meet somewhere for lunch outside of the Mavens. Amanda hated talking on the phone. But when I e-mailed her asking about Nationals, she actually called back in reply.

"You should put your name up for the Board," she began. "I know that this is Lillian's last year. She's started breeding King Cavalier Spaniels, of all things, and wants to spend more time getting that off the ground. I don't understand why writers just can't sit around and write. We're such an insecure lot, always worried that our current book will be our last. Anyway, she'll be gone and I couldn't sniff out any other serious contenders. The election is over a year away. If you started talking it up now, you could get a lot of support."

Hmm. Brian had never wanted me to become too involved with the RWA because he wanted me to play at all the parties rather than network. But now that he was out of the picture.... "I'll think about it," I told her. "What else?"

"The weather was cold and rainy. Fabulous shrimp. Louisa is roughly the size of a Hummer and she spent the whole week sipping Diet Coke and pulling carrot sticks out of her ass. Terry G. wore nothing but black leather the whole time. I know she's into her characters, but really. She might as well have had a cloak and false fangs. Barbara One and Barbara Two asked me about you. They are the sweetest women. Lots of new fan girls. If MaryAnn gets another facelift, she'll look like a Siamese cat."

I laughed. "Was it fun?"

"It's always fun. Worked my tired old ass off, but it's always fun. We're a great group of people. Everybody missed you. Really. People understood, so no damage done. Seriously, think about the Board. It could be a feather in your cap."

"Even if I'm leaving the fold?" I teased.

Amanda paused. "You're going to lose fans. No, that's not quite right. Some of your fans will not even try to read your new book because it's not a romance. It won't matter how good it is. You can't take it personally. Remember that. The RWA will forgive you as long as you let them know romance is your first love. In fact, start doing something about that new idea of yours. The sooner people know that you're back on the romance track, the smoother things will go."

I sighed. "Thank you, Amanda. You always have the best advice."

We hung up a few minutes later and I stared at the phone. Being on the Board of Directors of the RWA would be a big deal for me. I'd have to seriously consider this.

CHAPTER ELEVEN

I returned home just before Labor Day. My new bathroom was fabulous. It was the first thing Aunt Lily showed me when I got home. It looked like a spa: calm colors, elegant fixtures, ferns, and candles. I called Ben Cutler to thank him.

"It's amazing," I gushed. "Really. Better than I imagined. How can I ever thank you? How about I buy you dinner sometime this week?"

He chuckled. "I'm so busy for the next month I won't have time to breathe. In fact, the only free time I have is today for about ten minutes."

"Then how about coffee in an hour?"

He paused. "I could do coffee. In fact, I'd love coffee. Starbucks?"

I shuddered. "I can't. Long story. World Coffee?"

"Deal."

Thank God Westfield was the kind of town that could support more than one overpriced coffeehouse. We managed two armchairs by the window. He was attracting all sorts of looks from the morning-mom crowd. I was attracting pretty much nothing.

"When is David off to Yale?" I asked him when we got settled.

"I took him up this past weekend. He's so excited. He's a smart kid. He'll do well there." He seemed impervious to the stares. "Why not Starbucks?"

I related the story of Starbucks Marty. He laughed through most of it.

"I went out with someone like that once," he said. "I called her Black Cloud Carol. On our first date she choked on a chicken bone and had to go to the ER. I asked her out again, to be polite, and she was late because she set her kitchen on fire."

"You must date a lot," I said.

He looked at me quizzically. "Why do you say that?"

"You're straight, single, employed, and quite the hunk. A perfect catch. Don't you have women crawling all over you?"

"God, woman," he said angrily, "don't you realize that those other women mean nothing to me? You're the only one who matters." He bore down on her, taking her into his arms and crushing her to him. "You're the only one I want," he muttered, and then he kissed her, and she felt the earth beneath her give way.

Ben shrugged. "All the good ones are taken. You, for instance."

I felt a tingle. "Ah, yes. The Good Ones Who Are Taken. You know about us?"

He grinned playfully. "I've heard rumors."

"Go on."

"Well, I know that you're a quasi-religious group with strong political ties. When you're not dancing naked in a circle during the full moon, you're planning world domination through a series of leveraged buy-outs and subtle brainwashing techniques."

"Ben, I had no idea you were so aware. You realize, of course, that now I have to kill you."

He laughed. "Please don't. Your secret is safe with me."

I sipped my chai latte and grinned. "This is a goofy side to you I've never seen before."

"Well, mix physical exhaustion, no sleep, and a double shot of espresso and anything can happen. How's the book coming?"

I sighed. "Good question. I think it's done. Anthony says it's perfect and keeps wrestling me away from the computer. I had a habit, when I first started out, of over-thinking what I wrote. Then I would end up editing all kinds of junk out. Because this book is something new for me, I'm afraid I'm going to do that again. I sent it out to two friends of mine, fellow writers, and asked them to give me an opinion. One got back to me right away, and loved it. Amanda is taking longer, but I knew she would. She'll be an honest critic."

"Anthony isn't?"

"Usually, yes. I'm just feeling very cautious about this book. It means a lot."

He looked down at his watch. "Whoa. Gotta go. Thanks for the coffee. It was really good seeing you. Don't worry about your book. I'd trust your instincts. They've always been right before." He looked at me strangely, as though he was going to say something else, then shook his head. "I'll talk to you soon."

He was leaving. I stood up. "Thanks again for my bathroom. See you."

I watched him leave. Everyone else watched him too. I felt like calling out, "Hey, he's my plumber," but didn't. Let them think what they want. It felt good to be the object of so much envy.

~

Anthony, as it turned out, knew Mitch. When I explained that Mitch was no longer an object of ridicule and why, Anthony recognized Mitch's website, and then realized that Victor was a steady customer of Mitch's Jersey City store. The world, I swear to God, keeps getting smaller.

Mitch and I had spoken to each other about every third day for the past two weeks. He was in fact pretty bad at small talk, so we talked about bigger things, like movies and books and why Larry David was a genius and Bill O'Reilly was an idiot.

We decided to meet in Summit for dinner. I spent all Friday morning getting my hair done and, just to be on the safe side, another bikini wax, which was something I hated to do and which made me wonder about my subconscious. If I was willing to endure physical pain, not to mention normal, everyday embarrassment for the mere possibility that Mitch might want to see me naked, and therefore all the aforementioned pain and embarrassment would then be worthwhile, what kind of person did that make me? Simple enough answer: a horny one.

On Friday night my daughters all had previous social engagements. Aunt Lily was to meet with her fellow anarchists at an open mic poetry reading. But since I had a date, all other entertainment took a back seat.

"Why are you wearing that?" Lauren asked, frowning critically.

I squinted at myself in the mirror. I thought I looked pretty good. Simple navy dress with a splash of hot pink down the front. My ivory pashmina against the early fall chill.

"I look fine," I told her. "This is a universally accepted going-out-to-dinner outfit."

"Wouldn't you be more comfortable in pants?" she asked.

Actually, I would have been. I was wearing the dress for easy access. "I want to show off my new heels," I lied.

"But you hate heels," she pointed out. "You always say they're uncomfortable."

Yes, I did hate heels. But the extra few inches would make for an ideal kissing height. "These are very comfortable," I lied again.

"Why can't we meet him?" she asked for the fifth time.

I rolled my eyes. "Honey, you did meet him. At the shore, remember?"

Jessica appeared at my bedroom doorway, looking interested. "I think you have something to hide. Otherwise, he would come here and pick you up."

"I'm not hiding anything," I told them. "It's just easier to meet him halfway than to have him come all the way out here."

"If he was my date, he'd have to come to the door so you could check him out," Lauren observed.

I sighed. "I don't 'check out' your dates. I just make sure there's minimal piercing and no beer-breath." I gave myself a final look and went downstairs.

Aunt Lily and I had reached a very comfortable agreement last spring without ever sitting down and talking about it. She made coffee in the mornings and dinner when I was running late or rushed. She spent a great deal of time out of the house plotting or in her room reading and watching TV. She was available to the girls but not intrusive. She was pleasant and didn't ask questions. But tonight she was parked in the kitchen with Miranda and it was obvious they had been talking about me because when I came through the door, they both pounced.

"I don't think you should be running around meeting strange men in restaurants," Lily said. "It sets a bad example."

"Aunt Lily," I said, trying to be patient," he's not a strange man. And it is no longer 1958. My example is fine, isn't it, Miranda?"

My oldest shook her head. "What you shouldn't be doing is meeting anyone for a date in a minivan. Johnson is fine for carpooling and the food store, but for dates, you really need a red something. Maybe a convertible."

Miranda, Lily had just reminded me that morning, was getting her driving permit in nine weeks and four days.

"Johnson is just fine," I muttered as I grabbed my keys. "Don't call me unless there's a coroner involved."

I got to the restaurant a few minutes before he did, and was nursing a martini at the bar when he came in. I watched him make his way across the room. His hair was thick and glossy, his eyes warm, his features strong and chiseled. He moved easily and with a certain grace. His smile stole my breath.

After dinner, we walked through town, holding hands, and my skin felt on fire. We stopped in front of the library, under a leafy oak, and he kissed me. Hard. And for a long time. So long, in fact, I kept waiting for somebody to yell at us to get a room. When I came up for air, I looked around quickly—the street was deserted. We could probably take our clothes off right then and there and no one would notice....

"What are you thinking?" he muttered, his hands still moving.

"I'm thinking that I want to tear off your clothes. Right now. And teach you things."

"Things? Like what things?"

"You know. Things. Trashy things." I kept unbuttoning the top button of his shirt and then buttoning it back up. "To show you my vast world of maturity and experience."

He pulled back and looked skeptical. "Maturity and experience? How old are you anyway?"

"Forty-five."

"You're only three years older than I am," he pointed out. "What maturity are you talking about anyway?"

"Shut up, Mitch. I'm having a Mrs. Robinson fantasy, okay? Let me enjoy it."

He dropped his hands. "Does that mean I should pretend to be totally inexperienced?"

I grabbed his hands and repositioned them. "Probably not. Do you think it's too soon for sex?" I asked.

"Maybe. We should probably wait. How long would it take to get to your place?"

"Twenty minutes."

"That sounds long enough."

"But I have a dog, three cats, three kids, and Aunt Lily."

"Shit. Okay, my place then. I've only got one cat, and she ran off this morning."

"Oh, I'm sorry."

He was running his hands up and down my back. "No problem. She always comes back. Follow me in your car?"

It took us seventeen minutes to get to Chatham. I parked on the street and he met me halfway up the drive, grabbing my hand. His back door was heavy and old-fashioned, and we had to fumble up a few steps in the dark into the kitchen. Once inside, we were kissing again, and my back was up against the counter, and his hands were up under my dress, pulling down my panties, and I was done with his belt and working on the zipper when the door creaked, and a small voice called.

"Mitch?"

The light went on. I pushed Mitch away for a second, then stepped around to stand in front of him. Although my panties were halfway down my thighs, if I kept my knees together, no one would ever know. Mitch, on the other hand, had a belt, a snap, and zipper to deal with. Not only that, but he was, as we romance writers like to say, in *extremis erectus*, so I thought it prudent to shield as much of him as I could.

A frail looking older lady, who could only be his mother, was standing there, looking extremely embarrassed.

"I'm so sorry," she gasped. "I didn't see another car in the drive, and—"

"It's fine," I said quickly, smoothing my hair with my hands. "We were just making some, ah, coffee. I'm Mona."

I leaned forward, extending my hand as far as possible without moving from in front of Mitch or unclasping my knees. She took a few steps to take it.

"A pleasure to meet you," she said faintly.

By this time, Mitch had arranged things and had turned to face his mother, but I could tell by the bump I was getting in the small of my back that I'd better stay put.

"Hey, Mom, no problem. What's up?"

I choked back a giggle and he bumped me again.

"It's just that Lucy came back," she explained, "and I wanted you to know."

"Lucy?" I asked.

"Cat," Mitch said shortly.

"Well, that's great news," I said. "I have a cat I'm quite fond of myself."

Mitch's mom beamed. "Really?"

"Yes. Well, three cats," I went on. "And a dog."

"Oh?" By her tone, Mitch's mom was not a dog person.

"And three daughters," I finished proudly, which pretty much did her in. She smiled weakly, waved vaguely, and backed out the door.

I felt Mitch's hands on my shoulders. "Sorry," he said in my ear. "She usually doesn't come barging in like that."

My shoulders started to shake with laughter. "At least I managed to keep my underwear from sliding down to my ankles."

He was laughing too. "Yeah, that might have given us away. Where were we, anyway?"

"I think we were about to do a Glenn Close-Michael Douglas move on your kitchen counter, which, upon reflection, would have ended in disaster."

"You mean you can't be erotic and agile on granite?"

"I do much better on soft surfaces."

He grinned. "Just as well. I don't have any condoms within reach here in the kitchen."

I grinned back. "Not very forward-thinking of you."

"Follow me."

I did. The bed was huge. The pillows were plenty. And I didn't have to teach him a thing.

I didn't need to call him the next night. I just wanted to. "Hi, Mitch? It's Mona. Is this too late to call?"

"It's only ten o'clock Mona. Sometimes I'm awake 'till midnight. What's up?"

"My Aunt Lily just told me she's off to Brooklyn on Monday."

"Yeah? Are they posting 'Welcome to Earth' banners?"

Mitch thought the whole Aunt Lily thing quite funny. "I think it's just lunch with cronies. But the girls will be in school and the house will be empty."

"Poor baby. Maybe we could meet for breakfast?"

"That would be great."

"Then maybe a little afternoon delight?"

"I was thinking more of a midmorning delight."

"But then I couldn't sing to you."

'Maybe we could try afternoon as well."

He chuckled. "Your faith in my recuperative powers is touching."

"Actually, I'm counting more on my powers of persuasion."

"After last night, I'm not too worried."

"Me neither. We were pretty terrific."

He chuckled again. "See you Monday."

"Will you really sing to me?"

"You bet."

$\sim$

"Your voice is awful."

We were lying on my bed, sun streaming through the windows, and Mitch had just finished the last verse. During his performance, the vocal one, that is, I had been pressing my hand, fingers splayed, against the dark and springy hair on his chest. During his previous performance, the sexual one, I had other things to do with my hands.

"I'll have you know I played Nathan Detroit in my high school musical."

"You were a geek even then?"

"Pretty much since birth."

Lana jumped on the bed, gave Mitch a quick look, sniffed his pubic hair, and jumped back off the bed, tail high. He looked after her.

"Was that some sort of critique?"

"Maybe. Maybe not. But her tail held up like that usually means she's happy about something."

"Good to know."

"I like your chest hair."

"I look like a doormat."

"You're perfect."

"Thank you. You too."

"Yes, I know."

$\sim$

I hadn't heard from him in two days. I was practically sitting on my hands to keep from dialing when the phone rang a little after seven. I scurried into the living room to be alone.

"Hey."

"Hey, Mona. How are you?"

"Good."

"Yeah? What are you wearing?"

Oh boy. Our first trashy phone call. But I couldn't lie. "Gray sweat pants, an LBI sweatshirt and sneakers. Why?"

"Oh. That's a little disappointing. I thought all you romance-writer types lounged around in silk negligees and mules."

"Mules? You know mules?"

"Aren't they high-heeled slippers with fuzzy things on the toes?"

"Wow. You do know mules."

"Can I see you tomorrow night?"

"What did you have in mind?"

"Well," he said slowly, "we could get Thai food and eat it off each other's stomachs."

"Hmmm. What if I don't like Thai?"

"Mona, please. I could never consider a relationship with any woman who did not like Thai food."

"What if I don't like to eat naked?"

"Who said anything about eating naked? Maybe I just have terrible table manners. I think you spend way too much time thinking about people getting naked."

"Well, it was sort of my job for eighteen years. Does it bother you?"

He chuckled. "Hell, no. I consider it a perk. How about seven thirty?"

"I'm there."

~

"Are you seeing this Mitch guy again?" Jessica snarled. She had a new boyfriend and they needed a ride to the movies.

"Yes, as a matter of fact, I am. I'll take you both one way. Can't his parents pick you up?"

"No. We need a ride both ways."

"Well, I can't give you a ride both ways. I'll be with Mitch. We're having dinner. Thai."

"Why is your date more important than mine?"

"Because I'm the grown-up, that's why, and this ride you want is in my car that I pay for, with my gas that I also pay for. I do not feel obligated to compromise my social life for your social life. I can take you there. That's as good as it gets. Yes or no?"

"If Daddy were here, he'd give me a ride."

"Then call him."

She stormed out. Aunt Lily, leaning against the counter, made a small noise.

"Do you think, Mona, I should try and get a driver's license?"

"No," I blurted, then got my panic under control. "No, Aunt Lily, really. These kids are spoiled into thinking every wish is their command. They can walk to town or change their plans. I'm not changing mine."

"So, you're seeing this Mitch guy again?" she asked, eyebrows raised.

"Yes. I promise I'll invite him to dinner soon so everybody can get to know him."

"Dear," Lily murmured, "don't feel you have to do that. You don't want to send him running in the other direction, do you?"

"Now, Aunt Lily, we're not that bad," I protested.

She shrugged. "How old is he again?"

"He's forty-two."

She nodded. "Good age."

"That's what Patricia said. Why is that a good age?"

"Because he's three years younger than you, and a woman's life expectancy is three years longer than a man's. So, if you do end up together, and there are no unforeseen illnesses, you should both die together."

"How romantic."

"Romantic, hell. I'm a practical woman, Mona."

"That you are, Aunt Lily."

~

We did not actually eat off each other's stomachs.

"The girls are with their father this weekend."

"Really? Does that mean you don't have to leave in the middle of the night and go home?"

"Yep."

"That's great. Let's plan something. I'm in the store 'till six on Saturday, but we could go into the city and walk around Times Square."

"Have dinner someplace small and romantic?"

"Just like the tourists. Then we could get a room, someplace very expensive, like the Pierre."

"The Pierre? How rich are you?"

"Then we could have brunch and do more touristy stuff."

"Walk down Fifth Avenue."

"A carriage ride around Central Park."

"Oh, I haven't done that since the girls were little."

"Then tea at the Plaza. Like that little girl in the books? I kinda always wanted to do that."

"Tea? Like Eloise? My God, you're nerdier than I thought."

"What's wrong with tea?"

"Nothing. Should I tie a red ribbon in my hair?"

"Perfect. But the best thing will be waking up in the morning, and there you'll be."

"I have really bad hair in the morning and my skin gets all pinky."

"Now, there's a picture. Next you'll be telling me you have elephant breath in the morning."

"Dying elephant breath."

"Enough. Let me live the fantasy a few more days, okay?"

"While you're at it, put me in mules."

～

I was getting nervous about my book. I had met the October first deadline, sending Frannie a hard copy FedEx and e-mailing her the file. I was waiting for her to call me, and although it was not unusual for her to take a week or two to get back to me, I was feeling very anxious, and by day five I was jumping at loud noises. She finally called on a cloudy Thursday while Anthony was out getting Chinese food for lunch. I saw her number and pounced on the phone.

"Frannie? What did you think? Did you like it?"

She sneezed. "Hi, Mona. I've actually had a terrible cold, thanks for asking, but other than that, I'm fine. And you?"

"I've been feeling crazed. Seriously. What did you think?"

"Well, I was out sick when it got to my office, but Becca, my assistant, took it home and read it. She thought it was a riot, and she's one of those Sarah Lawrence grads who think the last great female writer was Virginia Woolf. She actually brought it to my house and I read it from my sickbed. I loved it. Congratulations, Mona. I laughed, I cried, I was a complete idiot. I was also on medication, but I read it a second time and still loved it. The whole office wants a look."

I felt weak from relief. I sank back into the couch. "Thank God. I was so afraid you wouldn't like it."

"Are you kidding? It's great. So funny, but a really honest story and wonderful characters. Sticking to your guns paid off big time. Always trust your instincts, Mona."

Anthony had come up and was pulling little white takeout boxes out of a paper bag. I gave him the thumbs-up.

"I've got a few suggestions, of course," Frannie went on. "Nothing major. But give me a few more days. We'll talk."

"Okay, Fran. Thanks a lot." I hung up and grinned at Anthony. "She loved it," I told him.

He punched the air. "Yes. Yes. Good. This is so good. Mona, you're a rock star. Honest."

"Yeah," I sighed. "I know. I need to call Patricia. And MarshaMarsha. We'll eat out tonight to celebrate. I may even take the girls shopping. I am so happy. And relieved. And hungry. No scallion pancakes?"

"Here they are. Can I come too?"

"Of course. You may have to drive in case I start celebrating too hard."

"My pleasure. Lo mein?"

I dialed Patricia's number, slurping noodles happily.

~

Fred was in love. The first time Mitch had come by the house, all Fred got at first was a quick peek before the bedroom door got shut in his face. But after Mitch had stopped by the house a few more times, he and Fred formed a real bond. Mitch would even get on the floor and rub Fred right behind his left ear, Fred's favorite spot. But the breakthrough came one Thursday morning, early in October, when the girls were at school and Lily was at her knitting class. I was looking forward to lots of nakedness, but Mitch looked out the window and suggested that we take a nice long walk first. With the dog.

That's all Fred needed.

"My dog is going to follow you home," I told Mitch.

"Fred drives?"

"Only if the car is already running. He has a problem turning the key, but if the van's in gear, he's off."

"This is a great neighborhood for walking."

"It's a great neighborhood, period."

"You must be very happy with your life here."

I thought about that for a minute. Yes, I was happy. The thought surprised me.

When Brian first left, it seemed like my life stalled. There were things that had to be done, the day-to-day chores of getting through the weeks and months, but my mind seemed frozen. Down at the shore, where Brian had never been around for weeks at a time, I felt a sense of normalcy return. Coming back to Westfield, getting back to a routine of school and going places and doing everyday things felt odd at first, because Brian was so definitely gone. But I realized, thinking about what Mitch had said, that I was in fact happy.

"I am happy," I said at last. "It's a different kind of happiness, because it's new. I'm living my life pretty much the way I always did, but it feels different. I don't miss Brian anymore. At all. I'm not angry all the time any more either. I'm working hard. I made a few changes to the manuscript, and I'm waiting to hear from Frannie again, but I'm already working on something else, something new. It feels really good to be alone, not that I'm ever really alone, but I mean, well, single. Single feels okay."

"Plus, you're getting fabulous company, not to mention great sex, from a hot young stud."

"Oh yeah, that's right. My hot young stud. I'm the envy of the neighborhood."

"Does Fred look thirsty?"

"Parched. I think we need to turn around right now and get him home. He may need emergency care."

"I'm very good in emergencies," Mitch said.

Mitch was very good. Period.

～

Against my better judgment, I thought I should introduce Mitch to the girls before they built up such an elaborate fantasy around him that I'd have to kill him off and hide the body rather than try to ask him to live up to it. My initial thought had been Sunday brunch. Eleven o'clock on a Sunday morning is the teenage equivalent of the crack of dawn so the girls would be slow to the point of sluggish, and they would be so ravenously hungry they would be incapable of complicated speech because they'd be too busy shoveling down goat-cheese omelets and croissants. However, I knew that I'd need more than a fluffy mimosa as fortification, and no straight vodka before noon is a personal written-in-stone rule for me, so I went to Plan B.

Plan B was dinner, but without anyone knowing. Mitch would just show up. I hoped that the element of surprise, plus homemade dessert on a weeknight, would be enough to keep at least Lauren and Miranda off-balance. Jessica was rarely off-balance, but I could always hope. Aunt Lily was just a case of "Pray for the best."

I decided on lemon chicken, roasted asparagus, and risotto, with pears poached in red wine for dessert. Since the risotto would require my constant attention, I could safely keep Mitch in the kitchen with me. My daughters stay out of the kitchen except when actually eating, because they're terrified I might ask them to put away a dish or, God forbid, wipe a counter, so I figured I could keep him safe until we were all at the table. By then, I would also have had a martini or two, to deaden the pain of whatever carnage might follow. The trick would be keeping them apart after he arrived. One at a time, my girls can be brutal but charming. As a single unit, however, they are just plain deadly.

I had told Mitch to come around to the kitchen door. Without the tolling of the doorbell, he might get into the house unnoticed. If the girls stayed in their rooms, which was their usual early evening routine, and if I could keep Fred from going ballistic with joy, Mitch's presence would go undetected until it was too late for planning, plotting, or going to Google for incriminating information. Not that there was any. I had Googled him myself and he came up clean. But Jessica would probably know of a secret website that stored fifty years worth of high school bios from across the country where she could dig up teenaged transgressions at a click of the mouse.

He arrived just after six, a little early, but with flowers and wine. He drank beer, so I opened a Rolling Rock for him while I tried not to mainline vodka tinged with vermouth. I stirred risotto, laughing with him while my ears strained for telltale footsteps. Six thirty-five came and went. I set out serving dishes, calling for the girls to come to dinner, and was feeling very smug. Mitch was pouring wine as they filed in. Only Miranda stopped to stare, then threw me a vicious look. Lauren and Jessica barely blinked, as though having a relatively strange man at the dinner table was no big deal. Aunt Lily, who'd been back in the garden, gave me a satisfied little smile.

"Everyone," I said casually, "this is Mitch Wallace. Mitch, do you remember my daughters?"

He smiled and nodded.

"And this is my aunt, Lily Martel. Aunt Lily, this is Mitch."

"Yes, I thought so," Lily murmured. "Very well done, Mona."

"Pretty sly, Mom," Lauren said.

"Thank you, honey."

"Mitch," Jessica announced, "has been to the nude beach at Sandy Hook."

Lily raised an eyebrow. "Recently?" she asked.

Mitch shook his head blandly. "Years ago."

"Ah," Lily said. "I imagine there were a lot of old men running around with very white, flaccid penises."

Mitch cleared his throat. "Pretty much."

"Aunt Lily," Lauren whispered loudly, "that's gross."

Lily shrugged. "Lauren, dear, you're not a child. I shouldn't have to worry about censoring my vocabulary in front of you. There's nothing wrong with discussing penises."

"No, Aunt Lily," I managed, "but maybe not at the dinner table."

She shrugged again and passed the risotto.

"Do you live around here, Mitch?" Miranda asked, her eyes never leaving his face.

"Chatham," he answered. "Not far."

"So," she continued, "I guess you'll be stopping in for dinner quite a lot?"

Mitch smiled. "I hope so, because this chicken is delicious."

"Thanks," I said, smiling into my dinner plate.

"But," Mitch continued, "I didn't just stop by. I was invited."

"Really?" Lauren looked at me with narrowed eyes.

"Yes," I told her. "I invited him last week."

"I can't imagine why you didn't tell us he was coming," Miranda groused.

"Oh, I can," said Lily, sipping wine.

"My mother," Jessica said to Mitch, "probably figured we'd try to ambush you."

"I don't know why you'd do a thing like that," Mitch said. "After all, if it hadn't been for you girls wanting your mother to date in the first place, we never would have met."

"Touché," said Lily.

I beamed at Mitch. The man was brilliant. Why had I been so worried? At that moment, I couldn't even remember what I had been so nervous about. What could the girls do anyway? Aside from mentioning a few harsh truths, like that I get hysterical at the sight of snakes, or that long fits of giggles send me running to the bathroom to pee, what could they use against me? More importantly, what could they say against Mitch? No matter what they might try to use against him, it could be turned around because Mitch had just hit them with the biggest deflator of all. Our being together was, ultimately, their fault.

Lily turned to me. "I do like this one."

"Thanks, Aunt Lily. Pass the salad, please?"

Mitch raised his wineglass. "A toast to all you lovely ladies. Now that we've all finally met, I hope we can get to know each other much better."

Aunt Lily rolled her eyes. "Good heavens, man, think about what you're saying." But she drank up anyway.

~

Miranda was turning seventeen. She reminded me of this on a fairly regular basis. When I asked her what she had in mind for a birthday present, she pretended to have to think about it.

"Something not too old," she said, "fast, hot, and maybe Italian."

I looked at her. "Honey, I want the exact same thing. And he wouldn't even have to speak English."

She flounced out in a huff.

Her sweet-sixteen party the previous year was an event on the same scale as Nancy Langhorne Astor's coming-out party. All that was missing was a horse-drawn carriage and a flock of wild white doves. Her birthday was going to be the first family affair post-Brian, since I don't count Halloween as a family holiday, no matter what my daughters say.

I'd been waiting for Miranda to start drawing up lists, and her lack of such activity puzzled me, until she mentioned, very casually one night right before Brian was due to pick them up, that he would be hosting her party this year.

I'd been scanning the freezer for a Lean Cuisine for dinner. I closed the freezer door carefully and looked at her.

"What did you say?"

"Daddy said he'd throw me a birthday party this year. He already spoke to Grandma. She's coming. And Aunt Rebecca and Aunt Marsha and Uncle Frank. Their kids won't be there, but Aunt Rebecca is bringing somebody, and Grandma is bringing along her student, Leslie. And I got to invite six friends."

"Ah." I waited. "When is the party?"

"The Saturday night after my real birthday. We're having it in a really cool restaurant in Hoboken. Dominique made reservations."

I was still waiting. "Dominique?"

Miranda shrugged. "She's good at parties."

So I had heard. Way back in April, when I dumped Rebecca's surprise party in Brian's lap, Dominique apparently pulled a Manhattan loft complete with a caterer and two bartenders out of her skinny butt and made a smashing success of the whole affair.

I couldn't stand it any longer. "So, am I invited?"

Miranda dropped her eyes. "I didn't think you'd want to come, with Daddy and Dominique and all. Do you want me to ask him tonight?"

My heart fell on the floor. I was surprised that my ears weren't ringing from the crash. "No, honey, that's fine. You're probably right, my being there wouldn't be such a good idea. We'll have a special dinner here on your real birthday, okay?"

She smiled and looked suddenly very young. "That would be great. Could you make homemade spaghetti sauce with meatballs?"

I nodded.

"And that chocolate cake with the sour cream frosting?"

I cleared my throat. "Sure."

She ran over and kissed me. "Thanks, Mom. I was really worried that you'd be mad, that's why I didn't say anything before. But Daddy was so excited and everything, I didn't know what to say."

"It's okay, baby."

"You can invite Mitch." Miranda said.

I was surprised. "Really?"

She shrugged. "Why not? He's nice. And you like him."

I nodded, and heard the car horn, meaning Brian was in the driveway. Miranda ran out the back door, and I could hear the twins going out the front, shouting their goodbyes.

I sat down slowly. Lana jumped up on the stool beside me and made a very sympathetic noise.

I needed to do something immediately. Mitch was in Chicago. Patricia was in Paris. MarshaMarsha had left earlier for a football game. Even Lily was out, prowling the streets. I closed my eyes and thought of what would cheer me up.

Onion rings came to mind. New black woolen pants. And a chocolate milkshake. That meant Johnny Rockets and Nordstrom. I needed to go to the mall.

The Mall at Short Hills is a little out of the way for me, but that's what made it special, like going the extra mile for a really great restaurant. It was deserted when I got there, being dinnertime on a weeknight, but that was fine with me. I bought the pants first, along with a red silk blouse, three sweaters, and gray suede boots. I made my way slowly toward my dining destination, hitting all the hot spots—Crate and Barrel, Chico's, William Sonoma. I was trolling Restoration Hardware for a new shower curtain when I heard my name. I stopped and looked around. Who would know me way out here?

Ben Cutler was standing there, smiling at me, looking like heaven.

"Imagine my surprise, dear lady, finding you here," he said, raising one dark eyebrow. She stepped back with a gasp, recognizing him as the dark stranger who had so enflamed her with his kisses. Her eyes moved across his chiseled face, half in shadow, and she smiled slowly, feeling the heat rise in her breast.

"Mona? How are you?"

I opened my mouth to say something, and then completely different words came pouring out. "I'm miserable. Miranda is going to have her seventeenth birthday with her father instead of me, and I may have to buy out the mall to feel better, and I can't really afford to do that, and my feet hurt because I forgot to change my shoes, and I'm so hungry my blood sugar is dropping and I may eat my new boots."

He laughed. "Don't do that. Shoe leather is a proven carcinogenic. Why don't you let me buy you dinner, instead?"

"I was thinking onion rings and a milkshake."

He shook his head and took the shower curtain out of my hands. "No, we can do better than that. How about crab cakes and a nice martini?"

I suddenly felt funny, kind of wobbly inside. Maybe it was hunger pangs. "You don't have to do that, Ben. Honest."

"Don't be silly. I want to. Come on. Legal Seafood is right here."

So we ended up in a very nice, cool booth, and after a few sips of martini and a shrimp appetizer, I felt much better.

"So, I'm here for therapy. What are you shopping for?" I asked him.

He was nursing a beer, looking very un-plumber-like in a button-down shirt and corduroy jacket. "A client. She picked out some fixtures from the Restoration catalogue, but I wanted to see them in person before ordering them. She's been driving me crazy, but she's got big bucks and lots of friends, so I'm being good." He grinned. "I'm branching out. After doing your bathroom this summer, I found that I really enjoyed the planning and design part, so I'm expanding my scope. Not just plumbing. I'm tired of getting my hands dirty, and my back could use a break."

"Really? That's great, Ben. Does Patricia know? She could drop your name in the right places."

He shook his head. "No, I haven't seen her in a while."

"She's in France right now. Paris. When she gets back, I'll tell her. We'll keep you busy."

"Thanks. So, what's with Miranda?"

I sipped more martini. "Brian planned a party for her, and she said she didn't want to disappoint him, but I think she's excited because it's going to be at a fancy place, expensive, and she got to invite a bunch of friends, and frankly, I couldn't afford to do something like that for her, not this year anyway."

He frowned. "Money problems?"

I shook my head. "No, not really. But things aren't settled with Brian yet, the financial part, that is, so I'm not exactly sure how much discretionary income I've got."

He dipped some bread in the sauce from the garlic shrimp. "What's the hold-up with Brian?"

I shrugged. "It's bullshit, is what it is. We've been going back and forth over stupid stuff ever since that day last summer, remember, when he came to the house? He's just busting my chops because I pissed him off."

"The guy is a jerk."

"Yep." I smiled at Ben. It was nice to be able to just talk to someone, and extra nice when the someone looked as good as Ben.

The waitress came and set down our dishes. Ben had the crab cakes, while I opted for grilled sole. I looked at my plate appreciatively. "This looks fantastic. And see, a normal portion. Last time we ate together, I had enough food for the Russian Army."

He laughed. "I didn't hold it against you, honest. But I must say, for our second date, this is a much better setting."

Date? Did he say date? "So, we're on an official date again?"

He took a bite. "Sure. Why not? As long as you don't mind that I didn't bring flowers."

I shook my head. The fish was delicious. "No, I don't mind. But I don't put out for just grilled fish."

He raised his eyebrows. "What if I buy you dessert?"

I sighed dramatically. "Sorry."

He smiled, and I watched him take another bite of crab cake. God, he was handsome. His hands were long-fingered and strong looking, and his eyes flashed electric blue. I glanced around the restaurant, and sure enough, at least five women at other tables were looking at us. At him. I felt like jumping up and screaming, "Hey, he just said we're on a date, can you believe it?"

We were on a date. Were we really? No, not really. We just happened to meet and he was being nice to a frazzled woman who happened to be his client and sometime friend. But being in his company was soothing. He was someone you could lean on. I suddenly shook myself. Thinking of him as someone to lean on took my brain where it usually went when imagining actually touching him in any way, and that meant naked skin and lots of sweat. Not the appropriate thought process for a quiet dinner.

"What are you thinking?" he asked.

I almost choked on a snow pea. I'd been thinking that if he'd just lean back on that nice leather seat, I could climb on top of him and have enough room to do whatever I wanted without knocking into the table.

"Good sole. Looking forward to the holidays?"

He made a face. "David has already asked to spend Thanksgiving with his roommate, who lives up in Maine, and Ethan is going to be in Florida. Disney, actually. His school's marching band is doing the Magic Kingdom parade on Thanksgiving Day. It's a big deal, and he's so excited, but it'll be a bust for me. Christmas should be better. We all go to Vail and ski over Christmas week. It's a great time."

I personally hated skiing. I had tried it once or twice, and could not understand the attraction to a sport that required you to spend hours in the freezing cold in clothes that made you look puffed-up and frumpy. The après-ski part sounded like fun, though.

She sank back onto the bearskin rug, aware of the raging blizzard outside, closing her eyes as the warmth of the roaring fire reached her. Suddenly, she felt him move against her, his hands running beneath the thin cotton of her shift. She opened her eyes and saw him, half-smiling above her, and she reached up to grasp his hair and draw his head down.

Good Lord, there I went again.

When dinner was over, we wandered into the mall, went back to Restoration Hardware and had a very detailed discussion about polished chrome versus pewter, and then he walked me out into the parking lot and to my car. He held the car door open for me, and after I got in the car, he hunched down so we were face-to-face.

"It was really good seeing you again, Mona," he said. "You don't have to just wait for a pipe to burst to call me, you know. If you ever want to talk or grab some coffee, just give me a call."

I was so startled that my jaw dropped. "Okay," I sputtered.

He smiled, straightened, and slammed my door shut. When I got home, the girls were back and I felt much better about just about everything.

Chapter Twelve

Striking back against the Miranda Birthday Debacle, I invited my usual crowd for Thanksgiving—that is, Brian's mother Phyllis, Rebecca, MarshaTheBitch and her husband Frank, their three almost-adult children, Patricia, Anthony, and, of course, Lily. Brian did not make the cut, nor did Dominique. I could have been hugely disappointed, not to mention embarrassed, by the number of refusals, but as it turned out, only MarshaTheBitch declined, citing dinner with her husband Frank's family as the almost-plausible excuse. I also invited Mitch, but he was taking his parents to Vicki's. She was thinking about moving to Florida, and this might be the last time they would all be together for a while.

So I called Ben and asked if he'd like to join us. He said yes. He also offered to bring wine and pumpkin pie.

I had not spent much time talking to Brian's family the previous summer. Phyllis used to come down to the shore house for a week or two when the kids were younger, but had stayed in Brooklyn for the past few years and had not even mentioned visiting during the few conversations I had with her. Rebecca had called me several times over the past six months, but we hadn't seen each other since a quick lunch date in May, when she gave me a blow-by-blow description of her surprise party.

I was a little worried about the Phyllis/Lily situation. Phyllis, after her initial reaction to the separation and pending divorce, seemed to have settled back into her Brian-the-good-son groove. Lily had, if anything, become more virulent in her anti-Brian feelings. The potential for disaster was high. I hoped that the presence of Ben would put all the women in the room, not to mention Anthony, in a much more benevolent frame of mind.

Thursday morning, Rebecca arrived at eight. She did that every year. It was a tradition, along with the ready-to-bake homemade cinnamon rolls she brought with her. God knows how early she had to get up to make them and let them rise, but they were perfect, hot and moist and sweet, with a crunch of pecans. She knocked at the back door, hands full of baking pans, a very distinguished gentleman trailing in her wake.

"This is Julian," she announced, pulling off one of several scarves. "I hope you don't mind him coming. It was rather last minute, but you always have so much food."

"Not at all," I said, meaning it, although if I had known I'd be receiving strange male visitors this early, I'd have been lounging in my kitchen in something other than ratty sweatpants and a T-shirt sans bra.

We played kiss-kiss. I popped the pans in the oven and poured coffee.

Rebecca is very tall, with silver hair swept up in a simple twist, making her appear ever taller and very regal. She has hazel eyes and pale skin. She's quite beautiful, even with wrinkles and laugh lines. She dresses in a kind of rich-hippie style, long skirts and gauze blouses, with lots of silk scarves and real gold.

Julian was shorter, but had the same silver hair swept back off a high, handsome forehead. He looked like Clark Gable would have looked at seventy, without the mustache but with a small gold hoop earring. He sat at the kitchen counter while Rebecca and I caught up.

"How's the divorce?" she asked, sipping coffee.

I shrugged. "Brian had been giving me a hard time, then suddenly he agreed to everything. We now have a court date. January eighth."

Rebecca nodded knowingly. "Dominique started pushing."

I looked sharply at her. "How do you know?"

Rebecca looked smug. "It seems that Dominique and Marsha have become very close. My sister seems to think that any day now Dominique will convert and become a perfect Jewish wife. There's about as much a chance of that happening as pigs flying, but Marsha is hopeful. Marsha mentioned that Dominique got tired of waiting."

"Is she pregnant?" I asked.

Rebecca made a face. "Don't think so. I think Dominique knows that if she really wants to marry Brian, she'd better do it soon before somebody else catches his eye."

I looked at Rebecca in surprise. "What makes you say that?"

Rebecca sighed. "Brian is a man who has proven his unfaithfulness. You'd have to be pretty stupid to trust him now.

Dominique is many things, but not stupid." She smiled at Julian. "Are we boring you, dear?"

He smiled back. "Your company is never boring, Rebecca, and your family machinations never cease to amuse."

She beamed at me. "Isn't he marvelous? How are the girls?"

"I don't know. None of them are speaking to me."

"Really? All three at once? That's a rare occurrence, isn't it?"

I nodded. "Yes. There must be some sort of distortion in the space-time continuum, because usually only two of them are mad at me at the same time. All three is rather sinister. I'm thinking End of Days."

Rebecca patted my hand. "As far as I know, there are no unusual metaphysical forces at work. It must be plain bad luck for you."

I sighed. "Well, it's good to know, I suppose, that it's just my life, not the universe, that's in the toilet."

Rebecca laughed. "Start at the top. What's Miranda's problem?"

I sighed again. "The car. Brian said he would give her five thousand dollars towards a car. Now she wants me to give her five thousand. Can you believe it? Ten grand for a car? When she can walk to everything? So I told her no. She could take the money her father gave her and get something perfectly adequate. She doesn't need anything fancy. God, my first car was a 1963 maroon Comet that had one hundred thousand miles on it."

"And I'm sure it was just what you wanted," Rebecca said gently.

I glared at her. "No, of course it wasn't. I wanted a Datsun 240Z with a moon-roof."

"I loved those cars," Rebecca murmured.

"I had one," Julian said. "Black with red pinstripes."

The house was starting to smell of sugar, which should have put me in a happy place, but I was on a roll. "Lauren has become a vegetarian. Just last week, in fact. She wanted me to make Tofurkey for today."

Julian looked puzzled. "Tofurkey? Is that a real word?"

"Yes," Rebecca said. "It's tofu pressed into the shape of a turkey, seasoned with herbs, and baked. It's supposed to be quite good, and tastes just like real turkey."

I snorted. "Rebecca, you know I love you, but that's a crock of shit. Nothing tastes like real turkey except real turkey. So she's in a snit and wailing that she's going to starve. We're having sweet potatoes, mashed potatoes, carrots, creamed onions, green bean casserole, roasted Brussels sprouts, stuffing, and two kinds of rolls besides the bird. And four different pies for dessert. I somehow think she'll find something else to eat."

Rebecca nodded in agreement. "And Jessica?"

"A tattoo."

"To be expected."

"Yes. And seriously, I wouldn't mind something small, like a Chinese character or a musical note."

"But?"

I sighed. "She wants this shoulder to elbow thing, all swirls and colors, and it will cost a fortune besides being something I know she'll regret if she ever decides to get married and wear a chic sleeveless dress."

Rebecca gave me a look. "Because we all know how likely it is that Jess will wear a chic sleeveless dress. Or even get married."

Lily swept into the kitchen. "Good morning, Rebecca. Lovely to see you." She gave Rebecca a kiss and Julian a hard look. "Is this the new beau? He was at Miranda's little fete, I'm told." She held out her hand. "Lily Martel."

Julian stood up and kissed her hand. "Julian Fitzpatrick. At your service."

Lily raised her eyebrows. "Oh my. Rebecca, I always knew you were the only one in that family with any class."

"Aunt Lily," I began, but she waved me off.

"Not to worry, Mona. I'm on best behavior today, promise. After all, it's not Phyllis's fault her son is an unmitigated jackass. Are those your famous rolls I smell, Rebecca?"

"Yes. About another ten minutes and they'll be ready. You're looking well, Lily."

"Thank you. I'm feeling quite good these days. Blue algae is the secret. I take it twice a day. Cleans out the system. Of course, your poop is bright blue, but well worth it. Mona is not a believer, but I think the girls are coming around."

Rebecca smiled. "Did you mention the blue poop to them?"

Lily shook her head.

"Well...." Rebecca said slowly.

Lily brightened. "Excellent idea. I'm sure that will do the trick. Can I help you with anything right now, Mona?"

I shook my head. "Nope. Good here. I'll call the girls in a bit."

"Excellent." She had poured herself some coffee and headed for the den. "Oh, I meant to ask, is Mitch coming?"

I shook my head. "No. Couldn't make it. But I asked Ben."

She stopped in the doorway to the den and gave me a sly smile. "Oh, how lovely. Do you think he'll take off his shirt?"

I almost dropped the carton of eggs I was taking out of the fridge. "No, I don't think so. But don't ask him, please?"

She looked sorrowful and disappeared into the den.

Rebecca had found a bowl and was cracking eggs into it. "Mitch? And Ben?"

"Mitch is the man I've been seeing," I explained, putting the frying pan on the stove to heat up. "About four months now. He's really nice, and the girls seem to like him."

"Is it love?"

"Not at all."

"Sleeping with him?"

"As often as I can."

"Good girl. Is he the rebound guy?"

I chuckled to myself and thought about Doug. "No, I had one of those. Mitch is the alternative relationship guy. You know, the-dipping-the-toe-in-the-water guy. For now it's good, but who knows how long it will last."

"And Ben?"

I pulled the rolls out of the oven and set them on the counter to cool. "Ben is my plumber. He's divorced, and his sons are away, so I thought it would be nice for him to be around people instead of all by himself."

Rebecca glanced over at me as she whisked the eggs. "Is he the same plumber who's really good looking with the hot body I've been hearing about all these years?"

"Yep."

"Sounds yummy. Is the table set?"

"Yes, but could you get the juice? I'll start the eggs in a minute." I went into the hall and yelled up to the girls, and the day began.

~

You'd think the hours between hot cinnamon rolls and scrambled eggs and the actual sitting down to turkey dinner would drag, but they don't. Rebecca and I can talk for hours, the girls sit and watch parades with Aunt Lily, and there's all that food to get ready. Around noon, the bird had already been stuffed and put in the oven. Patricia arrived, apple pie in one hand, a bottle of my favorite port and a huge bouquet of flowers in the other. She greeted everyone, dazzled Julian with a smile, mixed herself a martini, and supervised the setting of the table. She pulled glasses and bowls out of my breakfront that I forgot I even had, arranged the flowers beautifully, and started on her second drink. Rebecca watched the same way she always did when around Patricia: in utter amazement.

Anthony arrived a short while later, with cherry pie and Brie wrapped in pastry.

"We'll pop it in the oven for about twenty minutes," he said, "so we'll have a little something to nosh." Victor was with him, Victor of the beautiful yoga body and air of serene wisdom. Anthony gave him a tour, introduced him around, parked him with Lily and the girls, and came back into the kitchen frowning.

"Why is there an extra place at the table? I thought Mitch couldn't come."

"He can't," I explained. "But I invited Ben."

His face dropped. "Ben? Ben is coming here?"

Patricia, sensing a crisis, swooped in.

"Why did you invite Ben?" Anthony hissed.

I'd been trimming the Brussels sprouts, using a very sharp knife to remove the little stems and make a tiny slit in the tough end. "I invited Ben because I ran into him and he told me he'd always had a mad crush on you, and he wished he could spend a little time with you so he could ask you out. Too bad you brought Victor."

Anthony clutched the front of his cashmere pullover. "Oh, God, no."

"No," Patricia said firmly. "She ran into him, he told her he'd be alone, and she made a very friendly gesture by inviting him here."

Anthony was breathing heavily. "I could pretend to get really sick, have Victor take me home, then come back here by myself. What time is dinner? When did Ben say he'd be here?"

"Anthony," Patricia said, raising her voice. "Think a minute. Do you really imagine, even for a split second, that if Victor weren't here, Ben would suddenly look at you, give up a lifetime of women, and ravish you on the dinner table?"

"On the dinner table? Oh, God, would he really?" Anthony's voice cracked as he slumped against the counter. "I can't breathe."

I was trying so hard not to laugh that I could barely speak. "Anthony, I invited him after we had dinner together. And I never mentioned that you'd be here. Honest."

He straightened up and narrowed his eyes at me. "You two had dinner?"

"A few weeks ago."

"Why didn't you tell me?"

"Because when I mention his name, you get apoplectic, that's why. Calm down. We'll all have something really nice to look at besides Patricia's centerpiece and my turkey. The Brie should be ready now. Why don't you take it around?"

Anthony got his breathing under control, gave me a hard look, and grabbed the Brie.

Patricia also gave me a hard look. "You shouldn't do that to him," she chided.

"I know. I just can't help it."

"How are you cooking these?" she asked, nodding at the sprouts.

"Just salt, pepper, and oil in a hot oven; why?"

"Toss them with some balsamic. And pancetta if you've got it. Trust me. Why did you really invite Ben?"

"God, Patricia, why do you think? The man's beautiful."

"What about Mitch?"

"Nothing about Mitch. Mitch couldn't come. This has nothing to do with Mitch."

"If Mitch were coming, would you have invited Ben?"

I had to think about that one. "Probably not. But Mitch knows I invited Ben."

"Does Mitch know how good looking Ben is?"

"No. They haven't met."

Patricia raised an eyebrow. "Is this getting complicated?"

"No." I said firmly. I heard a car beep in the drive, and turned to yell. "Girls, Grandma's here."

I suddenly got choked up.

I had not seen Phyllis since before Brian left, and hearing the horn brought back twenty years of memories, most of them good. I loved Phyllis, not just because she'd been my mother-in-law, but because she was a warm, caring person who loved me and my daughters and had been very good to all of us. I suddenly ached to see her, so I ran to the door, threw it open, and swept Phyllis into my arms. She was shaking, crying a little, and we held each other for a long time until she finally pulled away, wiping tears turned black from mascara.

"Oh, Mona, it's so good to see you. I've missed you. You look wonderful, and your hair! It's so short! The girls told me, of course, put I couldn't picture it." She looked past me. "Miranda! Sweet girls, give me a kiss!" I watched, feeling a warm glow settle over me that was soon dashed by a cold voice in my left ear.

"Hello, Mona."

I turned. It was MarshaTheBitch.

My other sister-in-law is short, like Phyllis, curvy, with light brown hair and blue eyes, also like Phyllis. MarshaThe-Bitch wears her hair in a very short curly perm and is always perfectly made up, just like Phyllis. But MarshaTheBitch wears an expression on her face that looks like she just got a whiff of something unpleasant—not a sneer, exactly, but a slight curling of the upper lip. She had that expression on her face now, only more so, because although I knew she was intensely relieved that her brother was finally going to be rid of me, we were still technically family, and she still really didn't like me.

Which was fine, because I really didn't like her either.

"Marsha, what a surprise. Really. Because you told me you wouldn't be here."

She looked aggrieved. "Mom had a migraine all day yesterday, and didn't feel well enough to drive. I invited her to come to Frank's folks, but she insisted on coming here instead. So I sent Frank off with the kids, and agreed to bring her here. I hope you have enough food."

Perfect. My least favorite person in the world would be spending the day in my house. Not only would I have to be nice to her for the sake of the kids, but I'd have to be grateful that she'd brought Phyllis.

Phyllis tugged at my sleeve as MarshaTheBitch swept past. "I hope you don't mind, Mona, but I really couldn't drive, and if she hadn't come, I would have had to eat at Frank's family's house, and I don't think I could have stood it."

Having met Frank's parents on several occasions, I couldn't blame her. They were just like him, only ten times worse: pompous, boring, and totally devoid of a sense of humor.

"Of course I don't mind," I said. "It's worth it to have you here. Did you bring pie?"

She nodded and dived into the trunk of her car, bringing forth her specialty, the best pecan pie you'll ever taste in your life.

We went back into the kitchen, which now seemed very crowded, so I loudly suggested we take the Brie and some wine into the living room. Everyone filed out, but Anthony stayed behind, arranging more crackers on a dish. He looked up at me slyly.

"I'm sure Marsha will be quite interested to meet Ben," he said.

I closed my eyes. He was right. She'd never leave him alone. She'd assume he was with me and pump him ceaselessly for information. I didn't want to put him through all that. I wouldn't want to put anyone through all that.

"Ben can be Patricia's date," I said, suddenly inspired.

"Does he know that?" Anthony asked.

"No, of course not. I just now thought it up."

"Well, make sure you tell him," Anthony said. "And you might want to let Patricia know."

"Send her back here," I hissed as he went towards the living room.

I stood in the middle of the kitchen and took deep, cleansing breaths. Lily wandered in.

"I heard a commotion. Is Phyllis here?"

"Yes, Aunt Lily. And Marsha is with her."

Lily's eyes went cold. "MarshaTheBitch is here?"

"Yes. Listen. I need a huge favor. We need to make her think that Ben is Patricia's date. Otherwise, she'll assume he's with me and the entire day could get ugly."

"Very ugly," Lily murmured. "Not to worry dear, I can handle this."

"Handle what?" Patricia asked, coming in and looking concerned.

"Patricia, when Ben gets here, can he be your date? Please?"

"MarshaTheBitch?" Patricia asked. She's very quick on the uptake.

I nodded.

"Of course, Mona. Rather ridiculous, but I understand perfectly. What else can I do?"

"Get her drunk?"

Patricia beamed. "No problem." She and Lily went out. I turned, grabbed the phone, and called Mitch's cell phone.

He answered on the second ring.

"Mitch? Mona. Just wanted to hear your voice."

"What's wrong?"

"Are we playing the 'Who's Having a Worse Thanksgiving' game?"

He chuckled. "I wasn't planning to, but it sounds like fun. You first."

"My sister-in-law Marsha showed up."

"MarshaTheBitch?"

"Yep. Your turn."

"Vicki's new boyfriend is a twenty-six-year-old golf pro."

"That must be comfortable."

"Oh, yes. But I think you're ahead right now."

"Maybe. I'll talk to you later."

I took another deep breath, grabbed wine and some glasses, and strode into the living room.

Rebecca and Patricia had MarshaTheBitch surrounded on the couch. Anthony was making Phyllis laugh. Victor and Julian, the two relative outsiders, were apparently bonding over Fred, who was sitting between their two club chairs, getting his ears scratched and in obvious doggy heaven. Lily had taken over Brie duty and was making the rounds. Pure holiday bliss.

"Wine?" I asked.

Victor waved, so I headed straight over.

"How are you guys doing?" I murmured as I poured.

"Julian is a witch," Victor said excitedly. "He was just telling me all about it."

"Are you sure it's not warlock?" I said, puzzled. Julian rolled his eyes, so I left them.

I set the wine and remaining glasses down in front of the couch. MarshaTheBitch, holding a very full martini glass, looked annoyed.

"I've already got a drink, Mona," she pointed out.

"True, Marsha, but there are other people in the room," I reminded her, smiling. "Maybe someone else is thirsty."

She narrowed her eyes at me. "So, Mona, tell me what's new in your life. Your hair looks great, by the way. Why didn't you cut it years ago? You look much younger."

"Brian liked my hair long," I told her.

"Oh. Yes, he would. What else? We haven't spoken in ages."

How cute. She was being social. Probably for Phyllis's sake.

"Ah, well." I sat down across from her. "Actually, some good things have been happening. I'm going to teach an online class next year. Through the Gotham Writers' Workshop. They approached me a few weeks ago, and we're working out a class outline. I've never done any kind of teaching before. It should be a lot of fun and very rewarding."

"That's marvelous, Mona," Phyllis said, coming over to perch on the arm of my chair. "I've always wanted a teacher in the family. Not that you'll officially be the family anymore, but still. How nice."

She was getting a little misty again, so I hurried along. "I'm also going to put my name up to be on the Board of Directors of the RWA. The Romance Writers of America. It would be quite an honor to be elected, and a big responsibility."

MarshaTheBitch puckered her lips. "Haven't you been a member of that group for years? Why have you suddenly decided to become so involved? Are they running out of qualified people?"

I felt a burning behind my eyes. "Actually, it's something I always wanted to become involved in, but Brian didn't want me to spend all the time and energy needed to do a good job."

Anthony was hovering. I could tell he had his hackles up. "Not only that, Mona may be going on an extensive tour with the new book," he said. "Her editor loved it so much there were hardly any revisions. They'll be releasing it next fall, and if they go with hardcover, Mona will be on the road, all the major cities, signings and everything. That's something else that Brian never wanted her to do."

MarshaTheBitch set her glass down on the coffee table. "Well, Mona, it seems that your career has taken quite an upturn since Brian left." She sniffed.

There was a sudden silence. Phyllis cleared her throat. "Just what is the new book about, Mona?" she asked.

I looked steadily at MarshaTheBitch. "It's about a woman who gets dumped by her husband and turns around and has a much better life without him," I said loudly.

Phyllis blinked. "Oh."

Patricia turned to MarshaTheBitch with a brilliant smile. "Another martini? I know I could use one."

I followed Patricia into the kitchen. She put her hands on my shoulders and gave me a shake. "That woman means nothing to you anymore, Mona," she said slowly. "Leave her to me and Lily. Really."

I nodded. I checked the turkey. He, or she, was done, so I pulled out the pan and set it on the counter. I checked all the other pots and baking dishes. Everything seemed to be moving ahead. Patricia had mixed another pitcher of martinis.

"I'll take one now," I told her.

She tilted her head at me. "I know you deserve one, but are you sure?"

I nodded. "The bird is cooked and everything else looks good. Even if I pass out, dinner will be a success."

She nodded, found a glass, and poured. The first sip hit me like it always did. When I got to the third, I was in heaven.

There was a knock on the door. Patricia went to answer it.

"Ben, thank God," she said. "I need to explain something for just a sec." She closed the door behind her.

The fourth sip was not so much a sip as a long gulp. I closed my eyes to savor the moment.

"Mona?"

It was Rebecca. I opened my eyes and she was looking concerned. "Are you okay? Marsha is impossible. I'm sorry."

I smiled. "I'm fine. Honestly."

She was looking at the pitcher of martinis. "I've always wanted to try one of these," she said.

"Well, you can't get much better than Patricia's. You're not driving, are you?"

Rebecca shook her head. I poured her a glass, adding olives. She took a taste, and her eyes opened wide.

"Oh, my goodness," she said.

"I know."

Patricia came back in carrying a pumpkin pie in front of her like Donna Reed. "Ben made this himself, isn't he marvelous? He's bringing in the wine. We're all set. Rebecca, I don't know what you've heard about Ben, but for today he's my date, so keep your hands to yourself." She set the pie down and turned towards the den. "I'll let the girls know what's going on."

Then Ben came in, two bottles of wine in each arm. The cold had brought high color to his cheeks, and his eyes spar-

kled. He was wearing a black V-neck sweater and black corduroy pants. I felt a momentary rush of blood to my head.

*She was caught up in the heat of his hands and the sweetness
of his lips. She reached blindly, tugging at the linen of his shirt,
hungry for the feel of his skin against hers, and his lips moved
down her throat, searing her silken skin like a brand.*

"Rebecca, this is Ben Cutler. Ben, this is my sister-in-law,
Rebecca Berman."

Ben put down the bottles and shook her hand. "Are you
Glinda?" he asked.

Rebecca giggled. "You've been listening to Anthony,
haven't you?" she gushed.

He chuckled and turned to me. "Hello, Mona. Thanks
again so much for asking me here today. Do you really
want me to pretend to be Patricia's date? Isn't that a little
extreme?"

"Wait until you meet my sister," Rebecca said. "Then
you'll understand."

Ben smiled. "Mona, for you, anything." Then he leaned
over and kissed me on the cheek.

Now, my imaginary kisses with Ben usually involved lots
of skin and plenty of tongue, but it was still pretty special.
Patricia came in, slipped her hand through his arm, and
made a silly face.

"I can't believe you, Ben. I turn my back for one minute and you're flirting with the hostess. Come on through,
I'll introduce you." She snagged the pitcher with the other
hand and was gone.

Rebecca and I drank thoughtfully for a few moments.

"Well, he certainly is spectacular," she said at last.

"Yes, he is."

"I don't suppose he's a conceited prick?"

I shook my head. "No, he's very nice. Thoughtful. I can really talk to him, but not for too long."

"Oh? Why not?"

"My imagination starts to get the best of me and I start having concentration issues."

"Yes. Well I can see that happening. Patricia is a very good friend to put herself out like that. She'll probably have to be hanging onto him all day."

"She's a real gem. I'm lucky to have her." I reached over and patted Rebecca's hand. "And I'm glad we're still friends. I've missed you."

"Yes. I've missed you too. In fact, I don't know why I've stayed away so long. I've always liked you much better than I liked Brian."

Rebecca picked up her glass and wandered towards the living room. I yelled for Lauren. She came out of the den, her eyes glazed over from too many parades.

"I know you're still not speaking to me, but it's turkey watch time. You get the first shift."

She groaned. "Mom, come on. Why do we have to guard the stupid turkey?"

"Every year we watch *A Christmas Story*. Last year you saw it six times."

"So?"

"So, you know what happened to the turkey. When the mother set it on the table to cool?"

"Mom, do you really think a pack of animals is going to break into the house and eat the turkey?"

"We don't need a break-in. We have a pack of animals that live here."

She shrugged. "Okay. Mom?"

"Yes?"

"Why did Patricia say we should pretend Ben's her boyfriend?"

"Would you want Ben to be your boyfriend?"

She thought for a moment. "Well, he's kinda old, but yes."

"All right, then. Let the woman dream. We'll be eating in half an hour. Get your sisters in here to help."

I picked up the phone and dialed Mitch again.

"Ben and Patricia are pretending to be a couple so that MarshaTheBitch won't think he's my, well, you know."

"Does she know I'm your 'you know'?"

"No. Your very existence is a carefully guarded secret from all of Brian's family. Except Rebecca. Who thinks it's a good idea."

"Vicki is planning to deep-fry the turkey."

"That's supposed to be delicious."

"She bought fifty gallons of olive oil."

"That will taste awful."

"Probably."

"And doesn't olive oil have a lower flash point? Couldn't it catch fire?"

"I've already alerted the fire department."

"I still think I'm ahead."

"Yes, but the day is still young."

"I miss you."

"Me too. Got to go."

I hung up. The turkey looked perfect. Lauren was chasing Jane and Olivia out of the kitchen with a broom.

Good girl. I could hear Anthony's voice, telling a joke. Good boy. I straightened my shoulders and headed back to the living room.

It was a happy Thanksgiving after all.

~

The Monday after Thanksgiving, Mitch went out to California for a whole week. When he returned we had a very cozy reunion, complete with Brie, crackers, and champagne, all consumed naked. I was getting dressed, thinking about how cold it was getting and how I was going to hate driving home in the dark, when he told me that he was planning to return to California in a few weeks.

"But you just came back," I pointed out, pulling on a sock.

"Yeah. Well."

Something in his tone made me look at him hard. "What?"

"I was looking at an art gallery."

I frowned. "Really? I didn't know you were interested in art."

His eyes lit up. "It's not just art. It's animation art. Sericells, sketches, everything I've been selling on my website. I went out to check things over, and the place is fantastic. In La Jolla. It would be a terrific opportunity. I mean, it's the next step for me if I want to continue doing this."

I was getting a hollow feeling in the pit of my stomach. I knew how much he loved animation art, and I knew he was starting to lose patience with his retail stores.

"So, if you buy the gallery, would you run it?"

He nodded. "Yes. I'd really want to be hands-on."

"Ah. So I suppose that would mean you're actually moving there? To California? Unless you can afford your own commuter jet?"

He put his arms around me. "I'd be moving there, yes," he said softly.

"What about the stores?" I asked, pulling back to look at him.

"There's a buyer. The same guy has been after me for a couple of years now. It would be easy." He was looking very serious. "Do you love me, Mona?"

"No." The word came out before I could even think about it.

"I know. I'm not in love with you either. I like you a hell of a lot, and I'd miss you like crazy, but I don't think you and I are in a position where I'd ask you to move out there with me."

I shook my head. "No. And I wouldn't ask you to pass this by just because of me."

We sat there for a few seconds, sitting at the edge of his rumpled bed.

"We'll see how things go when I go back," he said at last. "Nothing has been decided. I have to see about financing, for one thing. It could all be a bust, and I stay right where I am."

I nodded. "True. And we could just keep on going just as we are," I said, but I knew that wouldn't be exactly the case. The summer romance was finally winding down. If he didn't go to California, there would eventually come a time when we would have to move forward, and it seemed that neither of us was in a place to do that.

~

The girls spent Christmas Eve with Brian. I spent it with Mitch. I bought him an antique Mickey Mouse watch. He bought me the complete Cary Grant film collection on DVD and an antique pendant, a single pearl with three tiny rubies. It was beautiful.

Christmas Day was quiet. We all woke up early, opened presents, ate Lily's blueberry pancakes and spent the day toasting marshmallows and watching Christmas movies. The day after Christmas, Mitch went back out to California. He stayed three days. He stopped by the house on the way in from the airport to tell me how it went, but he didn't need to say a word. I could tell by the way his face was lit up.

"You bought the gallery."

He nodded. We were standing in the foyer. He hadn't even taken off his coat.

I felt a huge lump in my throat. "When are you leaving?"

"I'm going back next week to look for an apartment, then again the beginning of February." He looked so happy. "Vicki is moving into the Chatham house with her boys, instead of going to Florida, so I don't have to worry about trying to sell in this market. The buyer for the stores should be ready March first, and then I'm out of here." He put his arms around me. "Mona, I'm so sorry to end this. We had such a great time."

Now the lump was in my stomach. "I know. I'm going to miss you. Who's going to make me laugh when you're gone?"

"Are you kidding? You'll probably meet Mr. Perfect walking out of the courtroom the day your divorce is final."

"I doubt it, but thanks for the thought. I hope you find somebody great in California."

He kissed me. "I hope I find somebody with real boobs in California."

I stepped back from him and took a deep breath. "Good luck, Mitch. And thank you for being exactly what I needed."

And then he was gone.

~

The day before Divorce Day, I went to David West's office, where I signed some papers and he walked me through everything that would happen in court the following day. I was feeling depressed and just a little frail. Mitch had left for California that morning. He'd be back by tomorrow night, but too late for me to see him. I had promised to call him as soon as I was out of court.

When I got back home I decided it would not be good to sit around and mope all afternoon, so I pulled on sweats and walked into town for a yoga class. I walked back a little slower, muscles aching. I was sitting at my kitchen counter, trying to decide between herbal tea and Absolut, when Brian came through the kitchen door.

I had not seen him since the summer, and he looked like hell. The lines around his mouth were harsher, more deeply drawn, and he was thin and tired-looking.

"You can't do that anymore, Brian," I said.

"What are you talking about?" he growled.

"I know that officially we're still a team until tomorrow, but this is pretty much my house now. You can't just walk in. Next time, knock. If it's a problem, just let me know. I'll have the locks changed."

He was frowning. "I'm sorry. I just—" He ran his hand through his hair. "Can I talk to you, please?"

I shrugged. "Sure. Tea?"

He shook his head. "No. Thank you. I think we made a mistake."

"We? Who we?"

"You and I we."

"What mistake?"

"Well, I think it's a mistake to get a divorce."

I stared at him. "What?"

He cleared his throat. "I think it will be a mistake going through with this divorce."

I shook my head to clear it. "Brian, wait a minute. There was no 'we' getting a divorce. It was you. All you. In fact, you sat in this very kitchen and said, '*I* want a divorce.'"

"Well, that may be. But you certainly didn't fight it."

I took a deep breath. "You moved out. Into a condo you had bought months previously with another woman. You sent me a settlement proposal the next day. You refused to see me, or even talk to me, except about the girls. How was I supposed to be fighting? And for what?"

He looked into my eyes. "Okay, Mona, then I made the mistake. Is that what you want to hear? Huh? I made a mistake."

My mouth dropped open. I had never heard those words come out of his mouth before.

He looked uncomfortable. "So, I'm admitting to you that I was wrong. Now, I know things are almost final, but I'm asking to come home. We can still call the whole thing off. It was crazy, but it's over now, and I'm ready to come back."

I sat down. Hard. "What did you say?" I whispered.

"I'm ready to come back, Mona, in spite of everything."

I couldn't breathe. "You're ready to come back. Here."

"Yes. And although I realize that while we were apart, you may have, well, been involved with other men, that's water under the bridge now. I'm ready to go forward again with our marriage."

I stood back up and leaned toward him. "And whatever makes you think I'd ever want you back?"

It was his turn to look stunned. "What?"

"You were a crappy husband the first time around, Brian. Why would I want to put myself through all that again?"

"But, but—" He threw his hands up in the air. "We were happy."

"You were happy. I thought I was happy because I was clueless. I didn't know any better. I thought every marriage was about one person doing all the work and the other person getting all the benefits. Do you know, Brian, the whole time you've been gone, I've never thought, gee, I wish Brian were here, so he could do this for me. Or that for me. Or anything for me. You know why? Because you never did anything for me when you were here. I never felt overwhelmed or unable to cope after you'd gone because I always did everything myself anyway. What the hell did I ever need you for? What did you ever do for me? What did you ever give me? Sex? Sure, but guess what, buddy, there's plenty of that around. Why would I ever need you back in my life?"

"We had a good marriage," he sputtered.

"You had a good marriage. I was in servitude."

"Mona, don't you love me anymore?"

.No, Brian, I don't think I do." Once I said it, I was a little surprised at myself. But only for a moment, because I knew it was true.

But Brian was fighting back hard. "Did you ever love me?"

"How can you ask me that?" I whispered. "I loved you with all my heart." I felt the blood begin to boil in my ears. "I loved you so much that I did everything you asked, and never questioned a thing. I took care of you and your children and your house and your life and I never complained or asked you to help me because I loved you. I never so much as kissed another man our entire marriage because I loved you. The real question here is did you ever love me?"

He came toward me, his arms open. "Mona, of course."

I took a step away. "Then how could you buy a house with another woman and leave me and your family?"

That seemed to stop him. "I can't explain it," he said at last. "Dominique was like a drug. She just got to me and I couldn't say no to her. It was an aberration. I swear it will never happen again."

I looked at him hard. "I'd have an easier time believing that if Dominique was the first, rather than the latest."

An ugly look crossed his face. "That skunk Doug," he growled. "He told you, didn't he?"

"Yes, Brian, he did. And you know why? Because he said that you would want to come back to me, and he wanted me to know exactly the kind of man you were so that when you did try to come back, I'd say no." I took a deep breath. "So that's what I'm saying. No. Please leave now."

"Mona—"

"I mean it. Leave. Right now. It's over. Completely."

He stared. Then he turned and walked out the door.

I sat there in the empty kitchen. We'd been married twenty years. We had three beautiful daughters. Last year, we had spent New Year's Day with our old picture atlas, picking out exotic places we might retire to. By tomorrow, it would all be over. Suddenly, finally, all the anger was gone. All that was left was the sadness.

CHAPTER THIRTEEN

January, in general, is a good month for me. Here in northern New Jersey, winter settles in for good in January. It's not the teasing, damp winter of Thanksgiving, or the maybe-you'll-get-a-white-Christmas winter of December, but the real thing: cold, crisp, lots of potential for snow. The girls and I spend lots of time watching the Weather Channel in January, praying for snow days.

I have lots of leisure time in January, time I spend looking through foreign travel magazines, especially the English ones, reading articles like "Schlepping through Skye" or "Cavorting in Cornwall." Mainly, I love to look at all the tweed, and fantasize about long, rambling walks in the crisp European air.

The food is always great in January, too. With the holiday cooking frenzy behind me, I bake lots of things with cinnamon and raisins in them. I start pulling out recipes for hearty stews and pot pies. I eat apple crumble and roasted squash, and drink gallons of hot spiced cider.

Best of all, January is about new beginnings. I'm a resolution person. I make a New Year's Resolution every year, and I really try to stick to it. I'm very reasonable about my resolutions. Last year, I resolved to learn to make a perfect piecrust. The year before that, I learned to say all my housekeeping requests in perfect Spanish. This year, I resolved to sign my name as Mona Quincy without giving it a second thought.

All in all, any day in January is a good one. But the day I divorced my husband Brian after he left me for someone fifteen years younger and thirty pounds lighter, was the best.

The morning began with no fighting, no wardrobe issues, no last-minute demands. Jessica came down for breakfast with a mohawk. She had gotten this haircut four days previously to show her new boyfriend that even though they were too young to be legally committed to each other, there were other ways of showing undying love and devotion, and since he had a mohawk, she'd get one too. The good thing about that particular morning was that when she came downstairs and I saw her, I didn't jump three feet into the air and scream in fright.

She came over to me and put her hand on my shoulder. "I'll get a ride home from school today, in case you want to, you know, get drunk after court. Okay?"

I nodded and tried not to tear up.

Lauren was next. She gave me a small kiss and a big hug. "Mom, I know this is going to be a strange day for you. Just know that I love you and think you're the best mom in the world." Then she grabbed a Pop-Tart and went out the door, leaving me tearful and elated.

Finally, Miranda came down. "I'm working after school today, babysitting at the Fosters," she said.

"I know."

"But I'll be thinking about you."

"Thanks."

"I love you, Mom."

That started the tears again.

Divorce is not a private affair. We sat in the courtroom along with several other couples awaiting dissolution. I noticed that Dominique had slipped in and was sitting in the back row. Brian must have neglected to tell her about his last-minute change of heart. When our docket number was called and we were going up to the front of the courtroom, I turned to sneak a look at her again and found that Patricia, arriving late and wearing a fabulous fur coat the exact color of old gold, had managed to sit directly in front of her. Patricia, much taller, waved happily.

So I stood in a courtroom and legally stopped being Mona Berman and became Mona Quincy again. Brian looked grim. Hirsch Fielding looked exactly like the jerk I imagined. David West was cool, comforting, and smugly satisfied. The lawyers talked, the judge talked, we answered questions, signed some things, and that was that. Then Patricia took me out to lunch.

When I got home, Ben Cutler's truck was parked on the street in front of my house. Aunt Lily was supposed to be at the library taking a class in something that I hoped wasn't bomb-building. As I came in the kitchen door, I saw Ben leaning against the counter.

He gave her a long, cool look. "I don't like to be kept waiting, madam." She smiled slowly and pulled loose the ribbons at her throat. Her cloak fell to the floor, and she stood naked in the candlelight. "I'll try to make it up to you," she said, walking towards him and watching his eyes widen with pleasure.

"Hey," I said. "What's up? Did something burst while I was gone?"

He shook his head. "Nope. Lily let me in before she left. I was just, you know, in the neighborhood, and knew today was the big day, so I figured I'd see how you were doing."

He was not in his usual plumber clothes. He was wearing a thick turtleneck sweater over his jeans, which were clean and pressed. He looked magnificent. The early afternoon sun was shining softly through his dark hair, there was just a suggestion of stubble on his perfect jaw, and his eyes were wide and twinkling.

"Can I get you some coffee?" I asked, shrugging out of my jacket.

I turned and he was right behind me. He grabbed me and pulled me to him, and he kissed me. Right on the lips.

It was the most astonishing kiss I'd ever received.

In my whole life.

Really.

It left me speechless.

And breathless.

When I finally pulled away, my entire body was quivering. Like a tightly strung harp string that had just been plucked. I stared up at him. I tried to form words but only managed "Whaa…?"

"I've wanted to do that forever," he said. "I'm crazy about you, Mona, and I could never do a thing about it. But you're a single woman now, and I want you to know how serious I am."

Holy shit.

"Serious?" I croaked.

"Yes. Listen, we've been spending more time together the past few months, and I was hoping you'd start feeling a little differently towards me. You know, like maybe I could actually be somebody important in your life."

I felt lightheaded. Maybe it was the kiss. I gotta tell you, it was something. "I need to sit," I gasped. He propelled me to a kitchen chair, sat me down, pushed my head down, and rubbed my back while I took long, deep breaths. When the world steadied itself, I opened my eyes. Ben was crouched down in front of me, his gorgeous eyes filled with concern.

"Better?" he asked gently.

I nodded, and he brushed the hair away from my face.

"Water?"

"No. I'm good." I took another long breath. There. That was better. What had he just said?

I squinted at him. "What did you just say?"

"That I wanted to be a part of your life."

"Oh. That's what I thought you said."

It was kind of funny, actually, that he wanted to be part of my life-life, since he'd been part of my fantasy life for just about as long as I'd known him. I'd given him all kinds of thought. Like what he looked like naked. How he'd look dangling grapes over my mouth. If he might be into licking ice cream off my stomach. If he liked to spoon after sex. If he'd prefer being on the top or on the bottom. And now, here was Ben, offering me the chance to answer all those questions and more. Ben the Kind. Ben the Thoughtful. Ben the Unbelievably Handsome. Ben who, now that I was single and he was obviously willing, I could take to bed and keep there as long as I wanted.

I looked at him. I opened my mouth to say something, but I could find no words.

"I know you've been seeing somebody else," he said gently.

My brain completely froze. Somebody else? Yes, of course there had been somebody else. Somebody sweet and thoughtful who made me laugh. Tall. Dark hair. Cute mole on his left nipple. What was his name again?

"Mitch," I blurted.

"That's his name?"

I cleared my throat. "Yes

Ben was frowning. "Is it serious?"

"Actually, we broke it off. He bought an art gallery in California. He's leaving. We weren't in love, so I'm not heartbroken or anything. I miss him, but he's gone."

"Good. I mean, I'm sorry you miss him, but maybe you can think about a future with me."

"A future?" I looked at him. "This is really weird."

"Mona, no it's not. Think about us. Think about how we are together."

I shut my eyes. Okay. Ben with clothes. Ben sitting in my kitchen. Drinking coffee. We could talk about everything. We *had* talked about everything. Our kids. My writing. We laughed together all the time. We'd even been on an actual date or two, and that felt fine. On Thanksgiving, he had been an absolute trouper. In fact, he had been such a doting companion to Patricia that I had to keep reminding myself it was all a charade.

"We're pretty good friends," I admitted, opening my eyes.

"Yes, Mona. We're very good friends. Is there a problem with us being more than friends?"

I had to think about that. "Yes," I said finally. "The problem is sex."

He opened his mouth to speak, stopped himself, and then started again. "We've never had sex, Mona."

"Well, yes," I said carefully. "That is literally true, but I've sort of been having sex with you in an abstract way for some time now. Years, actually. Sometimes in my head. Often, really, in my head. A lot in my books. You're one of my most repeated male characters, and you wouldn't believe the things you've done."

He had been looking at me, but shifted his eyes to the right. I could practically hear all the gears in his brain going round.

"Are you going to tell me about them," he said at last, "or should I just start reading?"

I touched his hand.

He was looking right at me now. "I love you," he said. "And I'm in love with you."

"What did you want to do about it?"

He shrugged. "Well, I figured if we started planning now, we could get some invitations printed up by spring and get married in June. What do you think?"

I stared. My jaw dropped. He smiled, closed my mouth with his index finger, and kissed me very gently on the lips. Off in the distance, angels sang.

"Or we could try dating," he said. "You know, dinner. A movie. Maybe Scrabble. I don't expect you to dive into this head-first. I'm perfectly willing to court you."

My lips were still buzzing but I managed a smile. "Court me? Is that a romance-book reference to score some points?"

He grinned. "Hey. Whatever helps." He tilted his head at me. "You seem really caught off guard by all this. Didn't you get the feeling that my interest in you was more than just polite professionalism?"

I sighed. "No. You see, I had a whole relationship with you in my head. I never thought of you as anything more than that. Now that I look back, I probably should have been a little more aware about what was going on. That's my problem. I mean, I'm not sure how to separate the real person that is you from the dark, brooding hero in my head."

He stood up. "You'll figure it out, Mona. I have." He walked across the kitchen and opened the door. "See, I had the same problem. But I managed to fall in love with the living, breathing Mona, in spite of the other Mona."

"What other Mona?"

He walked back to me. He pulled me to my feet and held me so closely that we were practically smoldering. Something electric was actually vibrating between us as he spoke. "The naked one. The one who keeps dragging me into bed. Touching me, stroking me, driving me crazy with her mouth." He stepped back and grinned again. "All God's children have fantasies, Mona."

Golly.

"Think about it, Mona. I know this has been an emotional day for you. But please think about what I've said."

"Okay," I managed.

"And call me. Anytime you want. For whatever reason. Okay?"

I nodded and he shut the door behind him.

I sat back down.

Ben wanted me.

Brian, who had sort of wanted me back, had just divorced me.

It was all suddenly too much, and I put my head down and started to cry.

I was sobbing so loudly I didn't hear the back door open again, but Patricia's voice came floating in, and I raised my head to see her leaning back out the door and yelling. Seconds later MarshaMarsha burst in. They sat down on either side of me, patting my shoulders.

"I was right to check on you," Patricia was saying. "I knew you were too calm at the hearing. Go ahead and cry, darling. Get it all out."

"I'm not crying about the divorce," I managed.

"The girls?" MarshaMarsha asked. "Did something…"

"No," I wailed.

Patricia grabbed my arm and gave it a little shake. "You haven't been reading Jodi Picoult again, have you?"

I shook my head, sniffing loudly. Tissues appeared and I grabbed them, blew noisily, and blurted, "Ben just told me he loved me."

Silence.

"Ben Cutler?" Patricia finally asked.

I nodded.

"But," she continued, "you're crying. Why would you be crying?"

I mopped my eyes. "I don't know. I practically fainted when he kissed me."

MarshaMarsha caught her breath. "He kissed you. Oh God, what was it like?"

"The best kiss I've ever had. In. My. Life."

"But," Patricia was soldiering on, "why are you *crying*? This is Ben. The best looking man never photographed for an Abercrombie and Fitch clothing advertisement."

"What did you tell him?" MarshaMarsha asked.

I took a breath. "I told him I'd think about it."

"But this is Ben,' Patricia said. "Who loves your kids, and your animals, and can have an entire conversation with Lily without the aid of pharmaceuticals."

I nodded. "I know."

MarshaMarsha leaned in close, disbelief on her face. "Did you tell him to go away?" she whispered.

I shook my head.

"Thank God," she breathed.

"Mona." Patricia was looking aghast. "This is Ben. Who is one of the best men I've known. Who probably has enough money to take you to Tahiti so you can spend the rest of your life sucking down coconut milk. And he'll fix all your toilets for free."

"I know," I wailed. "I know."

The front door slammed and Anthony's voice drifted in. "I thought you were back. Are you a free woman at last?" I saw him come into the kitchen through a haze of tears. He stopped and put his hands to his mouth. "Oh, Mona, don't cry. This divorce is a good thing."

Patricia stood up. "It's not the divorce. Ben is in love with her. We need a drink."

Anthony clutched at his throat with both hands. "Ben? My Ben?"

"Apparently," MarshaMarsha said, "*Mona's* Ben."

"He said he loved her?" Anthony gushed. "Ohmygod. Mona. You sly little vixen. Ben? I told you something was going on! Didn't I tell you?"

"She told him she'd have to think about things," MarshaMarsha told him with a groan.

He stopped and turned deathly white. "But, Mona. This is Ben. Who is a kind, generous man who likes your kids and—"

"I know," I yelled. "Stop it. All of you." I put my head back down on the table and started crying again.

Gradually, I could hear things other than my own sobbing. The heartwarming clink of ice against glass, for one thing. Then, voices.

"Well, I saw his truck parked in front of the house, but I mean, I just thought it was another toilet," MarshaMarsha was saying.

"And he kissed her?" Anthony asked.

"Yes," Patricia told him, "and she said it was the best kiss ever."

"Well of course it was. I mean, was there ever any doubt? So she told him what?" Anthony continued.

"That she'd have to think it over," MarshaMarsha said.

"I don't get it," Anthony said. "Gorgeous man, likes her kids, loads of money. What am I missing here?"

"It's shock, I bet," MarshaMarsha offered.

"It's crazy," Patricia said.

"She's crazy," MarshaMarsha murmured.

"But she's usually not that crazy," Anthony murmured back.

"Maybe it's about Mitch," Patricia mused.

"Aren't they over?" Anthony asked.

MarshaMarsha chuckled. "Well, I thought so, but maybe she changed her mind. Maybe she asked him to stay here after all."

"But I thought that was just sex," Anthony said.

"Maybe there was a little more to it than that," Patricia said.

"She turned down Ben for Mitch?" MarshaMarsha asked.

"She wouldn't follow him out to California," Anthony said. "Would she?"

I lifted my head. "I'm still in the room," I growled.

Patricia handed me a martini glass. A full martini glass. "Drink this. Now." she said.

I did as I was told. What a difference. My eyes cleared, my sinuses dried right up, and my brain shifted into focus. "These are amazing," I told her.

"I know." She folded her arms across her chest. "Do we need to talk about this? Does this have to do with Mitch?"

I shook my head. "No. It's Ben. And it's Brian."

"What?" MarshaMarsha looked shocked. "What about Brian?"

"He asked to come back. He wanted to stop the divorce."

"When!" Patricia demanded.

"Yesterday," I said. "He told me he had made a mistake. He wanted to come back and put the marriage on track."

"What did you say?" Anthony asked.

"No. I said no. What else could I say? Then he got all angry, like it was my fault. Can you believe it? My fault. I threw him out."

"Well good for you," MarshaMarsha said. "Really, Mona. That's exactly what he deserved."

Patricia came around and gave me a big hug. "Absolutely." She tilted her head at me. "But why would you be upset about that?"

"Because he's such a jerk. I can't believe he put us all through this, and then he changed his mind. Why did he have to start this whole mess in the first place?"

"Mona." Patricia gave me a shake. "If he hadn't started this whole mess, you'd still be married to a complete idiot. You wouldn't have written a terrific book, you'd still be running around trying to be Mrs. Perfect Berman, instead of doing what you want to do with your life, and the most beautiful man in the world would not just have told you he loved you. You shouldn't be upset." Her good breeding took over. "You should send him a thank-you note."

The phone rang. I waved at Anthony, who picked up the receiver, glanced at the caller ID, and said. "It's Oprah."

"Put her on speaker," I said. I have cordless phones all over the house, but the kitchen phone is kind of command central, with the answering machine, all sorts of speed dial buttons, and a speakerphone capability that's the equivalent of the PA system in Madison Square Garden.

"Mona, my God, you won't believe my morning," Sylvia blurted before I could even say hello. "It's been officially Mona Quincy day here."

"Here too," I told her. "I got divorced today."

"Congratulations, but that's not the only thing you've got to celebrate. I was on the phone with Frannie all morning, and your book was the hit of all the December conferences. Huge hit. Everybody loved it. You're getting a hardcover release, and they're pushing up the release date to June so you can get a big summer push."

My mouth dropped open and I looked at Anthony. He was doing his official Happy Dance, his hips going in one direction, his fisted hands in the other direction, his eyes closed and his head bobbing. "Sylvia, that's amazing," I gushed. "You're amazing."

"Yes, I am, because I sent the manuscript to Los Angeles, to a friend of mine. She stopped pimping book ideas a few years ago, and started pimping movie ideas. She liked the story and started discreetly shopping it around. Drew Barrymore loves it."

"But Sylvia, Drew Barrymore is too young to be Sydney."

"She has a production company, Mona. She made all those *Charlie's Angels* things, which made a bunch of money for her. She wants to start moving in another direction in her choice of films, and thinks your book would be a good start."

"Wow." I was impressed.

"And the character of the lady who sells Sydney the house? The one with cancer and the eight-year-old grandson? It looks like Jane Fonda might be interested. They might go straight for a sale. How do you feel about going Hollywood?"

"Sylvia, I'm ready. I'm so ready that I want to write the screenplay myself."

"What? Do you know anything about screenwriting?"

"No, but there are books. Hell, there's a software package I can buy where all I have to do is fill in the blanks. When I was writing this book, I visualized whole scenes. I know exactly what kind of movie it should be. I can do this, Sylvia. I know I can. Can you sell it?"

I could hear her thinking. The room was completely quiet. We were all staring at the phone.

"I might be able to if I ask for less money."

"Then do it," I said. "I don't care about the money. Just get me first crack at the screenplay. No promises, just the opportunity. If they don't like it, fine, but get me the chance."

"It will be a tricky contract, Mona. You are a total unknown to them. Nobody wants to risk time and money on an unknown."

"I'll have it to them in three months."

"Three months? That's not a lot of time."

I looked at Anthony. His eyes were blazing. "I can do it. Anthony and I can do it together."

"Okay, Mona, when they call back, I'll see what I can do. Later."

The phone went dead. I took a deep breath.

"Mona, why on earth do you want to write a screenplay?" Patricia asked.

I took a drink. "Because I've always wanted to go to the Academy Awards. I can't act or direct, but if I write a screenplay, and it's good, then maybe I'll get nominated for best adaptation and I can go to the Oscars. I'll finally be in the same room with Robert Redford and Richard Gere."

Aunt Lily chose that moment to come through the kitchen door, swathed in wool scarves and a long black coat, her purse draped over one arm.

"I'm always coming in late to the party around here," she groused, divesting herself of her outerwear. "What did I miss this time?"

Patricia poured another martini and handed it to her. "Well, there's Mona's divorce."

"Oh, that's right. Mona, thank God you're finally rid of that horrid man." She took a sip. "Anything else?"

"Ben is in love," MarshaMarsha told her.

Lily tilted her head. "Ben? With who?"

"With whom, Aunt Lily," I said. "With me."

"My. Imagine that."

I drained my glass. "And they're going to make a movie out of my book."

Lily frowned. "A real movie, or one of those silly Lifetime channel things?"

"A real movie. I'm going to write the screenplay, I hope."

"Well, if you do, don't put in one of those silly scenes where the heroine dances around in her pajamas and sings to some awful rock song while playing air guitar. Real women don't do that."

"Well, I do." I told her.

"Me too," said MarshaMarsha.

Patricia just shook her head.

Aunt Lily looked exasperated. "Why do you want to write a screenplay anyway?"

"So she can go to the Academy Awards," Anthony told Lily. He snuggled up to me. "Can I go with you?"

"No, of course not," Patricia said. "She has to take Ben. The man will look fabulous in a tux."

Anthony sighed. "True." He patted my hand. "We'd better get cracking."

"Writing?" I asked him.

He waved his hand. "That's not a problem. What we really have to work on is what you're going to wear to the Oscars."

~

I had about three minutes of relative peace between the time that my friends left and the girls came home from school. My daughters were trying to be sensitive to the fact that I was no longer married to their father, but they couldn't quite get over the excitement of maybe having a mother with a seriously awesome job.

"Will we move to Hollywood?" Miranda asked.

"No," I told her.

"If we do, then you can get back together with Mitch," she said.

I looked at her. The girls had liked Mitch, although they had not appeared to be particularly distressed at our break-up. I did not think this was the time or place to bring up Ben. After all, I had just divorced their father. I knew that if I mentioned Ben's name, I'd probably start grinning like the village idiot, which might prompt a barrage of questions and speculation, so I left him out completely.

"Mitch and I are over. If I thought there had been a real chance for us, I would have followed him out there, movie or not."

"But how can you write a movie here in New Jersey?" Lauren wanted to know.

"The same way I write books. I sit down, write, and press send."

"If we lived in California, I bet you'd let me have a tattoo," Jessica growled.

"Wrong."

"Will we meet movie stars?" asked Miranda.

"I doubt it. Even if they do accept my script, I don't think writers make the A-list parties. And I really don't think they encourage the writers' kids to come along."

"Will you get a column in *Entertainment Weekly*?" Jessica asked.

I frowned. "I doubt it. Why?"

Jess shrugged. "Diablo Cody did."

"I will never be as cool as Diablo Cody"

She sighed. "Probably right."

~

After dinner, the girls wandered off, Aunt Lily settled in front of the television, and I sat in the kitchen and stared at Lana. It was a little after seven o'clock. Was it too soon? I waited patiently what I thought was a respectable amount of time, about thirteen minutes. Then I called Ben.

"Hi. I was just wondering. When did you think you wanted to start this dating thing?"

He laughed. "What are you doing right now?"

"Wanting a martini."

"Would you let me buy you one?"

"I'd love it. Where?"

Half an hour later, we were sitting next to each other on barstools.

"This is the best drink I've ever had," I said.

Ben nodded. "Hits the spot." He took a long gulp of beer. "We seem to spend most of our time together eating or drinking."

"I noticed that. Believe me, we're going to be spending our future time together doing other things."

He grinned. His teeth were white and slightly uneven. Thank God he wasn't too perfect. "Like what?"

I looked thoughtful. "Museums? I love museums. And street fairs."

He nodded. "Antique shops? And salvage yards. I have a real thing for salvage yards."

"As long as we can look at doors and windows and things. I don't want to spend all my time looking at old toilets."

"Every old toilet has a story," he intoned.

"Maybe. But I don't think I want to hear it. Where do you like to go on vacation?"

"Is this more date conversation?"

"Yes."

"Well, I love to ski."

"I hate the cold."

"So if I skied all day, would you wait patiently by the fire, sipping brandy and looking lovely?"

"Actually, I always thought I'd be good at that."

"Good," he said. "Another drink?"

"Nope. I just needed one. And to see you." I looked at him. "You have got to be the best surprise of my life," I said. I leaned over to kiss him. I think the people in the bar stopped to watch us. At one point, I'm sure I heard applause. Someone may have been selling popcorn. I was flying, floating, burning, breathless....Oh. My. God. And this man loved me.

"Well," he said at last, "what now?"

"Scrabble?"

He smiled. "I was thinking we could work on one of your fantasies."

He spread his arms wide and bowed gracefully from the waist. "Your any wish is my command," he said in a soft, teasing voice. She bit her lip to keep from smiling. "Very well. You can start with your clothes. Take them off." His mouth twitched. "All of them, my lady?" She nodded. "Oh, yes, indeed. All of them."

"Not a bad idea," I said. "But I'd rather start working on something real."

Let me tell you—Ben for real?

I couldn't have written it better myself.

Acknowledgments

When I was a little kid, I started writing stories. I plunked them out on my mother's old Royal typewriter, and I decided that I wanted to be a writer when I grew up. As I got older, things started getting in the way—jobs, kids, paying rent. You know. Life.

Many years later, as a stay-at-home-mom, I started imagining what I would do with myself when I finally went back to work. One morning, while listening to Joan Hamburg on WOR radio in New York, I heard a woman talking about how women are always reinventing themselves, and she said that if you wanted to know what to do with yourself, think back to what you did when you were ten years old, because whatever it was, it was probably something that you loved. That's when I decided to start writing again.

Writing is a solitary occupation, but my friends and family have been reading my various manuscripts and cheering me on for years and they've become part of the experience. Thanks to all of you. My agent, Lynn Seligman, was a true believer from the first draft, and it was with her encouragement that I first published this as an e-book. I hope you've enjoyed this book enough to tell all your friends. I'd love to hear from you. I can be reached at dee@deeernst.com. Or you can check out my website, www.DeeErnst.com

About the Author

DEE ERNST, a Jersey Girl to the core, was born in Newark, New Jersey, and grew up in Morristown. She attended Marshall University, where she majored in journalism. Several years, career changes, and daughters later, she revived her dreams of being a writer after listening to the Joan Hamburg Show. A guest made the suggestion that if you want to be happy, you should go back to what you were doing when you were ten and try to make it a career. Since Dee was writing stories when she was ten, she decided that she ought to give it another go. After three novels and many rejection letters, she decided to self-publish *Better Off Without Him*, and did so to great reception and reader reviews. Her second book, *A Different Kind of Forever*, was released in April of 2012. Though Dee finds a lot in common with her heroine Mona, she is happily married and living in New Jersey.